"A TERRIFIC NEW VOICE IN HISTORICAL ROMANCE"
Elizabeth Lowell, author of *ONLY MINE*

His fingers wound into her hair. "You were very, very good, you know," he said the instant before his mouth closed over hers. There was rage in his kiss, possessive fire that he used as a weapon.

"What am I good at?" she dared to ask moments later.

"Why, at acting the innocent, of course. At making me believe you are a gentle thing to be cherished and cared for. Do not whisper so softly. Show me what you truly are."

"I did not come to you begging marriage, my lord," she managed to gasp. "It was you who insisted—against my wishes. If you do not love me, why do you kiss me?"

"Love?" His voice broke on a laugh. "There is no *love,* madam. Do not even let the word pass your lips."

"Let me go!" she cried, struggling to escape with all her strength. But he only gripped her tighter . . .

ONLY BY YOUR TOUCH

STELLA CAMERON

An Avon Romantic Treasure

AVON BOOKS ◆ NEW YORK

ONLY BY YOUR TOUCH is an original publication of Avon Books. This work has never before appeared in book form. This work is a novel. Any similarity to actual persons or events is purely coincidental.

AVON BOOKS
A division of
The Hearst Corporation
1350 Avenue of the Americas
New York, New York 10019

First Avon Books Printing: August 1992

AVON TRADEMARK REG. U.S. PAT. OFF. AND IN OTHER COUNTRIES, MARCA REGISTRADA, HECHO EN U.S.A.

Printed in the U.S.A.

RA 10 9 8 7 6 5 4 3 2 1

For Jayne Ann Krentz,
my extraordinary friend,
with affection

Chapter 1

⁓⁓⁓⁓

The chit was a necessary nuisance. An indispensable nuisance. Plain or fair, romp or bluestocking, the comeliness and nature of Miss Lindsay Granville of Tregonitha were entirely incidental to the matter at hand.

Court her . . . for as short a time as possible. Compromise if he must, offer for, wed, bed, and set her up comfortably but at an acceptable distance . . . also using as little time as possible.

On a wind-torn ridge overlooking the Granvilles' impressive Cornish estate, Edward Xavier deWorthe, the sixth Viscount Hawkesly, twitched his stallion's reins and absently rested a hand on the animal's quivering neck. The ride from Mevagissey had been hard, fueled by hatred and impatience. "Hold, Saber," Hawkesly murmured. "We're in the enemy's territory. Best study the lie of the land . . . until the land becomes ours." He smiled, flaring his nostrils, narrowing eyes he'd become grateful to know were considered "dark shutters on his soul." In the days ahead he would doubtless appreciate his considerable ability to hide emotion. In any case, he would employ all available means in the accomplishment of his deception.

And the prize for that deception? *Vengeance!*

"It's time." Straightening in the saddle, Hawkesly

applied the gentle pressure needed to spur Saber downhill.

From barren knoll backed by the wild English Channel, gathering speed across pastures where sheep huddled into hedgerows that offered meager shield against February's chill, Hawkesly moved as one with his mount.

Ducking beneath the naked limbs of drooping goat willows, he swept into a lane that would take him to Tregonitha's curving main drive. His breath rose in white clouds and he bared his teeth. Better his rage be spent on the ripping air than the man who would soon make the acquaintance of the Viscount Hawkesly for the first time. That man must sense no hint of the threat his visitor represented. Roger Latchett, destined to serve the only sentence acceptable for his crime, would unwittingly receive his judge and jury with courtesy, even with avid anticipation . . . and he would come to curse the day of their meeting.

Within minutes Hawkesly confronted the Gothic facade of the Granvilles' manor house. He made to dismount but hesitated, hearing the crunch of fleet footsteps on gravel behind him.

Hawkesly swung to the ground as a swirl of deep blue velvet, the impression of a loose mass of blond hair, darted level with Saber. Hawkesly registered the precipitous approach of a young female and took an instant's refuge behind his horse's massive flanks. Since the Granville girl was reported to be reserved and rarely seen, this was undoubtedly a servant or some visitor to the household, but he must take no chances.

"Didn't Calvin tell you to come through the woods?" A husky, breathless voice wobbled as its owner's pale face peeked around the horse's neck. "Do please be quick. If you . . . If you . . . Should you . . ."

Hawkesly found himself regarding wide and

troubled eyes the same color as the indigo pelisse which he now saw was shabby and several sizes too large. The face was perfectly oval beneath a heart-shaped hairline, the nose small and tipped, the mouth full and parted to show small white teeth, the lashes about those remarkable eyes thick and dark. Hawkesly squared his shoulders. The stunningly beautiful face was also ridiculously young.

"If I or should I what, young lady?"

"Oh." Fingers encased in extraordinarily heavy and serviceable leather gloves pressed to her lips and she blushed quite charmingly. "Oh. Well . . . If you care that Sarah doesn't get into quite terrible trouble would you please go very quickly around to the stables and hide your horse?" To Hawkesly's amusement, she dropped a speedy and definitely clumsy curtsy. "That is if you wouldn't mind." Those thick lashes lowered to brush now fiery cheeks.

He slapped his crop against a dusty Hessian. "Well, why not. Lead the way." The poor little baggage was obviously distressed and some excuse to approach Latchett from an unexpected direction might even prove an advantage.

The girl, for she was more girl than woman, being extremely small and evidently almost immaturely slender beneath the ill-fitting pelisse, surprised Hawkesly by grabbing his hand and rushing along the path from which she'd approached. Despite the thick glove, her hand was tiny in his.

"I should have known Sarah hadn't impressed upon you the importance of discretion. And I expect you forgot to stop at Calvin's cottage on your way." Her booted feet raced and she continued to tug as if Hawkesly weren't able to keep up nicely at a leisurely stride. His black ambled beside, still blowing from the ride.

"What exactly—" He glanced sideways at her. "What do you think Sarah failed to tell me?"

"This is really too much." She hauled him around a corner of the house into a cobbled stable yard. "I didn't believe her, you know. Sarah makes up such stories. I agreed to her plan because I thought it was all one of her games. But I really didn't think you truly existed."

"Oh, I exist," Hawkesly almost whispered.

The girl faltered. "Forgive me, please. I must sound rude, but I get quite ridiculously flustered. Everyone says I do. That and . . . well . . . Sarah should have made perfectly certain you understood how important it is that no one see you. Not just at the vicarage, but here, too. Please hurry."

No groom presented himself and Hawkesly allowed the girl to lead him into a stable, where she took Saber's reins. With the ease of one very accustomed to dealing with horses, she walked the black into a stall, tossed a blanket over his back and made sure he had feed and water.

"Now." She turned to him, brushing back shining curls. "You must be cold and hungry."

Hawkesly smothered a smile. An oddly fetching little piece, she seemed to have dampened his anger. Probably fortunate since he needed a cool head for what lay before him. "Am I to get a blanket and some hay, too?"

She frowned, stumbled as she slid the latch on the stall, then promptly blushed again. "You think I'm clumsy. Everyone does. If we don't waste time, we can go to the kitchen where it's warm. I expect I can find you something to eat and then we'll decide what to do. You've missed Sarah, you see. She's in Saint Austell with her papa. They won't be back at the vicarage for *hours.*"

"Perhaps you should summon the butler?" He'd taken the charade far enough. Clearly the child had mistaken him for someone else.

The huge, deep blue eyes didn't waver. "Sarah

really has made a terrible fuddle of all this. How fortunate I happened to see you arrive. This isn't where she lives, you know. This is Tregonitha. The vicarage is near the village. Several miles away." Slowly, the tip of a pink tongue appeared to be caught between those small, perfect white teeth. "Thank goodness Sarah described you so well."

Hawkesly grew restless, as restless as the horses he heard shifting in their stalls. "And how did this . . . how did Sarah describe me?" He hadn't given Latchett a definite time, or even a definite day of arrival, but now Hawkesly chafed to confront the man.

The girl frowned in concentration. "She usually talks about her brave officer serving with the Duke of Wellington and suffering from the pain of separation from her . . . I mean, she talks about you after she's been reading her romantical poetry. That's why I didn't truly believe her until today."

Curiosity detained Hawkesly. "And she says?"

"She says"—the girl regarded him intently—"tall, his dark curls windswept, fire in his black eyes, and his mouth—his mouth beautifully carved and firm. Fine broad shoulders to make of his coat a smooth perfection. And his legs—" Her mouth snapped shut an instant. "Oh, dear. *Please* don't tell Sarah I said such things."

Deeply amused, Hawkesly ran his fingers through "windswept dark curls." "I won't breathe a word to Sarah. Are you always so—" If he said "impetuous" he might embarrass her. Spontaneity was a rare and delightful commodity in young women of his acquaintance. "Are you always so outspoken?"

"Oh yes. Everyone says so." She showed no sign of chagrin that he could discern. "We must get into the kitchen before you're seen."

He followed her across the stable yard and

through an arched stone doorway into a walled
kitchen garden beyond. Signs of careless mainte-
nance were unmistakable in the scraggly remains of
winter-dead plants. Hawkesly raised a brow. For a
man who'd gone to deadly lengths to gain control
of an estate, Latchett showed remarkably poor concern for its upkeep.

"In here," his guide said.

A heavy door admitted them to a corridor at the
back of the house. Cold struck from stone walls and
floors as they passed the dairy, the meat and fish
larders. Then the girl ushered him into a surprisingly large and well-appointed kitchen where the
remnants of a fire burned beneath still spits.

"Sit down." A bleached wooden chair was
scraped toward the fire. "Here. Warm yourself."

The thought was not without appeal and
Hawkesly automatically sat, extending his hands toward the failing embers. This could indeed be a most
fortuitous development. Latchett, a known hanger-
on at the heels of Society, could not help but be
disquieted at a viscount's being shown into the
house via the kitchens! Hawkesly jerked the corners
of his mouth down.

"Where are the other servants?"

"I'm not . . . Oh. Yes. Cook has the afternoon off.
Deeds—the butler—is probably working on accounts. The others—" she waved a hand airily.
"When no guests are expected the staff all have tasks
elsewhere in the house."

"And you?" He regarded her over his shoulder.
"Who are you and where are you supposed to be?"

Her gloves discarded on the vast scrubbed table
in the center of the room, she paused in the act of
untying frayed ribbons that closed the pelisse. "I'm,
er—" A smile formed charming dimples in her
cheeks but didn't dispel shadows in her luminous
eyes. "You must know who I am, sir. I'm, er, Berthe. Sarah's maid."

She was a poor liar. Hawkesly frowned, oblivious of her reason, but convinced the chit was in the way of inventing a story. "Quite. You're Berthe. And what are you doing at this house if you're Sarah's maid at the vicarage?"

The painful rush of pink suffused her face once more. "Sarah shall hear of this. As she should have made clear, the reason for asking you to come to Tregonitha and wait in the stables was so that her papa—" She tiptoed conspiratorially closer. "Reverend Winslow is kind but quite old-fashioned about affairs of the heart, you know. Anyway, Sarah felt that if you were to come here and wait in the stables, she could come to you without her papa guessing the nature of her visit."

"I see. And did we—I mean, did Sarah warn you that this was to be the day of our meeting?"

"Oh, no. No." She appeared to glance into every cranny of the kitchen before dropping to her knees and working the broken corner of a flagstone free. This she set aside while she reached below and hauled out a bundle tied inside an old shawl. Puffing, the girl stood and dropped her bounty into his lap. "We must make haste. Sarah merely told me that it was likely you would come one day and we must be on the lookout. It was chance—a most happy chance—that I happened to see you arrive today. Here. There's game pie and cheese and apples. They should help fortify you for your wait in the stables. I'll bring you some ale when I can."

"You're too generous," he told her gravely, wondering if Latchett had any idea that his servants filched supplies from his larders to stock their own. Roger Latchett wouldn't hear it from Lord Hawkesly.

Shrugging, Berthe removed the heavy pelisse, rolled it carelessly and thrust it on a chair. Then she knelt to replace the broken flagstone.

Hawkesly drew in a sharp breath. This maid was dressed like none employed at his estate or the several other properties he maintained. Without the pelisse, his impression that she was small was verified. Small, yes. Childishly built, no. A muslin gown of palest lavender color offset her creamy skin. The unbound blond curls brushed about flawless shoulders and touched the tops of high, lush breasts in a manner that caused Hawkesly to shift in his chair. The dress had been well worn, as faded satin ribbon attested, but that ribbon circled her slender body in a caress that hugged thin fabric tightly over tantalizing curves.

"Why aren't you in uniform?" she asked. Brushing her hands together, she leaned over to check the stone, and soft smooth flesh threatened to entirely escape the confines of a too-small bodice. When she sat on her heels, the filmy straight skirt settled on gently rounded hips.

Hawkesly stirred himself with effort. He was not in the way of lusting after ladies' maids and serving girls.

"I expect you thought you'd be less conspicuous," she continued.

He realized he hadn't answered her question. "I expect so." He got up. "And I expect you'd like to return to the, ah, vicarage." He decided not to ask if she made a habit of journeying to Tregonitha every day on the off chance that Sarah, whoever Sarah was, had received a visit from her brave officer.

Another thought dawned. What was a maid from someone else's household doing hiding food in the kitchens here?

Berthe scrambled, none too gracefully, to her feet and stepped close. "There's something I ought to tell you."

Hawkesly was confronted by the delightful vision of dewy skin, shining eyes and tremblingly ripe young womanhood . . . near enough for him to see a pulse in the throat and the rapid rise and fall of tender breasts. A subtle scent of roses reached him. He momentarily lost his ability to speak.

"I would tell you," Berthe murmured. "I will. But I must make sure Sarah won't be angry with me first."

He swallowed. "Indeed. You must do nothing to offend your mistress. And now—"

She rested a hand on his arm. "Just let it be enough that everything isn't exactly what it seems. However, I'm certain that once you and Sarah are together again, all will be revealed."

"Undoubtedly." He restrained the urge to laugh. Instead he allowed himself the luxury of a light touch to her perfect cheek. His gaze flickered over her but she appeared not to notice. "Leave now. I'll find my own way." He wouldn't tell her where he planned to go or that he had no intention of mentioning to anyone how he came to be wandering from the nether regions of Tregonitha.

"No." She shook her head and her hair swished back and forth. "Sarah would never forgive me if I didn't take care of you."

A stimulating notion, Hawkesly thought. Immediately he set her hand gently from him. "I insist—"

The slamming open of a door stopped Hawkesly in mid-sentence. A paunchy blond man strutted into the room.

"What is this?" Thinning hair, swept carefully forward, cupped the edges of a round and florid face. Bulbous, moistly red lips held a pout while pale eyes embedded in puffy flesh took account of Hawkesly then Berthe. "Speak up, sir. What do you mean by intruding into my kitchens?"

His kitchens? So, this . . . this cockroach was Hawkesly's opponent, his unknowing quarry. "Good afternoon," Hawkesly said very softly. At the same time he rose slowly to his feet and set the bundle of food on the chair.

The man's small eyes narrowed to slits. His chins, stained a shiny puce by excess, wobbled against his stiff collar. "Who is this person? How long has he been here?" Latchett addressed Berthe and Hawkesly didn't fail to note how his attention lingered at the level of her breasts.

"He . . . I—"

"Enough!" Latchett raised a hand. "I'll deal with you later."

Hawkesly swallowed against acid hate. "I believe it is I whom you should take to task, sir." The man was a visible lecher and the manner in which he might prefer to deal with the girl took little imagination. "I fear I took a wrong turn coming here. This young woman was kind enough to set me on the right path." Whatever happened, he must not lose his head and move a moment sooner than would accomplish his purpose.

Latchett drew himself up on spindly, yellow-clad legs. His considerable girth strained against a rose brocade waistcoat. Hawkesly knew the other's age to be three and thirty. Excesses in living had made him appear many years older.

"Who did you want to see?" Latchett demanded.

"He rode the wrong way!" Berthe's clear voice burst from her. She wrung her hands. "You know how easy it is to take the wrong path from Fowey and come here rather than the village. I'll be glad to show him—"

"Silence!" Latchett's chest puffed up even higher.

An overblown country dandy, Hawkesly thought. Weak, self-indulgent, greedy . . . and deadly. How appealing was the thought of squeezing the life from Latchett this very moment. Appealing, but entirely too quick and merciful.

Hawkesly smiled at Berthe, who shook visibly. "I'll deal with this, my dear." To Latchett he said,

"There's been somewhat of an error, sir. I assume you are Mr. Roger Latchett?"

With a sniff Latchett said, "I am."

"As I thought. In that case I believe we have business to conduct."

"I—"

"Hush," Hawkesly told Berthe quietly. "It will be all right, my dear. Mr. Latchett, I assume you received my letter."

"Letter?"

"In which I expressed an interest in leasing Point Cottage—the property mentioned to me by my friends the Trevays of Mevagissey?" He heard Berthe's intake of breath but didn't look at her.

The stunned transformation of Latchett's face brought Hawkesly considerable satisfaction. "Point Cottage," he sputtered, taking a step backward. "Yes, yes, of course. Then you are . . ." His raised hand circled in a vague parody of a courtly flourish and he attempted a bow made difficult by his belly. "You are . . ."

"Viscount Hawkesly," he supplied, and clasped his hands behind his back. The Trevays of Mevagissey were, in fact, Bertram Trevay, private investigator. Thanks to Trevay, Hawkesly knew enough to make this sorry peacock squirm when the time was right. "I hope the property in question is still available."

"Ah . . . well, that is indeed a most desirable spot . . . my lord. But come, we'll have refreshments and discuss the matter." He fairly jiggled on the balls of his red-velvet-slippered feet. "Please, my lord, if you'll honor me with your company in my library?"

Muscles in Hawkesly's jaw cramped. "Of course."

Latchett gestured toward the door and Hawkesly inclined his head but paused in the act of following the other man to smile at Berthe. She stood as if frozen, her eyes dark with distress.

In that instant Latchett also fastened his gaze on

her. "This," he announced, "is the Viscount Hawkesly of Hawkesly Place in Devon."

Berthe's regard shifted to the floor and she dropped another awkward curtsy.

"My lord," Latchett intoned. "Allow me to present my stepsister, Miss Lindsay Granville."

Chapter 2

⁓◦◦⁓

The Granvilles had amassed a considerable fortune from tin and copper mining. Tithes collected from fishermen living on Granville lands also accounted for a tidy income each year. Tenant farmers poured a steady stream of blunt into the family coffers and it was rumored that Tregonitha could boast a worth to make the illustrious owners of more famous estates sick with envy.

Seated in a burgundy-colored leather wing chair, a glass of excellent brandy in hand, Hawkesly studied a diamond stickpin the size of a wren's egg in Latchett's cravat. Yes, the Granvilles had done very well indeed and this fat toad was obviously wasting no time in enjoying the benefits of their labors.

Latchett stood before the fire in the graciously proportioned library he called "his." From time to time he cleared his throat and rocked, his eyes darting to Hawkesly and quickly away again. Hawkesly was still mulling over the pleasant, if shocking revelation that the enticing wench masquerading as a maid was indeed the woman who would become his wife!

"I can't imagine why Deeds didn't hear your approach," Latchett said at last. His nasal speech was amusingly affected. "Embarrassin' that. Hope you'll forgive the imposition. Stablin' your own horse.

Bein' admitted through the kitchens.'' He shook his
head and fell into silence once more.

Hawkesly realized his free hand was clenched into
a fist on the arm of the chair. He spread his fingers.
Becoming installed as close as possible to his target
was of the utmost importance. Doing so rapidly was
also of the essence. If he'd ever doubted that, he
didn't now. Miss Lindsay Granville was unlikely to
be without a bevy of ardent suitors. Though none
was likely to get very far past the girl's odious stepbrother, the complication of dealing with competi-
tion was to be avoided. Not that Hawkesly doubted
his ability to dispose of any such nuisance. The
lovely Lindsay of the innocent eyes and delectable
body should prove an easy prize to secure, a prize
that would be far from a chore to unwrap.

He moved against the second flare of arousal in
one afternoon. Damn it all but the girl had affected
him as none had in the more mature of his twenty-
eight years.

''Point Cottage,'' he reminded Latchett tersely.

''Ah, yes.'' Latchett advanced upon a handsome
oak desk set before towering French doors. Beyond
was a narrow balcony overlooking a deep sweep of
lawn. ''Your letter says you are interested in leasing
Point Cottage for a year. You don't mention the purpose for which you might intend to put it to use.''

As a blind from which to pick off a bird of prey,
Hawkesly thought. He sighed, stood, and brood-
ingly stared into the fire. Miss Granville wasn't
the only one capable of dramatics. ''This is difficult.
Let us say that I am in need of a very quiet place
in which to, er, recover from a distressing disappointment—a place where no one will think to look
for me.''

Latchett cleared his throat. ''Quite. May I ask if a
lady played a part in this, er, disappointment?''

''You may ask,'' Hawkesly said. ''I hope, as a

gentleman, that you will understand if I decline to answer."

"Ah." Latchett nodded sagely. "I quite understand. I don't believe we've mentioned an appropriate, er, amount . . . ?" He let the question trail away.

"What would you consider acceptable?" Hawkesly's throat closed every time he looked at the man, and his body tensed. He'd never physically engaged a man who wasn't an able opponent and he didn't intend to break that record now, but he longed to see Latchett's eyes pop, to feel him grapple ineffectually at the hand Hawkesly could almost feel pressing into the soft flesh of the other's throat.

"It is a very desirable property. And in a magnificent location."

And the bloodsucker smelled more profits to add to the bounty he'd appropriated. Hawkesly said nothing.

"At Tregonitha we have no real need to look for additional sources of revenue."

But they wouldn't go amiss if they could be easily diverted for the purpose of helping support Latchett's considerable gaming weaknesses . . . another juicy detail Trevay had discovered.

"However," Latchett continued, "as Miss Granville's guardian—as well as executor of the estate—and, of course, as her loving stepbrother, I must lose no opportunity to make sure her interests are served."

No doubt the old clothes she wore were also in her best interests, as was having to steal and hide food in her own home. "Quite," Hawkesly murmured. Before he could curb the impulse he added, "How old is Miss Granville?"

Latchett's face swung abruptly up from his perusal of Hawkesly's letter. "She is almost twenty," he said sharply. "A comely enough young thing, but not blessed with the manners and talents so es-

sential in the female. She has been a great trial." He
raised his chin. "Of course, a fella does what his
duty dictates. I shall never shirk that duty."

Hawkesly swallowed brandy to hide his disgust.
"Admirable. I understand this *duty* came to you un-
expectedly."

"Indeed." Latchett moved to the French doors
and looked out. "My stepbrother William's death at
sea two years ago was a great shock. In battle,
y'know. The news killed my stepfather. In the absence of another . . . son, I had no choice but to
dedicate my life to my stepsister's welfare and the
protection of her inheritance.

"Her mother died at her birth and my own dear
mother—following her marriage to Broderick Granville when Lindsay was little more than an infant—
suffered considerable difficulty in caring for the two
offspring of my stepfather . . . not that she ever
complained. I am glad I have been able to give her
rest from that burden."

A prettily rehearsed story, Hawkesly noted. "And
your mother's health now?"

"My mother has done as well as can be expected
in the past two years. She adored my stepfather
and was inconsolable for months. Now she does
admirably, thank God. My stepfather was most
generous in providing for her and she continues to
live here."

The patterns of what he must deal with became
ever clearer to Hawkesly. He was already aware that
the widow of Broderick Granville continued to wield
considerable influence over her son and over Tregonitha. "You seem to have things well in hand.
What would you consider a fair arrangement for
Point Cottage?"

Latchett had moved closer to the windows and
didn't answer.

Taking his glass, Hawkesly strolled softly over thick

silken carpet, glancing at walls lined with shelves of leather-bound volumes until he could stand quietly a short distance from Latchett.

Then he saw what could pull the man's attention from what was obviously his favorite subject—money.

Lindsay Granville stood at the foot of a curved flight of steps leading down from the terrace. Despite the cold, she had failed to don the pelisse and stood in only the fragile muslin dress having an earnest conversation with a girl who was as strikingly dark as Miss Granville was fair. Sarah, no doubt, Hawkesly decided.

Miss Granville gestured extravagantly. The other girl, bundled in a conservative woolen riding dress, held her hands to flushed cheeks. Hawkesly speculated that he was the subject under discussion.

Latchett moved closer to the glass and Hawkesly saw him pass his tongue over his lips.

A pale sun shone through low, opalescent cloud and, in silhouette, Lindsay Granville's slim waist, her hips and legs, were cast in distinct outline. Her hair picked up shimmering highlights. Hawkesly drew in a deep breath and gritted his teeth. He couldn't afford to lose his objectivity simply because an innocent young piece ripe for the picking would become his to educate in the ways of the flesh. He switched his attention to Latchett. Clearly his stepsister's welfare played no part in what made him stare at her with such absorption.

"Name your price for the cottage," Hawkesly said abruptly. A new and disturbing idea had come to him. Latchett was only stepbrother to Lindsay Granville and as such there was no blood tie. Why hadn't the thought occurred to him before? As the issue of Broderick Granville's second wife by her first marriage, there was no legal impediment to Roger Latchett's marrying Lindsay Granville. Regardless of the sickening picture that painted for Hawkesly, there were other, far more pressing reasons to make sure such a travesty didn't happen.

"Your price?" Hawkesly prompted.

"There's no hurry on that, my lord." Latchett didn't move. "Make the place your own. Come and go as you please." His attention was obviously badly diverted.

"Thank you," Hawkesly said quickly. "We'll draw up the necessary papers." Any price would be worth it.

"I'll speak to my solicitor," Latchett said.

"Your stepsister seems a spirited girl," Hawkesly said. It would be necessary to start laying groundwork for what he would soon imply about the girl.

"Spirited?" At that Latchett swung around and regarded Hawkesly intently. "I assure you you are wrong, my lord. Lindsay is a very reserved and pious young woman. I have told you she is almost twenty—well past an age when she would have begun to consider marriage, had that been her wish."

Hawkesly kept his breathing even. "Surely not well past the age, sir."

"She refused a Season," Latchett said, lowering his eyelids. "Natural enough in a woman who has declared herself as a candidate for religious life."

A beat in time passed, and another before Hawkesly found his voice. "I don't think I understand you."

"It's very simple. And the burden of dealing with what will be left in my care will be great. But my stepsister is determined to become a nun."

"There, do you believe me now?" Lindsay thrust Sarah Winslow before her into the stables. "There. The black. Does he resemble any horse you've seen at Tregonitha before?"

Sarah's bonnet obscured her bowed face. Black ringlets bobbed alarmingly.

"Oh, Sarah. I'm sorry. I shouldn't have become angry with you. Please don't cry."

An explosive snuffle erupted and Sarah raised her face to reveal shining, upslanted dark eyes. "It's awful," she managed to say between giggles. "Absolutely, wonderfully awful. I wish I might have seen you talking to him."

Lindsay raised her shoulders, feeling the cold strike through her thin dress. She loved Sarah, who was her best, her oldest friend, but sometimes she could be so vexing. "I expect you'd have liked to see me giving him my old shawl full of bits of food I planned to take to Granny Whalen, too. I expect that would have made you very happy."

Sarah's giggles racked her shapely body. "Oh, I should. A *viscount*, Linny. A *viscount*!"

The Reverend Winslow's daughter was very impressed by the nobility—not that she'd actually come into contact with many of their number.

"I'll have to find a way to get to Granny Whalen with some food tonight. Thanks to Roger, she and her daughter can scarcely meet his demands for rent. I have to keep them fed."

Sarah became serious. "You are so good, Lindsay. There isn't always too much to spare at the rectory. And dear old Bostock keeps a sharp eye on the larder. But I'll bring what I can very soon."

"Thank you." Lindsay sighed. If her father were still alive there would be no need for the lengths she was forced to go to so she could help the luckless tenants Roger was steadily bleeding. And if dear William . . . Tears filled her eyes and she set her lips firmly together. For William's sake, for his memory and for what she had promised in his name, she could be strong enough to meet any challenge.

"You invented your brave officer, didn't you?" she said, smiling softly, indulgently.

Sarah spun around. "Fie. I might as well confess since you've had such a miserable time. Yes, I made him up. But he'll come one day anyway. Mark my words."

"One day," Lindsay said, still smiling. She reached into the stall to smooth the black's nose. "Someone wonderful will come for you, but not for me."

"Don't be silly," Sarah protested. "You're beautiful. You'll be married soon, you'll see. I expect this year you'll go to London for the Season and all manner of beaux will offer for you." A dreamy look had entered her exotic eyes.

Lindsay didn't bother to argue. Often she had wished she could share her burdens with Sarah, for there was no one else she could trust, no one but Antun, and he couldn't be expected to understand a female's fears and desires. However, he did understand the risks she took in the dark of many a wild night, risks that would terrify Sarah should she hear of them. Lindsay kept her appointments with the silent boats in Salters Cove against Antun's wishes, but her dead brother's best friend had given up trying to dissuade her.

"What are you thinking about?" Sarah asked.

"The Viscount Hawkesly," Lindsay improvised, not entirely untruthfully.

Sarah slipped an arm around her friend's shoulders. "Perhaps Point Cottage is an excuse. Perhaps he's heard about you and was simply seeking a way to meet you."

"Oh, Sarah." Lindsay laughed. "If you could see him you'd know better." Soon she'd have to find a way to send Sarah home. Tonight there would be business to accomplish.

"What does he look like?"

Lindsay frowned and pursed her lips in exaggerated thought until Sarah poked her ribs.

"Oh, very well. The viscount is tall. Very, very tall. So tall I had to almost snap my neck to look into his face. And his shoulders are broad. I don't think he'd need an ounce of padding to make his coat fit so. Or his trousers.''

Sarah chuckled. ''I thought you didn't notice too much about him. What about his face?''

''Very handsome.'' Lindsay considered. ''Tanned, as if by long exposure to sun. A strong straight nose and a mouth with a full lower lip, very firm and curving up at the corners. A little dip in his chin here''—she touched her own chin—''high cheekbones and black eyes that could get even blacker, if that doesn't sound silly. And his brows are straight slashes as dark as his hair. His hair is curly against his collar.''

Sarah caught at her own collar. ''Very handsome? Very, very handsome?''

''Yes. And with obvious character. I'd say the Viscount Hawkesly is the most handsome and upright man I've ever met. If I were the type of woman who might ever consider marriage, he'd be exactly the kind of man I'd hope would offer for me.''

At a sound from behind her, Lindsay turned around and her fingers flew to her throat. ''Oh, dear,'' she murmured. ''Oh, dear.''

Viscount Hawkesly smiled slightly and Lindsay quite forgot to curtsy.

Chapter 3

A ntun Pollack was a hard man. Everyone said so. Tall, muscular, red-haired and granite-eyed, twenty-nine and still unmarried, Antun was said to have a mind like a master cutthroat's blade and a hole where his heart should be. But Lindsay Granville was a hard woman and she wasn't about to be sent home like a little girl when there was something she desperately needed to do tonight. She also knew that much of what was said about the man beside her couldn't be more false.

"Antun, Captain Claude will be expecting you."

"And I'll not be there." Antun stood at the water's edge staring seaward from Salters Cove into the darkness. Fog shifted in tattered wreaths, driven by a stiff, cold breeze. "We'll not speak of this further. I'll ride with you through the woods. Light a candle in the window to signal when you're safely inside Tregonitha."

Lindsay drew herself up as tall as she could, wishing as she so often did that she hadn't been what William used to call "the runt of the litter." Dear William. How she missed her beloved brother. Eleven years her senior, he and Antun had been firm friends since childhood—a fact William had kept secret from Papa, who hated the Pollacks. Antun's father had been "that damn poacher" to Broderick

Granville. Lindsay hid a smile at the memory. Little had her papa known that the poacher of Salters Cottage, above the conveniently deep waters of Salters Cove, used his reputation with a gun as a clever cover for far more lucrative activities. Mr. Pollack had made a fine art of running undutied goods and, through his own necessities, Antun had followed in his dead father's footsteps. And for the past two years Lindsay had prevailed upon him to allow her to play a role in the business.

"I'll come out to the French smuggler with you. I can handle the—"

"No!" Antun swung toward her, the lines of his lean face hard in the eerie light of the moon filtered through fog. "By God, you will do no such thing, Linny. I should never have agreed to your getting involved in any of this."

"I gave you little choice," she reminded him demurely, while she looked directly up into gray eyes shadowed to black by the night. "I told you that if you wouldn't allow me to join your night runners I might find a reason to talk with Chief Revenue Officer Farr. And he would be very glad to find any excuse to talk with me, Antun. I know that by the way he looks at me."

"Enough," Antun thundered. He caught at his red curls and held on as if to control whatever he might prefer to do with his hand. "You'll stay away from that old lecher Farr. If he so much as glances at you I want to hear about it. I'll make sure he doesn't use his eyes on anything again, be it a maid or his damnable spying glass. I'll—"

"Antun"—Lindsay caught his arm—"we're wasting time. You said you can't go out to the Frenchman because Ned's sick and you need another pair of hands. I'm going to be that pair of hands."

He moved his big shoulders restlessly, but took her hand in both of his. "You don't fool me, you know, lass. You never did. You're reckless, but you're gentle—too gentle for the lot that's been dealt you.''

''Please, let us go.'' She made to tug her hand away but he held fast. ''You need the money for that fishing fleet you're trying to build. And we both know why I must earn what I can and quickly.''

''Our agreement . . . the agreement you *extorted* from me, lass, was that you would store the goods in Tregonitha's cellars in return for money to help the tenants that scoundrel Latchett bleeds. But keeper of the key is all you have to be, little one, nothing more. William would have my eyes if he knew I as much as allow you to ride the land at night, dressed like a boy and pulling carts of smuggled goods.''

''William is dead,'' Lindsay said softly. ''And he of all men would understand what I must do. I alone can ease the hardships of our tenants now.''

Antun swung away and paced the shingle. The tide rushed and sucked at the sand, the sound muffled by fog. A heavy salt tang assaulted Lindsay's senses. Her heart ached, for Antun's pain and for her own. She bowed her head. ''We have both lost so much. What we're doing to ease those losses is right.'' Antun must not yet know that the tenants' plight was but a small part of her burden.

''It should be my responsibility alone,'' Antun said, his deep voice barely audible. ''William was my best friend. I am the one to make sure that what he would have wished is carried out. You're no more than a maid.''

She laughed. ''As you said, a reckless maid. And William was my brother. We'll have no more arguments about responsibilities here. We both need money and the way to make it lies out there at anchor.'' Her hair hidden in a coarse wool cap, she nodded, indicating the sea. ''Come.''

Antun's resistance was spent. He led the way to a small wooden pier jutting out from the cove. By-

passing the seiner he would have taken out had Ned
and the other man who usually went with them not
failed to come, he dropped into a small boat and
handed Lindsay down. Steadying the little craft, he
leaned back to pull nets from the pier and dump
them in the bottom.

"If chance goes against us and we're stopped by
the revenue cutter, start throwing the nets," Antun
instructed, casting off. "We'll move out of the cove
before I raise the sail." He manned the oars and
began to pull through shifting shrouds of white. A
muffled thunk and dragging sound was made by the
oars straining against rowlocks bound with rags to
silence their noise.

Lindsay's heart thudded. She sat forward, straining to see through the fog. "They will wait for us,
won't they?"

"We can hope the merchantman is the only one
waiting for us," Antun said grimly, then muttered,
"I should never have allowed you to come. You'll
not say a word. Do you hear me?"

"Yes, but—"

"There'll be no buts, miss. The Frenchmen aboard
that boat have been at sea a long time. It wouldn't
do for them to know I've a woman with me."

"But the poor things are probably missing their
wives and daughters. A few womanly words might
ease their homesickness."

Antun groaned. "Womanly words? You'll be the
death of me. Say nothing. You understand?"

"Yes," she agreed meekly. Antun could indeed
be very harsh.

Once beyond the cover of the cove, the waves
picked up and the small boat was tossed. Water
sloshed into the well and Lindsay was put to work
bailing. "You see," she said, "I'm as good as any
man. And I'm brave."

Antun said nothing. He stopped rowing and

scoured around until he suddenly pointed. "There. Hear that?"

Lindsay listened. What she heard was the unmistakable sound of water slapping a hull. Then there was the faint winking of a lantern. Antun quickly sent a return signal. In minutes they were bumping gently against the side of a big schooner.

As Antun had instructed, Lindsay caught a line tossed from the larger vessel and held fast. Antun conversed with the ship's captain for several minutes during which time a number of casks were transferred to the smaller boat. Lindsay tried not to buckle under the weight of each load passed into her arms. Clearly the French captain was disappointed that the transaction was so much smaller than expected. Antun assured him that next time they would come with the seiner and the two men set a date and time.

Fairly popping from the effort of keeping silent, Lindsay was grateful when they pushed away from the schooner and Antun raised their own small sail.

He remained silent, ominously silent, and worked fast, tacking while he stared as if seeing something Lindsay could not.

"What is it?" At last she broke the silence. "Antun?"

"Hush. Cast the nets."

She did as he asked, glancing at him to see that he'd begun tying the brandy kegs to a long, thin line which he played out into the water. "What are you doing?"

The last keg disappeared beneath the surface. "Not a word," Antun ordered. "They're almost upon us."

Lindsay had noticed nothing. She spun around and clapped her hands over her ears. The fog had parted and clearly silhouetted in the moonlight was a revenue cutter. "What will they do to us?" she whispered, her voice rising to a shrill croak.

"If they catch us, we'll say we were fishing. *I'll* say we were fishing. Then we'll pray. But they may not catch us."

Lindsay's heart pounded so loudly she could scarce make sense of Antun's words. Resolutely, she bent over the nets trying to look as if she knew what she was doing.

"Heave to!" A voice roared through the wind.

"Don't," Lindsay squeaked. "Run! Run! They'll expect us to stop. They'll already be slowing down. Hurry! We may get away."

She was too frightened to tell Antun that his low chuckle vexed her. But he was doing what she'd suggested, crowding every inch of sail and heading for land.

"They'll only turn about and beat us to Salters Cove," Lindsay said miserably. "They'll wait for us there. We'll have to cut free the casks."

"You're right about one thing, my girl. Salters Cove is exactly where they'll go. But we won't." He chuckled again and inclined his head in the direction of the cutter.

Lindsay looked too and gasped. The fog, suddenly friendly, had thickened and drifted in a band to obscure their little craft from the revenue men's sights. She turned and smiled at Antun, who paused a moment, staring at her intently, before he set to work once more. He used skills born of being on the sea from when he was a small boy. Lindsay's lips parted in admiration when the boat came around the headland adjacent to Salters Cove and slipped neatly onto a narrow strip of beach.

Antun leaped ashore and lashed a line to a jagged piling. "Now you'll do exactly as I tell you," he said. Without ceremony, he plucked Lindsay from the boat, held her in his arms as if she were no more than a child, and marched with her toward the sloping headland.

"What of the boat?" she managed, puffing. "The brandy?"

"Don't you worry your head about that. I'll send you on your way and get back to Salter Cove alone."

"But the revenue men will be there."

"And the brandy won't. I'll sink it among the rocks, go back to the cove complaining bitterly about the shortage of pilchards, and return for the goods when it's safe."

Antun strode on, carrying her uphill over rough ground until they reached the cover of trees. All this was Tregonitha land and they both knew every inch.

"Put me down," Lindsay demanded. "I'm not a child. I can walk."

"And I can walk faster carrying both of us," Antun said tonelessly. "I carried you often enough when you *were* a child."

Through the woods, down the narrow, steep-sided valley behind Salters Cove, Antun walked on, not stopping until another stand of trees enveloped them. He set Lindsay down beside a swaybacked old horse that stood, quietly grazing, between the shafts of a cart.

"Go," Antun said shortly.

He behaved like this too often, Lindsay thought. He withdrew from her just when they had been closest.

"I'll unshackle the cart so you'll be quicker," he added.

"That was exciting," she said, wanting to discuss the night's adventures. Sharing the story with Sarah would be delicious but it was out of the question.

"It wouldn't have been had we been caught." He sounded gruff. "This mustn't happen again, Linny. You'll not come to sea with me, no matter what we must sacrifice. Nothing would be worth the sacrifice of you."

She thought his voice sounded funny, but dear

Antun was always a puzzle. "When shall I return for the casks?"

"I'll get word to you," he said. "Calvin will find a way to let you know."

Calvin was Tregonitha's gamekeeper. He'd been with the Granvilles for thirty years but Lindsay knew that he only stayed now because she was still there.

"It must be soon," she told Antun. "I . . . I need the money."

His fists landed on his hips. "My venture could wait. I've told you that. Take the money I've—"

"No! No it will not wait, and I will continue to do what I set out to do. These things are my responsibility."

"You are nineteen, Lindsay." He lifted his face and fell silent. "Twenty before too long."

"Yes?" she prompted him.

"It's time a lass—a young lady like you was marrying."

"That cannot be," she cried, turning from him to grapple with the shafts of the cart. "Never, never. I shall never marry now. It would be too dangerous."

"Why?" He caught her by the shoulders but she wouldn't look at him. "Linny, why would you say such a thing? How could it be dangerous for you to marry?"

She had been careless. Her stomach tightened. After two years of absolute discretion, she had made a foolish, careless comment. Arranging her features in a smile, she laughed. "Oh, you know me. I speak wildly. I've already told you I plan to go into a convent."

A dark expression she could not read entered his eyes. "That would be a waste."

She squared her shoulders. "That isn't for you to say."

"No, I suppose not. I understand some member of the Quality is taking Point Cottage for a while."

The swift change in topic disconcerted her. Since

yesterday's fiasco with Hawkesly she'd tried, completely without success, to put him from her mind.

"He's a viscount, so Ned says."

"Ned gossips too much," Lindsay said, feigning disinterest. "The viscount is evidently trying to overcome some disastrous affair of the heart, poor man." She sighed, envisioning black eyes and unruly hair, and a mouth that curved just so and commanded attention.

Antun hadn't moved.

"Why do you mention the viscount?" She wished her heart didn't do such odd things every time she thought of that tall, strong body, every time she remembered that briefest of touches against her cheek. Now she raised her hand to her face.

"I mention him because—" He stopped speaking abruptly, turned away and quickly accomplished the task she had started in unhitching the cart.

"Antun?" Lindsay rested a hand on his shoulder and felt his hard muscles.

"Doesn't it strike you as odd that a viscount, a member of the *ton* with a vast fortune and extensive properties, so I'm told, suddenly turns up in a place like this?" he asked.

"*I* love this place."

"So do I. But it isn't London."

"Say what you mean." Lindsay watched his back curiously.

Antun raised his big shoulders. "Couldn't it be that someone mentioned that there's a beautiful girl living here? Couldn't his lordship have decided to come and take a look at you for himself?"

"You silly." Lindsay laughed aloud. "Even if he had done that, he's seen me now. If he were looking for some decorative lady to entertain him, he would certainly have changed his mind about staying here, wouldn't he?"

Antun didn't respond.

"Well, wouldn't he? Instead of that, he's gone

back to Town to make arrangements to spend the next few months here. He's going to write, he says, and think and be quiet. He's really very nice, Antun, and kind . . . and very good-looking." She smiled at the thought. Hawkesly was all of those things. It was just as well that she'd be the last woman he'd look at other than politely, which was certainly what his gentle nature would dictate he do to even the plainest and dullest of women.

She roused herself to discover Antun had turned to face her. He studied her a moment, unsmiling, then caught her about the waist and, without ceremony, deposited her upon the horse. Dressed in pantaloons, she sat astride.

"I don't care what you think of the viscount," he said. "I want you to stay away from him. His kind are used to dallying with innocent young girls."

Sometimes Lindsay thought Antun the most "innocent" of men. "I assure you I'm not Lord Hawkesly's type." And if she were she'd be forced, for his own sake, to make certain he changed his mind.

"And what do you think his type might be?"

Looking down into Antun's face, Lindsay decided that he was also a most handsome man. She'd have to put her mind to persuading him to find a wife. "I think he would want a spirited person, someone who could keep him constantly entertained as he tried to guess what she would do next. And she'd have to be fashionable and witty and very clever."

"Is that a fact?" He crossed his arms.

"Oh, yes. I'm a very good judge of character. Everyone says so."

"Then you're probably right. This Lord Hawkesly wouldn't be interested in a dull little homebody like you. After all, what man worth his salt wants to know he can always find his woman by the fire with her needlework. Or practicing her music."

Lindsay frowned at him. "Belle says my needle-

work looks no better than a child's." Her stepmother frequently suggested that the sooner Lindsay
got to a convent the better, because there it would
be acceptable to dream over a still needle. As long
as she prayed at the same time, of course. Lindsay
winced. Her one real accomplishment, if it could be
termed that, was the ability to write down blood-
curdling romantical stories. That was something no
one knew, not even Sarah, who would doubtless
demand to read them and quite choke Lindsay with
embarrassment. The idea horrified her.

"You're blushing, Linny," Antun commented.

"I was thinking about my pianoforte," she fabri-
cated. "I do get so muddled up over my pieces."

"Hmm. You'd better work on those things,
Linny," Antun said. He gave the graying chestnut
a swat on the flank and she ambled off. "But stay
away from the viscount."

"He'll stay away from me," Lindsay called. Old
Catkin picked up her pace to a shambling trot. "Men
like him don't like dull women, I tell you." She really shouldn't wish that it could be otherwise.

Chapter 4

"The stories are false," the Dowager Countess Ballard announced as she sailed into her boudoir. Dressed in black satin from her beribboned cap to her delicate slippers, she paused to glance ominously at Hawkesly. Apparently satisfied with what she saw, she swished across pale blue carpets to perch her statuesque frame on the edge of a delicate chaise where blue-and-gold peacocks cavorted over heavy silk fabric. The countess steadfastly adhered to the custom started in her youth of entertaining friends and family who visited before noon in this intimate little jewel of a room.

A maid bustled behind to settle a tasseled pillow at her mistress's back, then withdrew. The countess touched iron-gray ringlets and arranged her skirts. A widow since her late twenties, some thirty years previously, she'd chosen black as her perpetual stamp of mourning . . . although the excessive quantity of fabulous gems that always adorned her person were the object of envious whispers among the ladies of the *ton*.

Hawkesly clasped his hands behind his back, smiled indulgently, and waited. There was the smallest kernel of doubt buried in his brain about the wisdom of the approach he'd decided to take with his aunt, but he had never been a man to give in to weaknesses and he didn't intend to start now.

"Did you hear me, Edward?" The countess flipped open the gold lorgnette they both knew she used mostly for effect and to help maintain her reputation for eccentricity. "I said the stories are false," she repeated, her bright blue eyes spearing him without the aid of the glasses.

"What stories would those be, Antonia?" Edward asked smoothly.

She waved him closer. "That I'm sick unto death, of course."

That jolted Hawkesly. He hurried to move a ridiculously spindly-legged gilt chair and sat, taking one of his aunt's bejeweled hands in his. "Tell me," he ordered. "What are you keeping from me?" He adored his cantankerous but exceedingly intelligent relation. Antonia had done her best to fulfill motherly duties for Edward and his brother, James, since their early years. The boys' own mother, Antonia's younger sister, had been a vapid woman too involved with the ill health she enjoyed to be concerned with her two children. After the death of Edward's father in a hunting accident, the then viscountess had lasted only months before fading away and dying, the physician said, of a lack of desire to live without her husband.

Antonia, plump and creaking slightly in her stays, smiled imperiously. "I'm keeping nothing from you, dear boy. But obviously you must have been told tales that I'm dying. Why else would you be here after managing to return from the islands who knows when, and then existing in Town for almost a week without coming to see me?"

Edward closed his eyes, shook his head—sighed. "I might have guessed your spies would report my presence." Please God she wouldn't discover he'd been in the country a month since.

"Spies!" She tapped his arm sharply with an

ebony fan. "You call the young woman you're going to marry a spy? Shame, my boy, that I have to
learn of your presence . . . and your impending
betrothal . . . from Lady Clarisse Simmonds."

Hawkesly's blood heated. "Lady Simmonds!"
Damn the hellcat. He'd thought his own long absence and neglect, added to a rumored infatuation
on the part of the Earl of Faddon, would divert the
woman from her quest to become the Viscountess
Hawkesly.

Antonia watched him curiously before saying: "I
see the excitement between you two young people
is mutual."

"Excitement?" Hawkesly sputtered.

One diamond-encrusted hand flipped open the
black fan, revealing an intricate pattern of emerald-
eyed butterflies etched in mother-of-pearl.

Hawkesly surged to his feet and paced. "What
did she say?"

"That you have been in Town to see your solicitors and that you are drawing up certain papers re-
lating to your marriage."

He stood still a moment, then snatched a crystal
decanter from a silver tray atop an Egyptian bronze
table and poured himself a hefty glass of Madeira.
This he finished in a single swallow.

"Edward?"

"Damn and blast the woman," he fumed. "Well,
she's right. I have been seeing solicitors about a certain matter. And when I discover which of the
scoundrels is accepting the hussy's favors in exchange for information on my private affairs, I'll
have him strung up."

"Edward!" Antonia fanned herself furiously.

His aunt's feigned exhibition of shocked sensibil-
ities had the desired effect. He laughed.

"That's better," she said, smiling. "I'll take a glass
of that myself. It is a little early. But for medicinal
purposes . . ."

A little early by most people's lights. Eleven in the morning was when Countess Ballard usually took her first "little medicinal draft."

Hawkesly poured another glass of Madeira. "I wouldn't marry Clarisse if she were the last woman alive." He calculated the timing of his next announcement.

"Of course not," Antonia said comfortably. "She's a very silly young woman. And very . . . shall we say, human?"

Definitely human, Hawkesly thought, remembering Clarisse Simmonds's sumptuous breasts thrust against his back, his belly . . . the clever way she used the rest of her body . . . and his. "Mmm," he murmured. "Silly and human." And relegated to his past.

"It's as well her family managed to marry her off early to old Simmonds," Antonia continued. "She would most certainly have disgraced them."

How true. At three and twenty, Clarisse, widowed for two years, was renowned for her considerable sexual appetite and the list of conquests she'd already amassed.

"So what were these papers you had drawn up?" Antonia pretended great interest in her fan.

"The formalities attached to my forthcoming marriage."

"Your—" Antonia leaned forward, recovered slightly, and drank deeply of her wine. "You just told me you have no intention of marrying."

"Not Clarisse Simmonds."

"Then who?" Antonia's voice rose. "Are you serious? Or is this your idea of a joke?"

"I couldn't be more serious."

"But you've only been back in England a short time. Who can you possibly have met that I haven't heard about?"

Hawkesly lowered his eyelids. From here on he

must tread very, very lightly. "You don't know the girl, aunt."

"I know *everyone*," she announced with pomp. "Everyone who *is* anyone. And why this secrecy, Edward? Why take days to inform me?"

She must certainly not discover that he'd returned from the Indies weeks ago. The time he'd spent awaiting final results from the investigator, Trevay, was a secret he intended to share with only Julian Lloyd-Preston, his best and oldest friend. And even Julian wouldn't be privy to the elaborate legal measures Hawkesly had designed with his lawyers to ensure that the ultimate closing of the net about Roger Latchett would be satisfactory and inescapable. Now everything was in place and Hawkesly was almost ready to embark on the most vital step in his plot . . . the ensnarement of the delectable and innocent Miss Granville.

"Edward?" Antonia flapped her fan with even greater ardor. "Do not vex me further with this. *Who* is this girl?"

He leaned against one of the white marble cherubs that flanked the fireplace, and crossed his arms. "I'm only telling you at all because you are my nearest and dearest relative. There will be no grand wedding, Antonia, no public fuss at all. When the marriage has become a fact, we will announce it, nothing more."

Antonia's lips set into a hard line. Edward was instantly reminded that this was the woman who had successfully administered her late husband's very extensive estate for thirty years. The Dowager Countess Ballard had remained a widow because she had everything she wanted: great wealth, power, and the freedom to take and discard lovers as she chose. She wouldn't tolerate Hawkesly's attempt at secrecy easily.

With regal grace, she stood. "Who?" she repeated.

Hawkesly held her stare while he took a long, slow swallow of his drink. "What I tell you is to go no farther than this room until I say the subject may be discussed."

She sniffed, but nodded.

"The young woman in question is heiress to a Cornish estate between Mevagissey and Fowey. She is the last living member of her family."

"An orphan?" Antonia's eyes narrowed. "And her bloodlines?"

"You will not be able to do other than love Lindsay," Hawkesly said, drinking more. "She is young—not quite twenty—completely innocent and . . . er, timid." Also artless, unschooled in polite manners and a country girl more at home with horses than people. Hardly qualities his aunt would consider desirable.

Antonia's silence unnerved him. "She will live at Hawkesly and probably never come to London," he said in a rush. "Being of so retiring a nature it's doubtful she would be less than terrified by a venture to Town."

"Retiring?" Antonia said slowly. "Terrified to visit London? Timid? Edward! *Who* is she? What have you done that you're forced to marry someone who cannot possibly be of interest to you?"

"You'll meet her soon enough." As soon as he could whisk her from beneath her stepbrother's nose—preferably with, but if necessary without, his consent. "At Hawkesly. And you will like her." The last was doubtful, but he couldn't allow such details to get in his way.

"Oh, I wish James were here," Antonia said and instantly sighed.

Hawkesly's back stiffened. "I too," he said quietly. "How much I wish he were here. If he were, he'd tell me to do whatever I consider right for my own life." And if James were here, none of this irksome maneuvering would be necessary.

"How did you meet this Lindsay. . . ?" She raised a brow in question.

"Lindsay Granville," Edward supplied. "She was introduced to me by someone who thought I would find her interesting." Not a total lie.

"And she is an heiress?"

"Yes." That was not a lie at all.

"Her title?"

"No title."

Antonia had turned away. She swiveled slowly back to face him. "*No* title?"

"I want her," Hawkesly said and paused. That was true, dammit; in a perverse way he did want her. Now he was losing his mind and that was a luxury he couldn't afford. "I am decided. I will marry Lindsay Granville and install her at Hawkesly. As I said, I'm telling you this because I hold you in high regard. I also trust you not to mention the subject until I give you the nod."

Antonia's expression underwent a subtle change. Her bright eyes took on an even shrewder light. "Is she pregnant?"

"No!" But that was certainly an interesting idea and one that might be employed if too much resistance was met.

"Then you must be in love."

He was incapable of response.

"How fascinating . . . and wonderful. All these years I'd thought you were at least in part your father's son. That is, incapable of particularly deep feelings for a female. This is good, very good." She began to pace with measured step. "But you cannot have everything your own way, my boy. No, that will not do at all."

"I don't understand—"

"You will. There's been no wedding date set?"

"No, but—"

"Good. The first change in your plans must be this foolish notion of burying the child at Hawkesly.

You will arrange to have her brought to London. Who is her guardian?''

''Her stepbrother, but—''

Antonia waved him to silence. ''I'm glad she isn't entirely without family. This stepbrother must be told that Miss Granville will come to London and stay with me.''

''What?'' He shook his head.

''Under normal circumstances, I would simply put my foot down and refuse to allow you to marry beneath you.''

Hawkesly laughed. Antonia had no right to tell him whom he might marry, but he knew he would be unwise to tell her so.

''You do know that this plan of yours has the potential to bring shame upon your family name?''

''You need not advise me of the obvious. However, I assure you that a quiet little wife hidden from the public view, one who does not present me with a child five months after the wedding, will do no more than make a mild ripple in the *ton*.''

''*Au contraire*, Edward. And you know it. Within hours of the news becoming public, you would be the latest and juiciest *on dit* in every London drawing room. The Season begins early this year as you know—with the Cumberland Ball, in fact. That's when your Miss Granville will make her first appearance in Society.''

''No.'' Hawkesly spread his hands. What Antonia suggested was unthinkable. She could not begin to imagine what she was suggesting. ''Lindsay Granville is a country mouse, I tell you—'' He paused, horrified at his careless outburst. ''I mean, she isn't suited to what you suggest.''

''I take it she is beautiful?'' Eyeing him with disapproval, Antonia sat down again, carefully smoothing her skirts.

''Yes.'' At least he'd had that much luck. ''Very beautiful.''

"Mm. Naturally. Then the subject is closed. You will ensure that she is delivered to me as soon as possible. I will attend to her wardrobe and schooling for her debut. We will hold off announcing the engagement until she is accepted. And she *will* be accepted, Edward. With my tutelage—and a nod from Brummel—there can be no doubt of it."

Hawkesly was speechless. Telling his aunt before completing his plans had been a mistake. Now he might have no choice but to comply.

"You are sure you haven't set a date?"

"No, not—"

"Good. I'll let you know when I think she's ready. Then we'll make the necessary arrangements. It will be the most talked-about wedding of the year."

Hawkesly silently cursed his bad judgment. He'd intended to move ahead quickly with his plans. Now he would have to positively rush and at the end be forced to wait through an infuriating period of social nonsense that had nothing to do with his plans.

"I take it this stepbrother will make no difficulties?"

"Latchett?" Hawkesly's attention snapped back to Antonia. For an instant he considered, then, slowly, a warm satisfaction spread through him. Why hadn't he considered this himself? "He'll make absolutely no difficulties. None at all."

Of course not. Hawkesly already knew that Latchett had attempted to wheedle his way into some of the more salubrious gentlemen's clubs in London—without success. The carrot that as guardian to the future Viscountess of Hawkesly all doors would magically be open to him should be enough to make Latchett beg Hawkesly to marry Lindsay—as long as the man didn't smell the poison that would be on that carrot.

"What are you thinking, Edward?"

He started, smiled. "Oh, nothing. Just that I long to see Miss Granville again."

"And you will immediately arrange to deliver her to me?"

As soon as he'd found a way to convince her she desperately wanted to marry him. "Absolutely, aunt." The task shouldn't prove hard. He'd already overheard her statement that if she were to marry, he'd be exactly the man she'd choose. He frowned. And in the next breath she'd spoken of her plan to enter a convent.

"Is there some problem?"

"Problem?" Yes, there was a problem. He might have to fight the Church for the woman he had to have. Not a cheerful thought. "No problem. Would you like more Madeira?"

"Thank you. You said she's a country mouse."

He chuckled. "Words. Terms. I am captivated by her innocence and gentle nature and scarcely know how to impart to you her pure and malleable spirit."

"I see."

That she saw anything at all about Lindsay Granville was something Hawkesly doubted. "I've always felt a man should have a wife who is completely manageable. There is enough to contend with in dealing with business and the matters only a man can deal with."

"Quite. So this woman will be perfect for you?"

"Perfect. I'm convinced you will also approve. She may be more naive and unschooled in manners than you might prefer at first, but I'm confident she will learn quickly." He slipped the stopper back into the decanter. "You'll take comfort, as I shall, from knowing that my wife will always be predictable."

"Predictable?"

"Predictable. She'll be happy with her home and children—her needlework or whatever else she'll deem appropriate to her position as my wife."

There was another creak from overstressed stays.
"And you're sure the young lady won't become
bored with this life you envision for her?"

"Not at all. Miss Granville isn't the type to as
much as consider gadding about or involving herself
in adventure."

Chapter 5

⌒◯◯⌒

The distant rumble of thunder didn't deter Lindsay. Dear old Minnie, the chestnut mare she'd ridden since childhood, refused to move at more than a tired amble. Regardless, Lindsay continued to murmur encouragements, urging the horse on.

A day spent with Sarah at the vicarage had ended on an unsettling note. After happy hours reading a volume from the Reverend Winslow's "secret" collection of novels, Sarah and Lindsay had taken tea with the Reverend. And that had been the cause of Lindsay's agitation.

The Reverend had heard about "the new stranger in their midst," the Viscount Hawkesly. With his kind brown eyes fastened on some distant point, Reverend Winslow had spoken of Hawkesly's past, and what he'd said had made Lindsay determined to go to Point Cottage the moment she could politely excuse herself from the rectory.

They had something special in common, she and the viscount. The instant they'd met she had sensed some indefinable bond. Now she knew what it was. If he would allow it, she'd try to help him.

Minnie clomped to the top of a bare knoll several miles from Tregonitha. From here, Lindsay could see the huddle of trees around Point Cottage on its vantage spot overlooking the Channel. A plume of chimney smoke rose and she felt a mixture of relief and apprehension.

The viscount must indeed have moved in. He must also be at home.

Minnie snorted and swayed on the downhill slope. From time to time she stopped as if she'd forgotten what she was supposed to do. "On, Minnie," Lindsay said gently. "Almost there, old girl."

The thunder rolled again but it was still a good distance away. Rather than the expected stillness, a wind had picked up to pluck at the skirts of Lindsay's dark green riding dress. Green didn't become her, she knew, but Belle had ordered the habit made over for Lindsay after Belle herself tired of it. The fabric was certainly still good. And at least the matching green bonnet was new and Lindsay loved the beguiling feather that curled at her ear.

Point Cottage was large, almost a small house, and stood in a clearing open on one side to give a view of the sea. Two-storied, of white stone, its roof was thatched. A general air of disuse clung to the place. Smoke rising from the wide chimney was the only sign of life.

No one seemed to remember exactly why the cottage had been built, but William had loved the place. Yards from the weather-beaten front door, Lindsay reined in Minnie and sat still a moment. Tears stung her eyes. There was much about William that was associated with Point Cottage. Here he had come secretly to meet Maria, whom he had loved so dearly.

Now wasn't the time to think of all that. She must do what any kind girl would do for a lonely stranger who obviously had such sadness of his own to deal with.

It was as well that she'd heard of his troubles today so that she could speak with him promptly. Tonight she must meet with Antun to get the money she needed for tomorrow. Tomorrow? Ah, yes, tomorrow with its promise of happy hours spent with the greatest joy in her life . . . after she overcame the dangers that always lurked between Tregonitha and the tiny cottage a short distance from the Jamaica Inn on Bodmin Moor.

Lindsay had waited two weeks for Roger to announce that he would again be leaving for London, and that Belle would be going with him. As soon as they were gone, Lindsay would tell Deeds that she was to spend two days with the Winslows at the vicarage. Then she would set off, on Belle's gelding rather than poor, slow old Minnie. On these occasions Lindsay was grateful that Gwyn, the maid she shared with Belle, also went to London.

Dear Sarah knew of Lindsay's adventures, but thought they were to take comfort to some of Tregonitha's more distant tenants. Antun knew nothing of the absences, must never know if she hoped to continue making her journeys without endangering the promise of secrecy she'd made.

Now she must concentrate on her reason for coming to the headland. Dropping from Minnie's back, Lindsay pulled down the soft string basket she'd hooked to the saddle. How should she approach him? What should she say? Would he be angry at her intrusion?

She was brave. Antun always said so and he understood her well. Noting that the handsome black named Saber stood in the ramshackle stable to the west of the house, Lindsay approached the low front door and knocked.

No sound came from within. No voice or footsteps.

"My lord," she called, tapping again.

Perhaps he was out gathering wood . . . not that viscounts were likely to gather wood. Or he could have fallen asleep. If the latter were the case she must not disturb him.

Lindsay frowned and toyed with the vine of a dormant climbing rose near the door. On the other hand, he might be ill.

She held a fist to her chest and tried to decide what to do. A third knock still brought no response. She spread her fingers on the door . . . and it swung open.

Hesitantly, she walked inside and looked around the main downstairs room. A fire burned brightly, sending orange sparks leaping up the chimney. The sparse furniture—castoffs from Tregonitha—was as she remembered: a scarred desk under the window, a square table of some pale wood and four chairs in the center of the floor, a couch and two wing chairs of a faded peach satin around the fireplace. On the floor were several fur rugs. There was no sign of anything belonging to the viscount.

Lindsay tiptoed to a door leading to the crude kitchen. The room was empty and cold . . . and more than a little dirty. She dare not go upstairs. If she went back outside and waited he would surely come soon and she could say what she had come to say and leave.

Yes. That's what she would do.

A sound. A sigh, or perhaps a groan, stopped her. Then she saw the boot, the shiny black boot extended over one arm of the sofa that faced away from her—toward the fire.

She rose to her toes again and went, step by careful step, to peek over the back of the couch. Lindsay covered her mouth to muffle a gasp.

The Viscount Hawkesly—Edward Xavier de-Worthe, as she now knew his given name to be—lay stretched on his back, one wrist supporting his head, the other arm outstretched to the floor. He was asleep.

Trembling, Lindsay inched past his foot and stood, looking down at him. He didn't appear ill. In fact, he appeared . . . wonderful. True, there was a shadow of darkness on his jaw. Because he hadn't

shaved recently, of course. She knew that was the
cause because she'd seen William in the mornings
and he'd explained. But the viscount's lashes were
thick and curly against his cheeks and his firm
mouth so gently curved and turned up at the corners.

The hand that trailed was big, but well shaped.
All of him was well shaped . . . and very big. She
swallowed and stepped back. His white shirt, full-
sleeved and ruffled down the front, lay open to his
waist. Lindsay swallowed again. She had never before seen a man's chest . . . not unclothed. This
chest was broad, ridged with hard muscle, darkly
bronzed and covered with sun-gilded black hair. Her
heart beat alarmingly fast. The viscount's soft, light-
colored trousers clung to legs as strong as those
she'd seen depicted in paintings of pugilists, and
the wide, buff-colored turndowns on his boots fitted
his calves so tightly it was no wonder he chose to
sleep without removing them.

His journey from . . . from wherever he'd come
from . . . had probably exhausted him. And from
the look of the kitchen he obviously hadn't eaten.
Well, it was just as well she'd brought food. She'd
go into the kitchen and see if she could remember
what their old cook had told her about making a
stew. The vegetables and the piece of mutton she'd
appropriated should work. And she would need water, a great deal of water.

"Don't leave me."

She jumped and cried out . . . and dropped the
basket . . . on top of the viscount.

"Oh dear. I *am* clumsy. Everyone says so." Hurriedly, she grabbed for potatoes and turnips that
rolled over his startlingly white shirtfront. Blessedly,
the mutton, cheese and wedge of fruit pie didn't
fall.

"Stop!" A strong hand caught both of her wrists

and she was deposited squarely on Viscount Hawkesly's stomach.

Lindsay felt a wave of heat rush over her. But she couldn't seem to move.

The viscount, still holding her wrists, eased himself onto one elbow. His action caused Lindsay to slip until she sat beside him on the couch.

"I'm so sorry," she whispered. "I didn't mean to shock you. I came to bring—" she nodded at the vegetables, now scattered on the floor around the basket. "I'd heard you were here and wondered if I could do something for you."

He continued to regard her, very seriously, and to say nothing.

Lindsay took a deep breath and continued. "When I was told about your arrival it seemed you might not have thought to stock your larder, or arrange for someone to clean and care for you. It's neighborly to make sure anyone new to an area is comfortable, particularly someone like . . . someone who may not be accustomed to dealing with minor household arrangements."

"Neighborly?" He smiled lazily. "And who explained these things to you? Your stepbrother?"

She watched his mouth. How extraordinary that she had remembered his voice so exactly. Deep, extremely deep, it was nevertheless soft and almost still . . . and ever so slightly frightening, although Lindsay wasn't sure why.

"Who taught you how to greet newcomers, sprite?" he asked. "Who has been your tutor in worldly matters and behavior? Your mother?"

"Why—" She frowned. "My mother died when I was born. And my stepmother—who is always very kind to me—my stepmother has never had time to instruct me. My father, when he was alive, allowed me to take classes with Reverend Winslow at the vicarage. The Reverend is a dear, kind man and he still answers any questions I have."

"Reverend Winslow would be Miss Sarah Winslow's father?"

Lindsay nodded uncomfortably, wishing she could forget the foolish mistake she'd made when the viscount had first come to Tregonitha.

"And did Miss Winslow's brave officer arrive yet?"

Lindsay shook her head. She couldn't help smiling. "No. You must think me very silly. I certainly wouldn't blame you."

"Loyal," he said softly. "Gentle and kind perhaps. But I would never think you silly."

She bowed her head, unable to look at him. What would he think if he knew what deceptions she was capable of, already guilty of even?

Moments slid slowly by while the viscount's dark eyes watched her. Lindsay shifted a little. She wasn't uncomfortable, quite the reverse, but she was aware of the viscount's proximity, of the undoubtedly inappropriate touching of their bodies . . . and of a certain unfamiliar heat in her own.

"I was asleep when you came," he said suddenly.

"I know. I'm sorry."

"Why?" The hand that held her wrists moved, covered her hands and held them against his chest!

The heat within her spread. "I—I'm not sure. Because you looked tired and I wanted you to rest, I suppose." The hair on his chest was thick and soft beneath her fingers.

"You were concerned for me? For a stranger?"

"I—" She'd read many novels about what happened when young ladies were alone with heartless rakes, but no one had actually told her how to behave with a man. In any case, the viscount was no rake. Lindsay raised her chin. "I don't regard you as a stranger. It happens that I now know we have much in common. And yes, I certainly was con-

cerned for you. I—I am concerned," she finished
with slightly less conviction.

"What do we have in common?"

She puckered her brow. This was the part she
should have rehearsed, the part where she explained that she understood why he'd chosen to
come to a lonely cottage and live alone for a while.
The subject should be approached cautiously lest he
think she doubted his strength of will and his ability
to overcome the heartbreak of loss.

"We are both, er, we are both generous people
who are capable of very deep feeling." There, that
was a good start.

"I'm sure that's true of you, sprite. What makes
you think you know anything about me?"

She should withdraw her hands. "The way you
didn't give me away to Roger when you came and I
made such a foolish mistake," she told him in a
rush. "You instinctively knew that I would be in
grave trouble if you told him the truth about our
meeting." She was skirting what needed to be said,
but even brave people needed time to assemble their
thoughts properly.

The viscount pushed himself to a sitting position
and released Lindsay's hands. "Would Latch— . . .
would your stepbrother punish you in some way?"

The sudden hardening of his features surprised
Lindsay. "Well—" She shouldn't talk about Roger,
not because she owed him loyalty or respect but
because she'd taught herself extreme caution on
the subject of Roger Latchett. "Roger is my
guardian. He takes his responsibilities seriously,
my lord."

"No doubt. My first name is Edward."

"I know," she said, caught unawares at the announcement.

"Really?" He laughed. "How do you know?"

She really should put distance between them.
"The Reverend Winslow told me." Lindsay held her

breath, waiting for the viscount to press on the subject of what else the Reverend Winslow might have said.

The questions didn't come.

"I brought some food," she said when it felt safe to continue. "And I thought you might like me to see if one of our servants could be spared to spend time here cleaning and cooking for you, my lord."

"You see?" His smile was positively wicked—and delightful.

"See what?" Her voice sounded squeaky.

"You are as generous and kind as I thought. And could you call me Edward, do you think? At least when we're alone?"

They shouldn't be alone. Simple she might be, and unworldly, but she was aware that a young lady should not spend time alone with a man. Certainly not practically sitting in his lap!

"I ought to go."

He swung his long legs around her until they sat side by side. Once more he took her hand. "Why?"

"Because . . . Because." Because what? No one expected her.

"I thought as much. You are perfectly free to stay as long as you please. And as long as you don't have some foolish notion about being a nuisance to me." He raised her fingers to his lips but looked directly into her eyes. "You are definitely not a nuisance to me. Has anyone told you that you have the darkest blue eyes? And that they are shadowed in the most mysterious way?"

"No, my lord." Her stomach did alarming things. "Edward?"

She glanced around. "Edward." Perhaps an open window would help her feel less light-headed.

"I've thought of you a great deal since we first met."

"You have?"

"Oh, most certainly. And I'm full of questions. I

hadn't hoped to be able to ask them so soon." His breath whispered over the backs of her fingers before he pressed them lightly to his lips and set her hand on his thigh. "I expect you are accustomed to men pursuing you."

What could he mean? "N-no."

"Come now. Don't be modest. How many offers were made for your hand last Season?"

"I . . . I have never had a Season, my lord."

"Edward."

"Edward."

"You have a most unusual voice, Lindsay." He said her name carefully, making of it two distinct, soft syllables. "Low . . . beguiling. A beguiling sound to the senses."

"Th-thank you."

His thigh was solid, completely unyielding. His hand, relaxed on hers, would not stop her from drawing away. Lindsay didn't want to draw away.

"I cannot believe my good fortune." He turned sideways to face her. "You are not betrothed?"

"No!" This was extraordinary.

He touched her hair so swiftly she was barely aware he'd moved. "Your hair is soft, and so pale. When I opened my eyes and saw you standing with the light behind you it was as if you were a spirit—a sprite."

No one had ever spoken to her so beautifully before.

"You blush prettily." His touch on her cheek was light but searing. "You are almost twenty, Lindsay? I don't have that wrong too?"

"How did you know?" And why would such a strikingly handsome and worldly man care?

"I asked. And I cannot believe you are not spoken for."

Some languid softening inside Lindsay made her lean toward him. "Life at Tregonitha is isolated, my . . . Edward. And I have plenty to keep me occupied.'' Plenty of important things that she mustn't forget. So why did she feel she wanted only to stay where she was, to feel his touch again, to hold and be held by him. She gasped.

He frowned and held her shoulders lightly. ''Do you feel faint?''

''Yes . . . No.''

Now he was so close she could see the lines that fanned from the corners of his black eyes. His brows slashed upward and one was raised slightly in question.

She was staring, but how could she do otherwise?

''The Reverend Winslow has been your tutor in worldly matters?'' he asked quietly, his own gaze shifting to her mouth.

''Yes.''

''What has he taught you of men and women?''

''I . . . I don't think I understand.''

Edward stroked her neck, ran a thumb along her jaw to the point of her chin. ''I think you do. You feel something now, don't you? With me?''

She trembled. ''Yes.''

''I knew you did. This is something I feel myself and it could only be so if we shared the moment equally. Such a feeling has never been mine before.''

''It hasn't?'' Shyly, she managed a small smile. What was this, this strange, hot longing?

''You are an innocent.'' He laughed shortly, but no light touched his eyes. ''A true innocent. I hadn't believed such a rare commodity still existed.''

He puzzled her. ''I read a great deal . . . Edward. The Reverend says I'm quite learned, perhaps too much so for a young lady. Not that I am so very young.''

''You are a child,'' he said softly. ''Think again. What has your tutor told you of men and women—together?''

Vague disquiet swirled in Lindsay's mind. Could it be that the viscount was somehow pulled to her by some force? By the terrible experience he didn't know they shared, perhaps? She ordered her mind. "He has told me that men and women are very different."

"That is astute of him."

"He said that there is some, er, chemical element that causes men—when they are with women who, um, attract them—to want to err."

His laughter startled her, but he held her still when she would have leaped way.

"Err?" He chuckled, then collected himself. "Did the good Reverend tell you what 'err' is?"

"Not exactly," she told him solemnly. "But I think I know."

"Aha." Bending over, Edward brought his cheek to hers. "And, from what you know, do you think this 'err' is wrong?"

His cheek was rough on hers, deliciously, mind-tinglingly rough. Lindsay rested a hand on his broad shoulder. "I don't think it can be. Not if the man and woman involved . . . care for one another."

"The Reverend is right in one thing. You are learned—certainly on this subject, sprite"—he tilted her chin up until she was forced to raise her eyes to his—"would you like to err with me? Just a little, to see if you like the experience?"

"I—" Unable to respond, Lindsay opened her mouth, trying to find more air.

Immediately, Edward settled his lips gently on hers. Lindsay stiffened and planted her palms against his chest, but Edward's arms, encircling her, crushed any resistance. With a small moan she closed her eyes, only to open them again when he started a rhythmic brushing of his mouth against her own.

"Do you want me to stop?" he said, stroking toward her ear, lifting her hair to kiss a heated trail down her neck. "I'm told that not every woman enjoys erring."

Lindsay ran her fingers inside his shirt, upward to his neck and shyly into his hair. "I think I like it very much."

"Your skin feels overwarm," he said, his lips at the corner of her mouth now. "Let me help you out of this jacket."

She couldn't think. Edward undid the row of buttons that closed the jacket and eased it back from her shoulders. Lindsay dropped her arms so that he could pull the garment away. Next he untied the ribbon beneath her chin and slowly took off her bonnet.

"Let me look at you." Rather than hold her again as she'd hoped, he rubbed her skin lightly from the bottom of her short puffed sleeves to her elbows and back. "You are very beautiful."

The way he looked at her, the bold passage of his eyes over her body, intensified the odd, roiling surges deep inside Lindsay. Was she bad? There were bad women mentioned in some of the novels she'd read, although she'd never been quite sure what that meant either.

Edward pushed her back against the pillows at one end of the couch and dropped his big body over her. "I would never grow tired of looking at you like this."

Surely he must hear the wild beating of her heart.

"You aren't afraid of me are you, Lindsay?"

She shook her head. "Oh, no." Oh, yes, she was very afraid, but as much of herself as of Edward.

"Good. I couldn't bear to frighten you." Slowly, he brought his mouth to hers again and this time his teeth parted over her lower lip. Lindsay sighed and wriggled to fit more comfortably beneath him. "So sweet," Edward murmured. "So very sweet."

The caressing brush of his fingers along the neckline of her dress caused Lindsay's breath to catch in her throat. But this must be all right. He'd said he would do nothing to frighten her.

He seemed heavier. And his hand at her neck spread wide over the soft flesh above her gown.

"Edward," she said.

"Mm?" His eyes when he looked at her were bright. "What is it, sprite?" But he didn't wait for her response. Instead he kissed her again, parting her lips and slipping his tongue just inside. Rather than horror, Lindsay felt swelling excitement and she arched closer to him.

"Yes, Lindsay. Yes." Edward nipped at her jaw and she felt him tug at the gathered bodice of the dress. "I think you are ready to err a little more."

Before she knew what he had done, cool air slipped across her breasts. He had pulled bodice and camisole down, baring her to him. Instinctively, she tried to cover herself, but Edward trapped her hands beneath him.

"Don't worry," he told her. "You are beautiful and meant for this . . . with me. Soon you'll understand completely. Trust me."

Lindsay looked down on the top of his head, at curly dark hair, moving, even as his mouth moved over her breasts. She blushed, and tried to struggle, but he seemed not to notice. Then a singed dart of sensation shot into her and she cried aloud. He had fastened his lips over her nipple and begun to suckle, flicking the hardened bud with his tongue.

Even as her mind formed a no, she strained against him the more urgently, keening out her need, her desire . . . for what, for what else? There was something else her body demanded but she didn't know what it was.

"Yes." Edward's voice sounded strange. "Yes, my small voluptuous sprite. Such breasts. Such a body. I had not dared to hope you would be as you are.''

His words made little sense, but she was past thinking.

Edward hooked a hand beneath her knee and pulled it up until her foot rested on the couch. When he pushed up her skirt, bunching it around her hips, she felt a fresh surge of mindless wanting and tried to capture his hand.

''Leave this to me,'' he said with a low laugh. ''Let me show you how wonderful it can be to err.''

She panted. Edward had positioned a cushion beneath her back, and her breasts, completely free of restraint, thrust upward where he could lave and play until Lindsay felt she would explode. He'd settled his teeth on her yet again when she felt another sensation that jarred her to every bone and nerve.

Stiffening, she grabbed for his shoulders—and her fingers slipped over slick and heated skin.

''No!'' She squirmed to free herself.

''Hush, sweet sprite.'' Edward's words came between gasps. ''This is for you. It will only bring you pleasure.''

''No-o,'' she moaned, but the light seemed to fade. His long, strong, clever fingers were between her legs, probing her most private places, parting soft folds, touching moist and aching flesh that wanted the touching to go on and on.

''Let go,'' Edward ordered. And his finger moved.

The darkness swept from the edges of Lindsay's vision to the center of her being, darkness tinged by bright sparks that melded into the fire Edward made. She writhed, no longer able or wanting to protest. There was a screaming instant at the brink of she knew not what, an instant when his mouth fastened yet again on her breast and his fingers stroked with deliberate mastery—then a fresh surge of pleasure came, so intense she felt consciousness slip, and she slumped in his arms.

Time passed. Lindsay felt it dimly, slipping away as she also felt Edward lift her, straighten her dress and settle her against his shoulder on the couch.

She sighed and snuggled close. What did it all mean? The heat within her began to ebb and she opened her eyes. In the fireplace, the fire had burned low. A crash sounded and she realized the storm that had threatened was upon them now.

"You will leave everything to me," Edward was saying.

"Mm." She would be happy to let him show her more of his marvelous knowledge, but not immediately. For a while she thought she would be too tired.

"I will be arranging for you to go to London to stay with my aunt."

Lindsay opened her eyes slowly. She must have misheard him.

"She is the Dowager Countess Ballard. My dead mother's older sister. I call her Antonia. She will tell you what you are to call her."

"What are you saying?" Lindsay sat up and tried, unsuccessfully, to order her wildly tousled hair.

Edward smiled at her. "It will be necessary for you to be accepted by Society before we marry and my aunt has very sensibly offered to sponsor you. There will be routs and soirees and balls and—"

"No!"

He frowned. "As I was saying, the sooner you go to Town the better. Antonia wants to introduce you to the *ton* at the Cumberland Ball. That is only weeks away."

Lindsay struggled to her feet. "No! What are you saying? London? Marriage? Impossible."

Edward rose slowly until he towered over her, his shirt now completely pulled free of his trousers, his fists planted on his hips. "Why impossible, sprite? A few moments ago you couldn't get enough of . . . erring, as you call it."

"I cannot marry. I will never marry." Frantically, she snatched up her jacket and struggled to replace it. "Forget I came here today." She crammed on the bonnet and fumbled to tie its ribbons.

Without appearing to hurry, he placed himself between Lindsay and the door. "How can I forget, sprite? I am a man of honor and as such I must go to your guardian and offer for your hand."

Lindsay let out a small, anguished cry. "If you care for me at all you will not do that." She had a sudden, terrible thought. "I am ruined now, of course. That is what you're telling me. What I did with you . . . I am a fallen woman."

She noticed the fractional lift of those straight brows and a faint change in his eyes, a passing uncertainty perhaps. Then the expressionless veil fell again. "Exactly. You are a fallen woman. You have been compromised and I shall do what is right by marrying you. If nothing else, we Hawkeslys are gentlemen."

Without stopping to button the jacket, Lindsay flung past Edward, eluded his grasping hand and threw open the door. He was on her heels by the time she reached the tree where Minnie nickered fretfully.

"Stop this," Edward ordered. "Do not make me have to deal harshly with you."

Rain had begun to fall and already the ground underfoot was slippery. Lindsay welcomed the cool deluge on her hot face. She tugged Minnie's reins free. "It is not necessary for you to be a gentleman in this case. The fault for whatever happened was all mine. I forced you. I took advantage of your—your tiredness."

Edward threw back his head and laughed. In the night, his teeth shone white. The rain had already plastered his black hair to his brow and he resembled, Lindsay thought with trepidation, a large and very powerful animal . . . a wild animal.

"I will come to Tregonitha tomorrow," he said as she mounted the saddle. "If you are wise you will merely accept with appropriate meekness the proposal I make to your stepbrother."

Accept? Dear God, what had she done? Please let her be able to escape this pickle, not for her own sake but for the sake of the one who could expect no other champion but Lindsay. Married to Edward, wonderful as that would undoubtedly be, she would be unable to do what she had promised to do, what she would do at any cost. Not that there was any question of marriage—for Edward's sake.

She dug a heel into Minnie's side and the mare whinnied a complaint. "Go," Lindsay implored. "Please, Minnie." She had not told Edward what she'd come to tell him and now there would never be another opportunity.

"I'll come for you tomorrow," Edward said. "Go carefully, my sprite. When you've slept you'll forget any hesitation."

"Never," she shouted. "Roger will never agree." And for once she was grateful for her hateful stepbrother's stifling control.

"We shall see." Edward was smiling confidently.

"Never, I tell you." Minnie had begun to move, but very slowly. "You and I will not meet again."

When she looked back, Edward was leaning against a tree. He raised a hand in an indolent wave. "Don't worry, sprite. We shall soon err together again."

"We shall *not*!" she retorted furiously. Mentioning the story she'd invented about the convent would be pointless. After her wanton behavior with him, Edward would surely laugh.

"Oh yes," he called after her. "I assure you that after I've presented my offer to Roger Latchett he will be in as great a hurry as I to seal the agreement.''

She almost wished she *could* take refuge in a convent. Lindsay screamed ''No!'' and Minnie broke into an uncharacteristic trot.

''Yes,'' Edward bellowed. ''Savor the anticipation, Lindsay. Of our next opportunity to err. Of our wedding day!''

Chapter 6

A varicious coxcomb.

Hawkesly regarded Roger Latchett from beneath lowered eyelids. Detestable, pompous fop. This afternoon Latchett sported a waistcoat of primrose yellow picked out with gold thread. His neckcloth, a fussy, badly executed effort Hawkesly recognized as a clumsy attempt at one of Brummel's masterpieces, was of a hopelessly informal flowersprigged yellow muslin.

"We're honored by your visit, my lord," Latchett said. "A neighborly gesture. We were to have left for Town several hours since. But when we received word that your lordship intended to grace our home again . . . well, we are more than happy we had not yet begun our journey. Yes, indeed. I'm sure my mother agrees."

Belle Latchett Granville, a plump, rouged, faded blonde of indeterminate middle years, inclined her intricately coiffed head with what Hawkesly took to be an effort at hauteur. But the woman's heavily jeweled hands, clutching the mangled folds of a lace handkerchief, revealed extreme agitation.

"I appreciate your hospitality, Mrs. Granville," Hawkesly said. He wondered how much of Belle Granville's finery was "borrowed" from Lindsay's inheritance. "With your permission—and with your son's, of course, I had hoped we might dispatch a certain delicate piece of business.''

Belle Latchett's pale blue eyes, fringed with carefully blackened lashes, darted to her son. Roger's pouting lips curved upward. ''I sent instructions to my solicitor asking him to contact your own, my lord. I'm sure we can reach a mutually agreeable arrangement on Point Cottage.''

''Just so,'' Hawkesly agreed. ''The cottage is exactly to my liking and should prove a most peaceful retreat.'' Peaceful and convenient, should he ever need a close vantage spot from which to keep an eye on this lecherous toad without the inconvenience of having to announce his own presence in the area.

''The cottage is, in fact, a most desirable property,'' Roger continued while he examined a pudgy hand that had been carefully dyed to a delicate pink with cochineal.

Hawkesly swallowed disgust. To cover his rising hatred, he prowled about the pale green drawing room, pretending deep interest in furnishings and ornamentations that were, admittedly, tastefully opulent—the design of the dead Broderick Granville and his first wife, no doubt.

''That chest is a valuable piece,'' Latchett intoned. ''Belonged to my stepfather's first wife.''

''Exquisite.'' Hawkesly had paused beside a black lacquer and giltwork cabinet, open to reveal boxes filled with needles and thread. A carelessly crumpled sampler spilled from one side.

Latchett cleared his throat. ''Are you certain you won't have brandy, my lord?'' He had already poured himself a generous measure.

''Quite sure,'' Hawkesly said, buying time while he thought over what he planned to say. He picked up the sampler. Even to his unpracticed eye, the stitching showed the results of a patient hand.

A loudly expelled breath drew his attention to Belle Latchett. Her impressive bosom rose inside a plum-colored brocade dress. A buffont of white gauze trembled over the tops of lusty breasts.

"Did you have a comment to make, madam?" Hawkesly smiled with difficulty.

"It's of no matter." Belle produced an ivory fan which she flapped, wafting the mass of tiny crimped curls about her face. "Lindsay—my stepdaughter—does embarrass me so. I should have been able to teach her to complete a creditable sampler years ago, yet she continues to struggle. No concentration. Quite hopeless."

"Quite," Roger agreed. "Hopeless, but harmless. I'm sure she will be a useful addition to some convent."

Hawkesly found himself pitying the fair Lindsay. She might be no more than a delectable tool to help him accomplish his designs, but the thought of her gentle spirit crushed by these vultures brought him no pleasure.

Carefully, without comment, he set the sampler back on the chest. "It is about Miss Granville that I have come to you," he said, keeping his voice neutral.

"Lindsay?" Roger touched each corner of his bulbous mouth with the tip of a small finger. "I can't think—"

"She's absolutely beyond control," Belle announced, waving her fan the faster. "She rides the woods and hills like a wild boy. A wild and common boy. I've told you, Roger, she should be restrained, and quickly. No doubt she has already annoyed the viscount with her intrusions. It's time you pushed that old fool Winslow to—"

"Hush, Mother." Roger's eyes had narrowed. He saw Hawkesly watching him and quickly fashioned a smile. "My mother is still not completely recovered from her loss. She cannot take the slightest strain and she does worry about Lindsay. We both do. But no matter. Please tell us what has happened.''

"What is it you want this Reverend Winslow to do about Miss Granville, madam?" Hawkesly paused to examine a very fine tapestry screen. He had the unpleasant notion that he already knew the answer to his question.

"My stepdaughter will pursue the religious life. Very wise on her part since she is totally unsuited to, er, other choices she might have made. Winslow is the local vicar. He is to guide Lindsay on this course she has selected. But he insists she isn't ready."

A wise man, the vicar, Hawkesly decided. But no time must be wasted. "I must plead for your patience." He swung to face Latchett and his mother. "What I have to say will not be easy . . . for any of us. I have come this afternoon to request your permission to marry Miss Granville."

Absolute silence cast the room like an intricate study in oils.

The splintering crash of Roger Latchett's brandy glass hitting a brass dragon on the hearth brought a sharp cry from Belle Granville.

Sputtering, Roger kicked aside a shard of crystal. "I've misheard you, sir. I must have misheard you."

Hawkesly attempted a pleasantly apologetic smile. "I fear you have not. And I completely understand your amazement. What I suggest is quite sudden. But, I'm sure a man of the world like yourself has encountered these rapid and overwhelming involvements of the heart before. I assure you I do not come to you impulsively, or without due consideration." Oh, a great deal of consideration. The trap was finally baited and Hawkesly could scarcely contain his excitement. He felt as he did at the gaming table when he had his opponents in the palm of his hand: *Exultant!*

"Roger," Belle said in a strained voice. "What does he mean? What has happened?"

"Hush, Mother," he said. "Don't overset yourself. We appear to have misunderstood you, my lord."

"Oh, no." Hawkesly affected an innocently disturbed expression. "I'm quite sure you have understood me well. But, before we ask Miss Granville to join us, there are certain matters to be resolved."

Paling, Belle flopped against damask cushions. "I am not well," she murmured.

"Madam, I assure you this will prove a most advantageous arrangement for all. I'm sure you will welcome relief from the burden of caring for Miss Granville. As you have both told me, she has been a considerable trial to you since her father's death."

"Lindsay could never be a burden," Roger insisted. "You are mistaken, my lord."

Hawkesly maintained his bland countenance with difficulty. He held up a hand. "You are too generous by far. Hear me out, please. My plans, of necessity, involve both of you and I do hope what I propose will not interfere too badly with your own arrangements."

"Arrangements?" Belle murmured weakly. "Roger, you must stop this before—"

"Be quiet, Mother," Roger said, his pallid eyes suddenly steely. "I fear you do not understand at all, my lord. My stepsister intends to enter a convent. I cannot imagine what has led you to ask for her hand—I believe that is what you are doing—but there can be no question of Lindsay marrying."

Oh, no. No question of her causing the control of so lucrative an estate to pass from this weakling's hands. "I believe," Hawkesly said, his eyes carefully downcast, "that when you have heard what I propose you will agree that my suggestions are most agreeable to us all."

Belle lolled, halfheartedly brandishing her fan.

"If you are ill, Mother," Latchett said sharply, "then be so kind as to go to your room."

"My dear people." Hawkesly laced his fingers together beneath the tails of his dark serge coat. "I am deeply moved by your concern for one who is, after all, not even of your own blood. But I expected your devotion to Lindsay and I will need your help in the weeks to come. . . . The weeks before our wedding."

Belle closed her eyes.

"My aunt, the Countess Ballard, my dear departed mother's older sister, will take Miss Granville into her Bryanston Square home and sponsor the young lady in Society."

"Bryanston Square," Belle murmured faintly. "Society."

"Out of the question," Latchett blustered.

Hawkesly slapped the other man's back. "Not at all, my good man. Don't give it a thought. This is not a favor. I'm happy to do it. Miss Granville will fill the bill admirably—the bill as my wife, that is."

"Out of the question," Latchett repeated, almost inaudibly.

"Dash it, man,"—Hawkesly laughed—"you're entirely too humble in this matter. I know my duty and my duty is something I never shirk. Of course, I realize asking you and your dear mother to be in London for the Season and throughout the tiresome but necessary formalities of the marriage is an outrageous imposition. But, as I'm certain you'll see, it will be necessary for you to move about in Society— to be seen as the type of people a man of my rank would choose as relations."

Hawkesly hardly dared look at Latchett. The change in the man's expression was almost laughable: from desperation to greedy anticipation.

"Are you suggesting my mother and I move to London?"

"An overwhelming inconvenience," Hawkesly

said. "But one which will only be necessary until your stepsister and I are married, when, naturally, you would return to what must be your most taxing duties here in Cornwall."

"Roger—"

"Please, Mother." Roger cut off his mother's querulous voice. "Perhaps you should reveal exactly what it is you are proposing."

"I thought I had." Hawkesly bowed and advanced to the silver tray where crystal decanters glistened. He lifted the brandy. "Do I have your permission?"

Latchett nodded and Hawkesly poured. This fat fly was primed for a very sticky web. "It is all extremely simple. I wish to marry Miss Granville. My aunt will school her in the refinements necessary to the wife of a viscount. You, my dear people, would be most graciously—and gratefully—received should you agree to be in London while these things are accomplished. Naturally, you would want your own lodgings. In anticipation of your acceptance, this is already arranged. A delightful little house in Chelsea, complete with a most competent staff." A staff presided over by one Mrs. Felling, a woman practiced in accommodating the more base tastes of base men. Hawkesly had found it a simple matter to discover Roger Latchett's distasteful sexual predilections. When the time was right, Mrs. Felling would assist in the man's descent to the gutter.

Latchett's eyes seemed fastened on a distant and wholly delightful vision. "And then I would return to Tregonitha," he said in a silky tone. He moistened his lips and held his hands as if in prayer.

Hawkesly hooded his eyes. "Tregonitha is a plum, but, as you can imagine, I already have more than enough to administer with my own estates. I don't need more responsibilities. Beside which, for all you have done for my future wife, I would consider it a

kindness if you would accept Tregonitha as a token
of my gratitude.''

''You would give your wife's . . . You would, if
this marriage becomes a fact, give away your wife's
inheritance?''

''I do not want you to think I don't appreciate the
value of Tregonitha. I do. However, it appears only
fair, in consideration of all you've done, that the estate should become yours.''

Hawkesly was aware that Belle Latchett had
straightened and moved to the edge of her seat.
Roger rubbed his palms together. He was without
guile. At the gaming tables the man would be like a
motherless chick awaiting the jaws of any passing
predator. Hawkesly suppressed a smile and drank
deeply of Latchett's excellent brandy. Those gaming
tables to which he knew Latchett was so very at-
tracted would become valuable tools in what was
about to unfold.

''I am aware that you will be most anxious to return here,'' Hawkesly told Latchett. ''However,
whilst you are in Town, I hope you will allow me to
arrange your use of one of my clubs—Boodles, perhaps—accounts to be settled by myself, of course.''

''Most civil of you,'' Latchett sputtered.

What his friends at Boodles would make of Latchett—
whom Hawkesly knew had tried unsuccessfully to join
several similar establishments—was of no moment in
the matter at hand.

''Why do you want to marry Lindsay?'' Belle
Latchett's voice cut through Hawkesly's almost
pleasant reverie. ''When did you meet the chit?
What has happened behind our backs?''

''Mama,'' Roger said, approaching his mother,
bowing slightly. ''I'm sure we have no need to go
into any of that. As you see, his lordship is—''

''Answer me,'' Belle demanded. ''*When* did you
meet my stepdaughter?''

Hawkesly hid a smile. ''I am a gentleman, madam.

Suffice to say that there are things a gentleman chooses not to discuss.''

Belle's face took on a purplish hue. ''I've always said there was more to that chit than meets the eye. Always missing. Never to hand when needed. Studying her lessons with the Reverend Winslow. Pah!''

''Mama!'' Roger made a strangled noise. ''His lordship has only been in the district a short while. I'm sure you cannot be suggesting—''

''That Miss Granville has been compromised?'' Hawkesly said softly. *That she has erred?* Not chortling took herculean effort.

''Has she?'' Belle's mouth turned down.

Had the charming Miss Granville been compromised? Unfortunately not in the true sense of the word. But the fair Lindsay's erring had been powerful enough to rob Hawkesly of his sleep last night. He turned toward the fire and stared into the flames. Visions of pale, voluptuous breasts, upthrust for his pleasure, had kept him turning in his bed, had kept regions of his body quickened. He would have her, every part of her, slowly, deliciously, as he coaxed her from innocence and into the full bloom of wild wanton sexuality he had felt barely leashed in her virginal body.

''Lord Hawkesly?''

''No, Mrs. Granville. The young lady has not been compromised.'' Her legs, encased in white stockings, had yielded willingly enough. She hadn't known what she felt, or why, but yes, she had been so very willing to find out.

''When would you want us in London?'' Latchett asked eagerly.

Above the white stockings, the girl's skin was soft, smooth. And when he'd touched her most secret places . . .

''If we are to take up residence there for an extended period we would have considerable arrangements to make before traveling.''

Her flesh had leaped beneath his expert fingers. Hawkesly closed his eyes, gritted his teeth. He was glad to keep his back turned, lest his condition be noted. ''I'd like to see Miss Granville. She should be consulted in these matters.''

''Not at all,'' Belle said. ''I will tell her what is expected.''

''Let us tell her together.'' These vermin must be watched at every turn.

At Latchett's command, Deeds, an ancient, stooped butler with wispy white hair, went in search of Lindsay Granville. Within minutes the old man opened the drawing room door again and admitted the girl. Hawkesly drew himself up tall and locked his muscles. She was even more breathtaking than his fevered brain had reconstructed in the hours since she'd ridden away into the previous evening's storm.

Miss Granville made no attempt to advance into the room, choosing instead to remain just inside the door. ''You wanted to see me,'' she said in a clear voice. Hawkesly realized she was unaware of his presence. Where he stood, his somber clothes and still form blended into the shadow of a paneled wall.

''Where have you been, you—''

''Mother,'' Roger interrupted smoothly, a beatific smile on his lips. ''This is a special day for Lindsay. The crowning day of her life. We must deal carefully with her to avoid overexcitement. Come here, my dear. Sit beside your mama.''

Lindsay opened her mouth and Hawkesly guessed she was about to tell Roger Latchett that her mama was long dead. Instead, some slight movement of his caught her eye. She stepped back, her hands seeking the door behind.

''Come, Lindsay,'' Latchett said, asperity replacing sugary coaxing. "We have an esteemed visitor come to see us."

She didn't move.

"What *have* you been doing to yourself?" Belle Granville snapped. She spread her hands in an attitude of resignation. "What his lordship sees in you, I cannot imagine."

Hawkesly eyed the older woman sharply. Of the two, mother and son, Belle was the more wary. She was far from convinced that in seeing her stepdaughter married she would not, in fact, be watching everything she held dear slip from her grasp. For the time being at least it would be his task to convince the woman she had no reason for fear.

"He sees nothing in me." Lindsay's unusual husky voice whispered across the overwarm room. Her great, dark blue eyes sought his and she stared at him steadily. "You have no cause to think of me further, my lord. *None.*"

Roger made a move toward his stepsister. "Lindsay—"

"It's all right, Latchett," Hawkesly said, advancing. "Miss Granville is gentle and retiring. I'm certain she is unaccustomed to being the center of attention." Certainly in this household.

"Hmph." Belle gathered her arms beneath her bosom. "Your hair is a fright, girl. And your dress. Where have you been? Riding through brambles?"

Lindsay Granville ignored her stepmother and continued to regard Hawkesly. Belle Latchett was correct in noting that the girl was disheveled, but Hawkesly would have described the result as charming. Her blond hair tumbled wildly about her face and shoulders as if she had ridden through the strong wind that blew across the hills this day. On any other girl, the obviously made-over brown wool riding dress would have appeared dowdy. On Lindsay, the worn fabric contrived to settle about softly voluptuous curves like the caress of a lover's hands, intimately molding to tease the mind into imagining what lay beneath. Hawkesly's gaze passed from hip, to breast, to mouth. Miss Granville slipped the tip of her tongue over full pink lips—and Hawkesly met her eyes.

The tightening in his belly was almost a blow. Young she might be, and inexperienced, but even in her innocence she recognized a man who lusted.

Roger Latchett cleared his throat, breaking a silence Hawkesly could have endured forever as long as he had Lindsay in his sights.

"His lordship has come to us with a proposition. He—"

"No!"

Belle flicked her fan at Lindsay. "Hush, girl. Mind your manners. Sit beside me."

Still Lindsay made no attempt to leave the door. Hawkesly almost expected her to turn on her heel and flee. In which case he would simply have to track her down and subdue her. Not an unpleasant prospect.

"You are to be married," Roger announced, his chest expanding inside its garish waistcoat. "At his lordship's discretion, you will travel to London to stay with his aunt, the Countess—" He raised a questioning brow to Hawkesly.

"Ballard," Hawkesly supplied. "Antonia, the Countess Ballard. She will prepare you for Polite Society and for your role as my wife."

"Her wardrobe," Belle muttered, more to herself than anyone else present. "She will have to be completely outfitted."

"That will be one of my gifts to my bride," Hawkesly said quickly. Money well spent in the pursuit of his aim.

"You are most generous," Belle said. Her cunning sidelong glance would be impossible to miss. "We will make the necessary arrangements here. I have a good woman with great flair who will do the work. When will you want Lindsay in London?''

Hawkesly noticed that the girl's lovely face was waxen, her eyes dark with evident fear. ''Within the fortnight. She is to make her debut at the Cumberland Ball. My aunt will require time with her first.'' He held out a hand to Lindsay and said quietly, ''Come, Lindsay. Your guardian and I have made arrangements that do not concern you, but still I should like to see some sign of happiness at your lot.''

As if mesmerized, Lindsay stumbled forward until Hawkesly could grasp her small, cold hand. She muttered something he could not hear. He frowned and leaned closer. Standing on tiptoe, she brought her mouth to his ear. Hawkesly bowed his head, fighting back the impulse to sweep her close.

''Do not do this, my lord,'' she whispered. ''I beg you, for your own sake, do not persist in this.''

He frowned and straightened, inhaling the elusive scent of her. Wildflowers and winter's wind off the sea. ''It is natural for a maid to be reluctant.'' He smiled. ''This will soon pass.''

At Roger Latchett's knowing laugh, Hawkesly's jaw clenched.

Lindsay pulled her hand from his. ''I will not marry this man,'' she said clearly.

Hawkesly drew in a long breath. He didn't want to employ desperate means, but he would do what must be done.

''He is a gentleman,'' Lindsay said breathlessly. ''First and always a gentleman. He told me . . . he told me as much when we . . .''

''When you what?'' Belle rose to her feet. ''I knew there was more to this than we were told. When did you meet? What has transpired? No, Roger.'' She waved Latchett to silence. ''Do not interfere. I could not believe that this man who could have any woman he pleases would choose Lindsay on a whim.

Clearly his design is to pull the wool over our eyes and escape the consequences of his vile deeds with the minimum of inconvenience to himself.''

"Mama—"

"Silence, I say. If this man of the world has ruined an innocent bound for the convent, he will pay far more than he suggests. Silencing us by allowing us to keep what we already have will not do. Oh, no. It will not be nearly sufficient. Neither will a loaned cottage in Chelsea—at our disposal until he can dispatch us from his sight again. Not nearly enough.''

The termagant's audacity won Hawkesly's grudging, if disgusted, admiration—for a moment. Lindsay's shifting as she stepped back and stood as straight as her slight height allowed drew his complete attention, and that of Latchett and his objectionable mother.

"You may forget all this, stepmother," Lindsay announced in a soft but completely clear voice. "Every one of you may forget the entire subject.''

"Now, now," Roger said.

"No." Lindsay tossed back her hair and planted her hands on her hips. "There is indeed fault here, but it is not the viscount's. It is mine entirely.''

"Miss Granville—"

"I beg to be allowed to finish," Lindsay said, interrupting Hawkesly. "I am indeed a fallen woman.''

Belle opened her mouth, gasped, and slipped to sit on the couch once more. "I knew as much.''

"You, sir, are a bounder," Latchett said, but deep satisfaction crinkled the corners of his eyes.

"No, he is not," Lindsay said. "I am fallen not because of any fault of his lordship. The fault is entirely my own. It was I who caused the chemical reaction between us." She looked boldly from one face to the other until she brought her blazing eyes to rest on Hawkesly. "I came upon his lordship

whilst he slept and I caused him to err. I . . . I seduced a sleep-befuddled man into erring with me.
And for that I apologize and release him from any
imagined responsibility toward me. Roger, I would
ask you to take me straightway to the convent, any
convent.''

Hawkesly, torn between embarrassment and the
greatest hilarity he had ever experienced, turned his
back on the room and went to gaze through the window at a dark and wrathful sky.

''I erred,'' Lindsay shouted.

He tipped back his head, closed his eyes, and
prayed for patience.

''Hawkesly?'' Latchett sounded uncharacteristi-
cally patient.

''She is very young,'' Hawkesly said, suddenly
weary. ''And naive. Which is as it should be. My
aunt will expect her as planned.'' And from that day
on, Lindsay Granville, soon to be the Viscountess
Hawkesly, would do and say only what pleased the
man who would become her husband.

Chapter 7

"You'll be caught, miss. See if you aren't."
Gwyn, officially Belle's ladies' maid, followed Lindsay back and forth across her bedchamber. "And if you are it'll be the worse for me. You see if it isn't. The mistress will have my head. That's if she doesn't dismiss me." The latter was said as if death might be preferable to being sent away without references and with no prospects of finding other employment without them.

Lindsay faced the girl and took a cold hand in hers. "There is only one thing I need to hear from you, Gwyn."

"Y—yes, miss?"

"Can I trust you never to reveal what I do these next few days? Will you promise to tell no one?"

"W-well . . ."

Lindsay brought her face close to the girl's, not liking herself for what she was about to say. "If you did tell, Gwyn, it would go badly for you. No one would believe your word against mine. I am simply giving you a chance to aid me on an important mission."

Gwyn's swallow made a loud click. "In that case, miss, you've got my word." She made a sign over her heart. "On my soul, I'll tell no one."

"Good. Then let us make haste." The delay in

Roger and Belle's departure for London had forced Lindsay to make unwelcome changes in her own plans.

"Oh, miss. I'm afraid. I know I'm timid, but—"

"Do stop fussing so, Gwyn," Lindsay said. Whatever happened, she must not allow the girl to see that the mistress was every bit as frightened as the maid. "I've done this many times before with no ill effects." Although not, Lindsay thought, with this dreadful pressing notion that she must forget nothing since she had no means of knowing when she might make the trek again.

"But a journey, Miss Lindsay. And for several days. Where can you be going with such stealth?" Gwyn touched Lindsay's arm. "And why alone?"

"Hush, Gwyn. I cannot take time to explain now." Or ever. No one would ever know why it was that against all odds she journeyed to wild Bodmin Moor.

Hawkesly. Lindsay paused, her trembling fingers clutching the rough kerchief she wore about her neck. Something must happen to avert the disaster that would be her marriage to the viscount. She would put her energies into bringing about her release from the arrangement Roger had made, but not until the work of the next few days was complete. And probably not until she had gone to London to start the charade. Once there she would set about showing the poor, honorable . . . poor, handsome . . . Oh, fie, but she must concentrate on ensuring that poor, charming . . . *The man must not marry her.* She had thought there would be years, the time until her twenty-fifth birthday, when she would inherit, to look for a way to deal with Roger and ensure what must be ensured. But the moment she married the estate would legally belong to her husband . . . at least it would appear so. Surely Roger would never allow such a thing. Why, in fact, hadn't he already refused Hawkesly's offer?

She imagined that gentleman's saturnine face, his darkly penetrating eyes with their suggestion of humor in their depths . . . his long, clever hands . . . How he had used those hands to fill her with strange, exciting sensations. How he had made her yearn for him never to release her.

Fustian! She must stop this silly girlish fluttering that started in her breast every time she thought of him. She should be deeply ashamed—she *was* deeply ashamed at her impure behavior. On his visit of two days previous he'd treated her with respect and kindliness when she deserved no better than any other woman of cracked reputation. Oh, the shame! Oh, how her skin flamed with mortification! Yet he had insisted that he intended to take his plan for their betrothal and marriage to conclusion.

Concentrate. Lindsay didn't know what Roger could be planning. Evil possibilities crowded her mind. He sought to benefit from Hawkesly's dedication to misplaced gentlemanly duty, that was sure. It was also sure that, after the marriage—or more likely before—Hawkesly would meet a violent end that would leave Roger with deeper pockets and with Tregonitha still firmly in his clutches. Had she misunderstood, or could Hawkesly really mean to make a gift of the estate to Roger? Could Roger believe that he did, and would the promise appease him? Lindsay shuddered. She could not endure such risks.

She proceeded to pull on a pair of dusty boots that reached over the bottoms of a small pair of men's breeches, and to button a coarse woolen waistcoat.

"Oh, say you won't go, miss," Gwyn wailed. "Say you won't. Say you won't never go again."

"Impossible. I have no choice. And I need you to come with me." To take adequate care of the one responsibility she must never shirk, it would be necessary to transport more supplies than one horse could carry. And a riderless packhorse trailed by a lone, overly small traveler might prove too enticing a prize for some ruffian.

At Gwyn's silence, Lindsay turned around sharply—and bumped into the frail-looking maid with her pleasant but homely features. Beneath a limp, frilled cap, those features were deathly pale now, her brown eyes wide and staring.

"Gwyn, what is it? Pull yourself together at once."

"C-come with you, miss? Ride a horse? Oh, I could not."

"You silly goose. You can and you will." Lindsay pointed to a ragged pile of cast-off boy's clothing. "Put those on. And say nothing to anyone. If asked, I shall say you are my small brother and that you are mute." Lindsay counted her blessings that Hawkesly had provided Belle with a maid at the Chelsea cottage, leaving Gwyn at Lindsay's disposal.

"Oh, miss," Gwyn said. "And how will you explain why you are a girl dressed as a man?"

"My voice has its advantages," Lindsay said grimly. "I have only to whisper hoarsely and no one will question that I am a man of small stature. We shall not be bothered. Haste, Gwyn. Please. We have far to go and only four days before Roger and Belle return from their buying spree in Town." Finally, just as Lindsay had come close to desperation, Belle and Roger had taken themselves off to London. Roger supposedly intended to inspect the Chelsea lodgings he was to share with Belle. Belle insisted she must personally select materials for Lindsay's new wardrobe, but at the same time, an aged mantua-maker from the village had been engaged to make over a number of Belle's gowns for Lindsay. Lindsay hoped she would be spared the embarrassment of having the viscount realize that his money had, in fact, been spent on new finery for his . . . She closed her eyes tightly, unable to say, even in her mind, that she was to become Hawkesly's wife, and Belle his stepmother-in-law.

Frantically, Lindsay cast about for the final touches to her disguise: a broad-brimmed hat and shapeless gray wool cape. There was no time to waste, certainly not on thoughts of the man whose handsome face and strong body sprang into her mind without bidding whenever she had an idle moment. There could be no wedding, *must* be no wedding, not if Hawkesly valued his life. But how could she, a mere female, prevent the disaster?

"Make haste," she told Gwyn, who had yet to don a single item of the clothing Lindsay had provided. "We have stops to make before we set off across the moors."

"The moors, miss?" Gwyn moaned and rocked. "It be snowing up there. My brother came that way the other night and said the way is nigh on impassable."

"Not if we stick to the path I know," Lindsay retorted, not without trepidation. "And you will go only as far as Jamaica Inn. The rest of the journey, I'll make alone."

"Jamaica Inn?" Gwyn's thin voice scaled upward. "There be cutthroats there. Smugglers and the like."

At that, Lindsay hid a smile. What would the gentle maid say if she knew her young mistress was— even if secretly—one of those very smugglers to whom she referred.

"Change," Lindsay ordered. "I have work to do below. Meet me in the stables."

Within the hour, Gwyn mounted on Minnie, Lindsay astride Belle's gelding, the two girls set off into an overcast morning. Remnants of frost etched grasses and teasel stalks along the barren hedgerows and wraiths of mist curled from frozen meadowland. Lindsay knew the way as surely as she did the path to Salters Cove. That path she had traveled the night before when she'd collected her share for the latest haul of fine undutied goods Antun had sold to willing agents for the Quality in Cornwall and farther afield. In pouches about her waist, beneath her cape and coat, Lindsay carried a tidy portion in gold coin.

It was Belle's habit to send most of the household staff—drawn from the village—home when she was not in residence at Tregonitha. She maintained this was an act of generosity to give the overworked employees a rest. Lindsay was not fooled. The small band of workers received no wages during their absence, thus saving money for the Latchetts. However, regardless of Belle's mean motives, today Lindsay was glad there had been no extra eyes to observe her actions. Even Deeds and Cook took advantage of their master and mistress's absence and kept to themselves. She had told Deeds her story about staying with the Winslows and he had shown no flicker of suspicion. He would if he could see Lindsay and Gwyn now.

A steady climb to the top of a knoll brought Lindsay and Gwyn into a copse of naked-limbed black poplars, their gray bark deep-scored with age. Beyond the hill, at the bottom of a wide gully, lay a straggle of cottages.

"Why this way, miss?" Gwyn said. She leaned far forward and gripped handsful of poor Minnie's mane as well as the reins.

"Hush," Lindsay said, preoccupied with what lay ahead. "As I told you, I have tasks to perform before we can get under way."

"I thought we *were* under way." Gwyn sounded pitiful.

Lindsay relented. "And so we are. I meant that I won't feel we're truly on our journey until we leave the estate. Be patient a little longer while I check on one or two tenants."

Evidently Gwyn decided events would progress the faster if she held her tongue. Soon Lindsay found herself glancing over her shoulder regularly to make sure her maid hadn't slipped away. Each time, Gwyn bravely raised a hand before clutching the horse once more.

Once at the cottages, Lindsay passed efficiently from one door to the next. She spoke briefly and kindly to each tenant, but made sure Gwyn did not see how she handed over a generous portion of gold in exchange for a cured ham wrapped in coarse sacking or a hogshead of salted pilchards, a bolt of warm woolen material, a sack of flour, or a crock of pickled vegetables.

Finally, both horses already hung about with precious cargo, she reached Granny Whalen's tidy cottage. On all sides stood carefully turned beds of earth. In spring these would bloom with the flowers Granny and her deaf daughter, Josie, sold at market.

Granny already waited at the door, her sharp brown eyes taking in Lindsay, Gwyn and the laden animals. "Trouble afoot?" the old lady said shortly. She pulled Lindsay into the one-room dwelling with its floor of brushed hard dirt. A fire crackled up a crooked stone chimney and rough cornmeal cakes stood cooling on the hearth. Josie, already middle-aged, bent over a spinning wheel. She smiled happily at Lindsay. Despite their poverty, with bunches of fragrant dried flowers, the bright colors of an ancient patchwork coverlet atop a sagging bed, and their own unflagging cheer, the Whalens contrived to make their home a welcoming place.

Turning her back on her daughter, Granny stared hard at Lindsay. "Is something amiss with—"

"No!" Inclining her head urgently toward Gwyn, who waited outside, Lindsay smiled reassuringly. "Everything's all right there. I'm on my way for a visit now. But I don't know when I'll be able to go again so I must plan accordingly."

"What's happened?" Granny kept her voice low. "Has *he* guessed anything?"

Lindsay sighed. "No. But there's something almost as bad. Someone has offered for me and Roger says I am betrothed."

Granny frowned. "But—"

"There isn't time. Please. I couldn't gather any food, but I've brought you this—" She handed over a heavy pouch that caused Granny to frown again. "Don't argue or ask more questions. Only promise me that if necessary you will find a way to go to Bodmin Moor for me and then send word if they have need of me there."

"Where will you be? How shall I—"

"Hush. Don't fret so. I'll be sure you know where I am. Use Sarah Winslow as a messenger if you must, or Calvin. Calvin is fearless and would find me if Sarah cannot. But make certain you reveal nothing of our secret. Now I must go."

When she and Gwyn rode away, leaving a worried Granny Whalen standing in her doorway, Lindsay felt better. She detested burdening the old woman, but trusted that the best possible plans had been made in case of disaster in the coming weeks.

Bags and bundles of Granny's precious herbs and potions had been added to the horses' packs. These would serve dual purposes: to be sold if the gold ran out, or to be used if the need arose.

Night had fallen by the time Lindsay led the way along the remaining miles atop the moor. Snow covered the ground and she bent her head against a fresh and driving fall. The last stop had been at a corn mill run by a silent but honest couple who beamed at Lindsay's much more than generous payment for the sacks of corn she bought.

Finally the dull glow of a lantern showed, then the low, huddled outline of Jamaica Inn. Lindsay rode on. She would entrust Gwyn to the innkeeper and his wife, who were rough but kind people. Then she would make the last leg of the journey alone. Despite her anxiety, and the edge of sad uncertainty she couldn't completely ignore, the thought of who she would see at the safe little cottage not far from Dozemary Pool made her heart soar.

"Miss Lindsay! Ooh, Miss Lindsay! Help!" Gwyn's shout became a scream and Lindsay whirled the gelding around in time to see the little maid dragged from Minnie's back by a raffish figure swathed in dark clothing.

Grimly, not giving herself time to think, Lindsay rode at the man. He turned, grasping a writhing, kicking Gwyn in his arms. "Get off the 'orse," he bellowed. "And stand away, or yer *man* friend dies."

Lindsay reined in her mount. "Certainly." Her pulse hammered in her ears. "Set . . . set him aside, I beg you. He has nothing you want."

The villain gripped poor Gwyn the tighter and laughed, a gurgling, lascivious laugh deep in his throat. "Oh, from what I feel here, there's plenty I want. But not tonight. The rutting will have to wait till I gets the two of you and your little hoard of goods somewhere where no one will find us." He laughed again and reached for Lindsay. "I'll just tie the two of you up snug and get me mate. We wasn't expecting to come upon treasure tonight. Nor a pair of tasty articles ripe for the pickin'. Come closer." He beckoned Lindsay.

She could run and probably make it away, but leaving Gwyn was out of the question. Slowly, she approached, carefully slipping a hand into her pocket as she did so. "My little brother's sick," she said, wishing her voice would be steady. "Let him go. I'm sure we can come to some arrangement."

"Oh"—he waggled his head—"high and mighty, ain't we. Little brother, my foot. Little brothers don't have what I feel here."

Gwyn screamed and Lindsay made a grab for her,

only to have her arm painfully twisted by the man.
"Stand still or she dies," he said. "Two of yer would
be better. But me mate and me can take turns with
you if it's all we've got." With that he scrabbled at
Lindsay's waistcoat beneath the cape, found her
breast and squeezed painfully. "Oh, my gawd! We
can do very nicely with you, my beauty."

"Let me go!" Whatever this oaf intended would
doubtless be worse than death. She must time her
move just right if she and Gwyn were to be saved.
"Let me go, I say!"

His fingers only probed the harder and, dropping
Gwyn, he pawed at Lindsay with both hands, tearing open her shirt. His panting was labored, his
breath foul on her face.

Then he reached for the top of her breeches. "I
won't wait. I'll have yer now. Nabsy can take his
turn when I'm finished."

Swallowing sickness, Lindsay pulled her hand free
of her pocket. "Someone's coming," she whispered
urgently.

The ruffian lifted his face . . . and Lindsay ground
the contents of her fist into his eyes.

It was the man's bellowed howls that finally
brought a response from the inn. Through the night
came shouts and a cluster of bobbing lanterns.

Pulling the quaking, mumbling Gwyn to her feet,
Lindsay shouted: "Over here! Quickly! Over here!"
Hurriedly, she straightened her clothes.

In seconds, the man she recognized as Denzil
Mollett, keeper of Jamaica Inn, arrived with a motley
group of oversized companions.

"Is it. . . ?" Denzil held his lantern aloft and
peered at Lindsay. "It is. It's the little miss. And
who've you got with you?"

"This is my, er, friend. I'd be obliged if you'd
look after, er, *him* while I go a little farther. I'll be
back within the day."

"Hm." Denzil looked knowingly at Gwyn before

giving his complete attention to the figure that still writhed on the snow. "And what have we here? Could it be Nabsy's mate?" He used the toe of a sturdy boot to kick the man over. "The very same. And I told him what would happen if he ever showed his face in these parts again."

More moans rent the air.

Denzil crouched, pulling aside the man's hands. Then he began to chuckle. He stood up and laughed aloud. "He should have knowed better than to tangle with you, Miss Lindsay. Where did you learn to be an amuser, then?"

She gathered Minnie's reins and climbed astride her own horse once more before answering loftily: "I read, Denzil. Amazingly useful, the lending libraries. All those books about the goings-on in certain unspeakable parts. It was in a novel by a certain 'lady' that I learned how these amusers throw snuff in the eyes of their victims and make off with their valuables."

Chortles rose from the group of men.

Lindsay attempted to maintain an aloof air. "Of course, I had no interest in robbing anyone. But I did think that just in case . . . Well, it came in most useful." She dug her heels into the horse's sides. "Please take care of things here until I get back."

"Oh, we will, miss. We most certainly will," Denzil said as she departed. "You're a brave one and no mistake. Any man would do well to know what he's about afore he tampers with Miss Lindsay." Even as she rode slowly along the narrow track that led from a point opposite the inn toward Dozemary Pool, Lindsay could still hear her attacker's agonized cries. She was grateful Denzil and the others had no idea how her teeth chattered and her body shook from her ordeal.

By the time she passed the pool, the snow had stopped falling. A crystal moon showed through shifting cloud to pierce the oddly calm waters where

Sir Bedivere was said to have thrown Excalibur at King Arthur's request. But Lindsay spared scant thought for old legends, or even for surroundings she had seen many times before.

At last she saw her destination. As always, a glow showed in the front window of the tiny cottage in a secluded clearing. Dear old Nanny Thomas kept a lamp alight every night, "just in case." Just in case Lindsay happened to come. Moonlight glittered on mounded snow atop the thatched roof, the bushes and the small barn where the cow and chickens were kept.

Leaving her horses by the door, Lindsay rapped once and walked inside the cottage.

"Oh, my!" The tall, thin woman who had been nanny to Lindsay and her brother, William, rose from a rocking chair by the fire and held out her arms. Her face flushed crimson with pleasure. "Lindsay! At last. I'd thought to see you two days since."

"And you kept the lamp alight in the window." Smiling, Lindsay walked into Nanny Thomas's embrace, the embrace she'd known as comfort and safety through her earliest years. "Events delayed me. Troublesome events. And now I have only tonight. Then I must be gone."

"But—"

"Please, Nanny. There is much I must tell you. And many plans to be made in case."

"In case of what?" A frown replaced the smile.

"Don't look so worried. Everything will be well." How she wished she didn't doubt her own words. "We must waste no time. But before we talk, let me see him."

Smiling once more, Nanny turned and walked to pull aside a curtain that screened a cradle. "Yes," she whispered. "Come and see him. He grows more beautiful and more like you every day."

Swallowing hard, Lindsay looked down on the

small sleeping boy who would soon reach his second birthday. ''Yes, John is even more beautiful,'' she agreed. ''Roger must never discover that he exists. If he does . . .''

Nanny took Lindsay's hand in hers and squeezed. ''Roger will never find out. Not until the boy is old enough to dispose of the murderous viper and claim what is his own.''

''That will happen,'' Lindsay vowed, as much to convince herself as Nanny Thomas. ''Somehow I will keep the promise I made to Maria before she died giving him life. Roger may have caused the murder of her husband . . . my dearest brother . . .'' Thinking of William, and the gentle wife he'd felt bound to keep hidden from his father until he felt the time was right to reveal the marriage, made it hard to continue speaking. That time had never come and now Lindsay was grateful, for the secrecy had probably saved the sweet, small life before her. She touched a red-gold curl against the boy's brow.

''What are you thinking, child?'' Nanny asked quietly.

''That Roger will pay dearly. He will not learn that William's son exists. Not until it is time for John to claim Tregonitha.''

Chapter 8

"**Y**es," Hawkesly murmured, quietly emphatic. "Oh, *yes*!" There at last was his town coach, the family's green-and-gold colors clearly visible. Urged on by a liveried coachman atop the box, four glistening blacks clattered past impressive stone mansions.

The net was closing mercilessly about Roger Latchett.

From a window in his aunt's third-floor boudoir, Hawkesly had the perfect view over Bryanston Square. The central gardens still bore winter's mark and the only people abroad on this blustery afternoon were a few servants and tradesmen. At the sight of the darkly sumptuous coach, several of these scurrying minions paused to gawk.

"She is here, then, Edward?"

Hawkesly started. "What?" He had momentarily forgotten his aunt's presence behind him.

Antonia's voice sharpened. "I said: *She is here.*"

"As you say." In the two weeks since he had last seen Lindsay Granville, he had endeavored—largely without success—to put her from his mind.

The rustle of silk and the clack of ivory fan sticks conveyed the countess's agitation. Antonia was unaccustomed to being ignored. But he could not turn

91

away from the window until he was certain his
quarry was safely delivered.

There he was. Even with his head and shoulders bent,
Latchett's silvery-encased midsection escaped his
many-caped greatcoat to take the lead as he stepped
from the coach. The man turned about to hand down
a figure in a billowing rose velvet cloak trimmed with
swansdown and a matching full-crowned bonnet. As
she joined her son, Mrs. Granville flourished a muff
of fashionably vast proportion. Hawkesly stood closer
to the window. The woman had obviously spared no
expense in dressing for what she assumed would be
the beginning of a new and glittering career in the Polite World.

Hawkesly drew his lips tight over his teeth. Belle
Granville was a nuisance, but a petty one, and easily
disposed of in comparison with the last passenger
to alight from his coach.

"Very well," his aunt said in haughty tones. "I
believe you."

Bemused, he glanced back. "Believe me?" Antonia's habit of announcing deductions that bore absolutely no relevance to whatever he happened to be
thinking could be amusing. But he was not of a mind
to be amused—by anything—at this moment.

She rose and swept to his side. "I *believe* that you
are besotted with this girl." Antonia inclined her
head and tapped him sharply on the arm with her
fan. "Therefore I shall put into action a little plan I
have devised."

He opened his mouth to make the enquiry she
sought, then remembered the scene below the windows. "I believe we should go down and . . ." The
thought trailed away. Latchett and his mother had
passed from sight, presumably to mount the steps
to the house. Left alone, the small woman who could
only be Miss Granville hovered uncertainly by the
coach.

Uncertain? Or reluctant to take the steps that

would bring her closer to him? He shifted irritably. Whether the girl was or was not anxious to see him again was of no matter. The choice was not hers.

"Ugh!"

Hawkesly stared at Antonia. "I beg your pardon."

"Is *that* your betrothed?"

He looked back on the scene outside. His coachman, at last realizing that Latchett had left Miss Granville unattended, had gone to hover at her elbow.

"What do you mean, Antonia—is *that* my betrothed? She is Miss Lindsay Granville. I'm certain you will find her quite charming."

"That remains to be seen."

It did indeed. He sent up a mental prayer that Miss Granville would keep blessedly quiet until she'd learned not to say the first naive thing that came into her head . . . her very pretty head. . . . With a sigh, he watched the coachman usher the girl toward the house. She was definitely far too appealing for his own good. Please God she had the sense to ably grasp and accept what little was expected of her: To look lovely and perform the social rituals Antonia was so qualified to teach.

"I thought you told me she would arrive with a suitable wardrobe," Antonia said, sniffing. "I said I would take care of the matter but you told me her family would do so."

"Exactly. I advanced Latchett enough blunt to outfit a bevy of women for a grand tour. Were it not for the silly business of that wardrobe, madam, we should have dispensed with all this formality nonsense a week ago at least. If I had my way, the betrothal would have been announced. The banns could have been called twice already and we'd be no more than a fortnight away from the damn—" He coughed. "The wedding could have taken place within the fortnight."

Antonia clasped her hands at her waist and studied him, her blue eyes piercing. "Evidently your ardor for this young woman is making you tetchy. I'll choose to overlook your impudence, Edward . . . for the moment. Kindly listen to what I have to say."

She made a stately return to the chaise and arranged herself against the blue-and-gold pillows. Hawkesly waited, vaguely amused but anxious to get on.

"The first point to be made. *Mustard yellow*, Edward?"

"Beg pardon?"

Antonia tapped the toe of a black-slippered foot. "I declare, young man, your hearing appears to be leaving you. I *said: Mustard yellow!* The girl is wearing a mustard-yellow gown with a brown pelisse. Totally unsuitable colors on what I took to be a rather fragile blonde. And, if my eyes did not deceive me, the whole is hopelessly outmoded." Her lorgnette, forgotten while she had made her minute inventory from a third-floor window, was now swept up for a perusal of Edward. "I trust *that* ensemble cost you very little."

He dared not tell her that he'd been too preoccupied with other matters to notice Miss Granville's gown. "It's of no account."

"It most certainly is. But I shall attend to that promptly. And there is to be no public whisper of the betrothal until she is launched."

"But—"

"*None*, Edward. Let her be seen as above reproach first. There will be speculation, of course, but that can be turned to our advantage. The instant there is the slightest suspicion that the elusive Lord Hawkesly might be considering marriage, every pink of the *ton* will want to see who could tempt the man considered the prime and unattainable catch of the Season."

Damn it to hell. ''I do not intend to wait—or to deal with would-be rivals.''

Antonia pointed at him with her fan. ''In this I know what I am about. Do I have your word that you will be guided by me?''

If he didn't agree she would undoubtedly find a way to make him wish he had. He did not have time for the added complication of a disagreement with his favorite relative. ''As you wish,'' he said coolly.

''Very wise of you, Edward. And for the rest, you are to remember that, by marriage, and distantly, of course, I am related to the Cornish Granvilles.''

Now she had his entire attention. ''Related?''

''Oh *do* stop parroting me, Edward. It really is a most annoying habit you've developed. Yes, I am related.'' She did not meet his eye, choosing instead to unpin a beautiful pearl-and-jet brooch from her bodice and study the craftsmanship. ''Distantly, very distantly, but nevertheless . . .''

Hawkesly smiled slowly. Clearly, preoccupation had befuddled his perception. ''And to think I had somehow forgotten such an important fact.''

''Yes. To think of that. The Granvilles are . . . You did tell me Miss Granville is the last of her line?'' She awaited Hawkesly's nod before continuing. ''Yes, you did. But, of course, I knew that. The Granvilles *were* an exemplary family. Fine stock. How appropriate that you should, to please me, come to consider marrying Miss Granville to at least ensure that so worthy a family does not entirely disappear.''

''Mm. Appropriate.'' Despite the unwelcome delay, Antonia's enthusiastic support and involvement could only help ease his path through the marriage while he concentrated on other, more important matters. ''Now, can we greet our guests?''

''No.''

Hawkesly stopped in the act of offering Antonia his hand. ''No?''

"Oh, really." She tutted and stood again. "You are becoming too irritating. You will remain here for precisely half an hour. *Then* you may present yourself."

"But—"

"*Then*, Edward. It is important to set the right tone. I realize you are overanxious to see your young lady, but if I am to be responsible for preparing her for Society, then *I* must see her exactly as she is . . . *without* the distraction of the two of you behaving like moonlings."

"Like—" Hawkesly checked himself. *Moonlings?* "As you wish, aunt," he said. This lovestruck nonsense was becoming a blight. But he need only play the pretense until Miss Granville was his viscountess and safely tucked away on his Devon estates. Yes, there in the country she would do tolerably well, perhaps very well, and they need almost never see one another.

Preparing to leave him, Antonia patted at her intricate cap. "Mr. Lloyd-Preston presented his card this morning. Evidently he'd been to Cavendish Square and failed to find you at home."

"I didn't know Julian had returned from Dorset." The Honorable Julian Lloyd-Preston had been the reason Hawkesly managed to weather his early years at Eton relatively unscathed by the "character-building" tortures visited on most younger boys by senior classmen. He'd had the good fortune to be taken on by the amiable Julian as his fag and the two of them had formed an unshakable friendship.

"I took the liberty of telling him to call this evening."

"This *evening*?" Hawkesly shook his head. "I mean, did you tell him to call on me here or in Cavendish Square?"

Antonia opened the door. "Here, of course. Once the Latchetts are dispatched to Chelsea and I've met Miss Granville, I shall retire early . . . after beginning her instruction, of course. I know you have other business to attend to this afternoon. But, should you wish to return . . .'' She cast him a knowing smile that warmed her eyes. ''Miss Granville will probably be glad of diverting company in her new surroundings. And Julian assured me he will not be here until *very* late.''

She left and Hawkesly slowly closed the door behind her. *Diverting company?* What very interesting possibilities that phrase presented.

From what little her discreet enquiries had yielded, Antonia knew Broderick Granville had been many years his second wife's senior. When they'd met, the then Belle Latchett must have been a beauty in a very full-blown way. Antonia forced herself to return Mrs. Granville's vacuous smile. Granville must have married the woman for her body. Her mind appeared to be virtually nonexistent.

''Hawkesly planning to join us, did you say, milady?'' Roger Latchett had ensconced himself in a wing chair near the drawing room fireplace. Ten minutes after introductions and he was already guzzling a second goblet of her excellent Madeira.

''*Lord* Hawkesly will be along shortly.'' This odious fop was already above his station. Why Edward should have chosen to involve himself with such people Antonia couldn't imagine. She studied Miss Granville and amended the thought. This lovely young creature had the makings of a toast any man would gladly lose his head for.

''Lindsay.'' Belle Granville frowned irritably at her stepdaughter. ''Do stop roaming. I'm sure her ladyship doesn't want you wandering among her beautiful things.''

''Let her wander,'' Antonia said, deliberately perverse. ''Long journeys are tedious, particularly on the young. She's been still enough for one day.'' True, Miss Granville's restless traipsing around the room was odd when she would have been expected to sit, hands in lap, silently waiting to be addressed. But then, everything about this situation Edward had manufactured was odd.

A delightful idea occurred to Antonia. "Forgive me," she said with sudden friendliness. "Mr. Latchett. You and your dear mother must be quite exhausted from your exertions. Please, allow me to have my nephew's coach convey you to your new lodgings at once."

"Oh, no," Belle said, her voice shrill. "We wouldn't think of leaving before we see our new relative. Not at all."

New relative! Antonia felt an unfamiliar sense of urgency. "I insist." She stood up and rang for Norris. Her butler of thirty years would quickly gather that haste was required. "Lord Hawkesly would never forgive me for my thoughtlessness."

The aged butler appeared and Antonia instructed him to show Latchett and his mother to the coach.

Belle rose reluctantly, disappointment etched in the downturn of her mouth. "But we cannot leave until we've seen his lordship. I clearly recall his saying we were to discuss my—er—the arrangements. And surely he'll want to greet Lindsay."

Antonia took an instant to digest that the "arrangements" had definitely not been made adequately clear to Miss Granville's family. That, or they had chosen to forget them. "He will greet Miss Granville soon enough. She will be staying here. But I'm sure you understood that. Are Miss Granville's trunks in the house, Norris?"

The butler nodded. "Yes, your ladyship." The angle of his nose showed disapproval of what he would consider unsuitable interlopers.

"But I thought Lindsay would be staying with us," Belle said. She distractedly retied the strings of her bonnet. "I thought she would be going about with us and that I would be accompanying her . . . and you, of course, my lady.''

''Quite so,'' Latchett said, relinquishing his goblet with evident regret. ''Least we can do.''

Antonia could easily imagine the fanciful plans Latchett and his mother had made for themselves. Upstarts. ''We wouldn't dream of such an imposition on your time. And I really shall need Miss Granville with me constantly in the weeks to come.'' She couldn't bring herself to say ''before the wedding,'' not yet. ''We shall meet again very soon. Don't hesitate to send word around if you need anything.''

Several more minutes were required to finally prod the pair from the room. Antonia, ever aware of the silently prowling Miss Granville, finally heard the coach leave. She let out the breath she hadn't been aware of holding and glanced at the delicate enameled clock on the mantel. Ten minutes remained before Edward would descend and addle the girl even further.

''Now,'' Antonia said, striving to sound more comfortable than she felt. ''We must get acquainted, Miss Granville. Lord Hawkesly has told me much about you, but—''

''He doesn't know anything about me.''

Antonia stood quite still and stared. Surely she had not heard correctly. ''I'm certain you will learn very quickly what is required of you and be a great credit as my nephew's wife.''

''I don't believe so.''

There was no doubt that she had heard very accurately this time. Antonia approached and stood at the girl's shoulder. ''You are nervous, my dear. Quite understandably so. It will be my job to help you through the difficult weeks to come.'' And very difficult they seemed likely to be.

''He does not know me at all.'' Lowering heavy lashes, Miss Granville hunched her delicate shoulders. She was the picture of abject misery. "This is all a terrible mistake and he is bound to send me away as soon as he comes to his senses."

The girl's husky voice was heavy with emotion. Overwhelmingly intrigued, Antonia held her tongue and waited.

"Lord Hawkesly is set on sacrificing himself out of his deep sense of honor." Dark blue eyes sought Antonia's face. "My lady, please, for his sake, implore him to give up the idea of this marriage."

Antonia flipped open her fan, closed it again, touched it to her chin. "Ah, how well I remember my own girlish fears when my dear husband offered for me." Deep sense of honor, indeed. And what, she wondered, did that mean? "Hawkesly is quite set on you and I can see why. You are lovely, my dear. Truly beautiful, in fact. In no time that nephew of mine will be wanting to rush you to the altar lest some young buck try to whisk you away from him."

Rather than seeing the desired effect of making the girl laugh, or at least smile, Antonia was horrified to see the start of tears. As Hawkesly had suggested, this was an exceedingly innocent, timid and gentle creature. Antonia straightened her already perfectly upright spine. Honor? Had that handsome scallywag . . . ? No, impossible. Not even Edward would . . . She looked at the flawless skin before her, the cascade of silvery blond ringlets, the vulnerable curve of neck, the swell of breast above the ghastly gown, the expertly but undoubtedly made-over gown. There was something more here than Edward wanted her to know, but she had to admire his taste in raw material. Antonia felt something special in Miss Granville, something rare; the makings of a celebrated toast with a good and kindly nature. She also felt what had always intrigued her most—*challenge*.

Searching for a way to draw the girl out further, Antonia indicated the painting over the delicately plastered Adam fireplace. "Lord Ballard," she said, not without pride. "My late husband."

The distraction worked. Miss Granville studied the painting. "A handsome man," she said. "His eyes laugh. I like that in a person. He looks as if he didn't take himself so very seriously. Most gentlemen seem so coldly distant and . . . self-involved. So important. I don't believe your husband was like that. I expect you miss him very much. How long . . . Oh." She brought her fingers to her lips and blushed. "Oh, dear. I talk too much. Everybody says so."

"Then everybody says wrongly," Antonia said, surprised by her own impulsiveness. "You are delightful. And very perceptive. My husband was a most unusual man and I loved him dearly. Unfortunately he died when we had been married only a few years." Dear Ballard, such a good, understanding man. She would always be grateful for his decision to make her his sole heir.

"So sad," Miss Granville said softly. "And you still mourn him."

Antonia hid a smile. The black she had never seen fit to discard had served her well. "For some more than others, the outward sign of bereavement is essential. I am among the number who wish to continue showing respect for the one I loved and lost." She spoke honestly enough. But mourning dress also kept certain admirers where she wanted them: close enough to be entertaining, but not too close. Dear, ardent Lord Airsly, the latest of her remarkable string of lovers, would be only too willing to enter into a permanent alliance. The fortune that would become his upon their marriage would replenish his shallow pockets nicely. Antonia had no intention of giving up her pleasures . . . or control over her own destiny.

Miss Granville appeared to have become deeply preoccupied.

"I am sorry to learn of your own bereavement."

The girl jumped and turned quite pale. "I'm sorry? Oh, you knew William?" Visibly confused, she brushed against a side table, rattling the collection of fine china pieces on its surface. "Oh, I'm sorry. I'm so clumsy. Everyone says so."

"Everyone," Antonia decided, had apparently done a more than creditable job of making this young woman insecure. "Don't give it a thought." William? Ah, yes, William was the brother who died in battle at sea shortly before the death of Broderick Granville. "I didn't have the pleasure of meeting William, or your dear father. It wasn't until Edward mentioned your family that I remembered the connection."

The girl looked blank. "Edward?"

Antonia opened her mouth to snap but managed to smile instead. "Yes, my dear. Edward. My nephew. The man who has asked for your hand in marriage." Was this obtuse repetition a new fashion among the young?

"Ah, yes." Again the lovely face was lowered.

Could it be . . . was it remotely possible that Edward's amorous interests were not reciprocated? Ridiculous! "Well, as I said, when Edward mentioned your family I remembered the connection."

"Connection?"

"Fie!" Ooh, she could not contain her ire completely. At the earliest opportunity she would consult with Ernestine Sebbel. As the mother of an aging but still hopeful spinster, Ernestine might know something of this twitterpated nonsense.

"Connection, er, my . . . your. . . ?"

Antonia managed another smile. "Call me aunt. Yes, connection. I recall that my husband's cousin— now deceased, unfortunately—but she had been married to a second-cousin—also now deceased, unfortunately—but he, the husband of my husband's cousin, that is, was related to the Cornish Granvilles." She should have rehearsed the speech but the girl merely looked politely interested . . . and confused. "So, since we are related—if very distantly—it is only appropriate that you call me Aunt Ballard, isn't it?"

"Y-yes. I suppose so."

"Good. And I shall call you Lindsay. Later I shall want you to tell me all about yourself. Perhaps tomorrow. But this afternoon we will begin your instruction."

"Instruction?"

Antonia closed her eyes. "There is much you have to learn." She eyed the girl quickly. "Although perhaps not so much. Perhaps I am presuming too much." Or too little, she thought with hope.

"Lord Hawkesly could make a brilliant match," Miss Granville said. Her beautiful mouth set in a surprisingly firm line. "I believe you should advise him to do so."

This was really the most extraordinary situation. "Edward would be unlikely to appreciate my telling him who he should marry. I take it there is no need to instruct you on the proper use of the fan?"

"I have never owned a fan."

Antonia barely suppressed a groan. "Then we do indeed have a few items to discuss. For today I will give you one of my own fans. Later—when we order the other things you need—you may help choose some fans that are to your liking."

"I think the one you have is quite beautiful."

The gentle shyness in the girl's husky voice caught at Antonia. "Thank you. I have another the same. It will be yours." She attempted to sound haughty. There was still a very good chance that Edward would come to his senses and cry off, simple enough since no official announcement had been made.

"I am a great trouble to you."

True, but unavoidable. "Not at all. Your dress. It is, er, interesting."

"Thank you. The cloth is good, I think."

"And you like it?"

Lindsay's great blue eyes looked straight into Antonia's. "It is serviceable. The cloth is good."

Antonia thought she could guess what had happened. Belle Latchett's traveling costume had been in high style and of the best quality. No doubt the woman had taken the opportunity to foist her own made-over gowns on the girl whilst spending most of Edward's allowance on a new wardrobe for herself. Detestable. But, despite questionable treatment by the Latchetts, the girl was determined to be loyal. Admirable, if foolish. "Edward said he had arranged for you to have a new wardrobe for your Season."

The furious blush that stained Lindsay's cheeks pained even Antonia. "I didn't need everything new," the girl said, almost inaudibly. "There were things that could be . . . This dress still has . . ."

"Quite." No point in making the poor little thing suffer further. "I expect you have many lovely new things in your trunks."

"Yes."

The deep unhappiness Antonia saw in Lindsay's face, in the winding of her hands in her skirt, angered Antonia. Regardless of what eventually happened between Edward and this girl, it would be gratifying to make sure the Latchetts suffered for their willful unkindness.

"I grieve for my brother."

Lindsay's announcement startled Antonia. "William? He died two years ago?"

"Yes. I would wear mourning for him yet, but the dark clothes I had became too tight."

The most cursory glance at the young woman's small but voluptuous body made her statement easy to believe. "Here," Antonia said, impulsively pressing the brooch she still carried into Lindsay's hand. "The jet will look wonderful against your beautiful pale hair. Wear it in remembrance of William."

Lindsay looked at the brooch in her palm. "Oh, but I couldn't. It's too valuable."

"Rubbish. It's a mere bauble. And I want you to have it. As a welcome present, too." Advancing years must be causing simpleminded softness. She assumed an austere expression. "Now. Can you dance?"

"Not really." Lindsay smiled and the effect was startling. Lights shone in her eyes and her mouth curved sweetly to show small, perfect teeth. "But my friend Sarah Winslow—Miss Sarah Winslow—plays the pianoforte tolerably well and often I—" The brilliant blush washed over her pale skin and she bowed her head.

"And you often what?" Antonia asked gently.

"You'll think me silly."

"Please tell me."

"I pretend I am in dancing class and make poses. Probably the most foolish poses, although Sarah says not. But she is my friend."

"And do you like to pretend you are in dancing class?"

"Yes, I do."

There was a marvelous freshness about the girl. Antonia began to feel excited. To bring a new toast, a true, unspoiled diamond of the first water to the Season, would be a diverting coup.

"Lindsay, you will be most happy with what I have already arranged. Shortly you will meet Monsieur Gondeau, an accomplished dancing master. He will begin your instruction."

If the announcement did indeed make her happy, Lindsay hid the emotion well.

Antonia pressed on. "And I have engaged another young man to make certain your skills with the pianoforte are adequate. Do you sing well, my dear?"

Lindsay's breast rose and fell with a great sigh. "I don't think so."

"No matter," Antonia said with a gaiety she didn't feel. "We will do the best we can. . . . And the best will be remarkable, I'm sure. First we will go through your gowns and plan shopping excursions . . . for any extra items you may need." Which would be virtually everything unless she was much mistaken. "You will soon be enthralled by the whirl that is London in the Season. By the excitement of it all. There will be balls and routs and salons and musicales. My dear, you won't have a moment to yourself to be concerned about a thing." She pressed her hands together.

Lindsay appeared . . . stricken? Only for Edward would Antonia endure this trial.

As if he had heard her think his name, the door swept open and her nephew strode into the room.

"Good afternoon, Lindsay," he said, his deep voice even but shedding some strong emotion Antonia was loathe to identify.

Lindsay made a pitiful attempt at a smile.

Edward, tall, strong, the picture of masculine command in his perfectly cut but somber clothes, continued to regard the girl and Antonia had no difficulty recognizing what lay in his black eyes. He harbored passion for the woman he had chosen for his wife, deep, fiery, utterly possessive passion. She experienced an instant of thrill . . . and trepidation. This was her nephew, the brooding, controlled man who had never been disposed to fall victim to any weakness of the flesh that might undermine his independence. In that moment she almost feared for the innocent he held fixed in his burning sights.

"Lindsay," he said more gently. "Tell me, my dear, how was your journey?"

"Well enough," she murmured.

Edward moved to stand behind her. "And you look more than well enough," he told her. "You look beautiful."

Love was blind? Antonia tried not to look at the

dreadful gown. True, Lindsay would undoubtedly look beautiful even in rags, but the frightful mustard thing must go. Love? She opened her fan and studied Edward from its shadow. This stark, tense attention he centered on the girl could be a sign that Edward was in love, not that she had ever expected him to fall victim to an emotion he'd told her, more than once, that he considered a myth.

Edward bowed over the girl. "You are pale. Don't be afraid, sprite."

"I'm not afraid, my lord."

"I told you to call me Edward."

The girl didn't respond.

Abruptly, he turned to survey the room, his expression changing to one of anger. "Where is he?" His voice cut the air like a blade on stone. "Where is Latchett?"

"Edward!" Shocked, Antonia covered her heart. "I'll thank you not to use that tone in my house."

"Where . . . I apologize, Antonia. Where are Miss Granville's stepmother and stepbrother? I had thought they were with her."

"They were," Antonia told him coldly. "Since they were exhausted from their journey I suggested they go to Chelsea. They will need to rest. There will be time at a later date to entertain them."

Frowning, Edward paced the room. He scarcely glanced at Lindsay, who had taken herself to a shadowed corner as if to disappear.

"Sit down, Lindsay," Antonia said, eyeing Edward with disapproval. "We shall have tea before you are shown to your rooms."

"I must leave you," Edward announced. He already stood by the door. Then, as if remembering himself, he advanced on Antonia and kissed her cheek. Barely above a whisper, he said, "Please forgive me. There will be a time to explain, but not now. Will you trust that I have something very important to do—a matter of honor that needs atten-

tion?'' When she murmured assent he added,
''Thank you. Do not forget that you need to retire
early.''

''Have a care, Edward. Whatever is afoot here,
please be cautious.'' The mention of honor disturbed her greatly.

''You have nothing to fear.'' His eyes met hers
briefly before he turned to Miss Granville. ''Fare-
well, Lindsay. We'll meet again soon. Very soon,
my sprite.''

Lindsay did not respond, only turned away. But
not before Antonia saw her blanch to the lips. Was
this the response of a virginal young woman who
was deeply affected by love for a handsome, worldly
man? Or could Lindsay Granville be overwhelmingly afraid of something . . . or someone?

Chapter 9

Candlelight reflected in the dressing table mirror, as did the glow of the fire. Emma, sent by the countess to be Lindsay's abigail, stood behind her. She wielded a silver-backed brush through the waves that fell about Lindsay's shoulders.

"Such beautiful hair, miss." Emma's plump, rosy face was untroubled, her brown eyes cheerful. "Like silver satin. With bits of gold in it."

Lindsay smiled. Nothing about her felt beautiful.

"We was all fair amazed when we heard about you," Emma said brightly. "You being her ladyship's relation by marriage when we all thought she didn't have no one. Lovely it is. Her having someone after all."

Lindsay's brain had reached an almost pleasantly numb stage. She allowed Emma's ministrations and made no comment.

Emma, a tall girl no older than Lindsay, leaned down and said, "Her ladyship does have *him*, of course. But you'd hardly think of that one as bringing a tenderhearted lady any comfort."

Despite the beautiful brooch the countess had so kindly given her, Lindsay wondered at anyone considering Lady Ballard tenderhearted. All afternoon that "tenderhearted" lady had relentlessly schooled Lindsay in the finer arts required of "young ladies of Quality" until Lindsay had longed to scream that she wanted only to rush out, leap upon a horse, and ride back to her beloved Cornwall.

Whatever was she to do? However was she to escape this frightful pickle? Whatever would Antun think if she didn't appear or send word shortly? She'd been so certain that the moment the viscount and his aunt saw her in London, saw how unsuited she must be to their lofty lifestyle, they would send her packing immediately.

"You wants to keep clear of *him*, miss. There's stories about that one to make a body shiver. If you know what I mean." Emma's industrious brushing pulled Lindsay's head, first one way and then the other.

The thought of telling Antun what had happened, about the proposal of marriage, had seemed out of the question. He would likely have flown into a rage and threatened Hawkesly's life. Poor Hawkesly. Little did he know that he was already in dire danger because of Lindsay.

She realized what Emma had just said. "Are you talking about Lord Hawkesly?"

"Aye, miss. *Him*. Handsome enough to make a girl all of a flutter, but a dark 'un and no mistake."

Lindsay stared in the mirror at the girl. "What . . ." She felt "all of a flutter" herself and the sensation was most unpleasant. "What kind of stories are there about him?"

Emma flourished the brush airily. "Just—stories. Like how he learned all sorts of strange, mysterious ways in the Indies. And how he's got a hard heart. And how he can have any lady he chooses but never chooses to keep one for long. He's said to be feared by men as well as women."

"Why?" Lindsay put a hand to her throat.

"Oh, I really couldn't say, miss," Emma said, commencing to brush once more with even greater vigor. "I only mentioned it because with you being in the way of probably having to keep company with him, it would be as well if you was on your guard. You being young and beautiful and all.''

Lindsay could scarcely take a breath. Her heart beat quickly, and low inside her there was an odd tightening, a heated tensing. Hawkesly was certainly dark. Just this afternoon, as he'd bent over her, she'd glanced up at his slanted black brows, his black, glittering eyes, his black hair. He'd smiled—before he became angry about she knew not what—and his smile had curved his mouth in a way that made her remember their time together in Point Cottage. His mouth had touched her then, touched her lips, her neck, her . . . She closed her eyes against the memory of his vibrant curly hair moving while he kissed her breasts.

''Are you all right, miss?''

Emma's shrill voice snapped Lindsay's eyes open again. ''Yes,'' she managed in barely a whisper. What a bad girl she must be. Perhaps she was what Mrs. Radcliffe referred to in some of her novels as a romp. Lindsay was certain a romp was not a desirable thing for a young lady to be.

''You don't look all right. Let me put you into bed. You've had a long day.''

Lindsay shook her head. ''I'm well. Really.'' And she was by no means ready for bed. She must think. And there were plans to be made. And, to calm her nerves and help her fall asleep, she would write a little on her latest story.

''If you say so. But tomorrow her ladyship will be taking you to Bond Street. And I heard her say you're to go to Mr. Ward's—the milliner—on the Strand. And she said her own *modiste* will be along after your lesson with Monsieur Gondeau. Then—''

''*Another* dancing lesson?'' Lindsay moaned. ''But I had one this afternoon and I'm sure Monsieur Gondeau wasn't pleased with me.''

Emma covered her mouth and giggled. ''He always looks like he's smelled something nasty. I expect that's what made you think he wasn't happy. I'm sure you dance lovely. A beautiful little thing like you must be ever so graceful.''

Rash and excessive as Emma was with her praise, Lindsay couldn't help but feel heartened by the girl. "Monsieur Gondeau did not find me graceful." She elevated her nose. *"Please, please, mademoiselle.* Not like the dry stick. *Bend! Sway!* Imagine you are the supple limb swaying in the warm breeze."

They laughed together and Emma set down the brush to fuss with violet satin ribbons threaded at the neck of the almost diaphanous white wrapper Lindsay wore over her nightrail.

"Her ladyship's a marvel," Emma said, giving a bow a final tweak as Lindsay stood up. "She sent Tom—he's one of the footmen—she sent him out to Thomas's in Fleet Street. Wrote instructions for what she wanted and they sent back these. Fit you like they was specially made they do. And they look lovely. Fair sight, you are. It's a shame there's no one but me to see—" She covered her mouth again, hunched her shoulders and blushed. "Beg pardon, miss. I forgot myself. You won't tell her ladyship? This is my first place as an abigail and I do so want to stay with you."

Lindsay patted the girl. "I want you to stay, too." She thought of telling Emma that, apart from Gwyn on a borrowed basis, she'd never had a maid of her own and didn't particularly want one . . . except as someone her own age to talk to in this confusing household.

As soon as she'd convinced Emma that her place was secure, Lindsay sent the girl to her own bed and tried to order her thoughts. Visions of Antun rose, interspersed with darling little John's face. How wonderful it would be when the day came to introduce Antun to his nephew, his beloved only sister's child. First there would be anger to dispel at her not having trusted him with the knowledge from the beginning. She wished she could tell him now, but the risk was too great. Until John reached one and twenty she must trust only Nanny Thomas and Granny Whalen.

She paced back and forth across the soft pink carpet in the beautiful bedchamber the countess had given her. The high, narrow four-poster was hung with silk drapes of the deepest blush rose. The same color, of a heavier silk and scattered with embroidered rosebuds, covered a small wing chair by the fire. She had never known such personal luxury. Her chamber at home was large and comfortable but very plain.

But there was no pleasure in any of this grandeur, not when she was needed elsewhere.

Passing in front of the mirror, she caught sight of the delicate, almost transparent white lawn that drifted around her. With the light behind, her body showed in clear outline. Lindsay looked away hurriedly. Unsuitably revealing the ensemble might be, but she loved the soft femininity of it. Again the countess had shown uncommon kindness in so marvelous a gift, although Lindsay was certain the wrapper and gown had been ordered because her hostess, who had insisted on being present while Emma unpacked Lindsay's trunks, was disdainful of her plain and serviceable sleeping garments.

She couldn't think. She couldn't plan. And she certainly couldn't write about poor distressed Lady Araminta waiting almost without hope for the arrival of the soldier lord who had promised to take her away from her cruel uncle. Lindsay admitted that Sarah's tales about her brave lieutenant had inspired this latest twist in the story—and that the uncle bore a remarkable likeness to Roger—but no matter.

The sooner she appeared to be resigned to learn what the countess wanted to teach her—which would suggest she was also resigned to becoming Viscount Hawkesly's bride—the sooner she would find a means to slip away to Cornwall. She closed out the enormity of the problems such a feat presented.

Hawkesly's bride. She folded her arms around her slender middle and shivered deliciously. *Edward's* bride. What would it be like to be his wife in what she understood to be the way women became men's wives? She knew that, although naturally men and women did not share a single chamber, they did occupy rooms that allowed them to spend night hours together in privacy. How would it feel to lie in a bed wrapped in Edward's strong arms—with his long, muscular legs touching her?

She must indeed be a romp and such thoughts must stop. There would be no marriage and therefore no lying in Hawkesly's bed. There. Now she was being sensible.

Aunt Ballard. Lindsay mulled over the idea that she had discovered a new relative. How strange that she had known nothing of the connection. But then, with her mother gone from the moment of Lindsay's birth and her father having been a silent man not given to idle chatter, there had been no chance to discuss family history.

Concentration. She must think only of what to do next.

The dancing was the most difficult. Not at all like the poses and steps she'd practiced with Sarah in the vicarage parlor.

Pointing a toe, she folded her arms behind her back and attempted to sway. Where was that silly chart of figures Gondeau had left?

On the table in the music room. As was the brooch the countess had given her and which Lindsay would always treasure regardless of what happened. How could she have forgotten to bring it upstairs with her? The countess would think her ungrateful should she find the gift before Lindsay could retrieve it.

Quickly gathering a candle from the sturdy Chippendale stand near the bed, Lindsay ventured from the room. On tiptoe, she slipped along the second-floor balcony to the top of the wide staircase leading down to the main floor. Pausing, she glanced upward at the area of the house Emma had said was the countess's domain. No light showed and there was no sound. Lamps glowed faintly below, but again Lindsay heard nothing. Everyone had retired for the night.

The music room with its glossy paneled walls and polished wood floor was situated at the back of the house behind a library. Lindsay flitted past this, glancing into empty, book-lined silence illuminated only by the suggestion of a glow from the hall. Opening the music room door, she edged inside. Carefully, she closed herself in. The afternoon's coals had burned to faintly glowing embers in the fireplace. Her candle gave scant light, but an ice-white moon sent a knife-edged shard through a narrow window and across the room.

Lindsay stopped, made breathless by the dramatic study the moon made of the room. She moved, more slowly, to the long table where Monsieur Gondeau had rested his violin whilst drawing the diagrams he had instructed her to follow. There was the paper, and the brooch.

The latter safely enfolded in one hand, she set down the candle and took the paper to the window to study. The patterns of marks were so intricate. She hummed, cleared her throat and hummed again the air Gondeau had repeatedly played on his violin. He had played, his eyes closed, and the sounds had been sweet. Each time he opened his eyes the music had stopped so that he might shake his head and snap out instructions at Lindsay.

Beyond the window lay a small, walled garden.

Moonlight touched elegant white statuary precisely placed in graceful, hedge-lined arbors where roses would bloom before many more weeks passed.

Enough dreaming! The room was tolerably warm. With everyone asleep she would not be disturbed. What better time and place to practice the silly figures.

Placing the paper on the table once more, Lindsay used the light of her candle to study Monsieur Gondeau's cramped marks. Then she stepped away into the moon's wash upon the floor and began to hum yet again. And as she hummed, she attempted to go through a sequence, watching her feet in the violet satin slippers that matched the ribbon in her wrapper.

She relaxed, feeling the tune, and began to drift freely. The light folds of the gown and wrapper floated about her. It was almost as if she wore no clothes at all. Lindsay smiled and twirled. ''I wish you were here, Sarah,'' she said aloud. ''You could play for me.''

''I will be delighted to play for you.''

At the sound of a masculine voice Lindsay cried out. She had heard the voice, deep and still, yet she saw no one. Her heart had become a wild thing. ''Who is it?'' Backing to the table, she leaned against its edge. ''Where are you?''

''It's Edward, Lindsay.'' He stepped into the moonglow. ''I didn't mean to startle you.''

She tried to gather the flimsy cotton tighter around her quaking body. ''I'm not startled.'' Strange ways, Emma had said. Hard-hearted. A man men as well as women feared. ''I, er, I came to retrieve something.''

''And you have found it?'' He came toward her. Shadow stroked the harsh planes of his face.

Lindsay watched until he stood inches away, a too big, too lithe male who moved with the grace of a wild and predatory animal.

"I asked if you had found what you sought," he said softly. "Or did you really only come to dance like a moonflake in the night?"

He confused her. His words were like those of a poet, yet they held some hint of threat. Or was she merely being the overimaginative wet goose William had been so fond of calling her?

"Well, my sprite?"

She was of a mind to tell him she was not "his" anything. "I have what I came for. Thank you, my lord. And now I shall retire."

He laughed. "Nonsense, little one. When I came you were busy. Do not let me stop your instruction. You were practicing dance figures, were you not?"

If she were not already wedged against the table, Lindsay would retreat farther. "How . . . How are you come, my lord? I did not see you."

"I was in the library when you passed."

"There was no light."

He inclined his head and took a step closer. "I am fond of my aunt's house. Particularly the library. To-night I had much on my mind, so I sat there, thinking. When I arrived the household was already retired. I had not hoped to see you, but—"

"I'm sorry I disturbed you."

"But fortune smiled upon me, Lindsay," he continued as if she had not spoken. "You are far more stimulating in the flesh . . . than in the imagination of the flesh. That is what I was doing in the library—thinking about you."

Heat raced down her spine. What manner of man lurked in dark libraries, watching and waiting—and imagining? "I should go." Regardless of the foolish mistake she had made in Cornwall, regardless of her ruined reputation, she knew they should not be alone, even here.

"When I came into the room you were engrossed, my dear. Or should I say transported? So much so that you did not even hear my approach."

She could not understand this unwavering concentration on her by so worldly a man, a man who "could have any woman he chose but didn't choose to keep one for long." Why should he want to choose her at all?

"Have I disturbed you, Lindsay?"

Her heart raced, faster and faster. "I fear it is I who disturbed you, my lord." She had the strangest feeling that he was somehow holding her captive here. "You came, after all, for solitude."

"I came, my dear innocent sprite, with hope that I might at least spend a few private moments with you. When I discovered you were already retired I was devastated."

"How . . ." She felt suddenly shivery. "The servants are in bed, my lord. How did you gain entrance?"

He shrugged and Lindsay saw the vaguely sinister glint of his smile. "I have my own key to the house," he said, so very quietly. "It's my aunt's wish that I come and go as I please. And I think I may please to do so very often . . . until we are wed and I need only open a door in my own home to find you."

A pulse thundered in her temple. "My lord," she said, barely above a whisper. "I really do not think this is wise."

"This," he said, clearly mocking. "What is *this*?" Another step brought him very near. He wore no neckcloth and the front of his full shirt hung open. Braced apart, his legs flexed inside tight-stretched trousers. This was a man other men must envy as well as fear. This was a body in need of none of the padding and artifice other gentlemen employed in their attempts to cut a dashing figure.

He reached to touch fingertips to her cheek, then chuckled. "Come now, little one. Don't shrink from me. Tell me exactly what you think *this* is. This whatever it is that exists between us."

"I do not know." She did know she both feared and adored the sensations tumbling through her body. "You must be very tired, my lord."

"Tired? Now that's an interesting thought." He tilted back his head so that the white glow touched the strong column of his neck. "No, I don't think I can be tired. Impatient, perhaps—to be with you as men and women are intended to be together. But definitely not tired. And, to you, I am Edward. Let me hear you say it."

"Edward."

"Again," he roared. "I can scarce hear you."

She cast about for a graceful means of departing. "The servants might hear."

"Oh, no. I do assure you that no one will come, Lindsay. We are completely alone here—and safe."

But she wasn't safe. Or she didn't feel safe. "I am tired," she said weakly. "Edward."

"Good," he said abruptly. "I like the sound of my name on your sweet lips. Dance! I shall play and you shall dance."

She could think of no reply. Goodness knew what he had already seen of her as she moved about unknowingly. To deliberately disport herself for his eyes was out of the question.

Hawkesly strode to the piano and positioned himself on the stool. From there he would have a clear view of her. "What do you think of Mozart?"

"I think—" she began hesitantly. Why should she not have opinions and voice them? Because the countess had warned her of the evils of a young lady's knowing too much—about anything. In fact, it was desirable to pretend to know nothing regardless, if one wanted to be considered an appropriate companion for an eligible gentleman. "I'm not sure." Fie! She was very sure. "Yes. Yes, I am. I am most impressed with Mr. Mozart's work. Particularly his piano concertos. There is . . . there is little music in my home but much in Sarah's. The Reverend Winslow does not play well. But he is enthusiastic and entertaining. And Sarah plays nicely. However, it is Mr. Edmonds, a curate who visits from time to time, who enthralls me.''

''Enthralls you?''

What very strange tones the man's voice produced sometimes. ''Yes. Mr. Edmonds is a marvel and what I enjoy most is the selection he plays from Mr. Mozart's twenty-first piano concerto. Sometimes it marches along and sometimes it is misty, dreamy. Very affecting.'' There. Would he want a wife who exhibited unbecomingly forward opinions on such subjects?

Rather than frown, Hawkesly raised a brow and smiled. ''You are indeed a surprise, Lindsay,'' he said, and notes began to issue from the piano. ''A most pleasant one. But it will be better that I enthrall you than Mr. Edmonds.''

The piece streamed forth boldly from obviously well practiced fingers. Drawn as a moth to a bright flame, Lindsay put aside her trepidation and went to his side. Bent over the keys so that she couldn't see his face, Hawkesly moved with the music.

She had understood that gentlemen of the *haut ton* did not spend time in the pursuit of playing instruments. They boxed and rode and fenced and shot—they did not play Mozart, their bodies moving as if possessed.

When he finished, Lindsay pressed her hands together, ecstatic and anxious to hear more. ''Play again,'' she implored. ''I have never heard anything so beautiful.''

''More beautiful than your Mr. Edmonds?''

''So beautiful you make me want to weep.''

He turned his face up to Lindsay's and the passionate gleam in his opaque eyes quickened her breathing. ''Dance for me,'' he said gently. ''There, in the moonlight. So I may remember how you look

tonight and during all the tedious time I must wait
to claim you."

She understood so little of what he said. Self-
consciously, Lindsay trod slowly to the place he indicated. "I feel foolish. I am a dry stick when I
dance. Monsieur Gondeau said so."

"At least *everyone* did not say so."

"I beg your pardon."

"It was nothing of importance. I will play a country tune that you may easily follow."

She recognized the melody as something else Mr.
Edmonds played, but did not ask its name. At first
she was so awkward she could scarce move. But
slowly she felt softened. Silvery notes flowed over
her and she moved with them, turned, raised her
arms above her head as she pirouetted as Monsieur
Gondeau had instructed her. And she began to hum,
to sweep her body from side to side. The music, and
the fabric of her gown like the touch of gossamer,
slipped about her.

The music had stopped.

With her arms still raised, Lindsay stood still, her
breath coming in shallow bursts. Hawkesly was
gone. Simply gone. A draft of cool air sighed over
her skin. She looked down and drew in a sharp
breath. He must have left to preserve her modesty.
There could be no doubt that every curve and line
of her was visible. She had danced before him like
a hussy displaying her wares.

"Don't stop."

For the second time, she jumped—and fingertips
passed from between her shoulder blades to the dip
at her waist. "Dance, sprite." Those strong fingers
turned Lindsay until her face was on a level with
Edward's almost naked chest. "You are so tiny. So
voluptuous, but such a little woman. Wherever I go
I shall be able to see you as you are this night. Your
soft form swaying, enticing. You entice me, my delectable sprite."

Lindsay could feel the heat of his body. "It is not my intention to entice." The hand at her waist burned as if nothing kept it from her naked skin.

"Mm. All the more fascinating. I doubt the stuffy Monsieur Gondeau taught you anything of the waltz."

Lindsay gasped. "Of course not! And the countess was most specific in warning me that the waltz is considered outlandish. For ladies and gentleman of the *ton*."

Hawkesly threw back his head and laughed aloud. "Antonia? Hah! I'll wager she can turn a pretty ankle in a waltz when the mood strikes. Why—" He shook his head, at the same time spreading his fingers so wide that the end of his thumb came periously close to her breast. "Enough of Antonia. I assure you, miss, that the waltz is being performed throughout *le beau monde*. Almack's excluded, of course. But you are not in the way of needing to be competing for vouchers to that establishment."

She could not resist asking, "Why, my lord? I understand every young woman making her debut feels she would die rather than be turned down at Almack's."

"Quite. And you shall see it in due course, if you want to—and as my wife. Which answers your question. The rooms are a marriage mart. You are not looking for a husband. You have already found one."

Lindsay managed to swallow. Supported by his large, firm hand she looked up into his face. "That was something I wished to speak to you about, Edward." He was more handsome than any man she had ever imagined, much less seen.

"I've decided to teach you to waltz. Put your hand in mine." He had a perturbing way of seeming not to hear her.

She glanced at his left hand. He'd moved closer, so close she must lean back to see him now.

"Just so," he said, taking her unresisting right hand in his. "Place your other hand upon my shoulder."

Hesitantly, her chest growing tighter and tighter, Lindsay rested the fingertips of her left hand on his upper arm. She thought to mention that since the top of her head barely reached his shoulder, to put her hand there would be exceedingly awkward.

"Now. Let my legs guide yours."

Lindsay drew in another sharp breath and tried to pull away. Hawkesly held her the tighter, so tight that her length was brought into intimate contact with his.

His soft laugh moved her hair. "Relax." He hummed, low, melodic, a sound that rumbled in his throat . . . in his chest . . . which was perilously close to Lindsay's face. "Be guided. One and two and one and two, and turn and one and turn and two. Very good."

It was not at all good. At every touch she trembled. At every step she stumbled.

"You are to relax," Edward said more firmly. "Follow orders, wife-to-be. It is time you started to learn what is expected of you."

"That is what I wanted to talk to you about," Lindsay said. She turned her face up to his. "I really do not . . ."

Hawkesly had bent his head. His intense gaze was on her mouth.

"I do not think . . ." Talking was so difficult when he looked at her like that.

"Then do not think, my love." His mouth met hers. Firm, yet soft, his lips brushed back and forth while he nuzzled her chin even higher. "So sweet. So ready to be mine." The kiss became harder and she felt a gentle sucking on her lower lip before Hawkesly licked a trail just inside.

Lindsay heard a small sound. Her own? A high, pleading moan? They swayed yet and when Hawkesly lifted his head a fraction he swung her once more, hummed once more, smiled a smile that crinkled the corners of those obsidian eyes.

She leaned against him now. How could she not when he held her so? Where his shirt gaped, her breasts were guarded from his flesh by only the thinnest layers of lawn. Lindsay closed her eyes and felt the solid power of him. Her aching breasts felt swollen.

"Ah, yes," Hawkesly whispered, almost as if he knew the sensations of her body. "Yes, sweet one. You are so ready. It must be soon."

Lindsay wriggled and only succeeded in rubbing against him more vigorously.

"Yes." His voice was husky.

When had his unyielding thigh found a path between hers? He pulled her up until she rode that thigh as intimately as he did his elegant black stallion. Helpless in the pull of sensations he caused, she let her head hang back.

"You are warm," he whispered. "And I want to see you." The marvelous sensation stopped while he untied the ribbon that closed her wrapper. He brushed it aside and down her arms. The fabric fell silently into a pool at their feet. "Come, Lindsay. It is time to teach you even a little more."

"More dancing," she said indistinctly, disappointed though she knew she should not be. "I do not think I want to dance anymore."

"The dance I have in mind will please you, I think."

Holding her hand, he led her around the table to the window where the moon still shone bright. Standing behind her, he put an arm around her and eased her back against his shoulder. "I want to teach you the dances of your body, sprite, the wonderful things it will do with my help."

"I do not . . . I don't understand you. . . ."

He had eased her hip forward. "You cannot know or understand everything at once, little one. Our pleasure will be the greater for taking time with this teaching, I promise you. Look." As he spoke, he flattened his hand over her breast, ignoring her futile attempt to stop him. "Watch how your body tells me what it wants."

Hawkesly took his time. The low neck of the nightrail barely covered her. Tiny tucks became ridges that incited her.

"Look, Lindsay."

Shyly, she bowed her face. His thumb scooped beneath the skimpy bodice to flick back and forth over her nipple. "Aah," she breathed and let her head fall against him once more.

Hawkesly laughed. "Watch, sweeting. See how the bud grows and asks for my attention."

She wiggled again, only to feel a probing hand between her thighs, seeking, rubbing. Twisting Lindsay he swooped and fastened his mouth over the wisp of fabric still covering her nipple. Exquisite seconds later he moved to the other breast and suckled again. She heard him groan and reached back blindly to find something to steady her. Her hand found his hip, then some part of him that was long and full and heavy and hard.

"Ah, yes," Hawkesly murmured. "Yes, yes. You learn fast, my sweet one."

With a cry, Lindsay snatched her hand away. There were mentions of such things, veiled hints . . . She had not believed them and she would not.

Hawkesly laughed again and lifted his head. "Now look, Lindsay. Look and see what your body tells me."

"No."

"Yes. Look."

Slowly, she let her eyes find what his clever mouth had made. The bodice of her nightrail was soaked where his tongue and teeth had left their mark. Through the wet fabric, Lindsay's nipple thrust, large, pink and begging for his attention.

''You see.'' When she nodded, he drove his hand between her legs. ''See here, also.'' But before she could move, he raised the filmy skirt, slipped it upward until cool air caressed her thighs . . . her belly.

''This should not be!'' But she would be bereft if he stopped.

''It will be,'' Edward whispered. ''It is.''

Gathering the skirt behind, he faced Lindsay and sank to his knees. The moist plucking of his lips and teeth at her belly stole her breath and she almost fell. Cradling her bottom in his hands he kissed and sucked, moving lower until his tongue found the most intimate folds of her body.

''No!'' She almost screamed, but the sound did not escape her throat. Thoughts turned to wild, flashing things. How could it be wrong to feel such pleasure?

''Lean against me,'' he murmured. And she did, seeking more and more of the wondrous sensations. Her back met the table and supported her, and Hawkesly's hands moved. He reached up to catch at her bodice. She heard the sound of tearing cloth as he bared her breasts. The ends of his hard fingers played over her stiff nipples and the sensation in her deepest parts broke wide open like flame-edged darts that seared up and drove her down against him.

A great, wild flash . . .

Lindsay sagged, reaching for and finding purchase by grabbing his vibrant hair. She panted. The moist place between her legs pulsed.

''I am . . . It is too much,'' she murmured, her hands slipping to his shoulders. ''This, this other thing, the erring between a man and a woman.''

''It is a wonderful thing.'' Hawkesly stood, let her skirt fall back into place, and cupped her breasts again. He stroked them, bending to kiss each one until she cried out and plucked feebly at him. She felt him smile against her skin. "You must remember this wonderful thing that has made it imperative that we become man and wife as soon as possible."

Lindsay wanted to lie down, to sleep. "I'm so very sorry that it would not be right to keep on bringing you such exquisite pleasure."

"Would you care to explain further, my dear?" He held her firmly in one arm while he found her wrapper.

"Is it as wonderful for you as it is for me? The erring, that is. If so, I can well understand how you would wish to do it again and again."

His silence perturbed her, but only slightly. She was too busy trying to help him replace the wrapper over the tattered nightrail. What would the countess think? What would Emma think? She must contrive to mend the gown, or better yet, to pretend to lose it.

Lindsay's mind became clear, amazingly, searingly clear. "Edward! Oh, Edward. I have it."

He had managed to tuck and tie her clothes together so that she could claim some semblance of modesty—at least until she returned to her rooms. "And what do you have?" he asked indulgently before chuckling. "Apart from the very delectable items I know very well you have."

She blushed at the suggestion she was sure he was making. "It is so simple. I cannot imagine why I didn't think of it before. Oh, Edward, this is perfect."

He braced a hand each side of her on the table. "Do tell."

"I would make you a terrible wife. You do see that?"

"No."

"Of course you do. It is the wonderful erring that has caused you to quite lose your senses. And I do admit that it would appear that you and I have what the Reverend Winslow calls a special chemical response to one another. But enough of that. We can still share this . . . We can be together this way when you can spare the time to come to me in Cornwall."

With the moonlight behind him, Edward's face was entirely obscured from Lindsay.

She persevered. "Yes, well. I, as you know, am firmly decided on a single life. I cannot . . . I mean, I do not choose to marry. But it really would be too bad for us not to share this very special gift we have together as often as possible."

"Mmm. Exactly my intention." He murmured something more, something that sounded like "And much more," but she couldn't be certain. Clearly, he added: "So we shall marry immediately. Don't you agree?"

"Not at all," she said sharply, annoyed that he could be so obtuse. "You shall marry someone suitable to be your viscountess and I shall not marry at all."

"I fear you are not making yourself clear, Lindsay."

She stood on tiptoe and quickly kissed the corner of his mouth. Before he could grab her, she ducked away and dodged around the table.

"It's all so simple, Edward. And so absolutely perfect. I've read all about these things. You will marry and I will be waiting whenever you want to come to me. Point Cottage will be our rendezvous place. I am going to be your *inamorata*." She covered her mouth, shocked at how wicked the word felt on her lips. "You will not pay for things for me, of course, since I do not choose to be a—er—ladybird. But we shall become lovers and err regularly."

"Lindsay—"

"I'll leave the arrangements for my return to

Cornwall to you. I would think as soon as possible might be preferable, wouldn't you?''

''Lindsay—''

''I'll await your instructions. Good night, Edward.'' Trying not to think that he sounded forbidding, she fled the room before he could say more.

Chapter 10

"**G**ad, Edward. You almost brought me to *my* knees."

Edward slammed the library door with enough force to rattle its hinges. "Damn you, Julian, for the slimy Peeping Tom you are."

The Honorable Julian Lloyd-Preston lolled, an elbow hooked onto the fireplace mantle. "Don't blame me, old man. A fella's only human. I came looking for you and thought I heard a mumble in the music room. More of a moan, really. A throes-of-passion moan, if you know what I mean."

Edward scowled. "So you slithered into my library and used the peephole I should never have shown you."

"Something like that. Only it's your aunt's peephole, don't you know. And I only peeped a moment."

"Of course you did, Julian. Only a moment."

One of Julian's finely marked brown brows rose. An aggrieved expression settled on his good-looking face. "I say, old chap. One's a gentleman after all. Deserve the benefit of the doubt, wouldn't you say?"

"Mmm."

Julian studied the fingernails of one long, well-shaped hand. "Fetching piece, I must say. Magnificent breasts."

"Why, you—" Edward made a move toward his old friend and stopped. "You shouldn't have looked. Not that I blame you for it," he finished under his breath. "Sit down. But pour us a glass of Madeira first."

By thunder, he was still hard. He couldn't remember sustaining the condition this long since he'd been a boy still peering down milkmaids' bodices. Not that he was totally oblivious to a good pair of breasts readily on display even now. The tense stretching against his thigh made him wince and turn away. Damn Lindsay Granville anyway. Why couldn't she have been the plain, chicken-breasted specimen he'd expected? Then it would have been simple. Do what must be done, and pack her away to Devon, where he'd manage to find the will to bed her for the purpose of producing an heir.

"Care to talk about it, old man?"

Edward grunted. His problem was more likely to become a difficulty in staying out of bed with the fair Lindsay.

"I do believe our iron-hearted maiden's dream is smitten. Got you where the need doesn't go away, has she?"

She had him where the need was *supposed* to go away much more quickly than it was. "Don't talk rot, Lloyd-Preston."

Julian nudged Edward's arm with a glass. "Finish this and I'll pour you another. If I ever saw a man in need of dulling the senses, it's you."

"Don't presume to read my mind." But Edward took the glass and drained its contents in a single swallow before handing it back to Julian.

"Disappointing, y'know," Julian said vaguely.

Edward heard the scrape of crystal as Julian removed the decanter stopper once more. Madeira gurgled into the glass.

"All right," Edward said, feeling peeved. "Tell me. What's disappointing?"

"Well, a fella hardly likes to complain, but it do seem a bit churlish to pull down the curtain before the end of the act, as it were."

Edward turned on him slowly. "Meaning?" he asked very quietly.

"Meaning that you had the chit—whoever she is—where you wanted her." He laughed, tipping back his head to display perfect teeth. "Exactly where you wanted her in the real sense. I was ready to see if your technique's any better than it was the last time I saw it. Parry and thrust—to the hilt. Remember those days?"

"Unfortunately most of us did foolish things in our youth." There were events, particularly during his days at Cambridge, that he'd as soon forget, particularly those involving one or two aging whores only too willing to help initiate tireless boys fresh from Eton into the more exotic ways of the flesh.

"There are those who aren't opposed to a little orgy even now, Edward. Why just recently some fella at White's was telling me I ought to stop by an abbey in a certain area at a certain time of night. Seems the Hell Fire club isn't completely buried."

Edward curled his lip in disgust. "Sharing harlots disguised as thirteen-year-old virgins with a gaggle of randy, frenchified old perverts isn't to my taste." In fact, there was only one virgin he could imagine having an interest in at this moment . . . perhaps at any moment . . . He drew in a sharp, surprised breath. "I didn't think that kind of thing was your style, either, Julian."

"It's not." Julian gestured broadly. "Don't know what came over me even mentioning such stuff. I suppose that little scene I just witnessed excited even my indolent interest in such things. Downright erotic, old man. Those breasts in the moonlight. The legs. Her—"

"That'll do, Julian," Edward said curtly, looking at his friend more closely. "I do believe you're foxed. Not like you to get in your cups, Julian. Having trouble with the ladies yourself, are you?"

"Pah! You know I don't have time for that."

" 'Course not."

Julian's affected disinterest in the opposite sex didn't fool Edward for a moment. As the younger son of a family that was respected but short on blunt, Julian always played close to the bone with money. Two Seasons previous he'd fallen quite madly for a girl, only to have her turn him aside in favor of a more brilliant match. On the day her betrothal was announced, Julian had managed to render himself completely foxed. The following afternoon, while Edward held his friend's head over a basin, Julian vowed never to love again. So far he'd held fast to that vow, but Edward knew the passions that ran beneath Julian's cool exterior.

"Been hearing rumors about you, Edward." Julian handed over another full glass. The lines about his mouth had drawn in tighter and Edward suspected the other man might also be remembering his lost love.

"What rumors would those be?" Edward asked. He flopped into a chair and stretched out his booted feet. Damn it to hell, but his body was still tensed.

"A match on the horizon. Must say I'm surprised she managed to snare you."

Julian had Edward's entire attention. He pulled himself straighter in the chair. "Where did you hear that? It wasn't supposed to be out until Aunt Antonia gives the nod."

"Even the inimitable countess herself wouldn't be able to keep the luscious . . . I mean the fair, Clarisse's mouth closed."

"Oh, that." Tipping up his glass, Edward slouched again. Clarisse must be taken care of. That would be simple enough. All he'd have to do was threaten her with embarrassment in every polite drawing room in London and she'd go scurrying back to old Faddon. Tomorrow or the next day would be soon enough to see the clever hoyden.

"It is true, then?" Julian asked.

Edward chewed his bottom lip. It was almost too bad that he wasn't the type of man who could choose to spill himself into a delectable and willing receptacle simply to find relief. Clarisse was certainly delectable . . . and *so* willing. But he wasn't that type of man.

"I must say, I'm surprised."

"Julian. Stop talked in riddles, man."

"Concentrate and you won't find me difficult to understand. First, I never expected you to shackle yourself to a jade. But since you're evidently about to do just that, why waste the energy you're going to need for the Simmonds on a serving girl?"

Edward stared, then bridled. "We aren't going to discuss my energy, Julian. Or what I can or cannot accomplish when the opportunity presents. I am not marrying a jade. And the girl you just . . . The innocent girl you just violated with your foul spying is no servant."

"Aha." Julian, in his place by the mantle, leaned forward, an avid twinkle in his clear gray eyes. "The Simmonds has been lying."

"Pay it no mind. I'll attend to her tomorrow."

"I pity her." With an exaggerated sigh, Julian removed a quizzing glass from his waistcoat pocket and swung it back and forth. "In that case, I understand perfectly what I just saw."

"You just saw"—Edward said menacingly, rising from his chair—"a man and his betrothed stealing a little private time together."

The supercilious smile was slow to melt from Julian's face. "You jest."

The shock that replaced the smile brought Edward immense satisfaction. "Not at all. And you, my friend, are going to swear to keep what I tell you to yourself until I give you leave to do otherwise."

"She's a child," Julian almost whispered. "A beautiful, voluptuous child."

Heat washed over Edward again. An unbearable tightening against his thigh made him shift. "*She* is almost twenty. For the rest, she is indeed beautiful. But that is neither here nor there." If only he could convince himself of that.

"But who is she, Edward? What is her name?"

Julian moved a chair close to Edward's, flipped aside the tail of his wine-colored jacket and sat down. "Tell me all. Hold nothing back because I know you too well not to pick out an intention to lie at ten paces."

"I was going to tell you," Edward said. He passed a hand over his eyes. "I may need your help. It's just that I've got to know you're with me."

"Tell me. By God, Edward. Tell me what's happened, man. Who can you trust, if not me? If it weren't for you I'd—"

"We won't speak of that." Edward waved the other to silence. The infamous episode of thwarted love had come within seconds of causing a far more permanent effect on Julian's life than a few too many bottles of Madeira. It had been Edward's hand that knocked the pistol barrel away from Julian's temple.

"There is something dire." Julian had paled. "I feel it. Damn, but I wish James were still with us."

"I, too," Edward said, swallowing bitter gall. "If he were, none of this would be necessary. Julian, do I have your word that you will repeat nothing that passes between us in this room tonight?"

Julian nodded.

"Of course." Edward let his eyes close. "I would trust you with my life. And tonight, I am."

"Edward—"

"Hear me out. James was murdered."

The silence lasted so long that Edward leaned to

clamp a hand on Julian's arm. "Did you hear me? He didn't die by a French shot. He was murdered. Stabbed to death by an Englishman, may God curse the bastard."

"This makes no sense. James died in battle at sea two years ago. You were informed by a messenger from His Majesty. What mischief is this? And what has the girl to do with any of it?"

"A man by the name of Kertz came to see me. He was a seaman aboard the ship where James died. He told me he witnessed James's murder." Repeating the words aloud freshened the pain Edward had felt at first hearing them. Since that fateful day when the seaman had come to Edward in the Indies, he had mentioned them to no one, not even the investigator, Trevay, who had certainly probed hard enough to find out the genuine reason for Edward's interest in the Granvilles. Trevay had made no attempt to disguise his disbelief that a man of Edward's standing would go to such lengths simply to find out more about a girl in whom he was interested.

"Go on," Julian prompted.

"I'm going to avenge James," Edward said, rising to his feet. "I'm going to avenge him slowly, with as much pain as I can drive into his murderer."

"I believe you," Julian said. He came to Edward's side and placed a hand on his shoulder. "Tell me what I can do."

"Support me. Help me in any way I may come to need. I will not put you in danger."

"So what if you do? Did this seaman tell you the identity of the man who . . . Did he tell you who murdered James?"

"He did not know the name of the man who wielded the knife."

"But he knew where and how you might find him?"

"No."

Julian pulled Edward around to face him. "Then how will we find him?"

"We won't."

"I don't understand."

"You will very soon." Edward smiled, a grimacing smile not born of humor. "The man who wielded the knife is not my quarry. My intention is to deal with the creature who sent that man. I will deal with him in such a way that he will grovel at my feet, begging me to save him. Only at the end will I tell him why everything he holds dear has crumbled. His shame, his eventual complete ruin and banishment will give me my revenge."

Julian dropped his head. "I'm glad I'm not this man. And you do know his identity, don't you, Edward?"

"Yes." The rage simmered afresh, white hot and frenzied inside the cold shell he'd learned to keep in place. "James died trying to save another man. This other man was attacked by a fellow while the battle raged. In the confusion, no one but James, and this Kertz who came to me, saw the assassin go about his business. James tried to intervene and was himself mortally wounded and left to die. Kertz, who went to his aid, listened to my dear brother's last words and carried a message back to me. He . . ." Sickness smote at Edward. He clamped the back of a hand to his mouth and leaned against a wall, rested his head against cool wood.

"Come away," Julian said, his voice heavy with worry. "My carriage is outside. We'll go to Cavendish Square. I'll spend the night and we can continue this tomorrow. You're exhausted now."

"I must finish. Then you will understand. The man I will destroy paid an assassin to kill so that he could gain control of what rightfully belonged to another man."

"Could you not put this in the hands of the authorities?'' Julian said. But his voice was devoid of hope.

"Evidence given by a seaman who took money for divulging the information and then vanished? Evidence of a crime already two years old? Even if the authorities could be persuaded to take on the case, their justice—if it ever came—would not satisfy me.''

Julian sighed. "I will do whatever I can for you, my friend. Ask—for anything, any help—and it will be yours.''

"Thank you.''

"But now, Edward, you must finish this tale. I have a feeling the worst is to come.''

Edward took measure of what he was about to reveal. "The girl you saw me with will become my viscountess within weeks.''

"Yes. But we can speak of that later.''

"No, Julian. The girl is at the very heart of it all.'' A fact he never intended Lindsay to discover. "Her brother was William Granville, the man my brother died trying to save. Her stepbrother is Roger Latchett, the filth who hired the assassin.''

Chapter 11

Lindsay flew up Lady Ballard's front steps. Before she could knock, the door opened and she was confronted by Norris, his nose at its customary elevated angle.

"Good afternoon, Norris," Lindsay said. Aunt Ballard, lecturing on the importance of commanding respect, had warned her to say little or nothing to servants unless she was giving orders. Lindsay found the rule silly. At home in Cornwall the servants were her friends. Why should she behave differently in London? Particularly since she had no intention of staying here long.

Norris bowed silently and opened the door wider.

"Do come along," Lindsay said over her shoulder to the new friend she'd made that afternoon and to Emma. "Do hurry."

Today the countess had complained of having taken cold and chose to stay at home while Emma was pressed into service to accompany Lindsay to a delightful little salon at the Berkeley Square home of a Lady Sebbel. As soon as they arrived at their destination Emma had been banished to the servants' quarters, leaving Lindsay feeling terrified.

Lindsay hadn't wanted to go at all, but now she was glad the countess had insisted, because she had found a wonderful new friend, and she needed a friend almost more than her own breath. She needed help from someone high-spirited and potentially sympathetic and she might very well have found just such a one.

The conversation at Lady Sebbel's had been so lively that Lindsay was at first afraid she would disgrace herself by seeming henwitted. But the subject had been romantic novels and the work of the dashing Lord Byron. Lindsay wasn't sure she would like Lord Byron, but she hadn't dared to say as much.

"Where is . . . Aunt Ballard?" she asked Norris. A week in the countess's house hadn't made Lindsay entirely comfortable with her newfound relation. "In her boudoir?"

The butler drew himself up. "It is after five in the afternoon, Miss Granville."

The implication being that his mistress only remained in her boudoir until noon. Lindsay, on the other hand, knew full well that the haughtily elegant lady frequently retired to that room at other times . . . notably when tall, distinguished Lord Airsly came to call.

"Her ladyship is in the drawing room," Norris intoned, taking Lindsay's cloak.

"Thank you," Lindsay said pleasantly. "Emma, thank you for accompanying me this afternoon. Would you please attend to that little task I gave you this morning?"

The maid stared for an instant before understanding showed in her eyes. "Yes, miss. I'll see to it at once." Her face flushed, she bobbed, then she ran eagerly upstairs.

Lindsay had discovered that Emma longed to learn to read and write. She'd also discerned that the girl had a quick mind. Already she could sound out and copy the simple words Lindsay wrote for her on a tablet. Any extra moments that could be invented for practice would be useful.

"Come," Lindsay said to her newfound friend. "Aunt Ballard will be delighted I've met someone my own age. She's been talking about finding some sort of companion. What a terrible thought. You must help me convince her I'm faring perfectly well as I am." She might have to implement certain plans, plans that would be impossible to accomplish with a paid watcher in residence.

Without waiting for a response, Lindsay opened the drawing room door. Then she paused. For one seemingly endless hour each morning, she walked back and forth in front of the countess with the dreaded book upon her head. *Glide, Lindsay. Glide. Chin up! Slower. Slower. Gentlemen are not impressed by ladies who gallop.*

Regardless of her stringent instruction, the countess was kind and Lindsay was determined to please that lady while, at the same time, finding a way to make Hawkesly change his mind about the wedding. There had been no word or visit from him since the night of her "offer." Mortified at the recollection, she tightened her mouth. She was undaunted. Eventually the infuriatingly stubborn man would give up. She intended to cajole, shame or shock him into doing so. If necessary a combination of tactics could be employed.

Sighing, she raised her chin, prayed her beautiful new gown of frosted lilac muslin wasn't wrinkled, and entered the room with gracefully measured steps.

"Lindsay." Seated near the fire, the countess smiled approvingly. "You are radiant, my dear. How was the salon? Did you enjoy yourself?"

"Oh, yes. I'm so glad I went." Until she could find a way out of her predicament and back to Cornwall, she might as well enjoy herself. There would probably never be another opportunity to see and do such wonderful things. "Lady Sebbel was most kind. And her daughter is dear. And we talked about—"

"Who do you have with you?" Aunt Ballard raised her lorgnette.

"Forgive me." Lindsay stepped aside and caught the hand of the young woman behind her. "I insisted you would be pleased if I brought Clarisse to meet you."

Aunt Ballard slowly lowered her lorgnette. Her frown suggested anything but pleasure.

"This is Lady Clarisse Simmonds," Lindsay continued, less certain now. "I told her I'm making my first visit to London and that I'm staying with you . . . And that you are my aunt—very distantly related through your late husband." Aunt Ballard sat perfectly still, her hands folded in her lap. Her face showed no particular expression now. "When Clarisse—as she has kindly insisted I call her—when Clarisse discovered I knew no one at Lady Sebbel's, she befriended me. It was such a help having her tell me who was related to whom and . . . and all the other gossip . . . I mean, *on dit*. I told her how eager you are for me to associate with other females of my own age," she finished hesitantly.

"I'm surprised Lady Simmonds didn't mention that we have already met," said Aunt Ballard. "Many times."

Lindsay looked questioningly at Clarisse, who turned the corners of her mouth up prettily. Dimples showed in rounded cheeks and her huge violet-colored eyes shone. "I wanted to surprise you, Lady Ballard. Wasn't it the most divine coincidence that Lindsay and I happened to meet! I, too, was wilting with *ennui* among those elderly bluestockings."

"Ernestine Sebbel could hardly be termed a bluestocking," Aunt Ballard said, sounding frighteningly severe. "And she's at least fifteen years my

junior. And isn't her Isabelle the same . . . no, no,
a little younger than you, Lady Simmonds? And
surely the Claridge sisters were there. I know
they—''

"Oh, la!" Clarisse swept to Aunt Ballard with
style and grace enough to make Lindsay green.
"There were so many people there, were there not,
Lindsay?"

"Well—"

"There. You see! Lindsay was overwhelmed, just
as I was." Clarisse executed a perfect curtsy. Her
dress, cut so daringly low as to be almost immodest,
was of finest batiste the color of sea foam. The shade
set off to perfection her heavy auburn ringlets and
creamy skin. Her full breasts all but overflowed the
scant bodice, and the fabric of the gown, close to
transparent, displayed the outline of a small waist
and curvaceous hips. Artfully tucked into the tiny
curls that framed her face were pearl-studded gauze
flowers of the same green as her dress. Lindsay did
think the outfit somewhat flamboyant for the afternoon, but Clarisse's personality seemed to justify a
degree of excess.

"Clarisse is so funny," Lindsay said, feeling de-
fensive of this exquisite creature who, despite the
discovery that Lindsay was no more than a distant
relative of the countess's last husband, had shown
her the greatest kindness. "And she's *met* Lord Byron!"

Clarisse batted her eyelashes in the way Lindsay
was supposed to master and which, as yet, had
proved ridiculously difficult. "Those seductive *un-
derlooks*," Clarisse said, her voice loaded with awe.
"I swear, when he looked *my* way I almost
swooned."

"No doubt," Aunt Ballard said crisply. "What else
did you speak of today?"

"Nothing that didn't entertain us." Clarisse
flipped her fan open and shut. "But enough of the

dull afternoon. Isn't this delicious? You and I already the best of friends, and now Lindsay is to become a dear confidante! I can hardly wait to act as the companion she needs. And since I am about to become a member of—''

"I trust Isabelle Sebbel is well," Aunt Ballard said, sounding oddly hurried. "She isn't a strong gel, y'know."

Clarisse's smooth brow puckered. "I don't know the woman." Her mouth turned down. "No wonder she's destined to remain on the shelf. Such a milk-and-water miss. Plain as Devonshire cream and equally without taste."

"There's nothing plain—or tasteless—about Devonshire cream, Clarisse. The best in the county is produced at Hawkesly, or so I'm told by people who travel miles to taste the stuff."

Lindsay whipped around, almost losing her balance. Hawkesly strode into the room and the expression on his face could only be described as thunderous. Her heart immediately tripped as wildly as it had when he'd taught her the waltz. She closed her eyes and took a deep breath. What had happened after the waltz must be forever banished from her memory if her heart was to continue to beat at all. This was the first time she'd seen him since that night, but the days between seemed vanished and, looking at him, it was as if there were no one but the two of them present.

"Edward." Clarisse's voice sounded entirely different—soft, sweetly reverent. "I knew you were in London attending to . . . well, certain business. Every day I have expected to see you. Oh, how naughty you are not to have come to me direct."

"I've been busy," Hawkesly said. In his wake came a tall, slender young man. "Julian and I have been busy, haven't we, Julian?"

"Most definitely."

Lindsay supposed many young ladies would find this Julian handsome. Indeed, he was very good-looking, his features fine with a strong jaw and well-made mouth. His slim brows arched dramatically over gray eyes and his brown hair, attractively tousled, tended toward blond as if sun-touched.

But beside Edward, Julian—whoever he might be—appeared as an insipid, if exceedingly well dressed shadow.

There was definitely a most remarkable change in Clarisse. She swayed, and dimpled and peeped up from beneath heavy eyelashes to twinkle at Hawkesly. Lindsay felt . . . Fie, she felt . . . She must not feel anything, least of all *jealousy*. What she had enjoyed with this man who was as darkly arresting as Satan should be eradicated from her mind at once. Not, of course, that she had any idea how Satan might appear. Reverend Winslow had made certain assertions, but even he admitted to having no absolute knowledge.

"I said, good evening, Lindsay."

At Hawkesly's smooth, deep address, Lindsay started and felt the dratted blush overtake her. "I'm sorry. Good evening, my lord." She stared resolutely at the toes of his shiny Hessians . . . and then at his knees . . . his strong, hard thighs . . . Lindsay looked quickly up into his night-dark eyes. They showed nothing but his intense concentration on her.

"Edward," Clarisse said. "This is really too marvelous. I have missed you so. And you making such wonderful plans in secret. Really, it has been hard not to tell everyone—"

"Oh, don't hold yourself back, my dear," Hawkesly interrupted. "It's perfectly all right for you to let your little circle of gossips know I have returned to London—not that I can imagine why they should care. Lindsay, has Clarisse told you that her late husband and my father were friends?"

Stunned, Lindsay shook her head mutely. Clarisse looked so young. Poor thing. Her family must have married her off to an old man when she was little more than a child.

"My dear husband was like another son to Edward's father," Clarisse said without looking at Lindsay. She sighed. "We had so little time together, Francis and I."

Lindsay's eyes filled with tears. "You are so brave, Clarisse. I never guessed you were suffering so."

An explosive cough made her look at Hawkesly's friend, who had produced a handkerchief and covered most of his face. He turned aside.

Hawkesly ignored the incident. "Clarisse is indeed brave. And I hope she will forgive me for not calling on her sooner. I will be doing so tomorrow, Clarisse. Shall we say at around eleven?"

"If you like." Clarisse's full lips formed a pouting smile. "Or earlier would be acceptable. As early as pleases you."

"Come into the room properly, Julian," Aunt Ballard said suddenly. "Really, I do wish you weren't such a hoverer. Lindsay—since Edward appears to have forgotten his manners—may I present the honorable Julian Lloyd-Preston. He and Edward were at Eton and Cambridge together. Did you come in your carriage, Julian? Or Edward's?"

"My own, my lady."

"Good. Lady Simmonds has undoubtedly overexerted herself enough for one afternoon. Perhaps you would be good enough to escort her home?"

"Oh, but I'm really not tired," Clarisse protested. "I'm sure Edward would like—"

"I would very much like to talk with you," Edward said, turning up the corners of his mouth. "But I think my aunt is telling us, with her usual lack of selfishness, that she is tired and would like a little time alone with her family." To Lindsay he added. "Clarisse and I are old friends. As she has told you, her husband was like a son to my father. So you will understand that Clarisse is like a sister to me.''

''Yes,'' Lindsay said faintly.

Aunt Ballard had pulled the servants' bell and Norris appeared with his odd motion that suggested a stiff and slightly crooked ice skater. Within moments Julian Lloyd-Preston had ushered the still-protesting Clarisse from the room, but not before she promised to call upon Lindsay very soon.

The moment the door closed, Lindsay turned away and began trailing between tables and chests bearing the countess's considerable collection of valuable porcelains, silver and gold pieces, and myriad other memorabilia.

''I considered the matter you raised, aunt,'' Edward said. ''About Lindsay's immediate welfare.''

Only with far more restraint than should be expected did Lindsay stop herself from facing him.

Aunt Ballard merely said: ''And what was that? Everything is going extremely well. Lindsay is, as you see, blossoming.''

''Blossoming indeed,'' Edward echoed in a tone that brought fresh heat to Lindsay's fair skin.

''She understands the plans we have made to avoid announcing the betrothal until she has gone about a bit in Society,'' Aunt Ballard told Edward.

Lindsay closed her eyes and prayed for guidance out of her dilemma.

''I have not had the opportunity to discuss matters further with Mr. Latchett and his mother,'' Aunt Ballard continued.

''I have,'' Edward said. ''Mr. Latchett is quite busy with affairs of his own and, so he tells me, very satisfied with the arrangements I have made for his, er, entertainment.''

''Quite.'' Aunt Ballard sounded tetchy. ''And Mrs. Granville?''

''I was about to mention the old . . . I was about

to comment that Mrs. Granville is also adequately engaged. It seems she is busy with some wardrobe intricacies. Although she did mention some, shall was say, frustration? She does hope she will get a chance to wear what she spent my— She would like to be included in some of the preliminaries to my wedding to Lindsay.''

''She does understand that nothing is to be mentioned as yet?''

''She understands that this is our wish. She does not like feeling, as she says, closed away and ostracized in Chelsea.''

''I will see to it that Mrs. Granville comes to tea. I'll arrange some suitable company.''

Lindsay's control broke. She swung around. ''Really! I *am* present. Do you think it appropriate to speak as if I were not here, or perhaps simply a mute shadow?''

''That was not our intention, Lindsay,'' Aunt Ballard said, unperturbed. ''Isn't that so, Edward?''

''Quite so.'' He barely flickered the corners of his unforgettable mouth while he watched Lindsay intently. ''You look beautiful today, Lindsay. But then, how could you ever look anything else?''

She dropped open her fan of stiffened violet lace and fluttered it rapidly. There were times when this little device she'd quickly mastered actually had some real purpose. Under Edward's intense gaze she grew predictably overheated.

''You will make a handsome couple,'' Aunt Ballard said, so softly that Lindsay glanced at her quickly. ''But we must not be too eager if propriety is to be observed.''

''Quite,'' Edward said, although his narrowed scrutiny, leveled minutely, inch by inch, from Lindsay's head to her toes, might be considered decidedly improper. ''And that is what I had come to speak to you about. The question of a companion for Lindsay in the weeks to come.''

"Had I mentioned that to you?"

"Certainly, Antonia."

"And then Lady Simmonds happened—"

"Quite," Edward said curtly. "When I was in Cornwall I made the acquaintance of Miss Sarah Winslow, a dear and close friend of Lindsay's."

Lindsay gaped. "You did? I didn't think—"

"Well"—he made an expansive gesture—"what I meant to say was that you spoke of her so vividly and with such fondness that I have come to feel as if I met her. Anyway, I have decided Miss Winslow would be the perfect companion for you. Do you agree?"

Sudden, incredible joy welled in Lindsay's heart. Sarah? Dear, wonderful . . . dear, *resourceful* Sarah. If persuading Hawkesly to give up on his outrageous notion proved to be too difficult, Sarah would be exactly what Lindsay needed. "Yes. Oh, yes, Edward. That would be lovely. Oh, do agree, Aunt Ballard. I know you would find Sarah agreeable. She's the daughter of a minister, you know," she finished, certain this last detail would dampen any doubts the countess might have.

Aunt Ballard sniffed. "The daughter of a country parson? Hardly likely to advance your studies in meaningful conversation, impeccable manners and deportment, would you say?"

"I—yes, yes, indeed. Sarah is most refined. Why, my own father, God rest his soul, used to remark upon how charming and accomplished Sarah is. She is far better schooled in impeccable manners and deportment than I. Everybody says so."

Edward made an odd sound that shifted Lindsay's concentration to his averted face. "You did meet Sarah, my lord. I had quite forgotten. It was only for a short while, but in the stables when I was telling her about the terrible mix-up when I thought you were her—"

"Exactly so. I had not forgotten but preferred not

to embarrass you. So"—he smiled charmingly at his aunt—"we are agreed? Miss Winslow shall be sent for immediately?"

Aunt Ballard looked dubious. "If you insist. I do hope that she is indeed refined."

"Definitely," Lindsay assured her. "Very refined."

"How is the wardrobe coming?" Edward asked his aunt. "Dashed nuisance—" He stopped and his glance slipped to Lindsay before he seemed to make up his mind to continue. "Not particularly pleasing to me to discover your stepmother chose to outfit herself afresh while she had her own old gowns cobbled over for you."

Humiliation weakened Lindsay's legs. "The gowns are not cobbled, my lord. They are extremely cleverly made over. And every one is of fine material."

"And deplorable taste," Aunt Ballard muttered. "It's of no matter, Edward. Perhaps we have misunderstood what happened. In any case, and to answer your question, my *modiste* tells me that working with Lindsay is, as she puts it, 'a dream.' The French are so emotional. The gown Lindsay is wearing is new, of course. There are many others nearing completion and, with Mademoiselle Nathalie's help, Lindsay is now entrusted with the selection of the rest of her wardrobe."

The amount of money being spent on clothing and fripperies staggered Lindsay and made her uncomfortable. She could feed the tenants at Tregonitha for several years at least on the amount. But she could not deny the excitement brought about by the endless array of dazzling materials and fashionable new designs and accessories that were almost daily paraded before her.

"You're smiling," Edward said softly. "Is it possible you are enjoying yourself—just a little?"

Lindsay instantly assumed a serious demeanor. "I was thinking of Sarah coming. When? When will she come?"

"At once," Edward said. "I see how much this means to you and it pleases me to please you."

His charming words flustered her.

Aunt Ballard cleared her throat. "The Cumberland Ball is only days away. You *will* be there, Edward."

"Damn . . . Forgive me. I detest balls."

"A man considered the best dancer in the land detests balls?"

Lindsay drew in a breath yet felt suffocated. Edward? Dancing? *Dancing with Edward?*

"Triviality abounds at such affairs, madam," Edward said to his aunt. "And I cannot abide triviality."

"This will not be a trivial event. It is essential as the starting point of our campaign to turn Lindsay into a toast. Brummel has promised to give her the nod."

"The devil he has!" Edward grinned and pulled a footstool close to his aunt's chair. "How did you manage that so quickly?"

"I have my means."

With Edward seated beside her, his hand holding hers, Aunt Ballard appeared softer, gentler as she studied him, her head tilted.

"You are good to me, Antonia," he said. "I really don't know why you bother."

"Don't you? I am not fooled by that sophisticated exterior of yours, my boy. I have known you since you were a very nice little boy. And he is still inside your sophisticated exterior."

"Bosh," Edward said, but he didn't pull his hand away.

Lindsay decided she liked the way the aunt and her nephew appeared together. Hawkesly might be a sardonic man accustomed to having his own way, but there could be a kinder side to him after all.

"Lindsay, accompanied by me, will arrive at the ball before you. Not too early, but before you. Perhaps we could expect you at, shall we say, midnight?"

"I had planned a few hands of whist at—"

"Yes, midnight. That will provide time for Lindsay to be introduced around and to dance enough to give the idea she isn't spoken for."

"I'd rather she didn't dance," Edward said, standing again, the stiffness returned. "In fact, I insist she doesn't dance with other men."

"Lindsay will dance," the countess continued. "Then you will arrive, dance with one or two other gels, then come to me. When you first dance with Lindsay it will appear you are being polite out of deference to me. As the evening progresses, it would be appropriate for you to, ah, request more dances with some degree of increasing insistence. The two of you might even wish to appear somewhat *engrossed* in one another."

"See here, Antonia—"

"Yes, that is exactly how it shall be done." The countess rose. "And now, I am tired. I would consider it a kindness, Edward, if you would spend a short while with Lindsay before you leave. I know you must have pressing matters to attend to, but Lindsay has not quite mastered making turns with a train."

"I'm not wearing a gown with a train," Lindsay said, desperate to escape what the countess was apparently suggesting.

"You will be wearing a train at the Cumberlands'. I do take it the gown you've decided on has a train. If not I must consult with Mademoiselle Nathalie."

"It has a train."

"Good. In that case, pretend you have one now."

She proceeded to the door. "Edward knows all about these things. I'm sure he won't mind sharing the burden of getting you ready for this marriage by watching and correcting your efforts."

Chapter 12

Edward waited for the door to close behind Antonia. His dear aunt was, despite her convincingly austere countenance, a romantic.

Lindsay stood, the fingertips of one hand resting lightly on the spine of an ancient Chinese porcelain dog. "Blossoming" hardly did justice to the charming picture she made.

"What are you thinking about?" He sat in the chair Antonia had vacated and rested a booted ankle on his other knee. "Perhaps that is a foolish question. Undoubtedly you are thinking about our upcoming wedding and how it will be when you are my wife." Intriguing thoughts indeed, particularly the latter.

"I would like to discuss matters with you, my lord." Her great, blue eyes sparkled: with imminent tears, or with defiance? "I had thought you would come to your senses without my help. But it seems the time has come for me to apprise you of certain details that will correct your faulty judgment."

Defiance.

"We'll not fence, Lindsay. Not you and I. And I believe we had got considerably past the stage of your addressing me formally."

"From my recent study of Polite Manners"—she raised her chin—"it would seem only correct for me to address you formally—since we do not know each other well.''

He laughed and leaped to his feet. ''Not know each other well? That's rich. I would have said that no young lady who knew a man as well as you know me would want to be on less than first-name terms.''

She wound her fingers together in the sleek folds of her dress but did not look away. ''There is no need to remind me that I have . . . I am evidently given to certain weaknesses and you are . . . You have been the one to unmask my base tastes. Now, sir. Given that you know these things about me, I accept responsibility for them and release you from any duty you wrongly feel toward me.''

Her breasts rose and it was there that Edward's gaze lingered. *She* released *him*? ''There is no question of that,'' he said softly. *No question at all.* And the reason was no longer as clear-cut as it had been on that blustery Cornish morning when he'd first seen this tender rose of a girl.

''Then I am forced to remind you of the suggestion I . . . The other evening I offered an alternative to dealing with our situation.''

He must not laugh. He must not even smile. ''You did indeed. Most generous, too.'' Unfortunately, her lack of sophistication served to inflame rather than dampen his fervor. ''I do believe you are afraid of me, Lindsay, and that you wish to run away and hide.''

Her pale throat moved sharply and he heard her dry swallow. ''I am afraid of nothing, sir.'' She made fists at her sides. ''I was simply offering you an honorable way out of an impossible situation. But, since my solution doesn't please you, you may say that we have decided we will not suit. Then I will return to Cornwall and we will forget we ever met.''

Edward knew a moment's uncertainty. But only a moment. It couldn't be that the chit found him totally repulsive. His original suggestion, that he had managed to frighten her, was undoubtedly the answer to this maidenly hesitation. From now on he must treat her more carefully . . . which would be a challenge since every time he saw her he had difficulty concentrating on his original reason for pursuing this marriage.

"Don't you think that would be the wisest choice?" she asked.

The tentative, almost pleading note in her voice plucked at him. "No, my dear," he told her, attempting to sound kind. "There are clearly things you do not understand. I will attempt to make them clear and concise. The agreement for our marriage has been drawn up." He would not tell Lindsay that these formalities had been largely attended to even before he met her or Roger Latchett. "Your stepbrother, who is your legal guardian, has accepted the terms. There can be no going back without incurring great difficulties, including a slur on my name. This I will never allow."

"But . . ." She came toward him. "I would make a terrible wife for a man like yourself. You have seen how unsuitable I am. My lord, please, there has been no formal announcement. Surely . . ." She faltered and hesitantly touched his chest. "It would be better, my lord . . . for you."

Her trembling lips, soft and pink, remained slightly parted. Restraint was supposedly one of his most admired attributes, but he was also human.

Carefully, slowly lest she bolt, he raised a hand to her cheek. He trailed his fingertips over smooth skin to her ear, then tested the feel of silken hair. Such flaxen, shimmering hair. White-gold strands slipped over and through his fingers. "No, no," he told her, smiling into her eyes. There, the color changed. Minute chips of black and violet reflected shifting candlelight. "No, Lindsay, calling off our wedding would not be better for me, nor, I think, for you."

With that, he bent to place a kiss on her neck—and felt her shudder.

"Edward." His name escaped on a sigh. "Please. I cannot think when you touch me."

He smiled, a secret, satisfied smile and bowed lower, to the beautiful, milky-pale tops of her breasts. Lindsay didn't try to move away. Her breath came in short, sharp little bursts and she rested her small hands on his shoulders.

Edward's muscles contracted hard and he tightened his belly, willing his body not to react. Impossible. But control himself he would. Fighting against the hot, black jabs into his groin, he eased the flimsy fabric of her bodice just low enough to allow his tongue access. Beneath his lips and teeth, her nipples became hardened buds.

"No," Lindsay said. But she clung to him and Edward supported her slight weight. "Stop."

He raised his head just enough to see what his lips had accomplished. The sight of her swelling, ready flesh almost undid him and he kissed her there again, lingeringly, dragging his tongue to the deep vale between her breasts before surrounding one with his hand and seeking out her lips. He kissed her with more force than he had intended. Holding back was beyond him. Her mouth opened beneath his and he tasted the sweetness within. Groaning, he plunged deeper, tested the softness beneath his hand more urgently. And she bent her body to shape with his, pressed him with blind and innocent ardor.

Not now.

"You see." Straightening, he heard his own harsh breathing. "There is indeed what you call 'something chemical' between us, my sweet one. Even if there were not already an agreement between us which cannot be ignored, I should be unable to give you up."

Lindsay stared up into his eyes, a flush over her

rounded cheekbones. Glancing at her still-bared breasts, he felt a fresh pounding at his gut and between his legs. Her deep pink nipples were taut and wet from his kisses.

"Perhaps, Lindsay, I should help you with this problem of the train on your ball gown."

Her indrawn breath was deep and did nothing to calm the raging within Edward. Confusion and distress sharpened her features.

"Show me how you would do this, my sprite."

Never looking away, she made an ineffectual motion of the hand behind her.

"Turn."

She did so, keeping her face toward his. Edward swallowed. This girl had the makings of an Incomparable. Never had he felt as he did at this moment.

Stepping toward her, he took her cold hand in his and passed it over her small rounded hips.

She had the power to undo him.

"That is all there is to it, little one. Flip as you turn. Then sweep away. And I promise you, my beauty, the eyes of every man in the room will be upon you."

As she looked now, every man in the room would be upon his knees. Curse any fool who looked at her too long. That fool would do well to keep himself from Edward's sight in the future.

Very deliberately, Edward spread his fingers and grasped Lindsay's hip. She made no attempt to stop him from urging her against the part of him that could not hide his need. Then, returning her fevered gaze, he adjusted her dress, prolonging the contact until he feared his legs might no longer support him.

This must stop. He had only one object and he would concentrate upon that end. Falling in love with the girl had never had a place in his plans.

Edward stepped away. Blood flowed back into his veins with a throbbing rush. *Love?* There was no love, not of the kind foolish poets wrote to fill the minds of weak females.

"I'm sorry."

"What?" Had he misheard the chit? "What did you say?"

She was crying. Without sound, but crying nevertheless. "I'm sorry I have no . . . I am so very . . . passionate? I have read about women like me but did not know I had such tendencies. It seems I cannot control what happens when . . . I don't understand myself."

Edward felt suddenly very old, very worldly. Poor little sprite. She desired without knowing what she desired. "Do not give it a thought, my dear. Simply accept that females such as yourself are better suited to the married state." He would have to hold back from her or she would addle his brain. He must avoid any threat of diversion from his purpose. The real test would come when they were married and he was completely free to do with her as he wished. Then his will must be ironclad if he were not to be distracted.

"Edward," she said, "I implore you to send me away."

There was only one answer. The marriage would remain unconsummated until Latchett was reduced to nothing and shipped from England.

"Please, Edward. I care too much for you to—" She clapped a hand over her mouth.

He narrowed his eyes. "The wedding will take place the minute Antonia and I—and your stepbrother—decide the time is appropriate." She could not possibly have been telling him she *cared* for him. Not other than in a casual way. If that. No, she was merely terrified of her own physical appetites.

"Edward." The abrupt straightening of her shoulders, the fresh spark of spirit in her eyes, took him aback. Lindsay tossed her disheveled hair. "I warn you. You would do well not to pursue this."

"You *warn* me, miss?" Admire her will he might. But enough was enough. "I shall try to forget you ever made some foolish attempt to threaten me."

"I mean this."

He turned away and crossed the room. "Enough," he told her, opening the door. "There will be no more discussion on the subject. Kindly do as my aunt instructs. I'll see you at the Cumberland Ball."

With that, he left her.

Chapter 13

R ain slashed out of the night to dash the carriage
windows. Julian leaned forward and passed a
hand over breath-clouded glass. Outside, huddled
shapes, their wet cloaks slapping, scuffed over slick
and shiny cobbles.

The carriage lurched, its wheels grinding. Julian
was jerked sideways and he glanced at Edward. Still
there was no hint of softening in those rigidly carved
features.

The silence between them had lasted long enough.
"You were in a hurry to make this visit, my friend."

Edward grunted and turned his face toward the
window on his side of the carriage, where he sat
pressed into a corner.

"By the time I had delivered her home, the Simmonds's disposition was foul."

"Pay her no mind. Tomorrow I will deal with that
strumpet."

Julian had no doubt that Edward would, indeed,
reduce Lady Simmonds to a model of subservience.
But there were greater concerns this night.

More quiet seconds passed as they bowled on
through London's streets. Despite weather bad
enough to chill a man's heart, Julian felt the seethe
of humanity that went about their motley tasks under the masking veil of wild elements.

"Are you sure this is a good idea, Edward?" His friend had appeared on Julian's doorstep a scant time after he'd returned home from Lady Simmonds's opulent house.

"Why would it not be?" Edward's tone suggested he was in no mood to have his judgment questioned. "Say the word, Julian, and I'll have my coachman set you down."

"You are in a black mood, my friend," Julian remarked, aware that his cool tone was belied by the worried set of his face. "Whatever this is about, I'm with you. As always."

Edward shifted irritably against the leather squabs. "This is, to use your expression, 'about' proving to you what manner of man I am set upon destroying."

"That is something I want to discuss with you."

"As I told you, there will be no discussion."

Regardless of how much he owed Edward, Julian would not entirely bend to the man's ill humor. "I think there must be more discussion. You have asked my help and I have already accomplished certain of your requests."

"Good. What manner of player is he?"

Julian shrugged. At Edward's request, for the past several days he had made a practice of engaging Roger Latchett in high-stakes play at Boodles. "Predictably incompetent and without subtlety. As you told me, he has a taste for hazard but clearly thinks whist is the preferred game of gentlemen. The man has no head. And the promise of backing from you has made him reckless."

"Good. Exactly as I had planned."

"How did you pull off his admittance to Boodles?"

"Someone owed me a favor. This is a more painless way to pay off than might otherwise have been extracted."

Julian cast a sidelong glance at his friend. There

was no mercy in that autocratic face. Pity the man who incurred the Viscount Hawkesly's hate. He had better find a very obscure hiding place.

"At the club, Latchett is looked upon with enough disdain to send most men rushing for the door. He seems oblivious and incredibly satisfied with his lot. I do believe he thinks himself accepted." Julian shook his head. "Have you noted his neckcloths? And the cut of his clothes? Pathetic."

"He is evil. That is my only concern. If just men are to find life tolerable, evil must be cut down."

Julian gathered his reserves of diplomacy . . . and courage. "Lindsay Granville is a beauty."

"If you say so."

"I do. And I know you are a man to appreciate a truly lovely female. She is innocent in all this, y'know, Edward."

"Lindsay is not the issue here."

Julian heard a very slight change in Edward's tone. A touch of defensiveness, perhaps? "I would venture the opinion that she is good. Am I wrong? In your opinion?"

Edward's expression became one of distant thoughtfulness. "No," he said slowly. "You are not wrong. I believe her to be good and . . . She is an innocent with banked fires of passion barely below the surface. It is unfortunate I did not meet her under—" He closed his mouth firmly.

"Under different circumstances?" Julian offered. "Exactly. I do believe, my iron-hearted friend, that this girl has the power to touch you deeply."

"Rubbish." A sneer curled Edward's lip. "No woman can touch me deeply. You know that."

Julian was aware of how unsuitable he was as a counselor in matters of the heart. "I know you decided long ago that you *wished* that to be so."

"And it is."

"As you say." Julian inclined his head. In this mood, Edward would refuse to consider any possi-

ble weakness of his own. "From what I saw of Lindsay Granville, and from Lady Ballard's evident liking
for the girl—and from your own, shall we say, *pleasant* disposition toward her?—anyway, these things
lead me to suggest that you may indeed have found
a most suitable candidate to become your wife."

"Thank you." Sarcasm hung heavy.

"Think nothing of it." Dash it all, diplomacy could
wear a trifle thin. "Edward. I'll not creep around
you, bowing and scraping and begging you to listen
to reason. Dammit, man! Don't use a lovely slip of
a girl the way you intend to use Lindsay. I know
you, Edward. You'll hate yourself for the rest of your
life. You aren't a man capable of pointless cruelty."

"Pointless cruelty?" The words exploded from
Edward and he rounded on Julian. "The pointless
cruelty was the murder of my brother. His honor,
and mine—and that of the family we were left alone
to continue—depend upon my avenging James's
death. That I will do and *nothing* shall persuade me
from it."

"But, why the girl? She has done—"

"She has done *nothing*," Edward said between
gritted teeth. "And I'll not harm her. I shall always
be grateful for the avenue she lends me. Without
her, suitable satisfaction would have been far more
difficult to achieve."

In this mood, Edward could be completely intrac-
table. "I saw the way she looked at you this afternoon."

Edward returned his attention to the window that
cast back his brooding reflection.

What Julian was about to say was an enormous
risk. He would take it. "Lindsay is falling in love
with you."

In the silence that followed, he heard the beat of
his own heart. Edward didn't move at first. Then he
turned, very slowly, his mouth flattened and pulled
back from his teeth. "That is ridiculous."

"I think not. Why hurt that love and toss it back at her? Why not take it and put this other aside? James is dead. You cannot undo that."

"You have grown soft," Edward muttered. "I told you I will not hurt Lindsay. She will be my wife and live in all the luxury that position can afford. One day, when all is accomplished, there may even be time for us to become friends. For now, she is merely a card, the winning card in the final game Latchett will ever play. And she is a card in my hand."

There was no reasoning now. Julian conceded this to himself. "Do not hurt her," he said, surprised at the intensity of his feeling for a woman he didn't know. "There was gentleness there. I saw it in her face, the set of her. Gentleness and strength. A powerful combination, Edward. Only a fool would waste a chance to call a woman like that his own."

Rather than the anger Julian expected, Edward turned an oddly thoughtful stare upon him. Perhaps he was thinking of Julian's own unfortunate brush with so-called love. That brush had brought him close to ecstasy, and closer to death. At that time Julian had vowed never to allow another woman to be more to him than a source of pleasure. Edward must think it odd for such a man to plead love's cause. Julian scarcely understood his own motives or feelings in the matter, but there had been an elusive quality about the Granville girl that moved him to view her as different from most other females.

The coach slowed.

"Chelsea," Edward said, stirring as if from a daydream. "We're almost there. Mrs. Felling has instructed us to leave the carriage where it cannot be seen from the house. Then we are to enter through the garden at the back of the building."

Julian moved to sit opposite Edward. "Are you certain there is nothing we should be wary of here?"

"Why do you question me? I told you that Mrs.

Felling merely seemed to feel it was necessary for me to come here tonight.''

"But what if Latchett or his mother sees us?''

"That is the reason for going into the house through the kitchens . . . and up a back staircase not known to Latchett and Mrs. Granville.''

Edward's reassurances only made Julian the more anxious. "You are sure this Felling woman doesn't plan something havy-cavy against you? Or is that why you wanted me with you? I would understand if you required my assistance during some possible mischief.''

"Mrs. Felling and I met several years ago. I did not mention the incident because there was no occasion or reason. She had been attacked by some ruffians near Vauxhall Gardens. I was able to be of some service. It was nothing. A trifle. But she has continued to insist that she wished to find a way to repay the kindness.''

The coach stopped. Before the coachman could get down from his box, Edward pushed open the door and jumped to the street. Julian joined him and they instructed the coachman to wait close by for their return.

As Edward would have strode away, Julian caught his arm. "And this Mrs. Felling is paying back your kindness by acting as housekeeper to Latchett and his mother?''

Julian saw the glint of Edward's teeth. "Not exactly. Although I'm sure that is how Mrs. Granville views her. Mrs. Felling is overseeing the domestic arrangements but she has certain other—ah—accomplishments?''

"Accomplishments?'' Julian tipped back his head. Understanding dawned. "I see. Mrs. Felling is a . . . What the devil has that to do with anything?''

Edward chuckled. "Probably as much as your little charade at Boodles. Mrs. Felling's efforts will doubtless hasten the fall of Mr. Latchett.''

"I don't see—"

"Enough of your probing, Julian. Mrs. Felling's message suggested she had important progress to report. She understands the need for revenge. I decided you should be with me to hear what she has to say. An eloquent woman on the subject of the need to bring evil men to their knees. Yes, indeed, very eloquent. She will persuade you that what I intend is just."

Further argument was unlikely to deter Edward from his mission. Julian, the collar of his greatcoat clamped to his neck, followed the tall, cloaked figure that walked rapidly along an uneven flagway. The houses they approached were terraced. Edward forged on without hesitation until he turned sharply to take a narrow passage leading to the back of the buildings.

"Edward," Julian whispered urgently. He caught up. "Why didn't she meet us somewhere? Why the need to risk coming here?"

"She was insistent."

And Edward always took notice of insistent women? Hah! "I don't like this."

"So you have made clear. Here we are. Through this gate. Quietly, Julian. If that's possible."

Julian swallowed a retort and hurried in Edward's footsteps through a creaking wooden gate in a high wall. Rocking beneath his feet suggested a path of loose, flat stones. The moon's absence made the way treacherous. Wind whined in creaking tree limbs. When Julian raised his face, rain dashed his skin and he inhaled the scent of wet leaves, and sodden earth.

"Shh."

Edward's outflung arm all but knocked the breath from Julian. He groaned and hugged his stomach.

"I said, be quiet. We'll use this door."

Julian looked to where the sky would be if he could see it and prayed for patience.

Once they were inside the darkness seemed even more profound. Julian grabbed for Edward and drew him near. "This is madness," he whispered. "We should—"

"Shh." Edward put his mouth close to Julian's ear. "I have learned never to question Mrs. Felling. What she does is always carefully considered. We are to go up a staircase. At the top we will find a room. She said we are to wait there until she has made a report of her progress. Then we will leave. In her words, we will leave quickly and quietly. And I, Julian, I, she said, will be more than satisfied."

And he, Julian told himself, was completely insane to take any part in this.

Through kitchens full of hard-edged shapes that reached out to jab at a man's knee, or his shin, or his elbow or hip, he followed Edward. Edward moved like a footsure wraith with the power to see all in the dark.

The foot of the promised staircase was found behind a dusty hanging. And the room they sought was easily located. The staircase led there and nowhere else.

"So," Julian murmured. "We have arrived. Where is she?"

"She will come." Edward sounded so calm that Julian almost relaxed. Almost.

They stood, shoulder to shoulder, and waited without speaking again.

Edward was the first to notice a red glow. He dug his fingers into Julian's arm and said, very low: "Look."

Julian did look. The shimmer of red showed through a square in one wall. With Edward still holding his arm, they moved forward and stopped only inches from the light.

"I'm damned," Julian muttered. "What in hell's name is this?"

Edward didn't answer. On the other side of the

wall, and in front of the opening, stood a latticed screen. Loosely woven of slender bamboo wands, the screen would hide the dark aperture completely. Candles, supported in crimson glass sconces, gave Edward and Julian a clear view into a room from which they could not be seen.

"What—"

The painful tightening of Edward's grip caused Julian to draw in a breath.

Edward leaned very close. "Be completely silent," he murmured.

As one man, they took the careful step that brought them close enough to see the entire chamber. Blood-red satin draped a large four-poster bed. The tented canopy drew up to a circlet of golden images, part human, part animal, their grotesque limbs entwined. Red silk covered the walls. Red rugs and a scattering of red and gold pillows lay upon the floor. Other than the bed, the room's only furnishing was a vast, black-lacquered chest, supported on clawed feet. Its many drawers were encrusted with the crawling bodies of ruby-eyed serpents.

"Good God . . ." Words died on Julian's lips.

The room wasn't empty. Before his startled eyes, a woman appeared. She had been concealed behind the bed drapings. Her loose wrapper gleamed incandescent white against the garish room. Hair as black as the night's sky spread about her shoulders in a river of waves. On her head she wore a garland of white flowers. This was the garb of a sacrificial virgin. This was a beautiful girl magically appeared as if from the air.

Julian heard the click of his own dry throat. She moved unerringly toward their hiding place. He would have stepped back, but Edward's grasp held him fast.

Now she stood scant inches from the screen, apparently staring straight at them.

His brain prickled. He remembered to take a breath.

Not a girl. A woman of perhaps eight and twenty. Perhaps thirty. But beautiful in the softly blurred way of one who bore more flesh than any sprig of a girl.

She smiled and narrowed her dark eyes. "Are you there, my lord?" Her light voice held traces of some country accent.

"Yes, Mrs. Felling," Edward said.

The fingers digging into Julian's arm let him know that a steady voice might be no measure of a man's feelings.

"Good. Don't you make a sound. Watch and listen. You'll be pleased. I can promise you that. Your slimy little worm was easily addicted to what I've been feeding him. His appetite gets bigger every day." She laughed, showing surprisingly strong, white teeth. "Tonight he'll learn that pleasure has its price."

"There is no danger to you?" Edward asked.

"No." She shook her head, pressed a finger to her lips and tiptoed quickly to the bed. Even as she climbed atop the satin cover a door began to open. But by the time a short, stout, blond man had entered completely and closed himself in, the woman lay supine, her hair trailing, her eyes closed as if in sleep.

Roger Latchett. Fascinated, Julian observed how the sash securing a black robe settled above a ponderous belly.

Once beside the bed, Roger raised the overlarge goblet he carried and drank deeply. Julian heard him belch and saw him sway. Then, when the man stared down upon the woman, he shuddered visibly. Bending—with difficulty—he pressed his pouting mouth to the woman's. When she raised the back of a hand to her brow and appeared to awake with a small cry, Latchett drew up her head and pressed the goblet to her lips until she drank a sip.

"Drink, maid," Latchett said, his voice slurred. "It'll go more easily with you." But he offered her no more wine. Instead he downed another great swallow himself and turned to the obscene chest. "After tonight you will welcome the attention of your lord, Satan."

Julian had seen his share of unnatural events. This ritual bore no similarity to any of them. It was as if the scene were rehearsed. Even Latchett's words had about them the monotonous tone of lines previously memorized.

Edward dropped his hand and Julian felt his friend's tension.

Latchett, ridiculous on tiptoe, slid the goblet on top of the chest. From a drawer he removed a length of braided gold cord. Then, moving as a man in a trance, he returned to the woman whose wide-eyed expression held terror.

"Don't resist, my virginal prize," Latchett intoned. "If you do, I shall have to beat you. You won't like that."

The woman shook her head vigorously and offered up her wrists. These Latchett draped loosely with the cord before urging his "prize" to slip from the bed and stand before him.

"I'm going to teach you how to please a man," Latchett said. Abruptly, he stepped back. "You are so fragile. So innocent. I cannot bear to keep you bound." With that he pulled the cord away and made as if to drop it at her feet.

The woman moved so swiftly, Julian jumped, and heard Edward draw in a sharp breath.

In a flurry of swirling white, Mrs. Felling caught the cord, whirled Latchett around and pulled his unresisting arms behind him. In seconds he was backed to a bedpost where the resourceful lady quickly secured his hands.

Rather than struggle, Latchett sagged. Even at
a distance Julian saw the glassy sheen in the
man's eye.

Slowly, Mrs. Felling unloosed Latchett's sash and
parted the robe.

"It is I who have wanted you," the woman said,
her voice sultry. "It is I who have lured you here.
And now you are mine. I shall do with you as I
please."

Uttering wild moans, Mrs. Felling pressed her
body to Latchett and pushed his robe from his
shoulders. He wriggled, and the noises he made no
longer sounded rehearsed. The industrious lady set
to work. "I want you," Mrs. Felling said, her long,
capable hands smoothing and caressing until Latchett's eyes rolled up in a manner that suggested either
overwhelming ecstasy or imminent death.

Latchett strained against his bonds.

"Not so quickly, my Satan," Mrs. Felling said.
"Now it's time for the maiden to get her share."
She untied the ribbons at her neck and dropped the
voluminous wrapper into a pool at her feet.

A nightrail of diaphanous gauze draped a body so
voluptuous that Julian gasped aloud. A hand promptly
clamped over his mouth, Edward's, stopped any other
sound he might have made.

The players showed no sign of having heard the
noise.

Again Mrs. Felling layered herself against Roger,
who groaned deep in his throat and tossed his reddened face from side to side. He made ineffectual
attempts to thrust at her with his hips.

"No, no," she trilled. Then she laughed and stood
back just far enough to leave a whisper's space between herself and Latchett. "You must be as patient
as I have been, my black devil."

Part of Julian longed to turn and flee. A stronger
part had to see this production to its conclusion.

Before he guessed her intention, Mrs. Felling caught at the neck of the nightrail and tore the garment to the waist, spilling forth magnificent breasts crowned with the largest nipples he had ever seen. She dropped back her head and laughed, swaying, touching those nipples to Latchett's chest, sliding them down his body.

Julian began to sweat—and harden. This was ridiculous. Outrageous. No man should view such . . . He drew himself up. A means to an end was all this was. A part of Edward's master plan.

The scene went on and on. When the woman had lavished her breasts and mouth on Latchett until his groans turned to hysterical giggles, she freed him, pushed his willing weight onto the bed and sat astride him. Julian watched her sink over the vermin, draw his loathsome cock into her once, twice, then sit on her haunches and laugh while he begged her to return to him.

"And now we want the best part, don't we, dearie?"

"Yes. Yes."

"And we shall have it. But first you've got to promise your little virgin something nice."

Latchett nodded senselessly. "Yes. Yes."

"Your virgin wants five thousand guineas."

This time the small noise in the watchers' cell was Edward's muffled laugh.

"I'll give you a beautiful present, my lovely one," Latchett promised.

"Five thousand guineas," Mrs. Felling said, soft yet clear.

Latchett whimpered. "Impossible. Take me. Please. You must." He managed to wrap his arms around her ample hips.

"Oh, now, now, my Satan. Not impossible, surely." She looked down on him, undulating her body enough to make her breasts sway. "Oh, don't you worry. I'll give you a little time. As long as you can keep showing me how much you appreciate me.''

''Oh, yes.'' Latchett panted, gazing up at the female flesh swinging enticingly above him. ''There'll be something soon. I promise. Please. Take me now.''

''Perhaps you won't have to manage the money all by yourself. I'm sure the Viscount Hawkesly would give me what I want, him being betrothed to your little ward like you said he was. If I went to him and said how you and me had an agreement, he'd be bound to help out.''

Latchett became still.

Mrs. Felling swayed on and as she swayed her voice became dreamy. ''Of course, maybe if I told that fancy aunt of his that you just don't have the blunt, she'd dig into those deep pockets of hers. I'm sure she would see how important it is to pay me. Particularly with you becoming a relative, and all. She'd probably be afraid of someone in her top-lofty circles not thinking much of our little games.''

''You wouldn't go to them.'' Latchett's arms slipped to his sides. ''You wouldn't tell.''

''Wouldn't I?'' Mrs. Felling puckered her brow. ''Of course, I suppose it might be a bit embarrassing to you if they found out you'd seduced a poor widow woman who was only trying to scrape out a living as a housekeeper.''

''Don't jest, Mrs. Felling.''

''Jest? Oh, I never jest. I understand you're becoming quite the gent about town. There could be those who wouldn't see you as suitable company if they knew what you make me do.''

''You said you like what we do.'' Latchett's whine sickened Julian.

''Well''—Mrs. Felling dipped coyly—''I do, darlin'. Only, a lady has to look after herself and her future. If I don't put a bit aside for my old age now, there won't be no way to do it later . . . when these aren't what they are today.'' She caressed her breasts. "Isn't that the truth, *Satan*?"

As if mesmerized, Latchett reached up and took one of her nipples between his fingers. His mouth opened and she bowed over him until he could suck what he wanted inside. When she finally pulled away, he grasped her hips. "You'll get your five thousand guineas," he said hoarsely. "I've got access to as much blunt as I need. It's my due."

"By tomorrow? When we come here to play again?"

"By tomorrow. It's my due, I tell you. I've been promised. There's a fellow at Boodles who'll advance me the ready against my vowels. Hawkesly's name's as good as gold there. He's sworn to cover me. And very soon the besotted fool will put Tregonitha in my hands for good. Anything you want you shall have."

As Mrs. Felling bent to Latchett once more, Edward pulled Julian from the room. They descended the stairs quietly and left the property by the route they had come.

In the passageway to the street, Julian stopped. Edward turned back. "What is it, man? Let's get away."

"So," Julian said quietly. "No doubt the poor fool will get his due. Your Mrs. Felling is indeed 'eloquent.' I would say she fulfilled her promise very nicely. She brought him to his knees well enough. I had not thought a man could be both completely satisfied and completely set on a path to destruction whilst kneeling before a woman."

"It is well begun." Edward strode on again. Over his shoulder he said: "I do not ever want Lindsay within that man's reach again."

Julian leveled thoughtful eyes on Edward's re-

treating back. A man who cared nothing for a girl,
but who thought of her safety while he would have
it believed that he was single-mindedly savoring imminent victory over his most hated enemy.

An interesting puzzle.

Chapter 14

This *must* work. It must. Lindsay placed her silver satin slippers precisely together and checked to be certain the folds of a matching, ermine-trimmed cloak completely covered her gown.

"Are you all right, my dear?" Aunt Ballard asked. Magnificently bedecked with sable-edged black velvet, she sat opposite Lindsay in the splendid Ballard town coach.

"Perfectly." Lindsay smiled at the countess with genuine warmth. "How could I not be when you've been so kind to me?" She regretted that soon, if she had her way, Aunt Ballard would undoubtedly never want to speak to her again.

"Your head is quite recovered?"

"Quite, thank you." For her own reasons, Lindsay had complained of a severe headache and contrived to remain in her bedchamber until it was time to leave for the ball.

The countess's eyes didn't leave Lindsay. "You are preoccupied, then. Will you share your thoughts with me?"

Sharing her thoughts with someone would be a wonderful relief. That was not possible now—here. "You worry too much about me." She smiled brightly and pretended to be entranced by the scene beyond their slowly moving coach. "This is so ex-

citing. So many coaches. There must be miles of
them. And all so handsome. And all the people
watching! It's almost as if they knew there would
be such a parade of finery."

The countess laughed and black plumes nodded
above the glittering band of diamonds and rubies
that secured them in her hair. "My dear little in-
genue, they *are* out to see the parade, as you so
charmingly call it. No major event of the Season goes
unnoticed by the people." With that she leaned toward the window, bent her head charmingly and
waved a gloved hand. Gems glittered in her hair
and at her ears and Lindsay decided she was the
most gracefully distinguished woman she had ever
seen.

The night of the Cumberland Ball. Lindsay shivered.
Despite the plan she would put into action, she was
excited by the glamour of the occasion. "Are *all* these
coaches going to the same ball?" How she wished
Sarah could see this. Perhaps she would be able to
experience some of the magic—if she arrived before
Lindsay managed to leave.

"Of course they are. Everyone who *is* anyone is
going to the ball."

They had reached the entrance to the Park and
continued to inch along in the gilded procession. If
she leaned very close to the windows, Lindsay could
see the spectacular liveries of footmen standing on
the backs of carriages. Lady Ballard also had footmen present, and two coachmen proudly stationed
on the tassel-trimmed box in front.

"How far is it to the Cumberlands'?"

Aunt Ballard continued to smile and wave at the
masses who pressed almost to the coaches themselves. "Not far. Their mansion is quite beautiful. I
know you will find it so. It overlooks the Park and
has the most grand gardens. Perhaps you will see
them."

Lindsay doubted that. In fact, she expected her

stay at the ball to be very brief. "If it isn't very far, why do we all drive? It would be so much less fuss and bother if those living close enough were to walk."

Aunt Ballard's trilling laugh jolted Lindsay. "My dear! You miss the point. We do this *because* it is slow and there is so much opportunity to be seen. It's . . . a ritual, I suppose we might call it. As much a part of the event as the ball itself. But you will come to understand these things very well."

"I see." Lindsay was not sure that she saw at all.

"I must remember to tell Edward how delighted I am with you, Lindsay. You have done quite outstandingly with your lessons. You will make Edward a wonderful wife. Exactly the kind of wife he needs." She leaned conspiratorially closer. "He needs someone with a little spirit, my dear. That young man is far too somber and brooding. A wise wife learns to be herself, get the things she wants and still have her husband in no doubt that he is lord and master. Remember I told you that."

Lindsay could not help but smile. "I shall. Thank you, Aunt Ballard."

"Make him learn to laugh again," the countess said, sounding suddenly distant. "Help turn aside the ridiculous gossip about his reputation. Edward is no heartless rake. When he was a little boy he laughed a lot. Despite that wretched father of his and my self-centered . . . Edward was full of high spirits. As you know, my husband and I had no children. Edward and James became like my own."

"James was Edward's brother?"

The countess looked at her sharply. "Edward has spoken to you of James? I suppose I shouldn't be surprised, although he has shown reticence on the subject with me."

"He hasn't mentioned James to me at all," Lindsay said uncomfortably. "The Reverend Winslow—who was my tutor—mentioned reading that the fifth

Viscount Hawkesly was killed at sea during battle. It became obvious that Edward is that man's younger brother. That is all I know. I did feel a certain bond since my own dear brother perished similarly. But Edward and I have never discussed these things." And they probably never would, she thought with regret.

"I would not suggest that you initiate any conversation on the subject," the countess said seriously. "Edward is still grieving. His grief makes him angry, I think. It would be unfortunate and undesirable for you to bear the brunt of any of that anger."

If events had progressed differently on the day she went to Point Cottage, there might have been a perfect opportunity for her to sympathize with Edward. They might even have helped one another with their anger and sadness.

Outside the coach, onlookers had dwindled to scattered groups. In the misty wash of a cool evening, the Park stretched away, blue-green and shadowy. Scarves of vaporous white furled over the grass and around the trunks of trees. Looking over her shoulder, Lindsay could see the glow of a setting sun that turned the buildings of the city to black skeletons that belched plumes of purplish smoke.

"You do care for Edward, don't you, Lindsay?"

She jumped and barely caught her tiny evening reticule before it would have slipped from her knees. "Yes!" Care for him? Lindsay passed her tongue over the dry roof of her mouth. "Yes, very much," she said softly. And it was true. It could never be that she should become his wife and spend her life with him, but she cared for him deeply.

The countess sighed and smiled. When she smiled like that she glowed and the spectacular young woman she must once have been was easy to imagine.

"You're happy?" Lindsay asked.

The flip of a long, tapered hand inside a black glove was a friendly, conspiratorial gesture. *"You* make me happy, my dear gel. I have prayed Edward would find the woman who could have spirit enough to handle him and make him forget the terrible thoughts I know plague him. You can do that, Lindsay. I feel it."

Lindsay fiddled with tiny loops of silver beads on her reticule. How cruel fate could be. What a sense of loss she already felt at what she might have enjoyed with Edward and his aunt had circumstances been different.

"You do know how much Edward wants you, Lindsay?"

"Yes," she said. And she now knew how much she wanted him. There was scarcely an hour when she didn't remember their times together, when she didn't replay what had passed between them. Predictably, she grew warm and that strange aching sensation began low inside her. If this was what wanton women experienced she could at least sympathize with the courses they chose for their lives.

"Tell me, child. What *are* you thinking? For a happy young woman soon to be united with the man you care for, and who cares for you, there is precious little joy in you."

Precious little joy indeed. "I am overwhelmed," she said, quite truthfully. Edward had told her it would be best for a woman of her passionate nature to be married. She believed he was right. Married to him. Oh, a pox on fate for showing her such wondrous possibilities when they could never be hers.

John. Yes, she would concentrate on little John and how she intended to see him again very soon. And Antun. Antun must be beside himself with confusion and worry over her sudden departure. She must find a way to get to him.

"We are almost there."

Lindsay turned from studying the Park. She heard

the cries of coachmen above the clatter of horses' hooves. On the other side of the coach lay a number of grand residences.

Her stomach did the oddest things, and her heart. Aunt Ballard patted her hair and fussed with the sable at her neck. "Now you know exactly what to do, Lindsay?"

"I think so." Her mind felt like an empty place. She *had* known all the little intricacies Aunt Ballard had imparted, but they seemed entirely forgotten.

Before Lindsay could try to remember what to ask about what she'd forgotten, the coach rattled to a halt. In seconds, a footman opened the door and presented steps for the ladies to alight.

"Chin up," Aunt Ballard said through her teeth, while she smiled haughtily on all sides. "*Glide*, Lindsay. *Glide*."

She did hold her chin up and she did glide. And she did hold her reticule so as to allow her fingers to keep her cloak securely in place.

"Oh, Aunt Ballard." She faltered, staring up at a house that had to be as large as a castle. Not that Lindsay had actually seen many castles—if any. "It's so marvelous. There must be hundreds of windows. And they all tremble with light."

"Glide, Lindsay."

"It's like stars shining on a castle of ice." Her heart thudded. Ladies and gentleman in dazzling evening attire preceded them to a bank of steps wide enough for several coaches to stand abreast. "Oh, they are all so beautiful." And she must seem a gauche country mouse by comparison.

"Do *not* gape," the countess snapped through lips that barely moved. "They will be watching. Anything that can be talked about *will* be talked about."

Lindsay felt dizzy. She had counted on providing plenty to talk about. But now she was frightened.

Up the steps past minions whose livery blurred to

a stream of gold. Silks, satins, the sparkle of gems. All swam together before Lindsay's eyes.

Then they were inside a great stone hall. White pillars soared. On all sides, rococo panels in palest green and white housed white statues in oval niches.

"The ballroom is on the next floor," the countess whispered. "Smile and talk to me as we go."

"What shall I say?" Lindsay faltered on the first step of a massive staircase that soared to a landing, bifurcated, and soared again.

"Tilt your head toward me and move your lips."

Lindsay tried.

"*You* are the mystery everyone is waiting to see," the countess said.

"But I've been about a bit. I've been seen already."

"And you've impressed people with your wit and unspoiled charm. And with your unassuming wisdom. Ernestine Sebbel positively gushed over you. She told me how you and Isabelle got along famously. Most people don't, you know."

"Most people don't what?"

There was a vaguest flash of impatience in Aunt Ballard's eyes. "They don't get along famously with Isabelle Sebbel. She is considered, shall we say, *astringent*?"

"She is very amiable, I think," said Lindsay. "Without the artifice of so many ladies. And she knows a great deal about literature."

"That was the other item mentioned. Evidently you are well read."

Lindsay lowered her lashes. "I do have a fondness for novels." She expected some rebuke for her lighthearted tastes.

The countess leaned closer. "So do I," she said softly. "We must compare our favorite novels very soon."

"I should like that." Lindsay wished that circumstances might have allowed her to have many discussions with Aunt Ballard.

"Good. And your smile is exactly the thing, my dear. They say you are like deep water, y'know."

Lindsay sniffed. "Murky at the bottom?"

The countess laughed and stopped. She batted Lindsay with her fan. "No! Still and intriguing. But that sort of reaction, my gel, is exactly what I want from you this evening. Be yourself. I could ask for no more."

Guilt lay heavy on Lindsay. "I will do my best." Yes, she could not go back from what she had to do. But she could do it with flair and finesse and show the confidence of manner the countess had so adamantly insisted upon.

"First we'll leave our cloaks in an anteroom," Aunt Ballard said as they reached the top of the stairs. "Then, remember, you stand with me. You will be asked to dance and I will give the nod, or not. Depending upon who asks. You understand?"

"Yes."

"A particular gentleman will smile at you and call you by name. He is Mr. Brummel. When he does address you, you are to give him your most gracious attention."

"Yes." Ahead lay twin sets of open double doors flanked by footmen. Music and laughter rose in bursts, but Lindsay couldn't see into the ballroom.

"Lindsay!"

Startled to hear her name, she halted, unsure where to look.

"Antonia, I'm so glad you're here!" It was Lady Clarisse Simmonds, resplendent in a daringly transparent gown of palest pink muslin. Clusters of pink satin roses, each bloom with a diamond at its heart, caught the neckline and hem into artful scallops. More rosebuds and diamonds adorned the delicate slippers that peeped from beneath her gown.

The countess's face had assumed the oddly expressionless quality Lindsay had seen in Clarisse's presence before. "Good evening, Lady Simmonds."

Clarisse curtsied. The diamond-and-satin rosettes coyly tucked into the curls at her crown were, Lindsay decided, a trifle too girlish. Perhaps the gown was also a trifle too girlish. But what did she know of fashion? This was her lovely friend and seeing her brought a measure of relief in this sea of strangers.

"Do allow me to help Lindsay check her toilette—"

"I don't think—"

"Oh, but I insist you allow me to do this." Clarisse's voice rose to a pitch that caught the attention of passing guests. "I know Lindsay will love seeing more of the exquisite furnishings before she has to be swallowed up by the silly old ball."

The countess nodded at several people, then her mouth tightened. She lowered her eyelids a fraction. "Very well," she said. "But please deliver her to me directly. I'll be at the far end of the ballroom—exactly opposite the stairs."

"Oh, thank you!" Lady Simmonds dipped another pretty curtsy. "It's so much fun to be with someone as charmingly *unspoiled* as Lindsay. She is amazed at absolutely everything."

Aunt Ballard's brows drew together. "Lindsay is merely politely *interested* in everything, Lady Simmonds. Kindly return her to me within a few minutes. There are a number of my friends who are anxious to be introduced."

When the lady turned away to be swept into the throng outside the ballroom, Clarisse seized Lindsay's hand. "La! I do love Antonia, but she can be such a termagant sometimes."

"Aunt Ballard is *not* a termagant," Lindsay said defensively. "She is merely concerned about me."

"Of course she is. I'm only chattering because I'm excited. Come. Let us rid you of your cloak and talk a while before we have to return." She giggled and rushed away, pulling Lindsay behind.

"In here." A door opened into the most beautiful boudoir Lindsay had ever seen. "Look at the mirrors. Aren't they perfect? I can see myself on all sides." Clarisse twirled and posed before floor-to-ceiling mirrors.

"Oh." Standing with her slippered feet pressed into Persian carpet in the deepest of pink shades, Lindsay felt at a lost for words. Swans had been etched in a border around each mirror and silver swans decorated panels of dusty rose silk in between. Matching fabric covered chaises and the seats of stools that stood before small dressing tables. Silver pots of lotions, powders and fragrant oils had been arranged on the tables.

Clarisse dropped onto a stool and leaned to study her face. "I wanted to talk to you alone. But I could hardly believe my good fortune when I found you so easily."

"I'm glad, too," Lindsay said. She felt very, very shaky.

"There is something I want to ask you," Clarisse said, looking at Lindsay in the mirror. "I need your help."

"Of course," Lindsay said, eagerly. "Whatever I can do, I will." Clarisse had been so kind to her.

Clarisse swung around. "Oh, I knew you would. I just knew it. And I do believe you *could* help me with this problem I have. But you have to promise."

"Promise? Tell me what I must promise."

Clarisse bobbed to her feet. "That you will tell absolutely no one what I'm going to ask you."

"I promise."

"Put your hand on your heart."

Duly, Lindsay flattened her hand on her breast. "I promise on my heart."

"Very well. We must be quick or the countess will be furious with me. Several days ago I had a . . . Something very unexpected occurred. I had been expecting certain things to happen and I was informed

that they would not. I do not believe the person who
told me this meant what he said. But he is evidently
under some duress from another quarter and I mean
to find out what it is and dispose of it. Do you understand?''

Bemused, Lindsay shook her head.

''Fie!'' Clarisse flounced to plop back on the stool.
She gazed at herself in one of the long mirrors. ''There
is a gentleman whom I know wants . . . Lindsay,
someone is standing between me and my blissful
happiness with the most handsome, exciting, daring . . . Oh, I am muddling. A man loves me more
than his life and I love him the same. He is being
forced to consider marriage with a woman he de-
spises, simply because he feels it his duty, and I
want you to help me convince him this would be
wrong. Will you?''

''I . . . I don't know if I can.'' How could she?
She was a hopeless neophyte in these lofty circles.

''You can. I know you can.''

''Who is this woman he feels he must marry?''

''That's just it.'' Clarisse made fists and waved
them. ''I don't *know* who she is. He won't tell me.
He pleads some sort of silly sense of honor to this
person. But I'm sure you are in a position to find out.
Then I will deal with her.''

''*Deal* with her?''

''Oh, don't be silly. I only mean to inform her that
she could never be happy with a man who loves
another.''

''I see.''

''Good. So—''

The door opened to admit a trio of breathless, gig-
gling young females. Each wore white muslin
trimmed with a variety of lace, ribbon and beads.
They ignored Lindsay and Lady Simmonds. The latter scowled most unbecomingly and motioned Lindsay to her side. She went, conscious that she still
wore her cloak and wishing she could contrive to

leave the house altogether—still wearing her cloak—
and never come back.

"He is said to be so very rich," one of the girls
bubbled. She poked at springy red ringlets. "But
doesn't he *terrify* one? That black stare that doesn't
quite see one. Or perhaps it sees one very well!"
She raised plump white shoulders and giggled
afresh.

"Mary! Do you mean he *actually* looked at you?"

"Oh, yes." Red-haired Mary solemnly regarded
her two more slender and nondescript friends. "At
the Gregorys' musicale. And Mama told me I was
to give him the cut direct. She says he is exceedingly
dangerous and that he has left a trail of beautiful
young women's hearts in his wake."

"No!" her audience chorused.

"Yes. *And* it is said that he practices all manner of
. . . well, that he is fond of strange practices."

Clarisse met Lindsay's eyes with a bored impatient stare and motioned her to sit.

Although curious about Clarisse's beau, Lindsay
wished she could get away.

"How do you know he's coming tonight?" a girl
asked.

"My mama said it's rumored he will," Mary said.
"She wished to warn me."

"What will you do if he asks you to dance?"

The redhead tossed her curls. "If he did, I should
refuse, of course. But he supposedly never asks anyone to dance anymore. Although I've heard it said
he cuts a magnificent figure in the dance."

"*He* is magnificent," one of the girls said breathlessly, clasping her hands together. "And he would
be such a brilliant catch. If he asked me to dance I
should swoon."

"Well he won't," Mary pronounced unkindly.
"The Countess Ballard is his aunt, you know. My
mama says that if he does come tonight it will only
be to please her. Mama thinks the countess is

grooming someone to become his viscountess. Of course, it will be merely a *mariage de covenance*.''

Lindsay clutched the edge of her stool, barely able to grasp what she heard.

"Mary! You do say *such* things."

Mary fluffed at her ringlets. "I know about these matters. The marriage will be purely for the purposes of producing a Hawkesly heir. As soon as that's done, he'll return to his wicked ways. Pity the poor soul is what I say."

Lindsay was grateful to be already sitting. She was certain standing would be beyond her.

"Who do you suppose this poor female is?" one girl asked. "Do we know her?"

Clarisse had leaned forward and Lindsay couldn't see her face. She prayed for time to make sure her own showed no emotion.

Mary tilted up her pert nose. Her eyes sparkled with importance. "Apparently she is some dowdy thing who was a distant relative of the countess's late husband. A complete nonentity, it's said. One could almost wish that such a victim might be spared her lot."

"Spared her lot!" The taller of the other two girls laughed. "I cannot say that marriage to the Viscount Hawkesly would be such a trial under any circumstances."

"How do you know, Bernetta?" Mary said crossly.

"I don't." A blush replaced a smile. "And I'm sure you are right, Mary. Perhaps we should return to our mamas before they decide we are lost."

The girls left in a flurry of white muslin and bobbing curls. The closing door cut off their chatter.

For what seemed a long time, Clarisse kept her attention on her hands in her lap.

Lindsay closed her eyes and willed herself far away. Chance was either her friend or her enemy. But for Clarisse's interruption, Lindsay would be in the ballroom already and would have missed the girls' gossiping.

A gentle hand stroking her shoulder snapped her eyes wide open again.

Clarisse stood at her side. "Lindsay, you poor dear. I see it all now. How could I have been so foolishly blind?"

Aunt Ballard had been explicit. No one must be told of the upcoming plans. "You have not been foolish, Clarisse. There is nothing to be foolish about." Of course, she would not be marrying Edward, and, besides, it seemed that word had somehow sprouted and grown even without any announcement.

"Ah, I see." Clarisse nodded sagely. "You have been sworn to secrecy. I understand and you may trust me."

"Clarisse—"

"No." Clarisse held up a hand. She dipped to drop a brief kiss on Lindsay's cheek. "I am your friend. Remember that. Your best friend in trying times. But, should anyone ask, I do not know what is planned for you. And if you choose not to tell me more I will never press you. But, please, promise me you will come to me if you need my help—in anything?"

Lindsay sighed. "You are very kind." And, regardless of who did or didn't know what, it was time to make her entrance into the ballroom. "We should return to Aunt Ballard."

"Yes. Take off your cloak. It will be safe here."

Lindsay remembered that Clarisse had been about to make a request. "You were going to ask for my help."

"La! Forget my foolish little problems. They can wait. We'll speak of them later if I cannot manage my own affairs."

"Very well." Lindsay was too oppressed to argue.

Trying not to see Clarisse's reaction, she undid the cloak and swung it from her shoulders.

Lindsay could not fail to hear Clarisse's gasp before she whispered a horrified "Oh, Lindsay, what *have* you done?"

Chapter 15

Paying no heed to Clarisse's amazed exclamation, Lindsay stood straight, fixed her eyes ahead and went to open the door.

"Lindsay! Wait!"

"Aunt Ballard will be wondering what has happened to me."

"Yes," Clarisse said, visibly trying to calm herself. "Yes, of course. We should go to her immediately."

In the hallway, Lindsay continued to stare ahead and walked with firm, smooth steps through groups of guests. As she went, with Clarisse flitting at her heels like an exotic pink butterfly, conversation faded.

"Remember," Clarisse murmured. "I am always your friend."

Grateful for the small comfort, Lindsay managed to smile. "Thank you." She walked through the ballroom doors.

A platform led to a wide and sweeping flight of steps bordered by gilt banisters. Here, as before, voices stilled. Lindsay gave her name to an intimidating man in a powdered wig. He wore a burgundy-and-gold jacket, white satin breeches, white silk hose and patent slippers . . . and disapproval shone in his ferociously hooded eyes.

"Miss Lindsay Granville," he announced, in a nasal voice loud enough to sound like thunder in Lindsay's ears.

Glancing around, she realized that Clarisse had been detained by some problem with the catch on a bracelet. Lindsay continued on resolutely. This was something she must do alone.

At the top of the stairs, she hesitated, looking over the whirl of dancers. By strength of will, she subdued any hint of a blush. Before her, impeccably turned out in either evening clothes, or military dress uniform, were hundreds of men partnered by gorgeously clad women. White and pastels predominated, each gown apparently more extravagantly trimmed than the last. Some more mature ladies wore brilliant shades. Jewels glittered. Music soared. Voices swelled, and laughter, together with the cascading notes from the orchestra.

Fixing her gaze on enormous chandeliers ablaze with thousands of candles, Lindsay began her descent.

Before she reached the floor of the glittering room, she felt a hush form among the nearest guests. Then they began to part, making a path before her.

Lindsay's heart pounded so wildly she thought she might faint.

Onward she walked—toward the spot the countess had designated.

"Jade!"

Lindsay flinched at the hissed insult. This was what she had planned, wasn't it? Enough stir to have Edward and Aunt Ballard send her packing back to Cornwall immediately?

Her progress was slow and steady. So was the pall of stillness that fell on dancers and the clusters of guests who had been talking together. The air of pause spread. The pathway in front of Lindsay opened like the falling away of tall grass before a strong wind. And as the dancing faded—and the music—the whispering grew.

Lindsay attempted not to listen.

"Strumpet." A woman's voice said clearly.

"Unaccompanied opera dancer," a man said in a low voice. "Got to be. Who let her in?"

"She should be asked to leave," said another woman.

Lindsay kept moving. The music dwindled away to nothing. Now they would have to let her go. Edward would never want to speak to her again. He *would* never speak to her again. It was as well for his sake that their sham of a betrothal had not been announced.

How would she get home? Her eyes burned. Home? That was in Cornwall. First she must find a way to return to Aunt Ballard's home, contact Roger and Belle and arrange transportation.

Roger and Belle. She'd scarcely thought of them since her arrival in London. And they had not contacted her. What punishment would Roger mete out when he was told she had disgraced herself?

"Outrageous," a male voice grumbled. "Who can she be?"

"I'm Lindsay Granville," she longed to shout. *"I don't like you either, you plumped-up popinjay. And I don't want to be here."*

Utter silence had fallen save for the shuffle of feet and rustle of gowns.

Lindsay drew a great breath, raised her chin even a fraction higher and stared ahead . . . straight at Aunt Ballard.

The pounding in Lindsay's breast nearly suffocated her. She blinked back tears. The few yards separating her from the lady who had become so dear to her felt like a wide and impassable ocean.

The countess looked into Lindsay's eyes. For an instant there was the faintest registering of shock. Then Aunt Ballard smiled and held out her hands.

"Lindsay! There you are, my darling gel. Do come and meet everyone."

Lindsay's legs came close to letting her fall. She faltered, fighting consternation.

"Come, come," Aunt Ballard said, so loudly that many must hear. Those who didn't were sure to know her words quickly since the closest guests sent a whispering wave over the assemblage.

Firm hands found Lindsay's and the countess planted a kiss on each of her cheeks. "I was just telling everyone how brave you are, Lindsay. We all think it incredibly noble of you to wear black in memory of your treasured *brother*, don't we, my dears?"

The group clustered about the countess drew a collective breath, then murmured assent. Lady Ernestine Sebbel, dressed in unbecoming red satin, shook her head so sadly that a feather curving from her purple velvet turban became dislodged and slid to rest on her considerable bosom.

Aunt Ballard smiled graciously around. "Lindsay is such a joy to me. She teaches me so much about generosity of spirit and learning to put one's own feelings last. I know of no other beautiful young woman who would choose to put aside her own comfort to honor a brave young man who died in defense of his country more than two years ago. But Lindsay wanted to share her pleasure in this evening with the brother for whom she still grieves. And so she chose to wear black."

A sympathetic murmur sounded.

Leaning to place another kiss on Lindsay's cheek, the countess whispered: "You will have to be much more inventive if you wish to outwit me, young lady. We will discuss your motives in this nonsense later." She kissed Lindsay's other cheek and added: "If you wanted to make yourself less appealing, you've failed miserably. I never saw a gel look more beautiful."

Aunt Ballard straightened. "You are noble, Lindsay," she said, her tone stridently enthusiastic. "A credit to the family."

Lindsay realized her mouth had fallen open and she closed it firmly. Aunt Ballard's words gushed approval, but the glimmer in her eyes, the faint quirk at the corner of her mouth, warned Lindsay that there would indeed be much said about her tactics at a later time.

"Noble indeed," a haughty-looking man said. His exquisite tailoring, the elaborate tie of his silk neckcloth, caught even Lindsay's inexperienced attention. "I am delighted to see you, Miss Granville," he said.

She could do nothing but allow him to raise her hand to his lips. This must be Mr. Brummel.

"Thank you . . . Mr. Brummel." It would be unthinkable to trouble Aunt Ballard further at this moment. "You are most kind, sir."

The faintest smile touched the man's mouth before he bowed shortly and moved serenely away.

Immediately, a hubbub of conversation broke out. The orchestra struck up, somewhat discordantly at first, before the strains became smooth once more. Dancers resumed their figures—all but those closest. These continued to stare and murmur. More than once Lindsay heard the name "Brummel" in awed tones.

"Stand beside me, my dear," the countess said in a more normal tone. "I've been talking about you and everyone can hardly wait to make your acquaintance."

Holding up her head, smiling, curtsying, took every scrap of Lindsay's strength of will. Names and faces became a nightmarish jumble.

"By all means," she heard Aunt Ballard say. "Be careful with her, Tony. She's been leading a very quiet life since poor William's death."

Almost numb, Lindsay found herself led among the dancers by a pleasant-faced young man in

spanking military dress. When he turned her to face
him, she noted that he seemed almost ridiculously
young.

He bowed, presenting a thick head of blond curls.
Then they entered the dance. "I cannot believe that
the countess has managed to keep your existence
hidden for so long," he said as they swung closer.
"I cannot believe it possible that a girl so lovely could
be hidden at all."

Lindsay realized she was gaping again and fashioned a smile. Surely he toyed with her. "You are
too kind . . . my lord." She vaguely recollected Aunt
Ballard introducing him as Lord something.

"I am Tony to my friends. And I certainly hope
you may consider counting me among your
friends."

So young. And so earnest. Lindsay nodded. "Yes
. . . yes, of course." He must, she realized, be at
least a few years older than she was, yet she felt his
freshness like a blow. Could the years since William's death have made her hard?

Ah, yes—William. Grudgingly, defeatedly, she
admired the countess's resourcefulness. The black
dress, daringly cut to attract as much negative attention as possible, had been Lindsay's master stroke,
designed to horrify the company. Young girls making their appearances in Polite Society were *always*
dressed in the palest shades, if not in white. Deep
colors were rarely seen at all, except on older
women, and *never* gowns of black silk cut so auda-
ciously as to be close to indecent.

"Your aunt says your home is in Cornwall."

"Yes." She would not be crushed by this setback.
When Edward heard what she had done, he would
be horrified. He would send her packing. She knew
he would.

"Dashed bad luck, your brother . . . and . . . and
all that."

"Thank you."

Lindsay remembered to look at her partner and instantly grew warm. His attention was fixed on her breasts. The gown's square neck barely covered her nipples. If she moved just so, the merest hint of delicate pink rims could be revealed. She held her body rigid. Earlier, waiting in her chamber, pretending a headache, she had experimented before a mirror. While she'd stood there, viewing the spill of her own pale flesh, her resolve had all but fled. Now she wished she *had* abandoned this outrageous idea.

She must attempt politeness. "You have seen battle?"

"I was at Albuera." There was pride in his voice.

Lindsay searched for some snippet of remembered information on the wars against Napoleon. "Albuera." Yes, Reverend Winslow had mentioned it. "In Spain. A very bloody battle. Were you terribly afraid?"

His shoulders jerked back. "I was doing my duty, Miss Granville." Then he smiled and his young face appeared even younger. But his bright blue eyes held a knowledge that made them contrastingly ancient. In a lowered voice, he told her: "It was a horror, Miss Granville. And, yes, I was very afraid. No sane man could not be afraid."

She liked him then. "I'm glad you are safe. Please call me Lindsay."

The pleased hint of a flush that touched his cheekbones amazed Lindsay.

"Thank you," he said. "I'm honored."

As the dance ended, he gallantly offered her his arm. The instant before he delivered her back to Aunt Ballard he said: "I doubt I shall manage to get close enough to ask you for another dance this evening."

Lindsay surveyed what lay ahead. Where Aunt Ballard should be, a bevy of eager-faced men crowded, all looking in Lindsay's direction.

"May I call on you?"

She glanced distractedly at her partner. "Oh . . . oh, yes. If you want to."

"I want to," he said, bowing low over her hand. Standing straight again, he added. "Until then, I shall think of nothing else."

In the next hour Lindsay hovered between extreme agitation and trembling excitement. Why should so many well-connected men wish to dance with her? She was twirled away by an earl with an unnerving habit of leaning close to murmur, "Enchanting. Absolutely enchanting," every few minutes. A duke old enough to be her father seemed to think she should know about his considerable holdings in Yorkshire—"Half the county, don't you know"—and the fact that he was a lonely widower who longed to share all he had with the "right" female.

From time to time Lindsay caught the eye of some other woman and she recoiled from the assessing stares. Why should the men in the company treat her so charmingly, while the women looked upon her with evident distrust and dislike?

And so many of the men requested her permission to call. Undoubtedly they were simply being polite.

At last she begged to rest. Promptly, a glass of champagne was pressed into her hand by a good-looking man in military uniform similar to Tony's. When she remarked upon this, the man, who had been introduced as Lord Bently, said: "Tony?"

Aunt Ballard was at Lindsay's side once more. "The Marquis of Gravistock," she informed Lindsay's current admirer. "He is evidently very taken with our Lindsay."

"Aren't we all?" the man said, but Lindsay thought his features sharpened. "May I call upon you, Miss Granville?" he added predictably.

When Lindsay had acquiesced and watched him move away, Aunt Ballard took advantage of a moment's privacy to murmur: "Lord Bently is a hunter. Shallow in the pockets at the moment, I hear. Had to go to an uncle for the blunt to buy his colors. Been through a fortune at Whites and several other, less salubrious establishments. I'll wager he thinks you may come with a sizable dowry."

"I see."

"I doubt you do. But you must learn the ins and outs of our world." The countess fixed Lindsay with an imperious stare. "And this *is* going to be your world, too, Lindsay. Never doubt that. For some reason—perhaps it is fear—you are resisting Edward's plan to make you his wife. Give in, dear gel. He wants you and be certain that whatever Edward wants, he gets."

Panic swelled afresh. She had expected, or at least hoped, that Aunt Ballard would hasten her away from the ball at the moment of her entrance. Actually coming face-to-face with Edward, wearing this dress, had seemed unlikely. Therefore, until this instant, she had not truly contemplated his reaction.

She flipped open her black lace fan and wafted it fiercely. "I . . . Aunt Ballard, I do believe I don't feel very well."

"The way you didn't feel well when you contrived to stay in your room earlier?" The lady smiled at several passing couples. "That wasn't very kind of you, Lindsay. To lie in order to accomplish such a flamboyant trick."

"I'm sorry," Lindsay mumbled honestly. "Please may I leave?"

"No."

"The coach could take me back and then return for you."

"No."

She would not beg. "Don't you think it would be better if Edward didn't see me like this?"

Aunt Ballard's chuckle startled Lindsay. "*Au contraire*, my pet. I can hardly *wait* to see Edward's reaction to you in that dress. My nephew is a man of deep passion. The way you look tonight would inflame the most narcissistic of dandies. Need I say more?''

A mariage de covenance. Poor creature destined to bear a Hawkesly heir before the viscount returned to his wicked ways. Lindsay swallowed. What wicked ways? It could be that she would have no choice but to go through with the marriage in order to obtain the freedom she needed afterward when Edward tired of her. But what manner of practices had first Emma and then the red-haired girl in the boudoir alluded to?

In a lull between dances, conversation buzzed. Glasses clinked and laughter ebbed and flowed. Above this, the intimidating voice of the master-of-ceremonies rose in a bellow: ''Edward Xavier deWorth, the sixth Viscount Hawkesly. And the Honorable Mr. Julian Lloyd-Preston.''

''Oh,'' Lindsay said faintly. Then she saw him. With the length of the ballroom and a great crush between them, she saw his tall, commanding figure at the head of the staircase.

''Quite a man, isn't he?'' Aunt Ballard said softly. ''And he wants you, Lindsay.''

She couldn't reply.

''Hello, Lindsay.'' A light, breathless voice was a momentary distraction. Clarisse, who had been absent since Lindsay entered the ballroom, stood at her elbow now. She rested a hand on Lindsay's arm. ''I've been trying to reach you, but I haven't been able to get away from all the men who want me to dance.''

''It's all right.'' Lindsay patted Clarisse's hand. She could not take her eyes from the tall man in black who made his way down the stairs. Beside him, all others paled.

''Gad,'' a man to Lindsay's right exclaimed. ''As

I live and breathe, it's Hawkesly. Thought he'd given up the real world."

Lindsay entertained the thought that this seemed anything but a real world, before she concentrated again on Edward. Surely she could slip away somehow.

As if she guessed Lindsay's thoughts, the countess positioned herself slightly behind and held her elbow. "I want to see his face when he sees you," she said—for Lindsay's ears only. "It will surprise me if you haven't accomplished quite the opposite from your evident plan, my dear."

There was no way out. She had barely blinked, barely taken another unbearably shallow breath, when a dark head became evident above most of the crowd. A dark head moving in her direction.

"You must not worry," Clarisse said conspiratorially. "I understand completely your effort to evade this odious fate. Leave it to me. I will divert him."

Lindsay scarcely heard.

Hawkesly had reached a group of men who detained him. The striking austerity of his impeccably cut black evening clothes only served to heighten the impression that he was a man like none other. Among his more extravagantly dressed peers he stood, straight and so very tall and powerfully built, like a lone bird of prey distinguished from the rabble of lesser creatures by the sheer force of his own confidence.

Lindsay heard Clarisse expel a quavering breath and patted her hand once more. This was not Clarisse's problem.

While he talked, Edward hooked his hands beneath the tails of his coat and appeared engrossed . . . until his unreadable eyes shifted. He looked past his acquaintances and the corners of his sensuous mouth turned downward. He looked directly at Lindsay.

Edward continued to listen to Lord Worthing's diatribe about problems with poachers on his Sussex estates. He listened. He did not concentrate.

All he saw with any clarity—with absolute clarity—was the temptress in body-hugging black silk. What in hell's name had possessed the little fool to come here so unsuitably dressed? He would find out soon enough. For the moment he feasted his eyes on her.

The contrast between her silver-blond hair, milky pale skin, and the black dress was dramatic. She contrived to appear both breathtakingly fragile and feminine, and overwhelmingly voluptuous. Beneath the scanty, square-necked bodice, a skirt so slim as to resemble a shimmering tube dropped from a high waistline to tiny silver slippers. A simple strand of pearls interspersed with silver beads surrounded her slim throat. Matching strands had been looped through her hair and allowed to trail where a mass of ringlets hung heavy from her crown. Soft, smooth curls framed her perfect face.

She was watching him.

He had no need to check her eyes to know she felt his slow appraisal. Inevitably, his attention had been drawn to the wisp of a bodice encrusted with jet beading. And Lindsay had taken in a long, slow breath.

He grew hot and heavy between his legs. Damn the girl. Her marvelous breasts rose, full, ripe . . . and untouched except by him. The barest suggestion of the tops of pink nipples showed. Edward locked his knees. Damnation. No other man would have the chance to openly lust after what was his. Not after tonight.

Could she possibly know what kind of effect she would have on any man who saw her? Perhaps so. Perhaps that had been her motive—to make him jealous.

That brought a smile to his lips. He was not a man to be made jealous. Angry perhaps, but never the other. She would learn soon enough that trifling with the man who would become her husband was a gross error.

"Have you met your aunt's little protégée?" Alistair McBride, more observant than the others, asked Edward. "Fascinating little piece, wouldn't you say?"

Edward cocked his head and pretended to study Lindsay afresh. Why not lay the groundwork for faster progress than Antonia had suggested? "Fascinating indeed."

"Word has it that she wore black tonight in honor of some brother who died in battle at sea."

Edward stiffened. "Is that so?"

"Mm. If she was aiming at making the picture of the demure, grieving little sister I'd say she failed by a long straw, wouldn't you, old chap? Makes a man think more of what it would be like to unwrap that delectable white body from that rustling black silk and let her hair fall down to cover what it might. Luxurious as it is, I'd wager a man could trust it to cover only enough to make his mouth water. . . . To say nothing of what else the exercise would accomplish for him."

Edward's every muscle leaped. "If you say so." He spared Sir Alistair a flat stare. The sooner he got what was his out of this damnable circus, the better. Knowing that in this room he could undoubtedly multiply Alistair's thoughts by the hundred did nothing for Edward's peace of mind.

"I think I'll ask her to dance," Alistair said, placing his glass on a passing waiter's tray.

"Have another drink," Edward said, picking up a full glass from the same waiter's tray and thrusting it at Alistair. "The lady's next dance will be mine."

With that, he shouldered his way from the group. Standing in front of Lindsay at last, he offered a short bow.

"Good evening," he said through gritted teeth,

making certain she would feel his fury. "May I have this dance?"

Extraordinarily, Clarisse Simmonds moved swiftly in front of Lindsay and offered him her hand. "Good evening, Edward. How lovely to see you here. And what a surprise."

He'd already made himself perfectly clear to Clarisse. Their little dalliance was over. "Good evening, Clarisse. I trust you are enjoying yourself." He ignored her hand.

"I am now." She smiled sweetly. "No one dances like you, Edward. How kind of you to ask me."

He disliked being totally cruel. Casting around, he located Julian and crooked an eyebrow at him. Reading the silent message they'd developed for such occasions, Julian made his way to Edward's side.

" 'Evening, all," Julian said, smiling the smile he'd cultivated to suggest somewhat mindless good humor. "Nice little affair, what?"

Edward didn't bother to respond. "Julian, we have two lovely ladies here and I cannot dance with them both myself."

"Rather not," Julian said. "Should have said that would be a bit greedy myself."

"Never let it be said that I am greedy." Edward caught sight of Antonia's face and all but guffawed. "Wicked delight" would describe her expression perfectly. "I'll give you the pleasure—if she agrees—of the company of Lady Simmonds."

Clarisse had already placed a possessive hand on his arm. He turned to Julian, whose innocent eyes betrayed nothing of his thoughts. He bowed and all but pried Clarisse from Edward. She went with him, her face scarlet.

"Shall we?" He offered Lindsay his arm, but turned a tight-lipped smile on Antonia. "Good evening, Antonia. Thank you. For *everything.*" He had no doubt that Antonia had been helpless to stop

Lindsay's little escapade. Clearly it had been his aunt who managed to salvage the situation. And at this moment she was savoring Clarisse's failure to divert his attention from Lindsay.

"Edward," Antonia said urgently. "May I have a word?"

Keeping a firm hold on Lindsay, he bowed toward Antonia.

"Be kind, dear boy. She is a gentle little thing. And perhaps frightened. I can think of no other explanation for this." Antonia pressed a long finger into his arm. "But she is right for you. In that you are absolutely correct. Do what you think advisable."

He thought a moment, then said: "Trust me. I will. Will you do something for me?" When she nodded, he whispered his request before quickly ushering Lindsay onto the dance floor.

The little baggage had taken her lessons well, he'd grant her that. Keeping her eyes averted from him, she moved surely through the figures. Only her heightened color and the evidence of her quickened breathing gave away her nervous condition.

Farther down the formation, he sighted Julian and Clarisse. She shot Edward a malevolent glare. He gifted her with a beatific smile that resulted in her stamping a pink-slippered foot in a way that brought disapproving stares from dancers on either side. Tossing her head, she looked away. He almost asked himself what he'd ever seen in the woman. But then he remembered and allowed himself a smile that was anything but beatific.

He returned his gaze to the small figure in black, a small, exquisite temptress unaware of her potential power as she puckered her smooth brow in concentration.

Every male glance sent in Lindsay's direction infuriated Edward. That rage must be contained. He would lull her from the anxiety that strained her hauntingly lovely face, then find the right moment to let her know she must never, ever, make him angry again. "Are you enjoying yourself, Lindsay?"

They moved together. "No," she said, so emphatically he raised his brows.

"No? Why ever would that be?"

"Don't play with me, please." Her husky voice slipped along his nerves like sweet fire. "I'm not accustomed to the odd charades you people concoct and I don't intend to become so."

There was spirit in this intoxicating little article. Whatever Antonia might think—and it might be true that Lindsay was somewhat afraid—the girl would never be easy to control. He smiled and contracted his belly. A little hostility, a little resistance, would undoubtedly spice the chase and the eventual winning of the prize. But win the prize he would.

"I do not like this dance," Lindsay said as they crossed over once more. "I'm tired and would prefer to return to Bryanston Square."

"You will return to Bryanston Square soon enough, madam."

She turned to face him once more. Her deep blue eyes flashed. "Soon enough is this instant, my lord."

They linked arms and Edward nodded at the man to his left. To Lindsay he said evenly: "I advise you not to take that tone with me, little one."

"I am not a little one."

"In some ways you are so correct. In others . . . well, little one, I think I am a better judge of these things than you."

"You, sir, are insufferable."

Excitement sparked in his blood. "Have you danced much this evening, Lindsay?"

"Every dance," she said defiantly. "And I shall dance every other dance once this misery with you is over."

"We shall see. Did you wear black in honor of your dead brother?"

She faltered. The glitter in her eyes faded. "No," she said, so quietly he strained to hear. "I wore it to disgrace myself and show you how wrong I am for—"

"Hush," he said, glancing around. "This is neither the time nor the place."

"When will there be a time and a place?"

"When and if I decide."

The sedate orchestral piece finished and partners addressed one another before starting to turn away.

Lindsay made to dart from his side, but Edward was too quick for her. He caught her arm and swung her around. And the music struck up again. Gasps and a wave of excited chatter gusted through the ballroom.

"A waltz!" a woman's voice announced breathlessly.

Edward sighted Antonia and sent her a secret smile of gratitude. She might not totally agree with such "daring" public displays as the very new and risqué waltz , but she had used her influence to carry out his request for one.

Firmly, Edward twisted Lindsay toward him. "*Never* attempt to walk away from me again."

Her face had lost every last trace of color. Her eyes were huge and touched with the black and violet chips that so intrigued him. She didn't flinch. A brave one was this fascinating enigma whom he'd expected to be no more than a dowdy spinster. Lindsay Granville a spinster? The idea was laughable now.

"I believe you promised me this waltz," he said, making no attempt to disguise his satisfaction.

Lindsay stood her ground, refusing to be pulled into his arms. Edward's gaze dropped to her soft mouth. She passed the tip of her tongue over her lips, leaving them moist and slightly parted.

"Shall we dance, madam?" he said. "Or will I kiss you right here and now in front of all assembled?"

Another deep breath brought those tempting traces of pink into view above her bodice once more. But Lindsay still held her ground, her stare declaring that whatever the next move, it would not be made by her.

Edward rested his right hand at her small waist and waited.

Standing close, her body almost touching his, she kept her regard aimed at his tucked shirtfront.

If she could wait, so could he. "Little hellcat," he whispered. "Termagant in the making. Give in. Look at me."

She didn't move.

He spread his fingers at her waist. The tip of this thumb met the soft underside of her breast.

She flinched and raised her face. Slowly, she rested a hand on his arm, put the other hand in his.

Edward felt the stares, heard the whispers he knew were spawned by the spectacle he and Lindsay must make. But now he was loathe to move. Lindsay's eyes changed as he watched them; dark blue to violet, violet to shifting cobalt and black. Those eyes held questions, and he knew she questioned some strong emotion in herself as much or more than she questioned his intent. Then her soft lips trembled and he felt what he had never felt before: overwhelming, possessive protectiveness. The sensation jarred him.

Insanity.

He caught the rhythm of the music and swept her into the dance. In Europe he had waltzed. In Paris he'd been hailed as the man every woman longed to dance with. But now, here with Lindsay, he waltzed as he never had before. Soaring strings bore him along and Lindsay was his perfect partner. But he could not think too intensely of her, not of Lindsay the girl trembling on the brink of passionate womanhood. This was dangerous. This threatened to weaken his resolve in the matter at hand.

Her face was turned up to his. He felt it, but did not look down.

"You are a marvelous dancer," she said, her honey-eyed voice breathless.

"Thank you."

"This is the most exciting thing I've ever done."

She was trying, his poor little sprite, to reach for him in her insecurity. In her ignorance, she believed she had done wrong. She feared and needed. And he couldn't be what she needed, *dammit*.

"Edward."

He whirled her, whirled her again. Her steps were so light she barely seemed to touch her feet to the floor.

"Edward, I have made you angry. And I understand why."

No, she didn't.

"I didn't wear this dress for William. Not when I planned it and talked Mademoiselle Nathalie into believing Aunt Ballard approved." She stared up at him until he was forced to meet her gaze. A tremulous smile almost undid him. "I wish I had thought of William as I put on the gown. Then my silly trick would have been worth something. Please forgive me."

He frowned. Not for an instant must he relent or he would be throwing himself at her feet like a love-sick boy.

"I don't want forgiveness for trying to dissuade you from insisting upon our marriage. Only for giving the impression that I mock the state of mourning."

"You talk entirely too much." And too eloquently. "You should scarce be able to breathe and dance at this pace."

"You can," she said defensively. "And I must ask

. . . no, insist again that you give up this ridiculous course you have chosen. Please summon my step-brother on the morrow and inform him that we have made a joint agreement to cry off.''

In that instant he knew what he must do. They had danced close to one of the many sets of French doors that opened onto a balcony. With a deft move, he simply swung Lindsay to one of these doors and whisked her outside.

Grabbing her hand, he strode across the white marble terrace and down curving steps to the gardens.

''Edward, stop!''

He slowed his pace to make it easier for her, but continued on, past wandering and curious couples, until they reached the path that would take them around the house.

''Where are you taking me?''

At that, Edward did stop. He spun to face her. Light from the windows cast the shadow of her lowered lashes on elegantly rounded cheeks.

There had been something in her voice. Expectation? Excitement? Hope? ''Where would you like me to take you, my sprite?''

She bowed her head.

Gently, he held her shoulders. ''Answer me.''

''No.''

Aha. She couldn't, or rather didn't want to simply order him to take her home. Edward felt his chest expand. His own sudden, darkly demanding excitement brought his teeth together.

He bent to touch his lips to the small hollow beneath her ear. ''Where would you like to go with me? Away, Lindsay? Somewhere we can be completely alone?'' He knew he teased himself as well as the girl, but he longed to hear in her voice desire to match his own.

She said nothing.

This evening must end quickly. But first he could

not deny himself another heady sampling of the
charms that had begun to haunt him night and day.

"Kiss me, Lindsay," he whispered. "Forget
whatever it is that troubles you and kiss me."

Her breath trembled out and she shook her head.

Edward lifted her chin with a finger and thumb.
With restraint that cost him much, he spread gentle
kisses along her jaw, over her closed eyes, on her
brow, against her sensitive ear. Beneath his hands,
she shook uncontrollably.

"Kiss me, Lindsay," he murmured urgently.
"Kiss me."

"I don't know how."

Triumph beat in his veins. "I'll teach you. Open
your eyes and look at my mouth."

The lashes fluttered and then she did as he asked
. . . and sighed.

"Stand on tiptoe."

Placing her hands on his chest, automatically slipping them beneath his jacket, she rose to her toes.

"Good. Now. I'll bend my head—this way. And
you bend your head very slightly the other way."

"Yes?"

"Oh, yes. And now you touch my mouth with
yours."

"I don't think I can."

"I do. Touch me, Lindsay. Touch my lips with
yours, my sweet one."

Slowly, slowly, she closed the space, arching her
neck, innocently pressing her breasts to his chest
until her enchanting mouth met his in a feathery,
totally maddening caress. *He would go completely mad
if he didn't have her. Here. Now.*

"Is that right?"

He barely trusted his voice not to break. "Exactly
right. Now, taste me, Lindsay. Like this." Feeling
himself swell unbearably against his trousers, he ran
his tongue along her bottom lip, dipped into a cor-

ner, and traced the pert bows above. "Like that, Lindsay."

This time she didn't protest. With a sensation in his groins and limbs like boiling lead, Edward closed his eyes and held still while Lindsay copied his lesson. Her tongue lapped delicately at his mouth, testing its lines. Then, suddenly bold, she closed her teeth on his lower lip and gently sucked.

The ground seemed to fall beneath his feet. He met that small, firm, thrusting tongue and forgot to temper his ardor. Until her moan entered his senses, he had no idea that he had backed her to a wall . . . or that he had lunged into her mouth with total abandon . . . or that her hair had escaped its bonds to fall riotously about her shoulders.

He did not know until he raised his head for breath that his errant hands had worked down what there was of her bodice to bare her breasts.

"Edward. We must not do this so much."

Her small, achingly innocent protest only inflamed him more. In the white light of the moon, her thrusting breasts enticed him and he kissed first one, then the other, cupping and pushing up their weight until he felt he would burst from the roaring ache in his loins.

"Sweet," he whispered against her skin. He sucked a nipple into his mouth and tugged gently, again and again, until Lindsay caught at his hair and cried out, her body writhing.

He wedged a thigh between her legs and dragged her along the solid line of his muscle until she whimpered her need. Edward framed her face, kissed her fully, deeply on the mouth and tangled his fingers in her hair.

"Edward. Oh, Edward." Feebly at first, but with increasing desperation, Lindsay ground herself against his leg. He grasped her hips to guide her.

"Edward? I say, Edward!"

"Damn." Slipping her to her feet, he caught

Lindsay violently to him covering her. "Don't move," he warned.

"Edward! You out here? It's Julian."

Edward cursed silently while he fumbled to pull up Lindsay's bodice and push back her hair.

"There you are. . . . Ah. Sorry, old chap."

"What the hell do you want?" Edward growled, holding Lindsay's face to his chest. Her fingers dug into him and she shook even more violently. "Damn it all, Julian. Can't you see this isn't the time?"

Instead of retreating, Julian came closer. He glanced fleetingly at Lindsay, then fixed Edward with a hard stare. "There's a little matter that needs your attention. You'll be very glad I found you, Edward. I'm sure you remember our project?"

Edward was immediately alert. "I remember."

"One of my contacts reached me here. He wanted me to know that our favorite racing pigeon is in trouble. It seems that greedy little Satan was caught cheating by another bird."

Julian's code was easily read. Latchett had got himself in some serious trouble. "Where is he now?"

"Oh, someone put him where he can't get away. I believe it will require a visit from you and some, er, tangible recompense to gain his freedom."

Gad! The evil fool was slipping almost too easily into Edward's trap. So now he'd been caught cheating at cards and had tossed Edward's name out as someone who would buy him out of the jam. And that was exactly what Edward would to—this time. And with the buying he would gain more of Roger Latchett's confidence in his "benefactor." And the easier it would be to push him into the hell he'd earned.

Lindsay pressed closer.

"Julian, Miss Granville seems to be taking cold. Kindly see her to my coach and accompany her to my aunt's home."

Disengaging her arms from his waist, he stepped away.

"Edward!"

He didn't trust himself to answer her plea. This was what he needed, something to refocus his objective. The moment before he strode away, he caught Julian's narrow and disapproving stare. There was no time to ask what that was about.

"Take her home," he called. "I'll make some excuse to Antonia."

What had just happened between him and Lindsay would not happen again until Roger Latchett was a memory. By then the murderer would have reaped his punishment. And by then Lindsay would be Edward's wife. Enforced restraint could only make final conquest more exquisite.

Chapter 16

A ntonia sipped a glass of sherry and pretended to be engrossed in the very boring novel that lay open on her lap.

"Beautiful roses Bently brought," she said, attempting yet again to draw Lindsay out. "Thirty-six red roses. Quite a posy. Surprised he could carry them."

Lindsay, reclining on a blue velvet chaise in the second-floor parlor, continued to stare into the fire.

"Lindsay!" Antonia shut the book with a slap. "For goodness sake, gel, tell me what is troubling you so terribly."

"Nothing." Lindsay smiled wanly. She was as preoccupied this evening as she had been throughout the three days since the Cumberland Ball.

"You aren't still fretting about the little matter of the black dress, are you, dear?" Antonia waited for the answer that never came. "Because if you are, please don't. You were naughty and I've told you I think so. But all in all the whole thing turned out quite beautifully. You stole the evening. Ernestine Sebbel told me she's thinking of encouraging Isabelle to wear black to the next ball. Evidently she's got the notion it would make the girl more striking."

"I'm tired," Lindsay said.

Antonia narrowed her eyes suspiciously. "That is

a pity. Perhaps you need a little something to help you relax. I'll have Norris pour you a sherry." It was entirely possible that Lindsay had decided to pretend a decline until she got whatever it was she thought she wanted. Antonia, however, did *not* for one moment believe that Lindsay was impervious to Edward. "Y'know, Lindsay, I won't be at all surprised if we start seeing a whole lot of black dresses on young gels this Season."

"You went into mourning when you were very little older than I am. And you still wear black all the time. Why is that?"

"Habit." Antonia had no intention of giving away too many of her secrets. She glanced at the mantel clock. Dear, flattering Lord Airsly would be along shortly.

"Tony is a nice man, isn't he?" Lindsay said.

"Very nice." And wasting his time in calling upon Lindsay three days in a row. "What was in the little box he brought you this morning?"

Finally, Lindsay smiled. She picked up the porcelain, heart-shaped box Lord Gravistock had presented that morning and carefully removed the top. From inside she extracted a brightly enameled bird. "It is a clockwork bluebird." She wound it up and tilted her head to watch its wings flap. "Isn't it enchanting? Tony said the blue feathers reminded him of my eyes." Instantly, she blushed and quickly put the bird away.

"Today a bird. Yesterday a music box. The day before orchids from his own hothouse. I'd say that young man is very taken with you."

"And that is pointless," Lindsay said. "I told him so today, but I invited him to be my friend. Tony is one of the nicest people I've ever met."

The girl's natural poise and charm amazed Antonia. Lindsay was in no way awed by rank and title. "What did he say to your offer?"

Lindsay sighed. "That he would not call again for

a while because it hurt too much not to be able to at least hope I would consider him as more than a friend. Really, this is all too much. One visitor after another for days. It really is exhausting."

"One *gentleman caller* after another for days," Antonia corrected. And Lindsay did not appear exhausted. Ethereal, her skin like apricot-brushed cream, but not tired. Much of her hair had been drawn into a braided chignon at her crown, but long, shiny ringlets framed her face. Thin, apricot-colored satin ribbon, threaded through with gold, wove in and out of the braids. Her India muslin dress was of the same apricot color. Gold rosettes decorated the low neck and the underskirt that showed here and there where the dress settled gracefully over her drawn-up feet.

"Are you not enjoying so much attention from the gentlemen, Lindsay?"

"No."

"Most young girls would count it a great triumph to attend one of two functions and immediately collect such a string of beaux." Antonia opened her book again, and cleared her throat. "Should we take the offers to Mr. Latchett?"

"Offers?" Lindsay's head jerked up. Her breast rose and fell rapidly. "What do you mean, offers?"

"Don't pretend you don't know. Gentlemen don't call on a gel again and again if they don't have something in mind other than worshiping at her shrine."

"Oh." She fell against the chaise and rested the back of a hand on her brow. "No. I am not interested in marrying any of them. I'm only sorry if I've inconvenienced them."

"Pah!" Antonia smacked the book shut again. "That is the chance men take in the marriage mart. Now. Tell me what is making you so feeble."

"Nothing. And I'm not feeble."

"Was there perhaps a man you hoped would come

but who has not?'' When she got Edward alone he was going to wish he hadn't played his little game of silence in the days since the ball. ''Lindsay? Was there someone you would have liked to see?''

''No!''

Mm. Much too emphatic a response. ''Are you sure you aren't missing that irascible nephew of mine?'' she asked softly.

''No!'' Lindsay rolled her head away. ''No, I am not. I hope I never have to see him again.''

Deeply satisfied, Antonia smiled. ''Of course, my dear. Silly of me to even entertain such an idea.'' Perfectly sensible of her to entertain it since it was true.

''Well,'' Lindsay said, her face still averted. ''I don't suppose there will be any more callers today.''

''Probably not.'' The gel was pining for Edward. How absolutely marvelous. ''Did you enjoy seeing your stepmother this afternoon?'' Belle Granville had come to tea. The longest, most exasperating tea Antonia had ever lived through.

Lindsay turned her head farther away and said nothing.

''She certainly has a great deal to talk about.''

''She has absolutely nothing to talk about that anyone would want to listen—'' Lindsay covered her mouth. ''That was unforgivable. Belle is a little . . . well, she hasn't had an opportunity to expand her mind.''

''No. I'm sure you're right.'' The truth was that the woman thought and spoke of nothing that didn't relate to her own vacuous concerns.

''I believe she had expected this visit to London to be a social whirl.''

''I believe you are right.'' The thought of Belle Granville flouncing and primping through the drawing rooms of the *haut monde*—and doing so as a future relative of Antonia's—sent a dart of horror into the brain.

"Edward was in the Indies, wasn't he?"

"Yes." The warmth of success curled about Antonia's insides. "For some years. He did very well there, too."

"I'm sure Edward would do very well at absolutely anything."

Antonia hid her broad smile. "So am I. He has been a determined male from the moment of his birth."

"Mmm. His personality is . . . magnetic? Would you say that was so, Aunt Ballard?"

"Oh, most definitely magnetic."

"And he is . . . He is a man whom one would have to be blind not to see as most . . . pleasant to look at."

"Oh, most pleasant to look at." She almost hugged herself with joy. What she had so desperately yearned for was happening.

"Do you think that somewhere in him . . . Somewhere in him . . . Could it be that in fact he has a kind heart, but that he is afraid to show it lest he be considered less than manly?"

"Yes, I do," Antonia said with complete honesty. "You would only have to hear him play the piano to know what a sensitive heart he has."

A muffled sound from the couch made Antonia lean forward in her chair. "What did you say?" she asked sharply.

"Um. I did hear Edward play. Just a little. It was on the night I arrived. I was unable to sleep and I happened to be in the music room. He had come to visit, but you were in bed. He kindly played a little for me and it was so beautiful I thought I would . . ."

"Yes." So, that secretive scoundrel had indeed managed time alone with the girl. On how many other occasions had he done so? Antonia wondered.

"He played as if his whole heart broke with the beauty of the music." Lindsay crossed her arms under her breasts and closed her eyes. "But that was only for a very short while. If he were truly kind he wouldn't keep me—"

Antonia leaned even farther forward. Color crept up the girl's face but she kept her eyes shut. "He wouldn't keep you what, Lindsay?"

"Oh, I don't know. I suppose I thought it might be nice if he took the trouble to see me. I'm certain he has concluded that I won't suit after all and is merely trying to decide upon a kind way to let me down. I wish he would just *do* it and send me home."

But that, Antonia thought smugly, was exactly what Lindsay did *not* want Edward to do and it was exactly what she was certain he had no intention of doing. Wherever her errant nephew was at this moment, she would wager that he was furthering his plans for the marriage he was set upon. Not that he could be excused for putting up such a shabby effort in the courting of his future bride.

The door opened and Norris entered with one of his cranelike steps. He cleared his throat, but before he could speak a young female darted around him and rushed to the center of the room.

Antonia was too shocked to react.

Dressed in a pale green traveling dress with a matching, rabbit-trimmed pelisse, the sturdy creature made a fetching picture.

"Hm, hm," Norris intoned. "Miss Winslow, milady."

"Hello," the girl said when she sighted Antonia. Blue-black curls sprang around her face beneath a chip bonnet lined with the same green as her dress. "I'm Sarah. Where's Lindsay, please?"

"Sarah!" Lindsay scrambled to sit up on the chaise. "Sarah! How did you get here so quickly? I didn't know you'd even been sent for."

Before Lindsay could get up, the other girl flew

over the blue carpet, sat beside her friend and gathered her into a tight embrace.

The two girls clung together. Antonia could see tears squeezing from beneath Lindsay's heavy lashes to course down her soft cheeks.

"I've had such an exciting time, Lindsay." Sarah sat up, untied her bonnet and dragged it off. "Why didn't you tell me *everything*? I thought you were just going to Town with Revolting Rog— . . . with Roger and your stepmama. When your handsome viscount came galloping to the rectory I thought poor old Bostock would have the vapors. Papa did almost have them. And I had them properly."

"Oh, Sarah, it's so wonderful to see you." Lindsay held the dark-eyed girl's hands in hers. "I've missed you."

"I don't believe you." Sarah set her bonnet on the chaise. "But no matter. Lord Hawkesly persuaded Papa that I will be well looked after here. How exciting to be your companion in *London*. His lordship said that you have quite taken the town by storm and that although the wedding will be small, it will be a most important event."

Antonia leaned back in her chair. *Wait* until she saw Edward. Insolent young puppy. Galloping ahead with plans he should not make without consulting her at every step.

"Oh, Sarah, what am I thinking of? This is Lady Ballard. Aunt Ballard, this is my dear friend—"

"Sarah Winslow. Yes, I gathered. I'm pleased to meet you, Sarah." Yes, this girl could be what was needed to raise Lindsay's spirits. "How was your journey?"

Sarah raised her shoulders. Her eyes shone as if she savored pleasant memories. "Mr. Lloyd-Preston was so kind to me. He explained everything we passed and he didn't think it at all silly for a girl as old as me never to have been outside Cornwall before."

"Julian?" Lindsay gave Antonia a bemused look.

Antonia shrugged—and then caught sight of a figure lounging in the doorway. Edward, a black garrick draped over his shoulders, watched the scene with apparent satisfaction. He caught Antonia's eye and put a finger to his lips.

"After the viscount had come and explained everything to Papa, Mr. Lloyd-Preston and a perfectly sweet maid came with the coach. Oh, dear, but we did have to do everything in such a hurry. There was no time for me to consider the additions needed to my wardrobe, but the viscount insisted that he would ensure the problem was attended to here in London. He said you would be able to go shopping with me in Oxford Street and the Burlington Arcade and all those wonderful places." She wiggled with anticipation. "Won't we have fun?"

"Yes, of course we shall." Lindsay's troubled expression suggested she might be thinking far beyond "fun" shopping expeditions.

"Do you know Mr. Lloyd-Preston?" Sarah asked.

Antonia frowned at Edward, who shook his head slightly. His self-satisfied smile grated on her.

"Julian is a very kind man," Lindsay said. Her choice of words and her sudden shifting on the chaise suggested to Antonia that there was something here of which she knew nothing.

Sarah sighed hugely. "I think so, too. He's of a gentle spirit, I think—and rather sad, as if bearing some sorrow he wishes to hide."

Now what was all this talk of young Julian Lloyd-Preston? Surely he had not managed to turn this artless young chit's head.

"I see you two are getting reacquainted." Edward moved from his place in the doorway and sauntered into the room, his garrick swinging. "Lindsay, my love, I'm sorry I didn't have time to consult with you before collecting Sarah. I had urgent business to attend to in Devon. I decided to speak with Sarah's father at the same time."

My love! Antonia opened her fan and used it to hide her smile. Lindsay, her hands pressed beneath her breasts as if to contain her heart, gazed at Edward with naked admiration.

"That was kind of you, Edward," she said softly.

"I wanted to please you." He stood beside her, looking down. "Pleasing you gives me pleasure."

My, but the boy could make a pretty speech when it suited him.

"Julian's on his way in. He's arranging for my valet's sister to be transported home." To Antonia he added: "Stoddart's sister was available to attend Sarah on the journey."

"How convenient," Antonia said. There was more to this, much more, and she didn't expect to wait long before learning what it was.

"Ah, there you are, Julian," Edward said as his ally strolled into the room. "Now our party is complete."

Bowing to Antonia, Julian went to Sarah's side as if that were his appointed place. Antonia smiled yet again. This was proving most interesting.

Edward spun a chair around and sat close to Lindsay. He took her hand in his and leaned over her. "Forgive me for not calling upon you sooner after the other night."

Instantly, a furious blush swept over Lindsay's face. "Think nothing of it," she said.

Antonia noted that it was Edward's firm grasp that stopped the girl from pulling her hand away. There had been the matter of the missing time between Edward's asking Lindsay to dance and his return to say that Lindsay was exhausted and had been taken back to Bryanston Square by Julian. . . .

"If there had been any other way, I would have postponed my trip to Devon, but—"

"I have been quite busy, I assure you." With her

spare hand, Lindsay took the lid off the porcelain box Lord Gravistock had given her. She removed the clockwork bird. "Isn't this delightful, Sarah? Wind it up. The wings flap."

"The Marquis of Gravistock gave it to Lindsay when he called today," Antonia said, feeling deliciously wicked. "And he told Lindsay the blue feathers reminded him of the color of her eyes."

"Gravistock?" Edward's lips flattened over his teeth. "What was he doing here?"

Antonia shrugged eloquently. "The same as Sir Stuart Long and your friend, Alistair, and Lord Bently—to name but a few."

"Alistair is no friend of mine," Edward retorted, getting abruptly to his feet. "And Bently's no more than a bounty hunter in fop's clothing, why . . . What exactly has occurred here?"

Antonia saw the way Lindsay caught her bottom lip in her teeth and developed a fascination for her fingernails. "The girl had spirit, thank God. She would need it with the possessive man who intended to own her."

"Antonia?"

She suppressed the desire to tell him to mind his tongue. "Our Lindsay made quite an impression at the Cumberlands'. And at the production we attended at the King's Theatre the following evening. To date there have been four offers for her hand."

"What?" Edward's eyes narrowed. "You allowed other men to come calling and offering for the woman who will become my wife?"

"You weren't in London," Antonia said innocently. "At least, I assumed you weren't. We didn't know where you were. Lindsay and I could scarcely be rude to such charming gentlemen. You agree, don't you, Julian?"

Julian's attention was entirely upon the winsome Miss Sarah Winslow. Antonia took an exasperated breath.

"What Julian does or doesn't think is of no consequence in this matter," Edward said in a terrible voice.

All eyes immediately centered upon him.

"I'm disappointed that I couldn't trust you to protect Lindsay," he said to Antonia. "But in future that won't be necessary. I shall deal with any unwanted attention myself."

"Edward—"

He held up a hand, silencing Antonia. "Please, I have other important matters to attend to, but first I want to make certain my plans for the next week are clearly understood."

"I say, Edward, don't you think you and Lindsay should talk about this alone?" Julian frowned worriedly.

"Not at all. This concerns all present." He nodded at Sarah Winslow. "I have already explained to Sarah that she will be Lindsay's bridesmaid. Julian, you, naturally will act as my groomsman. I've decided the wedding breakfast shall take place at Cavendish Square. Antonia, I would trust no one but you to oversee those arrangements."

She murmured assent, conveying none of the horror she felt at this cavalier exhibition.

Like a sleepwalker, Lindsay stirred and rose to her feet. "Had you thought to consult me on any of these matters, my lord?" she asked, far too quietly for Antonia's comfort. "Perhaps on the question of the calling of banns, or the style of my wedding gown. Or of whether I am *ready* for this marriage. Or *any* marriage!"

A small, appalled silence fell, before Edward recovered and smiled condescendingly upon Lindsay. "Don't overset yourself, my love. You are too highstrung to deal with these matters, so I have dealt with them—for both of us. Our engagement is to be puffed off in the *Post* and the *Times* tomorrow morning. The wedding will take place on Saturday next."

He appeared to calculate. "Five days, not seven. Antonia will deal with the matter of gowns and such nonsense. Julian, would you take Sarah and find someone to get her settled?"

"I'll summon Norris," Antonia said, feeling decidedly weak.

"No need," Edward boomed in a voice entirely unlike his own. "See to it, Julian, there's a good chap."

Antonia's concentration was on Lindsay's tight-lipped face, but she didn't miss Julian's air of disapproval as he ushered a clearly bewildered Sarah from the room.

"Now," Edward said when the door closed. "I must get on. Are there any questions?"

"Next Saturday?" Antonia said with total disbelief.

"A word with the archbishop was adequate. The special license will be in my hand by tomorrow."

"But, Edward, what will people say? The haste is indecent."

"Love is not indecent, madam. And there will be no infant presented in five months, so—"

"Edward!"

He had the grace to show chagrin. "I beg your pardon. These are . . . I have had a great deal to accomplish in a short while."

"The dress will be—"

"It will be made in time," Edward finished for her. "These details are for show after all. Of course, I will leave it to you to invite anyone you think fit. The fewer the better. The ceremony will be at nine at Saint Mary's. That has been arranged."

A flash of whirling apricot-colored muslin silenced him. Lindsay rushed to catch at his arm. Her eyes glittered. "And what of me, my lord? Do I not have something to say in all this? How dare you take such liberties with my life."

Antonia saw the briefest flicker of uncertainty in

Edward's black eyes. Just as quickly, it was gone. "You forget yourself, Lindsay," he said. "Since when has your life been your own to decide *anything* about? It has been decided that you will become my wife. Your legal guardian has accepted my offer. The necessary documents have been signed."

"Oh!" She backed away. "Oh . . . I do not care about you anymore. But I do care about . . . I will not marry you."

Edward's eyes narrowed to assessing slits. "You do not care about me *anymore*?" His tone was menacing. "A hopeful statement, madam. It suggests you have found yourself capable of caring for me until this point."

Antonia wished herself far away. She sat very still.

"I shall hope you may come to care for me again," Edward added without inflection. He strolled toward Lindsay, taking something from a pocket. "This is rightfully yours now."

Lindsay stared into the box he opened. From it he removed a ring set with an oval sapphire the size of a wren's egg. Rather than place it upon her finger, he turned her hand and dropped it into her palm.

"A blue to match your eyes, I think," he said with enough sarcasm to make Antonia flinch. "My mother wore it. And my grandmother before her. It has been in my family for hundreds of years."

"I don't want it," Lindsay said miserably.

He continued on to open the door. "It is already yours. Wear it on Saturday . . . when you become my wife."

Chapter 17

"**S**arah, this is madness!"

"Do be quiet, Lindsay. You always did talk too much."

"*I* always did talk too much?"

"Shh." Sarah pulled Lindsay through the shadows beside the wall at the bottom of the countess's gardens. "Please. Do as I say quickly and quietly. Then you will be glad you came. And then we can return to the house before we are missed."

Lindsay's arms and legs moved stiffly. Her entire body felt hot and cold by turns. This was the most horrible night of her life, or it would be until tomorrow night. Tomorrow she was to be married, which meant that by the time night fell she would be Edward's wife with all her careful plans of the past two years in ruin.

Sarah, bent almost double, ran toward a gate in the wall.

Lindsay was dragged behind.

Tomorrow she would be faced with the prospect of watching and waiting for Roger to make his move. And make his move he would. She had no doubt of that. A few days ago when Edward had been so hateful in his overbearing manner, she had almost convinced herself she didn't care what happened to him. Since then he had called upon her daily, show-

ering her with small but expensive gifts, mostly of
family jewels. But it was not the gifts that had
brought her to the point where she could think of
little else but his safety. Two simple words, "Forgive me," had stolen her heart. Two words delivered in a quiet, solemn voice while he looked into
her eyes.

"Through here," Sarah said. They slipped into a
cobbled way in front of mews quarters where married servants lived in rooms above the stables. "We
are to go quickly to the gardens in the middle of the
square."

"It's dangerous," Lindsay whispered.

Sarah ran on, her fingers tightly laced in Lindsay's.

There was Edward to protect and there was John.
But for now, Edward was more immediately vulnerable and, therefore, her first concern. "Forgive me,"
he had said. "I have been high-handed with you. I
have never felt I wanted to marry before. The discovery that I do now has unnerved me. Your life as
my wife will be a good one, sprite. This I promise
you." Edward had kissed her then, not with the hot
passion that had robbed her of many nights' sleep
of late, but with tenderness that made her heart and
soul ache.

Once in the square, Sarah rushed them to the gardens in the center and they passed quickly between
tall privet hedges until Lindsay felt swallowed by
the darkness.

"Lindsay?" A male voice rasped her name the instant before she was grabbed into a hard embrace.
"Lindsay, Lindsay. It *is* you."

Her chest tightened until she could hardly breathe.
"Antun?" The air burned her throat.

"Aye, Linny, 'tis Antun."

He held her away, but all she could see was the
silhouette of his tall, big body. Sarah hovered close.

"I've been out of my mind worrying about you,"

Antun said. "Why didn't you tell me you were going away?"

She cast about for a way to explain what had happened without alarming him. "I haven't told anyone about—" *Sarah must not know about the night runners.* "Antun, I'm safe. I am to be married tomorrow to a fine man who will be a good husband. But nothing will change between you and me. Do you understand?"

He was quiet and she took heart. Antun was too clever to say anything indiscreet in front of Sarah.

After what felt like an endless pause, Antun said: "If Sarah hadn't thought to come to me, I'd have been watching for you yet. Damn that highborn devil's hide. I knew he had more reason than he gave for settling so close to Tregonitha."

Lindsay slipped her arms around Antun's strong body and rested her face on his chest. "You are my oldest friend, Antun. William trusted you more than any man alive."

Antun's muffled oath shocked her, but she didn't release him.

"The viscount is no devil," she told him, although she had, more than once, put that intriguing gentleman into such a category. "And our meeting was purely chance." She would not inflame Antun by telling him that she wished she could avoid this marriage—for the sake of others involved.

"If you say so." Antun settled his big hands awkwardly on her back. "He'd as well be very good to you, Linny. If I ever hear otherwise it will cost him his life."

She smiled against his clean, rough clothing. "I should turn to you immediately if Edward treated me badly."

Antun grunted. He did not sound mollified. "I'm going to need your help, Linny." His urgent tone sent fear into her bones. "Soon. Very soon."

"How can Lindsay help you, Antun?" Sarah sounded bemused.

For an instant, Lindsay had forgotten the other girl's presence. "Is there some problem with the tenants?" she asked quickly.

"Um, yes." Antun had always been quick to grasp things. "There's a question of extra demands by . . . There are demands to be met and only you can deal with that effectively."

Lindsay frowned. Did he mean that Roger had pushed the cottagers for even greater portions? She raised her face questioningly to Antun. In the darkness, she could barely make out the glitter of his eyes and teeth.

He bowed his head as if to kiss her cheek. "Roger is threatening to put people out," he whispered. "I've done what I can, but I haven't had a good run with . . . with our foreign friends in weeks. One's expected soon. I'll need what I get then, and what's in the cellar at Tregonitha."

Lindsay nodded, her heart leaping.

"I can't get in the cellar without the key."

And the key was at Tregonitha. "How long do we have?"

"You two are whispering," Sarah said, sounding peeved. "I'm not a child. I can know about these things. I already do know that Revolting Roger's a toad."

Lindsay had to laugh and even Antun chuckled. "We all know that, young Sarah," he said. To Lindsay he added: "I'll get a message to you—when your help is needed."

"But what shall I do?" She stepped back, but kept a grasp on his woolen coat. "What *can* I do here?"

"Leave that to me. I'll get to you." Carefully, he took her hands from his coat. "And I won't embarrass you with this *viscount* of yours."

How she longed to tell Antun the weight of her concerns and beg him to help her.

"Lindsay," Sarah said. "We must return. Poor Emma is lying in your bed, pretending to be you in case someone looks into your room. But if someone did, I think she would expire."

"Sarah! Poor Emma. You do think of such dramatic measures. We'll go at once. Antun, when do you think I shall see you again." She looked around. "Antun?"

He was gone.

Julian cracked open the sacristy door and peered into the small side chapel where Edward and Lindsay were to be married. Measured footfalls behind him were a constant reminder of Edward's agitated pacing.

"More guests than I'd expected," Julian commented. "The countess is a remarkable woman. Can't think of another who could assemble such a distinguished audience at such short notice."

"Don't use the word 'audience,'" Edward said in a tone that echoed his evil mood. "This isn't a damned play, Julian."

"Some might think so," Julian muttered.

"What was that?"

"Shouldn't think so," he said hastily. "Very solemn affair."

"Very solemn," Edward echoed.

Julian contained a smile. Undoubtedly he was mistaken, but he might almost conclude that the unshakable Viscount Hawkesly was ruffled.

"Trevay made contact," Edward said. "He's heard rumblings that Latchett is trying to raise more money from the tenants at Tregonitha. Poor devils. The sooner we remove the blackguard, the better."

"He's in deep, Edward. Very deep. He's been telling his creditors he's about to come into a tidy sum. Which means that he expects this marriage to provide him with a completely free rein in Cornwall. As long as he has the constraints of acting as administrator for Lindsay, there are limits to what he can do. Without those constraints he'd bleed the place dry.''

''Fool. I'll have to keep him quiet for a decent interval.'' Edward fidgeted with his neckcloth and straightened his sleeves. Against all convention, he'd insisted upon wearing the black he favored. He swung to face Julian. ''I don't want Lindsay to get wind of any of this.''

Julian raised a brow. ''Of what you intend to do to Latchett, you mean?''

''Concentrate, man! I don't want her to know *why* I appear to suddenly change my mind about letting Latchett stay on at Tregonitha.''

''I see,'' Julian said innocently. ''You probably don't want her to find out why it is that you intend to drive the man from the country, either.''

''No! She's got a tender heart, Julian. Gentle little thing. Sweet. I couldn't tolerate watching her reaction if she found out it was her wretched stepbrother who arranged the murder of William Granville.''

''Quite so. And it probably wouldn't look too good to her if she thought you had married her simply to gain control of her inheritance.''

''I don't *want* her damnable inheritance.''

'' 'Course not. 'Course not.'' Julian fingered his own neckcloth and checked the church again. The chapel was almost full and the array of finery—and fine people—was awesome.

''All I'm trying to say,'' Edward said distractedly, ''is that I see no point in upsetting a fragile-natured little female any more than she's already upset by this precipitous marriage.''

Gentle. Kind. A tender heart. Fragile-natured. All this from a man who didn't give a damn about the girl? ''She cares for you, Edward.''

''What?'' Edward stood still and glared. ''What the devil are you blathering about?''

"Lindsay Granville is enthralled by you. I believe she very probably loves you." God help her.

"Poppycock!"

"And I think you care for her."

"Bosh! Your mind's been addled by mooning around after the Winslow girl."

It was Julian's turn to stare. He waved a hand. "You'll have to do better than that if you want to distract me. Edward, why not be honest with Lindsay? Tell her what you plan. Don't use her like this."

Edward pulled a fob watch from his waistcoat pocket and stared at the face.

"My friend," Julian said seriously. "There are not so many chances to share one's life with a woman worth loving. You have that chance. I beg you, don't waste it."

"It's time."

"Edward—"

"It is too late, Julian. And I will not be diverted. A female does not have the strength of mind or constitution to be involved in the kind of events I intend to manufacture."

Julian opened his mouth to try another protest. Then he changed his mind. This man was not one to be moved from a decision.

Organ music began to flow inside the church. "Very well, Edward," Julian said. "It is indeed time. You are about to become a married man."

Settling an impassive expression on his face, Edward led the way from the sacristy to the head of the chapel aisle. At the bottom of the altar steps, smile in place, Bible in hand, stood the minister provided by the archbishop.

With Julian at his side, Edward turned to face the congregation. He determinedly avoided catching the eye of Belle Granville, who sat pompously in the front row. He looked instead at Antonia and blinked. Not only had she abandoned black for silver-gray—for the

first time in his memory—but she dabbed repeatedly
at her eyes with a wisp of a lace handkerchief. Senti-
ment usually made him uncomfortable, but Antonia's
evident emotion moved him.

The organist played a transitional chord and broke
into a stirring but dignified march.

At the other end of the aisle, Lindsay appeared
and stood framed by an elegant Norman archway.
Edward clamped his teeth together and muscles in
his jaw flexed. Even at a distance she was breathtaking.

Slowly, with the odious Latchett at her side and
Sarah Winslow slightly behind and to her left, Lindsay proceeded toward Edward.

"My God," Julian whispered. "She's an angel."

"An angel," Edward agreed. "And she's mine."

"I was talking about Sarah," Julian hissed.

Edward frowned, amazed, and glanced at the vi-
vacious dark-haired girl dressed surprisingly in dark
green satin. "Quite so," Edward agreed. "But *I* was
speaking of Lindsay."

She was only yards away now. How Antonia had
secured such a gown in a matter of days he had no
idea. And he didn't care. Looking as she did, Lindsay would steal any man's heart and soul. She
could choose the hand of any eligible man in the
land and he would come willingly, gladly, to make
her his own.

No trace of a smile touched her beautiful oval face.
Her eyes were the darkest blue, huge and shining
with undisguised apprehension. Clever hands had
contrived to fashion the heavy hair into a braided
coronet on top of her head. Through this had been
threaded a rope of diamonds. But for the most delicate of curls about her face, her hair was drawn
back smoothly. A veil of white silk drifted from the
plaited coronet to float about a long train attached
at the shoulders of her satin gown.

Edward stood very straight. He smiled at her,

willed her to trust that he would care for her and that she had nothing to fear from him. She *was* gentle. And she *was* innocent of the sins of the foul creature at her side. He would protect and care for her. She would need time to adjust to her married state and he would give her that time. There would be no need to teach her all she must eventually know of being a wife until she became more accustomed to him—and until he had safely dispatched Roger Latchett and could concentrate on husbandly duties.

Lindsay arrived before him. Her trembling lips parted. A worried frown drew her fine brows together. He barely restrained himself from reaching for her hand.

"Edward," Julian whispered.

He ignored his friend. This girl whom he had expected to take as his wife purely as a necessary means to his own ends was a magical creature. The stiff white satin of her gown lent a luster to flawless, creamy skin. Her lush breasts rose to tantalizing fullness above the low, square neck of a bodice encrusted with flowers formed of pearls with a diamond at each center. Sleeves, puffed at the shoulders, hugged her slender arms tightly all the way to diamond-and-pearl-edged points at her hands. Strands of the same pearls and diamonds hung free from the high waistline and swung in a sparkling overskirt to within an inch of the gown's hem.

Rustling and whispering had begun to pass through the congregation from the moment Lindsay came into view. Edward glanced away from her and grinned with satisfaction. His aunt had contrived to take his lovely, virginal bride and turn her into a vision that resembled the perfection of starlight upon pure snow. And all those assembled here would remember the sight forever.

"Edward!" Julian sounded panicked.

With a smile, Edward faced the minister. Lindsay

came to his side and he looked down upon her young face, her shining, silvery hair, her softly rising breasts.

I will, he vowed in his heart. *Again and again, I will.*

Her new London home. Lindsay surveyed the dining room in Edward's elegantly masculine Cavendish Square house. Her first visit here and it was as mistress—as Viscountess Hawkesly, Edward's wife.

Overwhelmed, she stole a sidelong glance at the strikingly handsome man who had chosen to bring her into all this. He sat beside her at a table set with snowy linen and laden with fine Wedgwood dishes, heavy silver cutlery, old French crystal and myriad domed silver serving pieces. Branch candelabrums, each base wreathed with white roses, supported dozens of white candles. Fifty splendidly arrayed guests were assembled at the vast table.

Aunt Ballard, seated at Edward's other side, caught Lindsay's attention. "You have hardly eaten, my dear. Try one of the sugar peacocks."

Lindsay smiled but shook her head. "I'm not hungry."

"Give the girl a sugar peacock," boomed redfaced Lord Sebbel, whom Lindsay had never seen before today. "She'll need to keep her strength up, eh, Hawkesly?" He winked hugely and nodded appreciation of the guffaws that met his remark.

Edward turned to Lindsay. "Eat a little something," he said quietly. He waved aside a hovering servant and put one of the confections in question upon her plate. "You've had some difficult times, but there's no need to worry further."

"Thank you." Lindsay could only stare up at his lowered dark eyes. This man with the slender, serious face, with slanted black brows and strongly marked cheekbones, was spectacularly handsome. His straight nose, strong chin and full, clearly defined mouth would hold the attention of any woman, maiden or otherwise. Leaning close to add strawberries dipped in chocolate and curls of crystallized mint to the serving, the force of his size and power whipped her like a warm blow.

She was glad to be his wife. Lindsay's hands curled into fists in her lap. *She had wanted to marry him.*

Convivial conversation drifted around those seated for the wedding breakfast. With the exception of Belle Latchett, whose puce complexion suggested she'd taken too many glasses of everything offered, everyone present bore an impressive title.

Soon she and Edward would leave the party and retire to the chambers she had yet to see. A mix of fear and excitement clamored in her stomach.

"You look a treat, Lindsay, dear," Belle shouted lustily. "Done yourself proud, you have."

In the small silence that followed, sympathetic eyes turned in Lindsay's direction. She smiled sweetly around. "Thank you, stepmother. I hope Lord Hawkesly will not rue his choice."

Bawdy male reassurances rolled around the room: "Should say not." "Rather not." "Not a bit of it."

Edward leaned close. "Definitely not," he whispered.

Lindsay blushed. The women present sighed. The men chuckled knowingly.

She wanted to be with him—alone.

Lindsay tried to send him the message with her eyes, but Edward had already turned away. She toyed with the hardened sugar on her plate until it fractured and fell in a ruined heap.

"You look so lovely," Clarisse called from her seat much farther down the table.

Aunt Ballard had said there would not be room to include Clarisse but Lindsay had insisted that her friend be present. "Thank you, Clarisse," she said.

Someone was asking Belle where Roger was. Lindsay strained to hear the response but only

picked up the word "business" in the rising din.
She was grateful he'd chosen to absent himself from
the breakfast.

Julian sat on Lindsay's other side but, since all his
attention was on Sarah, who sat to his right, he'd
scarcely spoken to Lindsay. She began to feel very
alone.

Removable dishes were taken away and more
brought in their place. Heaps of fresh fruit, small
dishes of jellies and custards, baskets of succulent
pastries, chocolate pots and flavored creams were
spread before the guests, many of whom seemed to
have no difficulty eating more and more. And wine
flowed, a different vintage and variety to comple-
ment each dish.

And as the laughter grew, Lindsay felt Edward
become more quiet and withdrawn.

Tentatively, she brushed her small finger against
his hand on the table. He started and faced her.

Lindsay almost cried out. He appeared . . .
haunted?

"Enjoy yourselves, please," he said loudly, suddenly, and stood up. "There will be entertainments
later. Dancing. A game or two of chance for those
who wish. My home"—glancing at Lindsay, he offered her his hand and helped her rise to stand beside him—"our home is yours on this special day.
But we must leave you now."

Applause went up, so loud as to make Lindsay
smile and try to cover her ears.

Edward led her from the table. Immediately, Sarah
leaped to her feet to straighten Lindsay's train.
When they reached the mahogany-paneled hall and
the bottom of a gracefully curving staircase, Edward
turned back to Sarah. "Thank you," he said solemnly. "Please tell Emma that Lindsay and I wish
to be alone awhile. Lindsay will call one or both of
you when she needs you."

Coloring fiercely, falling into a deep curtsy, Sarah

bowed, then bobbed up and fled back to the dining room. She was to live at Cavendish Square as Lindsay's companion until she was more settled. And Aunt Ballard had spared Emma to be Lindsay's abigail.

Lindsay had never seen Edward move at such a slow pace. He was, she realized, climbing the stairs with deliberate care to accommodate the much smaller steps her gown necessitated.

The air seemed thinner and incapable of filling her lungs. Past beautiful hunting scenes in oils she climbed with her groom. Onward beyond a massed collection of exquisite miniatures depicting sailing ships Edward took Lindsay. The stairs were covered in deep-piled red Turkish carpet secured by brass rods. The wooden banisters, wound about with garlands of flowers for the occasion, gleamed. These were a testimony to an industrious household staff that had kept discreetly from sight during the festivities.

"Are you all right?" Edward looked down at her. His face seemed wiped clean of emotion.

Her heart thudded. "I'm well, thank you, Edward. A little tired, is all." She drew in her bottom lip. Perhaps a bride should not mention such things.

"This has been an emotional day for you," he responded tonelessly. "I hope you will approve of what I have done for your comfort here."

A corridor without doors led from the top of a second flight of stairs to what seemed an outer wall of the house. Here the passageway turned and at the end were large, double doors.

Lindsay's heart hammered wildly now. He was taking her to his rooms.

She faltered, and Edward turned back. Frowning, he placed an arm lightly around her shoulders and pulled her to his side. "Your apartments are here." He flung wide not one of the double doors but another that opened onto a large room to the right of the short passageway.

Inside the room he stopped and watched her closely. "What do you think? I consulted with an expert in these matters and he assured me this would suit."

Suit? They stood in a sumptuous bedchamber decorated, it seemed to Lindsay, entirely in deep blue and silver. Blue velvet drapes, tied back with silver tassels from three tall narrow windows, revealed silvery underdrapes of the sheerest silk. Dark blue carpet covered the floor. Diaphanous blue and silver draped a large four-poster and blue velvet to match the window drapings covered a chaise and several wing chairs. In one window stood a dressing table topped with an oval mirror and two jointed oval side mirrors. Lindsay's hand settled at her throat. All manner of silver-topped crystal pots and silver-handled brushes had been precisely set on the dressing table.

"Is it to your liking?" Edward asked, sounding as close to uncertainty as Lindsay had ever heard in him. "You have only to say the word and everything can be changed immediately. I had thought to surprise you."

"I *am* surprised. No, Edward, not a thing must be changed. It is all too much, too beautiful. I am so grateful."

"It is I who am grateful," he said gravely. "I suggested blue."

Lindsay raised her eyes. "You?"

"Yes," he said. "You wore blue that first day— when you were Sarah's maid, Berthe." His faint smile drove dimples beneath his cheekbones.

Lindsay stared, and swallowed. She loved him. Inside her trembling body, there was a sensation of falling. "I must have seemed a silly girl to you."

"You seemed a very beautiful, desirable girl." He rested a long forefinger on her temple and let it trail carefully to the point of her chin. "You still do. More so."

She closed her eyes.

"There is a sitting room here." Edward moved away and she watched him, regretting the loss of his touch. He pushed open a door leading to a sitting room that was also blue but in fabrics that rioted with silver flowers. On small gilt tables, beautifully delicate porcelains, crystal ornaments and dishes and whimsical papier-mâché figures were displayed.

Lindsay passed among the treasures, exclaiming as she went. "Everything is so lovely." A fire had been lighted in a small fireplace set with enameled tiles.

"I'm glad it pleases you." He stood, his arms crossed, observing her.

"Everything is perfect."

Edward's eyes didn't waver. He looked at her as if he could see into her mind.

Lindsay turned away from his gaze and wandered, picking up first one and then another of the pretty papier-mâché gewgaws some careful hand had selected to gladden her.

Why didn't he move? Why didn't he say something? Would he take her in his arms soon . . . kiss her again as she wanted to be kissed by him?

That aching heat built within her once more.

"That door leads to my rooms."

Lindsay raised her face and followed the inclination of his head to a far corner of the room. She hadn't noticed another door. This sitting room lay between his bedchamber and hers. So that was the way married people contrived to spend night hours together. She frowned.

"Does something trouble you?"

Shaking her head, she returned to the bedchamber he had prepared for her. Yes, she was troubled. Would it not be more companionable for a husband and wife to share the same bedchamber?

"Are you warm enough?"

"Yes, thank you." A fire had been lighted in here also, but she lied. In fact she felt chilled in the cool satin gown.

"There is wine and cheese in case you become hungry." Edward came close, took her hand and led her to a low table near the fire. "Let me pour you a glass of wine. It will calm you."

To say that she was calm would be a lie. Every nerve jumped.

"Your mother died when you were born?"

She frowned. "Yes."

"Did Belle Granville talk to you about . . . about how it is between a man and a woman after they marry?"

Lindsay couldn't quite draw in a breath. "No."

"The Reverend Winslow was indeed your only instructor in such matters?"

Such matters? She thought a moment. "He did not actually discuss . . . Um, the Reverend said such matters as the relationship between a husband and wife are easily taken care of when the need arises."

Edward's explosive oath sent Lindsay skittering backward. "Was it wrong of me to say as much? Oh, of course"—she waved a dismissive hand—"you wonder what exactly he told me about the evils of erring between men and women."

He appeared to stare through her. Lindsay tried not to imagine that his eyes shone black with an emotion that could be anger.

"I assure you that I believe I am well acquainted with the whole process now. I shall not be shocked or upset by *anything.*"

"Not by *anything*?" There was indeed a certain menace in his tone, wasn't there?

"Absolutely not," she said, attempting a happy lightness to her voice. "After all, we have practiced quite a lot and I'm afraid I enjoyed it all. As you told me, it is as well that I am a married woman because

I seem to have a certain—talent—or perhaps sympathy for these actions would be a better way to describe it.''

His back was so very upright, and stiff; his mouth so very set. ''Drink this.'' He poured a glass of wine and handed it to her. ''I want you to think of this house as your home in London. Soon I will be taking you to Hawkesly Place in Devon. There you will learn many more of the intricacies of being a wife.''

''Like the running of a household?''

He expelled a long sigh. ''Among other things.''

Lindsay sipped the wine and drew close. She held the glass to his lips. ''Drink, Edward. I think you also need to relax a little. Becoming a husband must be very fearsome to you, too.''

''Fearsome?'' He smiled for the first time since they'd come upstairs, and obediently covered her fingers with his to take a drink. ''We must be sure you can soon put any fear behind you.''

''Oh, I will.'' She turned her face up to his, waiting for his kiss.

Edward didn't disappoint her. His lips settled over hers, gentle at first and tasting of the wine they had drunk.

Lindsay closed her eyes and leaned against him. Her breasts began to feel too large and sensitive to be confined by the stiff bodice of her wedding gown.

''Damnation!'' Edward's oath fractured the soft sensuality of the moment. He set the glass down. ''You're going to drive me out of my mind.''

''Ed—''

His mouth, hard, punishing, cut off his name from her lips. The kiss was like no other she had experienced. His tongue forced her mouth open until he could plunge into it again and again. The violence of his embrace bent her backward over his arm and he used his teeth, his lips, his tongue, to assault her senses.

Ineffectually, Lindsay attempted to respond. Her

every movement was halted by the harsh control Edward exerted. He covered her face with his short, biting kisses, and her neck, and her breasts, up-thrust by her arched back.

Tears burned her eyes. "Edward," she managed to whisper. "I've made you angry?"

As abruptly as he had seized her, Edward released Lindsay and stepped away. "Angry?" He laughed, a bitter laugh that made her cover her ears. "Angry, you little fool? You are everything I could want in a wife. You are much more than everything."

He strode to the door. "I'll have my valet send your maid to you. I don't know when I'll return. It won't be soon." With that he left her.

Lindsay sank weakly into a chair. If she was everything he wanted in a wife, why had he become so angry? And why had he not given her the beautiful kisses and touches they'd enjoyed before? And why had he left her alone saying he did not intend to return soon?

A tapping brought her head up. "Edward—" Not Edward, but Lady Clarisse Simmonds peered at her. "Please go away." Lindsay could not face anyone now.

"Something is very wrong. I just knew it. I felt it. That's why I crept up by a secret way and waited."

Lindsay's control broke, but into anger rather than despair. "There is *nothing* wrong that could not be corrected if men were not such *idiots.*"

Clarisse came farther into the room. "Edward has left you. When will he return?"

"I don't know," Lindsay said, feeling snappish. "And I don't care. Please forgive me, Clarisse, but I don't feel like chatting now. Perhaps tomorrow, when I've discovered how sensible wives deal with impossible husbands."

* * *

Two bottles of Madeira had only managed to reduce him to a more foul-tempered villain. If that
were possible.

Edward tossed in his bed. He was vile. The girl
had suffered in her life, too. Not as he had, because
she was only a female. But she *had* suffered and he
had used her—and treated her despicably.

He raised up onto his elbows. A pox on Latchett.
A pox on all avaricious men who craved what belonged to others.

Perhaps another bottle of Madeira? He fell back
on the pillows and scrubbed at his burning eyes.
More drink could only worsen matters. Cold air
slipped through the open windows of his chamber
to stroke his naked body.

Lindsay lay in the blue-and-silver bower he had
designed for her. Her luscious, pale body would be
caressed by a flimsy white nightgown designed for
her wedding night.

He, not some lifeless piece of stuff, should be caressing her. His shaft throbbed and sprang hard.

"Wait," he said through gritted teeth. "Hold to your
word and wait until Latchett is sent from the country."

Just tonight he had been accosted at Boodles by
Latchett, who cadged two thousand guineas "for a
trifling debt." Later, while Edward had lounged in
a gaming hell where he could be almost anonymous,
Mrs. Felling had come to return the money. She'd
been pleased with the evidence that Latchett was
becoming ever more deeply ensnared. Edward had
insisted she keep the money "for her trouble." His
stomach turned. He must not forget that Mrs. Felling was hardened to the sickening likes of Latchett.

Lindsay. Lindsay. He drew up his knees against the
burning weight of his own desire. If he took her
now, would he be too distracted to finish what he'd
started?

Never!

Swinging from his bed, he snatched up the silk

dressing robe Stoddart had left for him and approached the door to the adjoining sitting room. Within seconds he had entered the small room with its dying fire.

One more wooden barrier and he could look down upon her while she slept. If he were careful, she might not even stir until he had slipped beside her and taken her in his arms. She was his wife, his virginal innocent ready for his expert grooming. It was his duty and right to make her his tonight.

Fresh knives of fire ripped into his groin.

Willing his breathing into silence, Edward let himself into Lindsay's chamber. Here, also, the fire had burned low. All candles had been extinguished and he could barely make out the small shape in the bed.

The thick carpets swallowed the footsteps that took him to her side. Seconds, and he had discarded the robe. Another second and he was beneath the covers, drawing her against him.

A scream rent the air. Edward's mind turned black. "Lindsay!" He grabbed for her flailing body. "Lindsay, it's me, Edward."

She screamed and fought him. Arms and legs more sturdy and strong than he had ever imagined beat at him.

"Lindsay! Be still. This will hurt you very little. I promise you, sprite."

"I am not Lindsay!"

"Be still, I say. Be—" Edward became still. The heat that had swelled and inflamed him ebbed as before a north wind.

The girl in his arms shook, but worked herself free.

Scrambling, he got from the bed, dragged on his robe and fumbled to light a candle. A flickering flame wavered faint yellow light over the bed.

"Who are you?" Edward asked the plump, disheveled girl who sat there, wrapped in a voluminous flannel nightrail.

"I'm Emma, sir. Miss—Lady Hawkesly's abigail."

His head pounded. "What in God's name are you doing in your mistress's bed?"

Emma clutched handfuls of flannel to her throat. "Miss Winslow said as I should lie there. In case anyone looked in. She said as anyone would just think it was the mistress and they'd go away again."

"Did she say *I* would just go away again?" he asked, barely containing his fury.

"Well . . . yes, I suppose so. Miss Winslow said as how Lady Hawkesly believed you wouldn't be likely to do more than look in and that wouldn't be for a long time."

"I see." Might he be preserved from the addle-pated notions of ignorant virgins. "And *why* is any of this necessary?"

The girl's pleasant face relaxed. "Because Lady Hawkesly had to go away—" Horror replaced relief. "Oh, dear. I wasn't supposed to tell anyone that, was I?"

Chapter 18

❝I told you to stay at the cottage and rest, Linny," Antun said. He looked up at her from a small fishing boat that bumped the dock in Salters Cove. "You're not a man. You're a maid."

Lindsay planted her fists on her hips. "And what of it?" She didn't regret her snappishness. "I'm as strong as many men." And any boy, which was exactly what she would appear to be on this unkind night.

Antun's man Ned climbed to the dock, tugged his cap at Lindsay and hurried to secure the lines Antun threw.

"Go back to the cottage," Antun ordered. "Sleep until I rouse you."

"I can't. I'm a married woman now. And I left my husband's roof on my wedding night. Two nights gone, Antun. And without leaving word. What must be done here must be done quickly so that I may return to London."

Antun looked toward Ned. When he saw that the man had run along the dock, he said: "If your husband had been where he should have been on his wedding night—with his bride—Sarah couldn't have brought you my message. And you'd not have been able to leave for Cornwall with me."

The truth smarted. Lindsay rubbed a hand over

burning eyes and dropped to sit on a coil of rope. "I won't speak ill of my husband . . . to anyone." Nigh on eighteen hours in the saddle, broken only by two rests of three hours when they'd changed horses, had left her legs stiff and sore.

Antun stared up at her. In the shifting light of a white moon through drifts of laden cloud, his gray eyes held some strange sadness that turned Lindsay's heart. Surely he hadn't held the hope that they could carry on as before—as unlikely friends who spent more time together than some married couples.

The slapping of water between the boat and the dock grew louder. "It'll rain soon," she told him, anxious to divert him. "When did you tell Calvin we'd meet?"

"He'll be at the forge by the mill. I sent word with Ned's brother-in-law. Calvin will wait until an hour before dawn. If we don't come, he'll return on the morrow."

"We've hours on our side, then," Lindsay said, relieved. "We'll make the forge in two hours and it's barely midnight now. While you were visiting Captain Claude I put the old horse in the shafts. We'll load what you have, then visit the cellars at Tregonitha."

The boat bumped dully against the dock. A freshening wind, loaded with the scent of wet salt and tar, swung the boom of the little vessel's single small mast. The lowered sail had yet to be lashed down and canvas scraped the decks. Antun continued to stand, arms akimbo, making no effort to move.

She needed, Lindsay thought desperately, to be done here and return to London. "Hand up the casks, Antun. I must make haste." By now Edward was bound to have discovered she was missing. He'd be in a towering rage. Doubtless Sarah and Emma would suffer for having aided Lindsay in what Edward would see as a foolish escapade. Not

that he must ever discover what she'd really been
about.

Running footsteps sounded—Ned, followed by
two other men Lindsay had never seen before. They
formed a chain and began stacking casks and
wooden chests at the landward end of the dock.

Lindsay stood back. What would she say to Edward? Perhaps she should simply go to Tregonitha
and pretend she'd fled London in a fit of pique.

Fie. She'd never carry it off.

The last of the cargo was handed up and Antun
swung himself to stand beside Lindsay. "Load the
wagon," he called to the men.

"Let's help," Lindsay said. "It'll go faster."

Antun settled a hand on her neck and turned her
toward him. "They'll go fast enough without us.
Don't go back to London, Linny."

She blinked. The tears that stung her tired eyes
made no sense. Except that she heard in Antun's
voice a deep concern for her—a love for her that was
as close to that of the brother she'd lost as she could
ever hope for.

"Did you hear me?"

"I heard you, Antun." But she couldn't explain
to him that the seemingly impossible had happened.
For all his strange, overbearing ways, Edward had
managed to make her fall in love with him.

"This match of yours is a sham. Why else should
a man leave so beautiful a bride on his wedding
night?"

She could only shake her head. Edward had said
he found her beautiful, yet, just when she'd thought
he would want to enjoy being with her again in the
way they'd already found so satisfying, he'd left in
anger.

"Answer me, Linny. Why return to a man who
abandoned you? He cannot be natural."

Distant thunder rolled, on and on.

"Stay here with me," Antun said, his voice low

and insistent. "I'll make a good place for you. You'll never want for anything."

He wanted to take William's place. "I can't." She wrapped her arms around his solid body and hugged him. Even if she hadn't somehow come to need whatever scraps of attention Edward might choose to spare her, she'd made a solemn vow before God and there could be no turning from that. And she'd also decided on the only safe course to take for John's sake as well as Edward's. She must make certain Edward didn't go back on his promise to give Tregonitha to Roger. Nineteen years remained before John could lay claim to his rightful inheritance. By then some solution would be found to dealing with Roger.

Antun framed her face in big, rough hands and made her look up at him. "You'll change your mind eventually, little one. And I'll be waiting."

She didn't say what she thought, that Antun would find a wife of his own one day and have children. Then he'd be too busy to worry about her anymore and she'd be glad for him.

"Tell me you'll come to me as soon as you need to." He pulled the coarse woolen hat she wore well down over her ears and brow and turned up the collar on her shapeless old coat.

"I'll always know you're my friend," she said, praying he wouldn't force her to make promises she'd never be able to keep.

"Antun!" Ned's anxious shout startled them both. "Antun!"

"Damn the fool," Antun muttered. "He'll wake the dead, to say nothing of the revenuers."

"Lantern lights spotted on the cliff path over yonder!" Ned puffed to meet them as they arrived beside the stack of French goods. "On the ridge. There. See?"

Lindsay followed the man's pointing finger. He indicated a heavily forested bluff to the east.

''Hurry,'' she said, stooping to heft a cask into her arms. ''It may be nothing. But if it is Revenue Officer Farr and his ruffians they'll take a while to reach the cove. By then we can be on our way north to the forge.''

''Give me that.'' Antun snatched the cask from her. ''Go! Now! Get to Tregonitha. They'll not go there.''

Lindsay's answer was to pick up another cask and struggle with it to the cart. Immediately, she turned back for another, ignoring Antun's muffled curse as she passed him.

Rain began to fall in earnest. In minutes, the clay soil underfoot turned to oily slime.

''Another light,'' a man called out. ''See? They're getting closer.''

''Hold your tongue,'' Antun said sharply. ''Sound carries on the cliffs.''

''The rain will muffle it,'' Lindsay said kindly. ''But we've no time to waste. If we leave anything here they'll have the evidence they want.''

She worked as fast as any of the men but Antun. Sliding on the squelching mud, they scrambled back and forth with their precious hoard. Fear curled in her stomach but she closed her mind to everything but what must be done.

''The last one,'' Antun said after what felt like much too long.

Wiping rain from her eyes, Lindsay glanced up to the west. ''I don't see—'' She pressed a fist into her stomach. ''There they are. Closer. Much too close. I didn't think they'd come that fast.''

''Ned,'' Antun rapped out. ''Sam. And you, Len. Run ahead. I'll drive the cart, but I'll need your help at Tregonitha.''

Before Antun could stop her, Lindsay hauled herself onto the horse's back. ''Go to the cottage, Antun. Go to bed and pretend you've been there

since you got back from fishing. Tell Farr the fish
aren't running."

He caught at the bridle. "Are you mad? Get
down!"

"Do as I say, Antun." She jerked the horse's head
around. "Ned, you and the others get home with
you now. You'll be safe. Go!"

Before she finished speaking, the three men ran
off.

"What—"

"Be quiet, Antun," she said with desperation.
"This is our best chance. I'll take the cart deep into
Myrtle Woods, leave it there, then ride on to Tregonitha. If those are revenuers, they're coming here.
If they find no one at the cottage or in the fish cellars, they'll be looking for tracks and they'll follow.
If you're here with a good story, you can take them
to see the boat as evidence, and delay them so long
there'll be no chance of them following me before
the rain washes out my tracks. Here, you keep the
key to the cellars at Tregonitha, just in case."

He caught the heavily wrought key she threw. "In
case of what?"

"You know the answer to that. If something stops
me, take care of the tenants. But nothing *will* stop
me so don't worry."

"I can't let you do this."

"You can because I won't let you stop me. Calvin
will be back at the forge tomorrow night. By then
we can gather everything and do what we set out to
do. Now, let me go."

"Linny—"

"Tomorrow night in Myrtle Woods," she said,
pressuring the horse to move. "The cart will be in
the hollow behind the ruined cottage. I'll cover it
with brambles. Be there an hour after dark tomorrow."

Clinging to the horse's bare back with knees that

already felt raw, Lindsay urged the patient mare on. "Come on, Catkin. Come on!"

Catkin strained. Casks of cognac and chests packed with tea, tobacco and fine French lace made a heavy load that drove the cart's wheels deep into the mud.

Lindsay cajoled and threatened, and slowly they began to move. A sudden burst forward almost knocked her off balance and she looked anxiously behind. The cargo was still safely in place. But Antun, his shoulder braced against the cart, had succeeded in making the wheels suck free of the miring sludge.

Catkin's hoofs slithered, then she found purchase and surged ahead.

Lindsay raised a hand to Antun and concentrated on guiding the horse.

In the first yards, she felt her heart lodge in her throat. They were in the open, with the horse blowing loudly and making scarcely any progress. Blessedly, the moon was completely hidden now. But the rain fell in a whipping torrent that plastered Lindsay's clothes to her body. Water dripped from her sodden hat and hair into her eyes.

If the approaching column was revenuers, and she knew in her heart it was, they'd take the only marked trail across the cliffs all the way to the cove. And that trail intersected the one path open to someone traveling with a cart.

"Go, Catkin," she called, as loudly as she dared. "Up, girl. Up."

The game old mare labored on. Behind Lindsay, casks and chests jostled and the wheels ground their way over rock and mud-filled ruts.

"Yonder! Yonder!"

The cry came, clearly at first, then snatched away by the same wind that had borne it. Lindsay closed her eyes and bowed her head. They'd sighted her. She dared not stop, yet to keep moving meant the approaching men would hear the cart and be led directly to her.

Being first to the point where the two paths crossed, and then reaching the trees, was her only chance. She bent over Catkin's neck and threw her own limbs forward again and again as if she could will the horse's legs to be stronger.

"A light . . . !" Again a fractured voice reached her.

"Oh!" The instant the sound escaped her mouth she clamped it shut and rode Catkin the harder.

Light? What light? They must mean that Antun had lighted lamps in the cottage already.

The trees were closer. Catkin struggled, her snorting breath sending steaming clouds into the darkness. The creaking of the cart became a tearing roar in Lindsay's ears. They must hear it. How could they not?

Spittle flew from the horse's mouth to coat Lindsay. "Go, Catkin." She worked her knees and body over the animal's slick hide. And they moved faster, painfully so, but faster nevertheless.

The crossing in the paths was just ahead.

Lindsay's tears mingled with the rain on her face. "Please," she whispered. "Oh, please let us make it."

The horse and cart trundled past the meeting of the ways and rolled on. Lindsay glanced upward, but saw no sign of the approaching men. Hunkering low over Catkin's neck once more, she rested her cheek and dug the heels of her ill-fitting boots into heaving flanks. She hated treating the horse so, but there was no other way.

They were there. The trees. Now everything depended on whether Farr and his men made the joining of the ways before she could send Catkin fully into the dense growth that overhung the stony track.

Wind roared. It screamed in the bending limbs overhead. And Lindsay blessed its raging. Even she could scarcely hear the wheels now. And the rain

beat relentlessly down, smoothing away telling
tracks.

She must stop an instant to catch her breath. And
allow Catkin a breath or two unhampered by her
burden.

Lindsay dared to peer back. If it were possible, her
skin grew colder. Through a gap she could see the
huddled outline of Salters Cottage and, approaching
it, a row of wavering lanterns.

Her heart expanded like a great, wild thing, then
broke into a thudding rhythm. She had not beaten
them. They had beaten her. They had reached the
crossing and passed over . . . before poor Catkin had
arrived with her load. By the time Lindsay had made
her agonizing last pull for the cover of trees, Officer
Farr and his men had dashed by, unaware of their
quarry's halting progress toward the prow of the hill
below them. In winning the race, they'd given her
the time she needed to elude them.

Now it was up to Antun. If he could delay long
enough she'd travel far into Myrtle Wood and find
the hollow safely. Leaving the cart behind, she'd
travel on with Catkin to Tregonitha. Since Belle had
told the staff they wouldn't be needed until she and
Roger returned from London, the house would be
deserted.

At Tregonitha, Lindsay could wash and sleep, and
wait until tomorrow. And she could decide what excuse she would give Edward upon her return to
London.

The horse Edward had secured at the last coach-
ing post was no Saber, but he'd traveled hard and
well. Now the beast pawed the ground and strained
at the bit, anxious to continue the headlong dash
they'd made over many a mile. Edward let the reins
slacken, controlling his mount with the pressure of
his thighs.

Damn the rain to hell. It impeded his vision. And

tonight he needed to see . . . to see very well. He
had found no trail to this vantage point above the
valley. The ground beneath his horse's hoofs was
slick and rock-strewn. He felt as much as saw copses
of trees scattered over the hilltop. Lower down the
slope would be the woods he'd been told about.
Then, beyond these, supposedly lay the valley floor
bound on its open end by a sickle-shaped cove.

Frustration boiled, and the blackest anger he'd felt
since learning the manner in which James had really
died. When he found his "gentle" little bride, her
backside had better be made of sterner stuff than he
had reason to expect. She had embarrassed and
shamed him in his own household. No man or
woman shamed a Hawkesly and went unscathed.

Once she'd gathered her terrified wits enough to
speak, Gwyn, the abigail he'd tracked down to the
village near Tregonitha, had sent him to the cottage
of a crone by the name of Whalen. A sprightly and
cautious crone she was too, he'd give her that. Only
when he'd announced that Lindsay was his wife had
she grudgingly suggested he go to Salters Cove to
look for her. "Antun Pollack might know where she
is," the woman had said guardedly. "If she really
came to Cornwall, which I doubt." And she'd had
the audacity to add, "A body would think a fine
man such as yourself would know where his wife
was."

Edward bared his teeth. Yes, a man such as himself *should* know where his wife was. And, after he
found her this time, he always would.

He smoothed his horse's sweating neck and
started a slow descent over the treacherous terrain.
On his last visit to the neighborhood, he hadn't
come this far west. He hadn't even known of the
existence of this ocean-tipped valley with its sheer
walls of rock narrowing to a cleft that drove inland.

The horse faltered, flicked up his head. Edward

reined him in and pushed to stand in the stirrups, straining to see through the dark and rain.

Then he saw it: a distant line of lanterns moving much below and to the right. "Whoa," he told the horse, gentling him with soft noises. "Whoa, boy."

Even farther away, but directly ahead of the lanterns, squares of light showed. That, he decided, must be Salters Cottage.

The foul rain, driven by a devil wind, near flayed him. Dragging at the wide cape he wore, he flung one side of the heavy garment over the other. Leather gauntlets helped him keep a steady grip on the reins.

"Up, Catkin! Go, girl. Go!" A voice reached him, carried on an updraft of the wind. It came from where he judged the woods to be. Unmistakably, wheels creaked and he heard the snort and blow of a hard-pressed animal.

Frowning, Edward descended some yards and drew closer to a stand of trees. Now he could make out the woods. They were much closer than he'd expected.

He looked again at the lanterns, closing on the cottage now, then back at the woods. Narrowing his eyes, he made up his mind. A controlled jerk in the saddle, the merest pressure of heel, and his mount stepped delicately, but rapidly downward.

The creaking grew louder, and the pleas for speed. "Come on, Catkin. You can do it. We're safe now."

Amazement overwhelmed him a moment. No. It could not be. His mind was playing tricks.

"A mile or two more. Good girl. We've beaten them. Antun will make sure they don't follow till our tracks are lost."

Edward's hands tightened. He wound his fingers into fists. Bloody hell. What was afoot here?

Damn, but he'd been played for a fool. He cocked his feet, ready to spur a headlong downward flight . . . then another noise came. Wind? Not wind. He stood in the stirrups once more and surveyed all around. In seconds he sighted the source of the noise. Racing past the lanterns, apparently along a curve that must be the shore, came two horses, their riders' cloaks billowing behind.

At first they set out for the east, but suddenly they changed course and veered inland . . . headed straight for the convoy of one that moved so slowly a few yards from Edward.

In only minutes the two riders would catch up with what must be their intended quarry.

Edward made up his mind. Hurtling forward, he moved as one with his horse. Slipping, back legs jutting, the animal proved what Edward had guessed, Saber he might not be, but he was a close second.

"Rider ahead!" The echoing shout went up from one of the two closing quickly on the woods. "I knew we couldn't trust Pollack's word."

Bending low, Edward shot beneath the limbs of the first trees. He peered ahead, swiping moisture from his face.

Almost before he knew it, he was upon the ruins of a cottage. In a hollow clearing that must once have been a garden stood a sway-backed mare with a scrawny and bedraggled rider. Behind the horse sagged a heavily laden cart.

He heard cries, and the sound of wheeling hoofs as the chasing riders drew up and tried to decide on a route.

He hadn't been the only one to hear the shouts. "No!" The pathetic little heap on the mare yelled but once. Then Edward swept down. In a single motion, he gathered the ragtag bundle of old clothes beneath one arm and galloped on, deeper into the woods.

He tossed his burden, facedown, in front of him across the horse. "Be silent," he ordered.

"You've made a mistake," that familiar, husky

voice managed to jar out between the horse's buck-
ing strides. "All those goods are already bought and
paid for."

"Be silent!"

"I'll pay the duty on the goods myself. And I'll
share the proceeds of what I get from the buyers
with you. This was all my idea. I go out to the French
captain myself. There's no one else involved."

Holy hell. *A smuggler!*

Even as he tried to decide what to do next, the
thunder of other hoofbeats resumed.

There was only one thing he could do. "One more
sound and you'll die before you make another."
That would silence the little fool. "I don't care a
farthing for your stolen goods. I'm taking you with
me."

"Kidnapping me?" came the squeaky reply. "You
cannot."

He worked his neckcloth free.

"Do you hear me, you big oaf? Let me down, this
instant, or I'll tell my husband. He's a very important man and . . . and I don't know what he'll do if
he finds out I'm a night runner."

Edward spared a beseeching glance heavenward
before he used his neckcloth to gag the gabbling
mouth that jounced against his knee.

"You would do well to worry, madam," he said
through gritted teeth. "I *do* know what your husband will do—at least until he gets to the bottom of
this. I know because I *am* your husband."

All struggling ceased.

Chapter 19

"**W**ake up, madam!"
Lindsay struggled to open her eyes and immediately squeezed them shut again. When had the sun begun to shine? Her head ached with every jarring thud. And every jarring thud rattled every bone in her sore and weary body.

"My lady! Wake up!"

She shot upright, grasping at air. Now she remembered everything.

"Sit still, you hoyden! And sit up. You're about to see Hawkesly Place, your new home."

Lindsay groaned and pushed matted hair away from her face. Somewhere in the endless hours of riding in front of Edward, she'd lost her hat and her hair had broken free of its braids to fall about her shoulders.

"Look well, madam. I hope what you see is to your liking because it's *all* you will see for a very long time. Perhaps forever."

All she'd seen so far was a seemingly endless gray stone wall overhung by thick ivy and backed by forest. "I hurt," she moaned. "We've been riding for days."

"Not quite." If Edward was tired, he showed no sign of it. Not that she'd actually dared to look upon

his face since the first horrible realization that it was
he who had swept her from Catkin's back.

"Can we stop?"

"Soon. Don't ask more questions."

"Edward—"

"And *don't* offer explanations."

"I wasn't—"

"Say nothing, madam. I still have my neckcloth
and I'll use it if I have to."

Lindsay let out a long, miserable sigh. Yes, at least
he'd removed the horrible, choking cloth from her
mouth and allowed her to breathe. Not that he'd
kept it there so very long. Not long at all. Only minutes, in fact. She scowled. It had felt a long time
and she would never forgive him for it.

His arm felt like a metal rope around her waist.
But at least he hadn't made her stay facedown over
his horse for longer than it took to ride clear of Myrtle Woods. While she had lain like that it had been
very degrading. She would never forgive him for
that either.

"You should have let me loose Catkin—"

"What?" he thundered. "Did I hear you speak,
madam?"

"No," she said softly. "I was only worrying
about Catkin. She's a very old horse and most gentle and—"

"Hold your tongue, you . . . you *criminal.* Never
mention that debacle to me again. And I shall en-
deavor to forget it, too."

He might forget, she never could. At least she
had thought to give Antun the key to Tregonitha's
cellars. She prayed he'd go ahead and gather the
goods stored there. If he did she knew she could
trust him to secure the money her tenants needed
to pay Roger off.

Oh, none of this was going to be easy.

Swerving, Edward wheeled his horse between
massive stone gateposts topped by stone stags, their

antlers magnificent against the pure blue of a late-March sky. The difference between yesterday's bone-chilling weather in Cornwall and this shimmering Devon day near disoriented her.

A wide carriageway stretched before them. Lindsay drew in a breath. "Edward. Is *this* your estate?"

"Yes. Now hold your tongue. God knows what the servants will think. Fortunately they'll have the sense to keep whatever they do think to themselves. Prepare yourself."

She had several miles to "prepare" herself. Edward kept his mount at a full gallop between groves of massive oaks. As they passed, deer raised their heads to stare and birds flew up in dark clusters. Fields of bluebells swayed like blue goose down cast upon miles of grass. Here and there, clumps of daffodils and narcissus nodded their cheerful new heads. The danger and fury of the previous night seemed a dream . . . or a nightmare.

The fury of the rigid man who held Lindsay was entirely real.

Ahead lay another thick wall, bisected by a massive stone gateway above which, and forming a bridge, stood a gate house which would give a view for miles around. Inside this second wall, Lindsay saw a great courtyard in front of a massive house. By the time the horse's hooves hit flagstones, a rotund, florid man in baggy clothing appeared at the foot of stairs leading to the gate house.

"Halt!" he cried, brandishing a spyglass. Almost immediately he fell back and doffed his battered hat. "Master Edward, sir? Is it you?"

Edward wheeled the horse around. "No, Sains, it's my ghost, man. And be grateful I don't whip your wretched hide for your impudence."

"Edward," Lindsay said, horrified. "How could you speak so harshly to an old man?"

Edward cleared his throat. The man scuttled to lift a brass hunting horn from hooks on the wall.

"Please, Edward," Lindsay said. "You have quite befuddled him."

"*Women,*" Edward muttered. "Afternoon, Sains. Her ladyship and I are, er, visiting. That is—I'm visiting. Her ladyship is . . . Oh, damn it all."

All but ignoring Edward's mangled attempt at politeness, Sains had raised the horn to his lips. A piercing blast sounded. It cracked each time the old man paused to draw more breath. The noise sent Lindsay's hands over her ears.

"Too much," she heard Edward exclaim. "He'll have the whole blasted household out."

"There, sir . . . I mean, my lord," Sains said, smiling proudly. "The Hawkesly horn has been sounded. Welcome home, my lord."

"Yes, well—"

"And . . ." Sains tottered closer to peer up at Lindsay. "You did say this was *her ladyship,* didn't you, Master Edward?"

"I did."

"Well, well. And very—er—interesting she looks, too." Sains stood aside, rolling his already mangled hat. "A new mistress for Hawkesly Place. Quite an event. Quite an event, indeed."

Muttering words Lindsay was grateful she couldn't quite hear, Edward set off at a trot. She leaned to wave at Sains.

"Do not fraternize with servants, madam," Edward said into her ear. His explosive "Damnation" jolted her exhausted body afresh. "I'd forgotten the damn horn. He's got every one of them out. All the way down to the scullery maids by the look of it."

Lindsay looked. On either side marched beds of budding roses surrounded by immaculately trimmed, low boxwood hedges. In a wide circle amidst these lay a pool in the center of which the effigy of a woman with the stature of Boadicea held aloft a water-spurting urn.

"Another castle," Lindsay whispered in awe.

"I beg your pardon."

"Another castle." She dared to twist around and attempt to smile up at him. "Like the Cumberland house in London. Surely, they are castles."

The corners of his mouth dimpled in a way that delighted her. Did she see a crack in his formidable facade?

"Why, there are dozens of chimneys and thousands of windows and balconies, and—"

"A large house, I'll allow," Edward said, but his voice had definitely lost some of its ire. "But hardly a castle. You are about to meet your staff."

Only then did Lindsay see what unfolded on the wide and curving steps leading up to impressive, brass-studded oak front doors. Beside each elegant stone balustrade, descending apparently with careful consideration to height and symmetry as well as rank, stood a line of servants.

"Oh, my," Lindsay whispered. "Oh, Edward, I cannot."

"You cannot what, madam?"

A groom ran forward to take the horse's reins.

"I cannot meet all these people now . . . not looking like this."

"You have no choice and the fault is entirely your own."

Without another word, he dismounted, grasped Lindsay about the waist and lifted her to the ground.

Instantly her stiff legs buckled. Edward caught her before her knees would have hit the ground. He swept her into his arms.

Dimly, she heard a rising ripple of whispers. "Put me down, please," she said urgently. "I simply tripped. *Please* put me down, Edward."

He frowned into her face. "You look unwell."

"I am perfectly well. Put me *down*."

If Edward heard the muffled giggles, he gave no sign. "I should not have made you ride so far without rest."

"No, you should not," she agreed tartly. "Now, put me down. This is to be my staff, correct?"

"Correct." That irresistible smile hovered about his generous mouth.

"Then allow me to greet them appropriately." Whatever that might be. Apart from what she had read in various novels, she had little idea how these matters were conducted.

"As you wish." Edward set her on her feet and murmured, "Precede me. Smile. Nod. Nothing more for now."

Lindsay obeyed, finding to her mortification that hours in the saddle had produced a limping gait. She arrived at the first of several very young girls with shiny faces and flapping caps who made rapid and awkward dips at her approach.

"Good afternoon," she said valiantly. "Ouch!" A muscle behind her right thigh cramped and she stopped to snap the leg straight.

A slender, gray-haired man of indeterminate age but obvious importance stepped before them. "Welcome home, my lord. We heard the news. On behalf of Mrs. Gilley, the staff and myself, please accept warm congratulations on your marriage." His eyes moved from Edward to Lindsay without as much as a flicker of emotion. "And welcome to you, my lady. We shall all do our best to serve you well."

"Thank you, McBain," Edward said. "Thank you, Mrs. Gilley." He smiled warmly at a plain but pleasant-looking woman who wore black relieved only by the glitter of many keys hanging at her waist. "Lindsay. McBain is our steward here at Hawkesly and Mrs. Gilley is housekeeper. And very efficient they are."

"I'm sure," she murmured, smiling too, and wishing fervently that she hadn't arrived looking like a tinker.

Limping, the heel of each too-large boot alternately clacking and scraping, Lindsay attempted to proceed with some dignity. Grateful to follow Edward's instructions, she nodded and smiled briefly at each servant.

Unfortunately, there was the necessity to acknowledge those on either side of the steps. She scuffled first in one direction, jerked her head, turned up the corners of her mouth, then dragged back again.

Something bumped her knee. She glanced down and saw that the knotted end of the rope she'd used to tie the too-big pantaloons around her waist had worked loose. Horrified at what might follow, she grabbed a handful of the pantaloons through the still slightly damp woolen coat.

After a few steps, she halted, completely out of breath. Hot blood pounded in her cheeks. She was dirty and disheveled and must appear ridiculous. Suspicious snuffling noises served to embarrass her further.

Edward came to stand beside her. He looked, she thought, suspiciously close to laughter himself. Lindsay narrowed her eyes at him.

He cleared his throat. "Her, um, ladyship is a little tired. The ride was somewhat . . . hard on her."

A titter was quickly suppressed.

"She'll finish meeting all of you at a later time."

"Nonsense." Lindsay attempted to push her hair from her eyes. It simply fell back. "We small people are hardy, are we not?" she said to a diminutive parlor maid who bobbed and smiled delightedly.

"You don't have to do this," Edward said under his breath.

"Yes I do," she responded in the same tone.

And somehow she scuffed and limped and smiled and laughed her way to the top of the steps. Once there, she turned, one hand still firmly clutching her pantaloons, and waved. "Thank you all for welcoming me," she said.

Applause broke out, and a few cautious cheers,

before Edward took her firmly by the elbow and ushered her into an entry hall as big as the chapel where he'd married her.

Apprehension settled on Lindsay. Edward said nothing more as he walked her across echoing stone tiles, past darkly paneled walls covered with vast oils depicting the serious faces of what she took to be his Hawkesly ancestors.

There was little time to do more than gather an impression of great, richly furnished spaces before she was drawn into a book-lined room with high mullioned windows. A fire glowed brightly in a large fireplace beneath what Lindsay now recognized as a plaster rendition of the Hawkesly coat of arms.

A heavy mahogany desk, untidily stacked with papers, had the most prominent place in the room. "My study," Edward said perfunctorily. "Now, madam. Sit."

Gathering the ragtag collection of clothes she wore more tightly about her, she sank gratefully into a burgundy-colored wing chair.

"You were magnificent out there, Lindsay." When she might have smiled, he added. "I admire your courage, but it has already proved your potential downfall. We'll speak more of that later."

If she weren't afraid of what was to come, she'd close her eyes and rest. To meet Edward's rage she'd need to be wide awake.

"I can explain it all," she began. "All I need is a little time."

He sat on the edge of his desk and crossed his arms. "You can explain how it is that the woman who became my viscountess five days ago is a smuggler."

"A night runner."

He arched a brow. "Oh, do excuse me, madam. Is there a difference?"

Lindsay shrugged, sniffed, sat more upright. "In a way. But it's too fine a distinction to explain." Particularly since she didn't know of a difference other than her own preference for the sound of one over the other.

"Obviously you settled upon this dangerous and foolish prank to punish me," Edward said, sounding almost disinterested.

"You think—" How very convenient. She should say nothing to make him consider otherwise.

"Your pride was bruised," he said, hitching one strongly muscled thigh onto the desk. "You were irked by my departure on our wedding night and decided to try gaining my attention by outrageous means. Men have better things to do than chase the countryside after addle-brained wives."

Men could be so vain and obtuse. "I'm ready." She kept her eyes demurely downcast.

"Ready?"

"For whatever you've decided to do with me."

"Really. Are you sure?"

"Quite. But there are one or two things I expect you to promise me, too."

He rose abruptly and turned his back. Not a good sign, Lindsay decided. Nor was the oddly explosive sound he made. She felt very warm. "I'm sure you don't think I have any right to make demands upon you. But I would like to appeal to the finer side of your nature."

"The finer side of my nature?"

"Yes. Please, do not be angry with Sarah or Emma. They begged me not to leave, but I am . . . Well, my lord, I'm afraid I am very headstrong."

"So I've noticed. I shall consider your request."

It wasn't much, but it was a start. She prayed Sarah and Emma had stayed true to their promise to say she'd made the decision to go to Cornwall independently. She didn't want Antun involved in this. Already he'd be beside himself with worry over her sudden departure.

"Perhaps I could wash and put on clean clothes."

"Suitable clothes, you mean?"

"As you say?"

"Soon enough, lady wife. First I will tell you what I've decided about your immediate fate."

What an ominous sound that had.

"You are to remain here at Hawkesly Place indefinitely."

"But—"

"*No*, Lindsay. Do not even think of arguing this. You will not leave this estate. You will never again go *anywhere* I do not suggest you go unless you have my permission."

"But—"

"No, Lindsay!" He swung to face her. "Hold your irrepressible tongue. You will find your quarters here to your liking, I'm sure. In time, if you can show me you can be trusted, you'll go out and about again. We'll discuss that further when next I return from London."

She stared at him aghast, the import of his words dashing her like cold waves. "You are going away, Edward? Now? And leaving me here?"

"I have no choice." He avoided her eyes and picked up a pile of envelopes from the desk. "You will be well cared for."

"No!" She shot from the chair and hurried to him as fast as her aching legs would allow. "Please don't leave me." Grabbing his arm, she momentarily forgot her pantaloons.

Before she could rectify the situation, Edward gently pulled her near. He unbuttoned the shabby coat, pulled up the offending garment, and tied the rope at her waist as he might have had she been a child.

"There," he said. "Safe . . . for now." His marvelous dark eyes met hers. He smiled with his mouth, but there was quite a different emotion in those eyes. "Ask me again, Lindsay."

Mesmerized, she watched his lips move, the

glimpse of strong, white teeth. "What should I ask you?"

"Ask me not to leave you." He caught both her wrists in one long, strong hand. "Or perhaps that wasn't what you meant?"

Lindsay swallowed. What was this? Why was it that the instant she was anywhere near him—and he wasn't raging at her—she lost reason. "It was what I meant, Edward." She lowered her eyes. "I'd like you to stay with me. I . . . I care for you."

For an instant, his grip on her wrists tightened almost painfully. Then he dropped her hands. "You don't know what you say, madam."

She did know. He was the one who didn't understand such things. "May I prove that I mean what I say?" Automatically, she rose to her toes and tried to kiss him.

He held her off—an instant—then he gathered her close. "All right, little one. Show me."

Remembering his delicious lesson in kissing, Lindsay touched the tip of her tongue to the corner of his mouth. Very carefully, very slowly, she traced the outlines of his lips. First beneath the full lower lip and then over the sharply defined lines of his upper lip. Nibbling, she gradually drew his bottom lip between her own. Gentle sucking brought a groan from his throat. Lindsay drew herself up, wrapped her arms around his neck and kissed him deeply, darting her tongue playfully in and out of his mouth until he made a strangled noise and crushed her to him.

"You are a little witch," he said against her cheek. "A temptress with the angelic face of an innocent. But I will not be distracted."

Her head fell back and she stared up at him. Her mouth felt swollen. Edward's face was taut. Muscles in his jaw jerked. He pushed a hand inside her baggy shirt and exclaimed as he covered her full, naked breast.

"You will never, ever, run the countryside dressed like this again. Do you understand?"

"Yes, Edward."

"You could have fallen among thugs who would have taken advantage of you. Do you understand?"

"Yes, Edward." She could scarcely breathe. His thumb worked back and forth over her straining nipple.

"Now. Your task is to learn everything necessary to make me a good and obedient wife. Do you understand?"

"Yes, Edward." Lindsay leaned against him and her eyes flew wide open. His lower body met hers and the hardness there pulsed. It jabbed as if independent of the man. "Edward! That part of you is moving!"

His mouth opened. He shook his head, then laughed. "You are so—" Again he laughed. "I have to leave. Now I *really* do have to leave."

Lindsay felt close to tears, but she would not beg. "You are very angry with me. I don't blame you. I really couldn't blame you if you locked me up here and never came back."

Drawing a breath that expanded his broad chest, he bent to plant a small, hard kiss on her lips. He gathered the pile of letters once more and crammed them into a pocket before striding to open the door.

"I could blame myself if I didn't come back," he said. "I could agree with any man who suggested I be committed for insanity if I didn't come back to you."

Lindsay smiled. "Thank you," she said softly. "I shall do my best to learn very well how to be a good wife."

"Do that," Edward said as he left. He popped his head back into the room and added, "But don't worry too much. I'll regard it as my duty to ensure nothing remains a mystery after I get back.''

As his boots rang on stone she heard him say: ''That part of you is moving.'' And his laugh echoed until the great front doors thumped shut.

Chapter 20

His mood was exactly as it needed to be, Edward decided. *Volatile.*

He strode into the hall of his Cavendish Square house, sending minions scuttling back into the shadows. His staff had been well chosen. They knew exactly when to be absent.

The burgundy barouche and the slightly shabby phaeton drawn up before the house had warned him of what he would likely find in his own drawing room. Or should he say whom he would find?

"Afternoon, Antonia," he said before he'd fully opened the door to the room. "Afternoon, Julian. I do hope you're enjoying my hospitality."

Silence met his salutations. Frowning, he surveyed the tableau spread before him. Antonia, seated in his favorite chair near the fire, continued to read. Julian, leaning over Miss Winslow, one hand lightly touching her shoulder, appeared to be teaching the chit some card game!

"A pretty scene indeed," he said, strolling in and tossing his gloves and crop on a chair. "A fit opening to the best of productions at the King's Theatre. Genteel domesticity encapsulated at its most genteel."

"Sarcasm doesn't become you, Edward," Antonia said without raising her face. "Neither does your behavior of the past week or more."

"*My* behavior." He snorted, swinging off his cloak. "After what I've suffered, you call my behavior to task? I take it my message preceded me from Hawkesly? I had a small piece of business to attend to before leaving Devon, but I thought you'd be awaiting word of my *dutiful* wife."

"You, sir, are an insufferable boor on occasion."

Julian's comment, delivered with quiet vehemence, stilled Edward as he would have dropped the cloak. "Beg pardon, Julian?"

"I think you heard me well enough."

"Perhaps I did. Since when has it been your place to criticize my conduct?"

"Since you took it upon yourself to verbally attack innocent young ladies."

Edward paused, considering, before laying down the mud-spattered cloak with deliberate care. "I regard myself as entirely just in whatever course of behavior I've chosen."

"Gad!" Julian straightened, but his hand remained on Sarah Winslow's shoulder. "You can be . . . be . . ."

"An overbearing, pigheaded, unjust"—Antonia paused and glared at him—"*jackanapes!*"

Edward clasped his hands beneath the tails of his jacket and walked with springy steps to stand with his back to the fire. "Jackanapes, hm?" He narrowed his gaze on Sarah Winslow. "We have not heard from you, Miss Winslow. Don't tell me you have nothing to add to this diatribe."

Her large dark eyes met his. "You . . . you were so *angry* with me, my lord." To his discomfort, great tears welled and began to slip soundlessly down her overly pale cheeks. "Poor Lindsay. She is so good and kind. She has always tried to help those less fortunate than herself. And now . . . and now, you have *banished* her somewhere."

Before Edward's awfully fascinated eyes, Julian
dropped to a knee and drew the girl into his arms,
where she sobbed quietly against his shoulder. Julian's rigid face rained disgust on Edward.

"Leaving your bride on your wedding night!" Antonia smacked her book shut and rose to her feet.
"First you manage, by some means I fail to compre-
hend, to force the poor innocent into agreeing to a
marriage. Then, the moment your arrogant control is
as much as tweaked by the masculine attention such
a purely lovely creature commands—rightfully—from
the *ton*, you rush ahead, making wedding arrangements with the most unseemly haste I have *ever* had
the misfortune to witness."

"I hardly—"

"*Ever*, Edward. You removed any joy the poor gel
might have found in the event. Never, for one moment, did you consider that Lindsay is an intelligent, lively young person whose will must be
supremely strong." Antonia's bosom rose beneath
layers of black silk and multiple strands of jet beads
interspersed with diamonds. "Did it not occur to
you that for anyone—*anyone*—to retain the wit and
sense of humor that young woman has, whilst living
with the likes of Roger Latchett and Belle Granville,
makes her extraordinary?"

"Well—"

"No, of course it hadn't. You are too consumed
with the business of exerting your rights of ownership. And you deeply upset Sarah, Edward. Something else I shall be hard put to to forgive."

"Here, here," Julian echoed staunchly, still on his
knee beside the girl.

Edward glared at his friend. Damned if the man
wasn't besotted with the featherbrained little baggage.

"And Emma. *Emma*, Edward."

Wearily, he faced his aunt once more. "Am I now

to be berated because a foolish maid allowed herself to be found in—''

''Don't!'' Sarah leaped to her feet. ''Please don't speak of that, my lord. It is too embarrassing. And you frightened her so that Emma has scarce come out of her room since.''

Edward looked from one accusing face to another. His body ached from too much riding over too many days and not enough sleep. And, damn it all, there might be a grain of truth in some of what they said. His little Lindsay, standing on the steps at Hawkesly, holding up the ridiculous pantaloons and managing to appear dignified for the servants, was something he would never forget.

''You're filthy, Edward,'' Antonia said. ''Your boots are caked with mud.''

''I know.''

''The least you could do would be to appear suitably dressed in Polite Company.''

''I've been in the saddle for days,'' he said defensively. ''These have been difficult times.''

''Not only for you,'' Julian said, his tone grave. Then he raised a brow at Edward in a manner that promised renewed communication between the two of them.

''I have waited long enough for you to say what I want to hear,'' Antonia said imperiously. ''Now. And kindly don't waste my time with devious responses. Where exactly is she?''

He ran his fingers through his hair. How quickly could he dispatch his mission in London and return to Lindsay?

''Edward. Where *is* she?''

He felt dazed. ''Where is she?''

''Oh, really. Do not begin that nonsense again. Where is Lindsay now? What have you done with her?''

His brain cleared. Not long at all. No, he need stay but a short time before returning to Lindsay and

doing what he had dreamed of for far too long . . .
claiming her completely.

He smiled briefly at Sarah. "Forgive me if I was
harsh with you, Sarah," he said. "Please remember
that I have never been a bridegroom before and such
responsibilities bring their own tensions."

Her lips curved prettily.

"And be so good, if you would not mind, as to
tell Emma we shall do well to forgive and forget any
. . . awkwardness."

"I will tell her," Sarah said with mirth in her
voice.

"Antonia." He gave his aunt his full attention.
"You certainly make some good points in your ti-
rade. Now I must change."

She slapped open her fan and frowned at him over
its ivory sticks. "That doesn't answer my question."

"The answer to your question is simple. My
viscountess is where she belongs. In Devon. At
Hawkesly Place. Lindsay is attending to her duties as my wife by overseeing our household
there."

He aimed another smile in all directions before
leaving the room.

"Latchett?" Edward swung away from the window in the library to face his large, sharp-eyed butler. "He's here, Garrity? At this hour?" Midnight
had come and gone.

"Yes, my lord. I put him in the drawing room." Garrity coughed. "He appears somewhat—disturbed?"

Edward paced. He'd been engaged in deciding
where and how soon he should confront Latchett.
Now the decision had been made. "Bring him to me
here."

Within minutes, the door burst open. Latchett,
red-faced and perspiring, elbowed Garrity aside.
Mopping his brow with an overlarge handkerchief,

he approached Edward, then turned back and waited until they were alone.

"Know it's late," Latchett said. "Decided you wouldn't want me to put off coming."

Edward seated himself on the window seat and rested a shoulder against dark green velvet drapes.

Latchett approached a silver tray of crystal decanters. He raised a hand and looked at Edward. "You don't mind if I, er. . . ?"

Edward shook his head and Latchett poured himself a generous measure of brandy.

"Dashed awkward this." Latchett gave Edward a sidelong glance. "Sure it's all a matter of timing. But you see, old chap, timing rather has me by the short hairs as it were. If you see what I mean?"

Edward shook his head again. He crossed his legs and laced his fingers around one knee. Not one word of assistance would this worm receive.

Latchett began to pace. He took measured steps, pointing each toe to trace the pattern in the green Persian carpet before sliding forward again.

Edward uncrossed and recrossed his legs. And he waited.

"You do remember the agreements we had?" Latchett said.

"Refresh my memory."

"Oh, dash . . . Well, if there is some point you've forgotten, I suppose . . . Yes. At your insistence, I availed myself of the, er, entertainments offered at Boodles. Damned nice. But damned expensive, too."

Edward raised his chin.

"Not too expensive for such a fine establishment, of course," Latchett quickly added. "Anyway, it seems that you have forgotten to, er, settle accounts?"

Edward allowed several seconds to pass before he said: "What can you be speaking of? I *always* settle my accounts. And I'm amazed that my affairs should have been discussed with you."

"No, no, no." Latchett grimaced. "I have not made myself clear. It is *my* accounts that have not been settled."

"Oh." Edward studied the fingernails of one hand. "Did you want me to ask them to extend you a little more time to come up with the blunt?"

The choking sound coming from Latchett made it unnecessary for Edward to see the effect of his own words.

"You said *you* would take care of my expenses," Latchett managed explosively. "It was part of our agreement. That and the little matter of any other *necessary* outlays during my own and my mother's stay in Town."

Edward raised deliberately blank eyes. "*Other* necessary outlays? What can you mean?" No doubt the good Mrs. Felling came under Latchett's interpretation of "necessary." And his gambling debts.

"If it were not for your desire to have my mother and myself present in London to give that—to give Lindsay the necessary family backing before her marriage, Mother and I would not have incurred the considerable expenses necessary to the running of the Chelsea cottage."

A mere five thousand guineas of incurred expense on one occasion, Edward thought. And a mere two thousand here and three thousand there. And then there had been the unsavory necessity to secure Latchett's release from a certain establishment in Jermyn Street where he'd been accused, probably falsely, of cheating. Since that particular gambling hell was infamous for its wickedly dangerous hazard tables, it was probable that Latchett had been the victim. Not that Edward cared.

"I did intervene on your behalf in Jermyn Street," he said quietly.

Color raged in Latchett's face. "Yes, well, damned good of you. But there are Mother's little fripperies to be paid for . . . and a number of minor amounts outstanding in Chelsea."

"How much, exactly, in Chelsea?"

"Ooh"—Latchett raised his shoulders—"fifteen, perhaps."

"Fifteen guineas?"

Latchett stared. "Fifteen *thousand* guineas. But that does include my mother's fripperies."

Edward frowned and said nothing.

"But let us deal with the matter of Boodles first. This evening I was refused admittance. Damnably embarrassin'."

He must not let his satisfaction show. "Surely you are not asking me for another loan?"

"Loan?" Latchett opened his little eyes wide. "Loan? Not a bit of it. I see you have forgotten, my lord. You agreed to *pay* my expenses at Boodles."

Edward bent forward, hands on knees—paused—then pushed slowly to his feet. "We seem to have somewhat of a problem. A minor misunderstanding. I agreed to *sponsor* you at Boodles, Mr. Latchett. And that I have done." Much to the ire of many other members. "I most certainly did not undertake to make good any debts you incurred there."

Latchett's lips parted and remained so. His head stuck forward on his fat neck. "But . . . but, surely you did. If there had been any question, *any* question at all, I would have conducted . . . That is to say, my lord, that I am considerably taken aback at being expected to pay my own debts."

"Really?" Edward laughed. "Most men, sir, *gentlemen*, expect to pay their own debts."

"But the bill is considerable." A large draft of brandy filled Latchett's cheeks. "I certainly had not thought to use my own funds to pay for the style of living to be expected of a viscount's relative—of the stepbrother of his future wife."

Edward watched him closely. "Our misunderstanding has been established. That being the case,

surely you will be forced to use your own funds."
Now would come the truly interesting part of this
little scene.

Refilling his glass without asking permission,
Latchett favored Edward with a dark scowl. "We
will return to the topic of Boodles later. But let us
deal with the subject of my own funds. The necessary papers for the transfer of Tregonitha to my
name have not been received by my solicitors."

"Transfer, Mr. Latchett?"

Latchett's eyes bulged. "*Transfer*, my lord. You
have been married to my stepsister for over a week
and as yet you have failed to complete your side of
the marriage settlement."

Edward removed his fob watch from a waistcoat
pocket, looked at its face, and swung the gold in-
strument back and forth by its chain. "This is awkward. I fear you have badly misinterpreted my
intentions. I believe I said that I would be loathe to
remove Tregonitha from your administration since
you have had the burden of caring for Lindsay since
her father's death—her blood brother being also
dead."

"Quite so."

"I never said I would *give* my wife's inheritance
to you, sir. That would be a grave injustice to her."

Latchett's normally florid face turned purple. His
mouth opened and closed while his nostrils became
pinched. He made the most objectionable sounds:
part gasp, part retch.

"Are you ill, sir?" Edward asked.

"What?" Latchett's next breath screeched in his
throat. "What exactly do you believe your settlement on Lindsay to have been?"

Edward spread his hands. "That I would care for
her—now and for the rest of her life. She bears the
title of my wife with all that entails. I believe I am
being more than fair in providing for anything and
everything she may need or desire."

"But what of me?" Latchett blustered. He shook visibly. "Am I to do no more than return to the position I already had before the little chit opened her legs for you?"

If it were possible, Edward turned colder. "I would remind you that you are speaking of my wife."

"I'm speaking of the succulent little piece you could hardly wait to drive yourself into, *my lord.*" Latchett moved closer until Edward saw veins standing out in the other man's temples. "I'm speaking of what you *bought* from me. A fine big pair of bubbies any man would pay dearly to get his hands upon."

"Mr. Latchett—"

"Don't interrupt me, *my lord.*" Clearly the vermin was beyond caution. "You purchased a body. A stallion you were, straining to rut the prime filly I had to offer. Oh, you spoke a pretty speech, but you wanted to be the one to pick the virgin's flower, *my lord.* A ripe and ready toy for whatever pleased you, she was, *my lord.* And by now you'll have used her for your pleasure aplenty."

The rage Edward knew he must contain made his face and body feel like bleached granite. His blood was ice in his veins. He scarce dared face the man.

"How did you find her?" Latchett continued. "Willing, was she? Quick to learn? Offer herself to you, did she? Or did she scream and try to hide? All the better if she did, say us men of the world. Aren't I right, *my lord*?" Latchett's laugh held the kind of evil men made a joke of.

"I think you are in your altitudes, sir," Edward said, swallowing bile. He made fists in his pockets. A safer place to keep his hands at this moment. "Have your coachman take you home, where you may sleep off this . . . this sickness."

"You bought," Latchett raged. "And now, by God, you'll pay. Starting with the debts you told me to incur at Boodles. Then I have considerable debts to clear in Chelsea. Very considerable. I had to amuse myself while I was being excluded from your *marriage* arrangements. Add to that my mother's expenses. I'll use a pen now to tot the sum and you can settle. Your check will suffice.''

''No.'' Edward strolled to stare down into the fire. This was what he'd worked for, dreamed of, yet he found he had little stomach for dealing with the true dregs of humanity.

''No?'' Latchett came to stand beside Edward. ''I misheard you surely.''

''I said''—Edward turned his face toward Latchett—''I said no. I will not pay your debts at Boodles. Neither will I pay a penny toward your expenses in Chelsea.''

''But Mrs.—'' Latchett coughed and made a visible attempt to collect himself. ''We'll not argue. We're relatives, after all. Just deal with the transfer of Tregonitha to my name first thing in the morning and we'll be on perfectly amiable terms, I assure you.''

''There will be no transfer,'' Edward said. ''I cannot imagine what made you assume there would be.''

Latchett plucked at the sleeve of Edward's dark jacket. ''You said I deserved it because of all I'd done for Lindsay.''

''I believe that upon Lindsay's marriage, the estate becomes her husband's.''

''Yes, but—''

''I am not a fool, sir. I did not say I would give it to you.''

''I can prove you did.''

''Really. Did we sign something?''

Latchett looked aghast. ''A gentleman's word is his bond.''

''We'll not speak of matters about which you

know nothing. And now I'm tired. So, if you'll excuse me?''

"Then I'm to return to being nothing more than a hired overseer to the estate that should have been mine anyway?''

Edward shook his head.

"If that fool of a stepfather of mine hadn't cocked up his toes when he did none of this would have happened.''

"Make yourself plain.''

"Oh, it's obvious.'' Latchett swung wide an arm. "With his milksop of a son dead he'd have been grateful to make me his heir. Broderick Granville wouldn't have risked passing on what was his to a fool woman, or to some son-in-law not of his choosing.''

Edward smiled. "Too bad Lindsay didn't follow her *calling*. Perhaps you should have tried to deny my offer. With the girl in a convent, there could never have been a husband or an heir to contend with. The estate would have been as good as yours.''

"Exactly,'' Latchett said. His speech was already slurred, but he downed more brandy. "But you said it would be all mine and I believed you.''

"And you believed wrongly,'' Edward said softly. "Please leave my house.''

"It'll cost the estate dearly to pay off my debts here,'' Latchett said, swaying forward on his toes.

"It won't cost the estate a penny.''

"How do you . . .'' Latchett turned his head and tried to focus on Edward. "What do you mean by that?''

"A new overseer for Tregonitha has already been hired.'' Edward pulled the cord to summon Garrity. It was no accident that the butler was extraordinarily young and fit for his position. "Garrity will see you out. You have a week to clear your possessions from my Chelsea cottage. Another week and I'll expect your goods out of Tregonitha.''

"You'll . . . You can't do this."

"I already have."

"I'll see you dead first."

Yes, Edward thought, you will if you can. Vigilance would be the watchword from now until this man was finally, irrevocably dealt with.

"Garrity," Edward said when the butler came into the room. "We discussed what is to be done now. Kindly accompany Mr. Latchett to Chelsea."

Latchett made a dash at Edward, who warded him off with a single forearm thrust. Garrity grasped the man's collar and hauled him to the balls of his feet.

"Your mother," Edward said, "is a vain, stupid woman. But only a woman, after all. I have arranged a place for her on an estate in Yorkshire. Since she is without skills, there is little she can do. A friend there has been kind enough to say she may take over the care of the estate chapel."

"Why . . . why . . ."

Edward left Latchett to Garrity and swiftly climbed the stairs. How many hours had it been since he'd left Lindsay, his darling little Lindsay, staring at him with adoring blue eyes that beseeched him not to leave her?

Adoring?

Edward paused at the top of the stairs to watch Garrity bundle a loudly railing Latchett through the hall. This night was only the beginning of the end with that murderous scoundrel.

Lindsay had looked at him as if she adored him? He walked slowly along the hall. Love? Could it be that the girl loved him?

Did he want her to love him?

He leaned against the wall and sunk his hands into his pockets. He *wanted* her, wanted . . . Latchett's foul babblings flooded through Edward's brain like fetid slime and he clamped his back teeth together. How dare that whoremongering coxcomb speak of a man's wife . . .

Damn it all. He didn't know what love was, *if* there was such a thing. And if there was, it was only for poets and fools and he was neither.

A night's sleep and he'd set out again for Devon . . . and Lindsay.

Passing the door to the chamber he'd prepared for her he hesitated an instant. His body, tired as it was, reminded him of how she'd looked, trembling, delicately voluptuous in the white she'd worn to become his bride.

Before two days were up, his bride would truly become his wife.

In his own rooms, he was met by a pleasantly blazing fire. Stoddart had laid out a dressing gown and left a decanter of brandy and a glass beside the bed.

Edward poured a small brandy and went to stand before the fire. He swirled the amber liquid in its finely cut glass and drank it down in one draft.

He didn't want to be here. Not without Lindsay.

Setting down the glass, he loosed his neckcloth and pulled it off. He stripped away his jacket and his shirt and braced his hands on the mantel, allowing the fire to warm his skin.

A small sound startled him, but before he could react, slender arms surrounded his waist. "My poor Edward," a light voice said behind him. "I knew you would need me tonight."

He didn't move a muscle—except for his shaft. That part of him that was beyond his total control sprang hard inside his trousers.

Against his back he felt the unmistakable pressure of a woman's substantial breasts. Distended nipples probed his skin like round pebbles.

He straightened slowly and the hands that had been crossed about his ribs started their practiced massage. Almost dispassionately, Edward watched those smooth, clever fingers make circles over his

belly and press downward . . . until he stopped
them.

"I know how to make you relax." The brushing
at his back closed Edward's eyes. "Let me touch
you, Edward."

Drawing in a jerky breath, he clasped one slim
wrist and spun to face Lady Clarisse Simmonds.

Chapter 21

Temptation came in many forms, but usually men made at least a little effort to search it out. Rarely did the stuff of the most heated carnal fantasy offer itself like ripe grapes poised over the open mouth of a man with a taste for sweet fruit.

Edward held himself erect. The woman swaying before him in a loose gown of pale blue satin had gone to great pains to present herself as a hedonistic feast.

"You look tired, my dearest love," Clarisse said, her voice a purr. "But I know how to turn that tiredness into heavy, satisfied sleep. You know that, don't you, my stallion?"

The very term used by the filth, Latchett. Edward flattened his lips over his teeth. "Don't do this, Clarisse. Collect yourself and go home."

"Go home?" She made her beautiful but avid eyes huge. "I could not leave without giving you what you need."

His chest expanded with the deep breath he drew.

Clarisse spread her fingers over his hair-rough skin. "I dream of your body when I sleep," she said. "And when I'm awake, I see it. This black hair on your chest, and on your long, strong legs . . . and elsewhere." She smiled with mock coyness. "People prattle about nothing of importance but I do not care because I can ignore them and look at you in my mind. *All* of you. I can even taste you.'' She looked suggestively at the bulge in his trousers.

Sarcasm was wasted on this woman, but he said: ''I trust you do not belch too loudly, madam.''

Clarisse only laughed. When she moved, throwing back her shoulders, Edward was hard-pressed not to gasp. He saw why it had been possible to feel her flesh on his as if it were naked.

The fullness of the gown was an artful device to hide the true cut—until the wearer wished to reveal the designer's cleverness. Clarisse hung her head back, and vertical slashes in the gown parted over her big breasts. The satin opened to present those white mounds that had once intrigued Edward. Even now, his male drive strained at the erotic image she made.

''Touch me, Edward,'' she whispered, undulating, arching her back. ''Use your teeth and tongue the way you know how. *Use* me, Edward. Be rough. I want you to be rough.''

He swallowed, unable to look away from her nipples. His belly contracted. Wide areola and their stiff centers glistened red with some oiled rouge.

''Taste, stallion.'' Her tongue, pink and glistening, flickered around her parted lips.

When he made no move to touch her, she rubbed her own fingertips over her nipples, moaning softly, shuddering. Then she touched his mouth, spread the sweet-tasting oil along his lips. ''Taste it, Edward. Taste me.''

Slowly, the haze she had cast upon him cleared. He breathed deeply once more. The woman had moved into her own erotic trance. She was her own sexual fulfillment. His role was only to aid in her fantasy.

Her body was luscious, a libertine's delight.

''Take me,'' she crooned. Her nimble hands sought the fastenings of his trousers and in seconds she worked them down his thighs. "I will be for you what that insipid little waif you married cannot. No wonder you left without bothering to bed her."

Edward said nothing. He let Clarisse do her work.

When his shaft rose heavy and pulsing, he felt no shame. He felt nothing but the lustful, searing need that was a man's nature.

"Mmm." She surrounded him, stroking, parting her thighs and sliding him against her cleft on top of smooth satin that was immediately damp from the mingled essences of their bodies. Closing her legs to hold him, she raised his hands and spread them over her breasts. Sighing, crooning, Clarisse made sucking noises with her pretty, practiced mouth.

Then she stepped away and dropped to her knees. Looking up, her eyes were glazed. "It's been too long," she murmured. "I've missed you and you've missed me."

She took him into her mouth and the sucking took on a different sound, this one full and purposeful. Her head moved over him, her thick auburn hair sliding over his thighs.

Edward locked his knees. "Enough," he said when he trusted himself to speak.

Her giggle was near-hysterical. With a prancing bounce, she leaped to her feet and rent the neck of the gown, let it fall to her feet in a shimmering puddle of blue. Running, laughing, she jumped onto the bed and crouched in its center like a waiting, predatory animal.

Disgust lashed Edward. Self-disgust as well as sickening revulsion for the mindless woman who waited, breasts dangling, moist readiness at her core, for him to do what they'd done many times before.

No more. He might not deserve the gem of a sweet little wife with whom he had been presented and he doubted he could bring himself to risk committing the deepest parts of himself to her or anyone, but

by God he'd make her happy. And he'd give her his
faith.

Turning away, Edward pulled on breeches and a
shirt. He closed out the whining sounds that came
from the bed. Soon he'd donned top boots and a
warm, serviceable jacket. With a cravat loosely in
place, he strode from the room.

Waiting longer was unthinkable. His ride to Devon
would start tonight.

Behind him, whines turned to enraged screams.

Stoddart, struggling into a robe over his night-
shirt, stumbled from his quarters to meet Edward.
"My lord? What's afoot?"

"Abed, you mean, Stoddart," Edward said, taking the stairs downward two at a time. "Please see
that the lady gets home. And, Stoddart, I suggest
you prepare yourself for physical attack. I'll be at
Hawkesly Place—with the viscountess."

By the time he gained Hawkesly, the evening of
the second night since leaving London had swept
in, bringing with it the mist of a light but warm rain.
The air was heavy with the scent of early roses.

He'd been unable to stop Sains from sounding the
gate house hunting horn and by the time his horse
clattered to the bottom of the front steps, two
grooms came at a run from the yard and the great
doors to the house were flung open.

Grinning, Edward hauled his punished body from
the saddle. "Treat him well," he told the grooms,
referring to the third horse he'd used on his headlong ride.

He looked up, smiling still, expecting Lindsay to
make a shy appearance.

It was McBain who descended toward his master
with unusual haste. "You were not expected, my
lord."

"No." Edward pulled off his riding gauntlets. "I
had not thought to be through with my business in

Town so quickly." He wasn't through, but the rest could wait. "Where is her ladyship?"

Mrs. Gilley appeared behind McBain. She stared at Edward, turned back toward the house, then spun toward him again. Her hands clutched the bundle of keys at her waist and he saw, even from a distance, that she trembled.

Alarm turned his stomach. "What is it? What's happened here?"

"Hm. Well, my lord, I scarce know where to begin," McBain said. "It's most unfortunate. Most unfortunate."

"What's unfortunate?" Edward mounted the steps. "Where is my wife?" A deep dread swelled within him.

McBain spread his hands.

Edward found he could scarcely breathe. "Has something happened to my wife?" Fool that he was. He should never have left her alone in such strange surroundings. Attending to Latchett could have waited.

"She's . . . Lady Hawkesly isn't here, my lord," Mrs. Gilley said. "She had a, um, *visitor*. She had to leave immediately."

"What visitor?"

"A woman," McBain said. "Of the lower classes, I would have said. Her ladyship became most upset and said she must go."

"Go *where*?" Edward roared.

"She told us she was sure she'd be back before you came home," McBain said, sounding desperate. "If your lordship were to come in and rest himself. Eat. Sleep. I'm certain her ladyship will return in no time."

Edward spun away. "Groom! Bring me Saber." To McBain he said: "Answer me one question direct. Do you think my wife may have headed for Cornwall?"

McBain nodded. "I think so, my lord. The person

who came spoke like a Cornish woman. She said her ladyship had unfinished business to attend to." McBain gulped visibly. "Oh, dear, I'd hoped not to have to tell you this. I heard the woman say that a risk of death lay where they were going."

This time Edward did not pause on the ridge above Salters Cove. Daylight revealed clearly the land he'd traveled in cloaking darkness on the night of his previous visit. Instinct had brought him here again this morning. He did not believe he'd find Lindsay at Tregonitha and there was the chance that Latchett might have returned there. Time enough to confront that quarter again. On his previous visit, the old woman had sent him to find this Antun Pollack of Salters Cove. Today he'd start with Pollack.

By skirting the woods he was able to find a path leading down to the cove. He eased the pace. Only a fool stormed an unknown stronghold. The cove opened, just as the old woman had described, like the graceful blade of a sickle. Edward reached a fork in the path where a second track led back toward the woods. This must have been the way Lindsay took with the cart. He stayed on the main path, which led directly to Salters Cottage.

An incoming tide left barely a rim of dark gold sand at the water's edge. From the land jutted a sturdy dock with two boats moored alongside, one a small craft with a single mast, the second a rugged seiner rigged for deeper sea fishing. Edward paused a moment. Painted black with green scrolled chevrons along her sides, the seiner made a handsome picture. He noted her name: *Linny One*.

James had loved the sea.

Edward blocked out the thought and wheeled away—and confronted a man with bright red hair.

"Who are ye? What's your business here?" The man's eyes were as gray as this Cornish sky on a winter's day.

The same instinct that had brought Edward directly here told him he'd found his man. "Antun Pollack?"

With his big fists on his lean hips, his strong legs braced apart, the other raised his chin. A breeze off the sea moved that unruly thatch of hair. "Who wants to know who I am?"

"I'm looking for Antun Pollack." Edward wasn't certain why he hesitated to give his title. "The Widow Whalen told me I'd find him here."

Instantly, the combative stance relaxed a little. "I'm Pollack."

Edward was rarely conscious of another man's physical size, and evident power. With Antun Pollack, neither could be ignored, anymore than the fact that he was handsome.

"The widow thought you might know where—" He paused, irritated at having to consider what to call his own wife. "She thought you might know the whereabouts of the Viscountess Hawkesly."

For an instant Edward thought he'd imagined that Pollack's large body tensed. A look at the man's face removed any doubt that it had.

"So it is you," Pollack said through clenched teeth. His swift move to grasp at Saber's bridle caught Edward off guard. "You took your time coming, didn't you? Any normal man with such a wife ready to share his bed wouldn't leave her alone on her wedding night. And if she disappeared that night, he wouldn't take nigh on a fortnight to decide to come looking for her."

Slowly, Edward dismounted. He hooked a hand above Pollack's on Saber's bridle. "How do you know what did or did not happen on my wedding night?"

He saw the man swallow, the slight shifting away of his eyes. "I have my ways."

"Lindsay came here to you, didn't she?" He'd

give the man a chance to tell the truth—and prayed the truth would be better than he feared.

Pollack's clear eyes met Edward's squarely. "Aye, she did."

"And you involved her in activities that could have cost her life."

So swiftly that Edward almost lost his balance, Pollack grabbed him by the shoulders. "How do you know? Where is she now? Is she hurt?" He tried to shake Edward. "Tell me, man. I've scoured the countryside for her. The cart was there in the woods. But so was old Catkin. There were the tracks of a horse. Farr's man, no doubt. I thought he'd have taken her to Saint Austell but there's no word of her there."

Edward threw off the other man's hands. He'd wager his soul that what he saw before him was a man who harbored tender affections for Lindsay. "It wasn't Farr's man who took her—whoever Farr is. It was me. I'm her husband and I came to collect her. Just in time, too. What would possess a man to involve a woman scarce more than a girl in such activities?"

"Is that what Lindsay told you happened?"

Indeed, there was some attachment here that Edward disliked intensely. "Lindsay would tell me nothing about what happened here. She would not as much as acknowledge that she knew your name. But a genteel girl doesn't become a smuggler unless she's forced into it."

Pollack's smile came and went quickly, but Edward knew he'd seen that smile. "We'll not waste time discussing these matters," Pollack said. "I don't understand why you come looking for her now. You say you took her away ten days past."

Edward seethed at the indignity of admitting his own inability to control his wife. "I left her in Devon while I completed some business in London," he said. "Upon my return I discovered she had . . . I understand she decided to visit Cornwall again."

"You don't know your bride very well, do you, my lord?"

Edward didn't fail to note Pollack's first use of the title. It was done with unwitting respect and eased the acid in the man's suggestion. "Answer me this, Pollack: Have you seen my wife since the night you used her for your own illegal ends?"

"I did not *use* her! I could never use Lindsay."

"Are you telling me it was her own idea to transport undutied goods through the countryside with revenue men chasing behind?"

Pollack squinted into a pallid sun. "You married a gem. It cannot hurt to tell you that your wife is beyond price. If I thought it would go better for her, I'd gladly say she was involved in the night running against her will. I don't believe that. She needed money. That's why she did it."

Edward regarded the other man narrowly. "As my wife Lindsay needs nothing, sir."

"She might not if she trusted you. Evidently she does not."

Edward checked an urge to strike the man for his insolence.

"Have you met Roger Latchett?"

The question startled Edward. "Of course."

"Is he your friend?"

"I hate . . . That is hardly your affair."

"You've given me my answer, my lord. I thank you for it. Since her brother died—when Lindsay was barely past sixteen—she has done all she can to stand between Latchett and Tregonitha's tenants. Latchett as good as steals from them. Lindsay finds ways to ease their hardships. The money she's made—at her insistence—from the night running has gone to the poor devils scraping a living on Tregonitha lands. She has more courage than any man I've met. And she's gentler than any maid."

Edward considered the long speech. "Latchett will pay," he said, not caring who heard. "His payment has already begun."

Pollack didn't respond. He turned his face away. "If you took Linny with you, why come looking for her now?"

If Pollack knew nothing of her whereabouts, and Edward was convinced he didn't, there was no point in involving him further. "My wife is safe." He prayed he was right. "I came to discover the truth behind what I found here before. Now I have that truth." And he admired his viscountess the more, although he might, he decided ruefully, come to wish she weren't quite so venturesome.

Edward mounted Saber. "It might be better if no one knew of our meeting."

"They'll know nothing from me." Pollack stood in Edward's path. "Will you allow Linny to send word to me? I was her brother's friend. She was as much a sister to me as . . . as the sister I once had."

"I'll give your request consideration," Edward said.

Pollack stepped aside. "Good day to you."

"Good day."

Edward rode past the man without looking back. He turned Saber inland, but not before catching sight of the seiner once more. *Linny One*. Pollack's name for Lindsay, the girl who had been like a sister to him . . . ?

Without hesitation, Edward rode back the way he'd come, crossing the hill and several more behind it until he came to the dale where he'd found Widow Whalen's cottage.

He ignored a man who stopped digging in a cottage garden next to the widow's and went to dismount. Before his foot was free of the stirrup, a flurry caught his attention. Waving both hands, a pleasant-faced woman of middle years hurried down the path between tidy flower beds crowded with budding plants. Clearly she motioned him to remain in his saddle.

As was his preference, he rode bareheaded, but he bowed as the woman approached.

"Good afternoon," he said. "I'm Lord Hawkesly. I visited Widow Whalen once before. I'd like to speak to her now."

The woman shook her head, glancing around. "Follow," she said, her voice loud. Without waiting for his reaction, she hurried in the direction of a treeless meadow.

Edward trotted Saber behind.

"Stop," the woman shouted when they were some distance from the cottages. She pointed to herself. "Josie Whalen! Deaf! You're Lindsay's husband?"

He nodded. "Yes." Once more the dread swelled in his belly. What had Lindsay been through alone since her brother died? And where could she be now?

The woman smiled. "She loves you!" Her words echoed.

He felt an unaccustomed tightening inside. "You've seen her?"

Josie frowned.

Edward looked around and raised his palms. "Lindsay?" he said, feeling desperate and helpless.

Slender, surprisingly smooth hands caught at his arm. "With my mother. Supposed to get back before you."

The relief that swept in made Edward euphoric. "Where?" He turned up his palms again and repeated: "Where?"

"Bodmin," Josie said. "On the moor. Cottage is near Dozemary Pool."

He knew a moment's heavy exhaustion. On his way from Devon he'd passed but a few miles from the spot Josie spoke of.

From a pocket inside his jacket he produced a sov-

ereign and pressed it into Josie's palm. She looked
at the coin and her face reddened. Shaking her head,
she tried to push it back at him. Edward forced himself to pause long enough to close her fingers over
the money, and to smile. "From Lindsay," he said.

Josie appeared to consider before she, too, smiled.

Edward left, but when he reached the top of the
next rise he turned back. Josie stood where he'd left
her. She waved and he raised a hand in response
before flicking his crop and spurring Saber into a full
gallop.

The last weak rays of a setting sun shivered on
the breeze-driven ripples of Dozemary Pool. If Saber
and his rider had been less than exhausted, they'd
have reached their destination an hour or more
since. Edward squeezed his prickling eyes shut.

Saber walked now and Edward made no attempt
to hurry the animal's pace.

The scent of smoke reached Edward and some of
his heaviness lifted. There was a cottage here somewhere then. Josie Whalen's instructions had been
vague enough but he'd followed out of desperation.
Only as the hours and miles passed did he begin to
doubt, to consider that he might find nothing once
he got to his destination.

He'd barely entered a group of trees on the far
side of the pool when he broke into a clearing and
stopped. In the center stood a small thatched cottage
and a well-tended barn. Grazing contentedly near
the barn was a mule—and the horse Lindsay had
ridden the day she came to him at Point Cottage.

The first day . . .

Edward swung from his saddle. The innocent girl
who had come to him then was as innocent today,
but now he knew what he couldn't have guessed at
then: she was courageous beyond measure. From
now on he would find a way to do what he'd set

out to do—for both of their sakes—and be the husband she deserved.

Pushing aside his fatigue, he strode to the cottage door and knocked. No doubt she was here to help some other poor unfortunate soul. There must be no more dangerous running around the countryside. He'd make her trust him enough to allow him to do what she thought needed to be done for those she felt responsible for.

Minutes passed. Edward had raised his hand to knock again when the door swung open and he was confronted by Lindsay. She held a young child in her arms.

"My God, do you know how you've worried me?"

She shook her head and backed away.

Edward followed, trying to reach for her.

Lindsay eluded him. Tears began to course down her cheeks.

"My dear one," he said. "I know everything and I'm not angry. You should not have tried to fight Latchett alone."

Widow Whalen sat in a rocking chair while another woman stood near a table where she'd been preparing food.

"Lindsay, don't look like that." He touched her arm and felt her tremble before she jerked from him once more. "We will find a way to make sure everything is taken care of. Justice will be done. Trust me."

"Josie," Widow Whalen said. "Josie's told 'im."

Lindsay looked at the old woman, then at Edward. "She doesn't talk to anyone but you and me, Granny."

"She talked to me," Edward said quietly. "She said you loved me."

"Yes," Lindsay said, her breath coming in pants. "Yes, I do. And I cannot let you live with a lie. It wouldn't be fair."

He shook his head, bemused.

She hugged the child to her, cradling his head against her neck. "He was very ill with a fever, so they came for me. But he's not going to die. He's almost better."

"Good. Lindsay—"

"Josie lied for my sake. He's my child. John is mine. Do you understand? Mine!"

Edward's arms fell limply to his sides. The shouting had awakened the child. Scrubbing a fist into his eye, he turned his face toward Edward. The boy blinked. His eyes were dark—dark gray. His hair, damp from sleeping, shone reddish brown.

"What are you saying, Lindsay?"

"This is John," she said defensively. "He's almost two years old and he's mine."

Slowly, the cooling in his veins turned to pumping heat. He stepped closer. *Red hair and dark gray eyes.* "Yours?"

She nodded. The other women seemed as pale, motionless shadows. "It would be a slur on the Hawkesly name forever, wouldn't it? If anyone found out you'd married a woman with a child? Reverend Winslow told me that's what cuckolded means. To marry a woman who already has a child."

Dimly, he tried to make sense of her rambling. It didn't matter. "No one will find out," he said grimly.

"Good. Then leave me here and forget me. When you're in London, say I'm in Devon. When you're in Devon, say I'm in London."

Heat turned to a raging burning blaze that threatened to consume Edward. "Give the child to the old women," he said, and to Widow Whalen he added, "one word of this—to anyone—will cost you more than you have to give."

The woman shook her head, clearly terrified.

"You'll hear my instructions soon enough. Come with me, *my lady*."

She opened her mouth as if to argue, then mutely gave up the boy to the woman he did not know.

Rather than watch while she gathered the jacket of her riding habit, he walked outside.

Innocent? Only when it came to the finer points in defining certain terms. He hadn't been Lindsay's husband when she'd conceived her child. He hadn't been cuckolded, only made the complete, the unbelievable fool.

Waiting, his clenched fists crossed over his chest, he visualized a name written in green letters on shiny black: *Linny One.*

Antun Pollack would pay for his part in this. But Lindsay would pay first.

Chapter 22

❧

John would get well, thank the Lord, but everything else Lindsay cared about was in ruins.

Saber dwarfed Minnie. Edward held the stallion in check so that Lindsay's little chestnut could at least keep almost abreast of the great black animal.

Would Edward tell Roger about John?

What would Edward do to Lindsay herself?

Heading north into the gathering night he'd said not a word since they'd left Nanny Thomas's cottage. To Lindsay he presented the unyielding figure of a tall, cloaked man staring straight ahead. She wanted to touch him, to say, *"Josie told the truth. I do love you. But I'm doing what I must do—for William and Maria, and for John."*

At least he'd been easily persuaded that John was Lindsay's rather than William's child. She was still surprised that Josie had been able to explain the circumstances of William's death. When he'd first arrived at Nanny's, Edward had said he would deal with Roger himself. But now he seemed to have quite forgotten the ill Roger had done William. But then, a cuckolded man could be forgiven such a reaction.

"I'm sorry," she cried out. "And I would have stayed at Hawkesly Place if I hadn't received word about John's illness."

306

For minutes she thought he would not reply. When he did, she wished he hadn't. "There is no John," he said savagely. "Remember that, madam. From this night on his name will never be mentioned. You will forget he exists."

Lindsay drew in a horrified breath. "I cannot! He has only me. Surely you would not be so cruel—"

"As to deny a mother access to her son?" He laughed, never turning to look at her. "You have no son. And to think I was ready to treat you with the respect due a courageous woman."

He made no sense.

"Pollack thinks he has duped me yet again with his pretty speeches about your charitable defense of Tregonitha's tenants against Roger Latchett. I planned to help you—despite the fact that it is no woman's place to involve herself in the affairs of men. I planned to forgive you your stupidity. I had already done as much!"

Lindsay pressed a hand to her breast. "You spoke with Antun? He told you about the way Roger has ill-treated our tenants?" Could it be that there had been no mention of John being William's son? That no one had mentioned the child to Edward before he arrived on Bodmin Moor?

"I congratulate you on a most touching excuse for your actions. No doubt designed between the two of you against the possibility that I might discover your alliance."

Lindsay thought rapidly. There was little doubt that she had misinterpreted Edward's meaning upon his arrival at Nanny Thomas's cottage.

"Will you mention any of this to Roger? The night running? Or John?"

Edward brought his horse around and Lindsay reined in Minnie. "*Nothing* will be said to Roger Latchett. Not by me, and not by you. Do you understand?"

"Yes."

"How did you manage to—" His eyes were terrible in the gloom. "How is it possible that no one knows about the bastard child—except for Pollack, of course?"

"John is—" No. She must not say anything to suggest John's true parentage. "Antun doesn't know about John. He must not."

Edward maneuvered his horse until he could look directly down upon Lindsay. "You did not tell the bastard's father?"

She blinked, opened her eyes wider. "You think Antun is John's father?"

"I *know* he is. But it is just possible you didn't tell him, isn't it? Making fools of men is something you do so very well."

Her heart squeezed in her breast. If Edward discovered the truth he would undoubtedly go to Roger and inform him that Tregonitha could never be his. Roger had killed once to gain the estate. Lindsay was convinced he would kill again. Bad enough that she must worry about Edward's safety. John could be kept from all this. "Antun must not know," she said, making her voice firm.

"Hah! You have my word on that, my lady. Neither Pollack nor Latchett shall ever discover your true colors."

Even while she cringed beneath her husband's blazing stare, Lindsay dared to hope that in allowing Edward to believe Antun to be John's father she could protect the people she loved.

"You are a practiced actress," Edward said. "A loss to the stage."

"Thank you." He so often said things she didn't understand.

"I could not have guessed that you had given birth to a child. As for the rest—" He raised his head and she saw his angular jaw in stark outline. "Erring, as you charmingly put it. Ah, yes, we must speak more of your experience in the art of erring."

Lindsay had been with Maria when John was born. She remembered the horror of her sweet sister-in-law's pain . . . and the bitter sadness when Maria had died. It was true that families had similar features, and John did resemble Antun. This was fortunate, since Edward would have no reason to look elsewhere for the man with whom she had supposedly done whatever was necessary to the production of a child.

She dared another glance at Edward but could make him out only as a great, angry shadow. Could it be that the kisses they had shared would lead to a child? She did pray so, since he would probably never kiss her again. And if she could have Edward's child she would find a way to gentle the man's heart. He had seemed kindly enough toward John until she'd told her lie.

"We have a fair measure to travel yet, my lady," Edward said. He wrested Minnie's reins from Lindsay's hands. "From now on I will lead the way for you . . . in all things."

"Yes," she agreed meekly, finding a purchase on Minnie's mane. He did not *sound* as angry as he had.

"Except, of course, for those things in which it would give me pleasure to allow you to lead me."

On Lindsay's first day at Hawkesly, after Edward had left for London, Mrs. Gilley had proudly displayed the freshly made over bedchamber that had been prepared for her new mistress. On that sunny afternoon, shades of yellow in draperies and silk wall hangings had assumed the richness of warm butter.

In those few days before Granny Whalen had arrived with the news of John's illness, Lindsay had begun to revel in the sumptuousness of her surroundings. She had taken pleasure in Edward's having ordered pretty things for her comfort. Her clothes had been sent by family coach from London and a *modiste* arrived within hours

to measure Lindsay for a number of stylish riding
habits and for gowns suited to the more subdued
life of the country.

And Mrs. Gilley had been deferential, making
clear Lindsay's position as mistress of a great household whilst discreetly guiding her through formidable new duties.

Now all the pleasure would be gone.

For at least an hour, since her arrival from Cornwall with Edward at around midnight, Lindsay had
lain in her big, soft bed dully watching a flickering
glow from the fireplace turn her lovely marigold-
yellow bed drapings to deep gold.

When she and Edward had appeared, McBain and
Mrs. Gilley had presented themselves, looking as if
they neither had been abed, nor needed to go to
bed. Lindsay received the same deference as before
from both, and from the abigail Mrs. Gilley had
helped select. But Edward's brooding stare before
he strode away from her in the hall was all Lindsay
could see or think about clearly.

Lindsay tossed, first one way and then the other.
He was downstairs—probably in his study. And he
was angry. With her! He would probably be angry
forever and she would be forever under sentence of
that anger.

It was not to be borne! She was not a shrinking,
simpering, whimpering milk-and-water miss! She
had smuggled with the best of smugglers! She had
managed to care for a tiny child and for the tenants
of her family's estate without arousing the suspicion
of an evil, dangerous man! Lord Hawkesly would
not be allowed to turn his wife into something she
had never been—a helpless weakling. He would not
close her out of his life without her at least trying to
make peace.

Lindsay threw back the covers and got out of bed.
The ridiculously flimsy white nightrail she wore had
been one of Aunt Ballard's many wedding gifts. Dear

Aunt Ballard. How Lindsay did miss her. Shivering, she pulled on a lace wrapper. Threaded with yards of violet satin ribbon, the cobwebby Belgian lace was quite beautiful, but as much use against the night chill as the nightrail beneath.

A thud stopped Lindsay on her way to light a candle. The noise, like something dropping—or being thrown on the floor—came from the other side of the wall between her own chamber and the one she knew to be Edward's.

She almost scrambled back into her bed. "No," she said as loudly as she dared. "You will not intimidate me, my lord."

Using the firelight to find her way, she crossed the room with exaggeratedly careful steps. In the wall between the two rooms was a door. This, she'd been told, led to Edward's dressing room—and his bedchamber. Lindsay had never opened that door.

If she went to him and . . . And what? What could she say to make peace between them without endangering John?

She could try simply saying she was sorry there were things about her that displeased him. Lindsay opened the door and stepped quickly into the space beyond. Her heart beat suffocatingly in her throat. With the aid of the faint illumination from her room she made out the dim shapes of hanging clothes. A simple couch stood to her right, along the wall common to her room.

Lindsay bowed her head, willing her pulse to slow. She would simply tap on his door and, if he granted her admittance, go and plead for some measure of civility between them. That would be a start.

Resolutely, she raised her face . . . and saw Edward. For an instant her knees threatened to buckle. She opened her mouth but could make no sound.

"Exploring, my lady?" His voice had a still, cold quality. Behind him, on the back of the door he must have entered the dressing room by, was a mirror in which Lindsay could see herself as a pale wraith.

"You must have been here first, my lord," she managed to say. "Were *you* exploring?"

Edward stretched out his arms and braced himself between shelves that ran the length of the room at the level of his shoulders. "I have no need to explore," he said, raising a brow. "This is *my* dressing room."

"And it leads also to *my* room," she said, scarce able to breathe.

"It does indeed. And, of course, you know the reason for that."

She shook her head.

Edward looked at the ceiling. The front of his full-sleeved shirt gaped open to the waist. "Do not play with me further, my lady."

"If you intend to continue in this foul mood I had better return to bed."

He moved then, so swiftly he had passed her before she realized his intent. "You shall return to bed, madam. When and where I decide suits my preference." The door to her room slammed shut and she heard a key turn in the lock. Immediately, the dressing room was plunged into total darkness.

"Edward! I cannot see."

She felt him somewhere near and reached out. Her fingers made contact with warm, hair-covered skin. His chest. As quickly, he moved away.

"Edward," she said, trying to be calm. "I don't like the dark."

"I do."

He was to her left. Lindsay turned, grabbing, closing her fingers on air.

"I've always had this uncanny ability to manage with very little light."

He had moved to her right. "Edward?" She searched for him again. And again found nothing.

"Each of us knows how the other looks," he said.

"I shall try hard not to think of that. You look far too lovely, my dear. Far too lovely to be what you really are."

Deep within Lindsay some primitive sense of alarm flickered. "Why are you doing this?"

"You came to me tonight, Lindsay. I can only assume you intended to start leading me in the things you do well. And I believe I've decided to let you. Only I don't think I could bear to look at your face while you do so."

"Please open the door."

"What's wrong, Lindsay? Do you prefer to attend to these matters only in your own way?"

"These matters?"

"Very well," he said, behind her now. "Play your games. We will call what we are about *erring*."

Lindsay spun around. "You're making fun of me."

"Ah, but it was you who first made fun of me, Lindsay."

"Let me out of this room."

"All in good time."

He'd passed her again. She swung around once more, flung out her arms and rushed forward—and collided with a very solid body. She inhaled shakily and stood still against him. At least with him close she didn't feel so horribly afraid.

"Eager, my lady?" He sounded like a complete stranger. "Good. I've changed my mind. This time we shall play your game of erring by my rules. I think you will like them very much. They will be completely in keeping with your nature."

"Please, Edward," she whispered.

His fingers, winding into her unbound hair, were a shock. He twisted the hair and pulled her head back until tears of pain came to her eyes. He would not hear her cry. She held her teeth tightly together.

"You were very, very good, you know," he said, the instant before his mouth closed over hers. There

was rage in his kiss, possessive fire that he used like
a weapon. His lips forced hers wide open and then
her mouth was used by his tongue. He seemed bent
on a bitter and total possession.

He paused an instant, breathing heavily against
her cheek.

"What am I good at?" she dared to ask. Her
mouth felt bruised and swollen.

"Why, at acting the innocent, of course. At making me believe you a gentle thing to be cherished
and cared for. Do not whisper so softly. Show me
what you truly are."

"I don't understand you." The sudden firmness
of her own voice surprised Lindsay. Her legs shook,
but her jaw had grown rigid with her own kindled
anger.

"Don't you? I think you do. You acted your part
well. And you caught a fine fool to use for some
purpose I'm sure will eventually become clear."

"I caught—" His mouth on hers closed off the rest
of her protest. The weight of his big body pushed
Lindsay against what felt like more shelves. The
wood hurt her back.

These kisses of Edward's were unlike those she
had come to yearn for. These wounding kisses
grazed the tender skin on her lips, whipped her head
from side to side. And all the while one of his hands
remained tangled in her hair while the other covered
and kneaded her breast.

Once more he raised his face to breathe.

"I did not come to you begging marriage, my
lord," she gasped out. "It was you who insisted—
against my wishes."

"Silence!"

"I begged you not to persist in your suit."

"Be silent, I tell you."

"If you do not love me, why are you kissing me?"

He made a noise that reminded Lindsay of the
animals that sometimes howled in winter. "Love?"

His voice broke on a laugh. "There is no *love*, madam. Do not even let the word pass your sullied lips. Or any other word unless I ask you to speak."

Lindsay struggled, but Edward only gripped her tighter.

"Let me go." She made a grab for him, caught at his shirt and heard the fine linen tear. With all her strength, she twisted her body. "You're hurting me, I tell you. Let me go, now! Now!"

Again he used his mouth to silence her. And he ripped at the fragile lace wrapper.

Lindsay's last shreds of control snapped. "Don't." She bit down on his lip—and tasted blood.

His curse hissed through the close, dark space. The tearing of lace screamed in her ears.

She pummeled his head and shoulders with her small fists, and kicked, crying out against the agony of her bare toes meeting his unyielding legs.

Edward's response was to drive his thigh between hers, lifting her from the floor. He dragged her most sensitive parts along his stone-hard thigh, forcing the air from her lungs in a helpless rush.

The blackness in the dressing room became a blackness in her mind. She squeezed her eyes shut and saw blinding red behind her closed lids.

Lindsay fought.

Edward found her mouth again. And she bit him again, driving her teeth into his bottom lip until he jerked her away. His blood was warm on her tongue.

With a single sweep, he rent her wrapper and gown from neck to hem. She felt cool air slap her burning skin.

Edward's hand was instantly between her legs, his fingertips urgently probing the softness there. She felt her own moistness spring against his fingers. He was making her feel as he had done before! No! She would not allow him to make her feel so when he was hurting and abusing her.

A hot dart of sensation shot from the little spot he seemed to know so well.

"No! Stop it." She arched back, fumbling on the shelves for something to use against him. "Stop it, I tell you!"

His teeth, fastening on a nipple, brought a scream to her lips. She writhed. The heat grew. Burning, aching shards that speared through her body. He sucked, used his tongue to flip the bud of her nipple erect. Lindsay struggled afresh, straining to stop her mind from submitting totally to him. Her fingers closed on something cold—the stem of a metal goblet.

"This is what you like, then, my lady?" Edward licked the swollen flesh of her breast. "You like to fight. I am glad to oblige." He filled his mouth with as much of her other breast as he could pull in.

"Fight!" Lindsay brought her hand over her head, struck at him with the heavy goblet. "I'll fight you." The blow glanced off his shoulder.

Edward yelled. He grappled to find her wrist and shook the goblet from her grasp.

Then she fell, her heel caught in what tattered remnants of her gown still hung from her body. As she would have risen again, Edward pushed her down.

"I will fight you. I will fight you." Her words were panted on jarring sobs. But he held her on her knees and she felt him move above her, heard the unmistakable sounds of fabric scraping across skin.

He was undressing! In front of her! A beat in time in that sightless space and he shifted again, jerked her against him. "Show me your skills, madam *wife*. Vixen. Temptress. Do what you know so well how to do. What you have been taught and learned so very, very well."

"You are wicked, my lord," she whispered. "Enough of this wickedness."

"You threaten me, vixen?" He laughed, and with

both hands brought her face against that part of him that jutted and pulsed. "Now it's your turn to use your mouth, *my lady*."

It was the part of him she'd felt leap against her before. He could not mean . . . Lindsay grasped at his thighs. No, he could not.

"Come, come. Let us get this done." He spoke, she knew, through gritted teeth.

Lindsay screamed then, and clawed at him. She surged upward. And was as quickly tossed to her back on the jumble of what must be his clothes and the remnants of hers.

His hand covered her mouth. And his body covered hers. "That will be enough, madam. The servants may begin to concern themselves if our passion is too loudly abandoned. Spend yourself in your bodily efforts now, my little wild one."

She writhed. He was heavy and hot and hard . . . and so very different in feel from her own softly rounded body. Even as she struggled, some white searing hunger licked at her core. Half fear, half intense pleasure surged, stronger and stronger. His power was to be feared, but it also brought a kind of fierce wanting that forced her to arch up against him.

"Yes," he said against her neck. "Oh, yes, my delightful one. It is time." Holding her wrists above her head, he kissed her yet again, nuzzling, darting his face away as she made the move he must now recognize as an attempt to bite. "Amusing. Viciously amusing."

"I will amuse you," she whispered vehemently. "You shall remember this night."

His answer was to shift his firm mouth from her face to her neck. Sliding his tongue, working his body down, he brought his lips between her breasts, down her ribs to the dip in her belly and lower.

Lindsay's eyes flew open. She made to cry out,

but could not. She could not move. His tongue pressed into the soft hair between her legs and curled about that little nub he'd taught her could feel so . . .

"Aah!" She pulled uselessly against his trapping hands. "No!"

Edward made no reply. With his mouth and tongue he pushed and pressed and stroked, until Lindsay rolled her hips from side to side.

She panted, half crazed with desire, on the edge of some sensation she wanted desperately. "Edward!" Lindsay's hips jerked up, beyond any control of hers. "Please!"

"God, yes!"

The instant she thought this torrent of sensation would break, break gloriously, his mouth left her.

"Edward?"

"Yes, yes. You shall have what you want."

He pressed her wrists to the floor again and, where his mouth had been, she felt some stiff, foreign probing. Lindsay became completely still. Her heart bounded.

The probing went on. And Edward was moving over her, breathing against her ear. His skin, where his chest ground against her breasts, was slick and rough.

"*Yes.*" With one mighty rocking motion, he slid higher on top of her. And the rigid thing at the entrance to her body drove inside.

Lindsay convulsed under his weight and around the solid intrusion. A pain shot from that point, a burning pain, and the raw, hot sensation that her flesh was torn.

Her scream caught and died.

"Lindsay!" Edward's voice rose; different, desperate. "Lindsay! What in God's name? I can't stop now!" He surged once more and there was a burst of smooth wetness before he slumped onto her.

She drew in rasping little sobs.

"What in God's name have I done?" he cried. "Why? Why did you let me think . . . Oh, my God. No! No!"

Edward stumbled to his feet and threw open the door to his chamber. As rapidly as he dared, terrified he might hurt her more, he swept Lindsay up into his arms and carried her to his bed. Tossing back the covers, he set her gently down on the white sheets and covered her.

The water Stoddart had brought for Edward to wash was still warm. Quickly, he poured some into a bowl, picked up a cloth and brought them to his bedside.

Lindsay stared up at him, her great blue eyes like the night sky about a risen moon.

"Why did you tell me the child was yours?"

She stared at him silently.

Edward shook his head and moved the covers aside. Her lovely body filled him with awe—and with self-loathing. He had abused an innocent who had pleaded that innocence to his disbelieving ears. He was loathsome and undeserving of what she had offered him: trust.

The truth about the child must wait. She was too shocked now to explain, not that she owed him explanations after what he'd done to her.

He bathed her face carefully, and her neck and shoulders, her perfect breasts. With another soft cloth, he dried each inch of cleansed skin. And finally, he tried to ease her legs apart. She cried out and covered her face with her hands.

"It's all right, dear one. I only want to soothe you." She relaxed and he saw what his masculine pride had wrought. With fresh warm water, he washed away the telling traces of blood and held

the moist heat against her, willing away all traces
of the discomfort his violent possession had
caused.

When he had finished he covered her again.
"Sleep, sweet Lindsay. You have no more to fear."
He turned away.

"Don't leave me."

"What did you say?" He must have misheard her.

"Please don't go away. We have so much to learn
about each other, Edward. Is it permissible for you
to lie here with me?"

He returned to her side. She was doubtless delir-
ious from the strain to which he had subjected her.
"No one will harm you again."

"No." She shook her head and offered him her
hand. "What just happened? That is how women
come to have babies, isn't it?"

His stomach turned. "Don't think about those
things." *Fool.* He was a complete fool and he'd
thrown away a prize no man could hope to deserve.

"Hold me." She sounded drowsy.

Afraid that at any moment she would scream
again, he joined her under the covers. When she
turned against his chest, threading her arms around
his neck and resting her face against his throat, he
thought his heart might stop beating. Because of him
she was like a needy, hurting child.

Very gently, he smoothed her hair. "You are my
beloved one," he said quietly. "What has happened this night is unspeakable. And ultimately I
will be the one to reap the results of what I have
done."

In the next hours she slept fitfully, clinging to him
ever more tightly if he tried to leave the bed. At last
he was able to slip into her room and find a fresh
nightrail. She murmured and awoke when he pulled
it over her head, but promptly slept again once he'd
finished.

Dawn had crept into the sky before she com-

pletely stopped muttering and reaching for him. She
had fallen into a deep sleep from which he hoped
she would not awaken for many hours.

In those hours he would take the only course left
to him.

Chapter 23

The note was on the pillow, pinned there with an exquisite sapphire brooch of a design to match the ring Edward had given her before their marriage.

Lindsay had awakened reaching for him, and found the place beside her empty—except for the letter. The covers had been settled carefully over her and she soon realized that she wore a clean night-rail.

Then she remembered the previous night: the wildness turned to passion such as she'd never thought possible, the fury turned to gentle ministration that had filled her with both love and regret. She should have trusted Edward enough to tell him the truth. He would have to know now. There was no other way.

When she sat up, her body felt stiff and there were places where she expected to find bruises. But she wanted only to see Edward.

The room was warm. While she'd slept, the fire had been kept blazing and she perched on the edge of the bed whilst quickly unfastening the brooch.

She'd never seen Edward's writing before, but his name, written in a large, firm hand at the bottom of the paper, confirmed that he'd left the letter for her.

Lindsay held the brooch tightly in her palm and read:

Dearest Lindsay:

If there are words to express what I feel, I do not know them. I leave you as a desperate man aware that he deserves no peace.

Perhaps the day will come when we can at least be together as friends. I will pray for that. Meanwhile, dear wife, your every need will be met. You have only to say what will please you and it shall be yours. Your comfort will be my constant concern.

Please know that you have no further cause for fear. Unless summoned, I will never intrude upon you again. Mrs. Gilley will be waiting outside the chamber when you are ready for assistance. She is a good and discreet woman.

I am, my dearest lady, your champion and protector.

                              Affectionately,
                              Edward.

P.S. The matter of your tenants' hardships will be attended to. There will be no further need for you to risk your own safety in dealing with these issues.

Lindsay stared at the page until the words blurred. Then she folded the paper carefully and held it in her lap. What Edward had written touched her heart. He had come to her at Nanny Thomas's ready to be her "champion" only to be made to feel the fool. Yes, he touched her heart. *And he made her furious!*

"Men! If they could only learn to do what women do so well—*talk!*" She hugged the bedcovers around her. "Mrs. Gilley!"

The door opened almost immediately and that lady hurried into the room, her hair slightly awry but otherwise as immaculate as ever. "Oh, my lady. You are awake at last. How do you feel?"

Lindsay felt her skin turn red. Surely Edward had not . . . of course he hadn't told anyone exactly what had passed between them.

"Lord Hawkesly said you were not feeling well. He gave very strict instructions as to your care."

Lindsay found her voice. "I am perfectly well. Is Hawkesly at breakfast?"

Mrs. Gilley appeared astonished. "No, my lady." She went to open the draperies, letting in sunlight. "It is afternoon. Lord Hawkesly left for London early this morning."

Disregarding her scanty nightrail, Lindsay threw aside the covers and stood up. "He went to London?"

"Yes. He rode out when dawn was scarcely in the sky."

"The fool!" Lindsay paced. "Are all men crazed, Mrs. Gilley? Are they all complete rattles?"

Mrs. Gilley smiled faintly.

"Arrange a horse for me. At once. I'll follow my husband as soon as I can dress."

"Oh, oh, no."

"Oh, yes, Mrs. Gilley."

"No, my lady. Lord Hawkesly would never forgive us. A lady could never be allowed to *ride* to London."

"Hm. His lordship has had little difficulty dragging me all over—" She checked herself. "I'm going."

Mrs. Gilley straightened her back. "Not on horseback. If you insist upon going to London, a coach will be made ready."

Lindsay prepared to argue, until she met Mrs. Gilley's outraged stare. "Very well. Make a coach ready. But I will expect to leave before nightfall."

* * *

There had never been another moment such as this in Lindsay's life. Since her departure from Hawkesly Place days and nights had become all the same, all one. She had refused to stop, except to allow for changes of horses and for the coachmen and outriders to eat. Sleeping when even the jolting of the coach could no longer keep her awake had brought brief respites from continual practice of what it would soon be time to say aloud.

Standing at the top of the steps leading to the front door of Edward's Cavendish Square house, Lindsay was aware of the dusty, gold-trimmed Hawkesly barouche that waited in the street. Mrs. Gilley had tried her best to insist that a maid accompany Lindsay. Lindsay had prevailed and come alone. Now she almost wished she had brought a companion.

She rang the bell a second time. Surely *someone* was in.

At last the door was opened by Stoddart. Lindsay turned and waved the coachmen on to the stables.

"Lady Hawkesly," Stoddart said, sounding harried. "Thank goodness you have come."

In the rich hallway, Lindsay allowed the valet to take the hooded gray velvet mantle she had worn over a carriage dress of a slightly paler shade. Satin ribbon in deep orange circled the dress's high waistline and the frilled hem of a satin slip in the same color showed at the ankle.

Lindsay held her embroidered reticule in both hands. "Where is Garrity?" she asked, surprised to find Stoddart performing the butler's duties. "Is he ill?"

"Lord Hawkesly has requested that all members of the staff—except myself—remain in their quarters until further notice."

"I don't understand."

"Don't you?" He cleared his throat. "I mean, I'm

sure you'll be able to set things to rights, your ladyship.''

''Yes.'' Lindsay wasn't at all certain she knew what she was supposed to set to rights. ''Have some of the staff members annoyed his lordship?''

''No, my lady.''

''Then this is most odd. I take it you have been attending to meals?''

''If he's eaten a proper meal, it hasn't been here. And he hasn't left the house since he arrived from Devon.''

''Two days!''

''More like three. He must have ridden here like a madman.'' Stoddart put a finger to his lips and drew closer. ''He's in his study, my lady. Apart from a few hours in his bedchamber, he's been there almost all the while and something's troubling him very deeply. I know it's inappropriate for me to ask, but do you know what it could be? He needs help but I can't reach him.''

Lindsay poked at her hair, certain it must look a fright. ''You may leave Lord Hawkesly to me, thank you, Stoddart. In fact''—she gave the best confident smile she could muster—''I believe it would be a very good idea for you to take the rest of the day off.''

Rather than argue, Stoddart bowed shortly and left, muttering profuse thanks.

Lindsay had never seen Edward's study but easily discovered its location. Evidently he had a piano in the room; an unusual arrangement. Treading hesitantly past the dining room where she had sat at her own wedding breakfast, she followed the strains of a haunting piano piece to a room at the back of the house.

The door stood slightly open. Lindsay hovered awhile, listening. She'd only heard him play once before yet she knew it was Edward who drew such fluid beauty from the notes. She stepped just inside the room and saw him.

With his back to her, he sat on a long bench before
a piano of glistening rosewood. Devoid of a jacket
and wearing a full-sleeved shirt of the type he'd
worn when . . . Lindsay wondered at the surge of
passionate tenderness the sight of him invoked.

She stepped farther into the room. His black hair,
always unruly, was tousled as if repeatedly assaulted by those strong fingers she longed to touch
and be touched by again.

The music was unfamiliar. Edward's heavily muscled shoulders moved with the melody. Only one
lamp lighted the room and the fire had burned low.
Shadows crowded corners and all but hid the details
of a handsomely proportioned study.

She had to touch him.

Lindsay hurried across the carpet—until she arrived within a few steps of Edward. She saw the
sharp line of his jaw, his closed eyes, the downward
turn of his firm mouth.

On tiptoe, she reached him, turned and sat on the
end of the bench, facing away from the piano.

The music stopped.

"Play for me, Edward," she managed to whisper.

"Lindsay—"

"Please, play. It's so beautiful."

"You came."

"I had to."

"You could have sent a messenger with whatever
request you have."

"No messenger could have been trusted with the
message I have for you."

"Tell me."

"Play. *You* tell me. About the music."

"Sit closer."

Holding her elbows close to her body, Lindsay slid
until she sat with her shoulder touching his arm.

Edward began to play again. "Pachelbel," he said.
"His *Canon.*"

"I've never heard it before. It touches my heart."

"It was written for trumpet and strings."

"It's perfect on the piano."

"The melody is so simple."

"So haunting."

Edward took his hands from the keys and rested them in his lap. "You are haunting and perfect. You have touched my heart as I never thought possible. And I shall always regret my . . . my violence toward you."

Lindsay pressed her fingers to her cheeks. She leaned against Edward's shoulder. "You were angry. More than angry and I made you so. But, Edward, John is not my child."

Seconds passed before he gently stroked back her tumbled curls. "I know, sweet one. My dear untouched one."

"You knew when . . . when we . . ."

"Yes. These are things a mother should tell her daughter. In her stead, someone else should have given you instruction. Many men would not agree, but I believe it is criminal for a girl to go to her husband with absolutely no knowledge."

Lindsay smoothed her skirt. "What happened between us—that is the way babies are begun, isn't it? And you could tell that I had no experience?"

"I could tell. But"—he sighed unevenly—"such things should not be done in anger, Lindsay. That man you saw was not me, not truly me. If . . . There will never be such bitterness between us in the act again."

She wished he would do more than touch her hair. Instead, Edward returned his hand to his lap.

"I must tell you all the truth now, Edward. It's only right."

"Truth? You sound so concerned." He laughed. "What is the truth? That the child is one more of your causes? Truly, the Church lost a great boon when I snatched you from her. You would have served her well with endless acts of charity. But I am glad I married you first." She heard him swallow. "I hope I can dare to hope that you may become glad one day."

"I already am."

Edward turned on the bench and put his arm around her. He inclined his face to look at her. "I am afraid to press you for your meaning."

She smiled shyly. "Do not be. Edward, we have to talk about serious matters. And I do have a favor to ask of you. John is related to me. He is also related to Antun, although Antun does not know of John's existence and must not do so—not yet."

"Something tells me you've been about one of your harebrained schemes, madam wife."

"Harebrained, no." She shook her head. "I only wish it were all a game. John is my brother's son."

Edward's arm tightened about her.

Lindsay grew rigid. "I feared telling you. Tregonitha is not and should never be mine. But I have known since John's birth that it is my trust to preserve his rightful inheritance. Edward, Roger would do anything to gain ownership of the estate. *Anything.*"

He took her chin between finger and thumb and turned her face up to his. The feverishness in his black eyes disquieted her but she was not afraid of him.

"Tell me your story," he said. "Everything."

"My brother married in secret to Maria Pollack, Antun's sister. Our father and old Mr. Pollack were in the way of being enemies. Father considered Mr. Pollack a poacher of the lowest kind. Only Nanny Thomas and I knew of the marriage—until Maria became so ill when John was born. Granny Whalen came to try to help then, but it was too late. Maria died."

"Why didn't Antun know of his sister's marriage?"

"Because he would have been enraged at William's decision to keep the marriage a secret. And afterward, after Maria died, I could not tell him in case he revealed John's existence to Roger.''

She poured out the rest: the pledge made to Maria that John would be kept safe until he was of age to inherit, the night running to pay for a safe haven for Nanny and the boy, the story Antun had been told of Maria dying whilst in service in another county.

And, until she finished, Edward kept silent. Then he said: ''Why were you so certain Roger might harm John?''

There was more she must say before telling him the rest of the truth. ''Please will you help me to keep Roger appeased? Have you made the arrangements to pass Tregonitha to him?''

''No.''

She looked at him sharply. ''You must do so quickly. I beg of you. Any delay may cause events I cannot bear to think about.''

''What events?''

''I must keep you and John safe.''

Edward framed her face with his hands. ''Keep *me* safe?''

Lindsay twisted to wind her arms around his neck. ''William did not die in the battle. Roger had him murdered.''

''You know?'' He bowed his head. ''You know William was murdered?''

''Yes. And I fear Roger may try to kill you, too, if you don't give him what he wants. Oh, Edward, that is why I was so afraid when you wanted to marry me.''

''You were afraid for me,'' he said quietly. ''And you knew William had been murdered. All this time I thought I was the only one who deserved revenge.''

She threaded her fingers into his hair and tugged lightly until he looked at her. ''What are you talking about?''

"My brother, James, my older brother, he was killed by the same villain who took William's life. James had tried to intervene. A seaman by the name of Kertz came to tell me while I was still in the Indies."

Lindsay stared into Edward's eyes. "It was a man named Kertz who came to Maria and me with the news. He witnessed the horror."

"And you paid for the information?" Edward said.

Lindsay nodded.

"Yes." He smiled bleakly. "You will not concern yourself further with Roger Latchett. And do not fear for the child. He is safe."

"Tregonitha is not mine," Lindsay said tentatively. "I have no dowry."

Edward laughed, tilting back his head to show white teeth. "You have a dowry. You brought me yourself and that is all the dowry you will ever need."

His strong throat invited Lindsay's touch. She made herself look away and open her reticule. "The brooch you left for me is beautiful. As beautiful as the ring. I brought you a gift." She withdrew the gold man's watch that was her dearest possession and gave it to him. "This was William's. Antun heard about his death while he was in Plymouth talking to someone about fishing boats. He went to see what he could find out and brought this back. Will you accept it from me, please?"

Edward turned the well-worn gold over in his hand. On the back were the engraved initials W.B.G. "Thank you for wanting to give it to me," he said, slipping it into his pocket. "I will keep it until we can give it to John."

She had not been wrong in her very first assessment of him. Edward was a truly good and honorable man. Lindsay blinked away tears. "I would like to send word to Nanny Thomas and Granny Whalen that I am well and safe. I fear they may have been worried about me after we left them.''

''I fear they may indeed,'' Edward agreed with mirth in his voice. ''No doubt they think you are married to a monster.'' Edward was suddenly somber. ''I could not blame them for thinking so. Any more than I blame you, my dearest. I am still amazed that you decided to come to me.''

Men could be so obtuse.

''I'm afraid I may have terrorized the servants. I'll find someone to attend you. You must be exhausted after your journey.'' He stood up and offered Lindsay his hand. ''You'll need food and sleep.''

''Don't summon anyone,'' she told him, rising. ''I know the way upstairs and I'm not hungry.''

Edward stood over her. Surrounding hers, his hand was warm and firm. Wordlessly, he led her into the hall and to the foot of the staircase.

''I think you will find everything you need,'' he said. ''Please . . . please do not be afraid in any way. I will remain in my study.''

Rather than allowing him to relinquish her hand, Lindsay deliberately entwined their fingers. She climbed a stair and looked back. ''I'm not sure I do remember the way,'' she said, and held her bottom lip in her teeth.

Edward frowned. ''You'd like me to call for a maid?''

''No.'' She shook her head emphatically.

He continued to frown.

''Show me the way, Edward.''

Chapter 24

He stepped slowly up beside her. Lindsay climbed another stair—and Edward joined her. Then he moved ahead, leading, smiling back at her.

At the door to her chamber, he paused. "So much has happened since I first brought you here, yet it was not long ago."

"It seems a lifetime to me," she told him.

"The fire is alight," he said. For the first time she saw in him some unease. "It has been kept burning because . . . In case . . ."

"In case I came home to you?"

His smile drove the deep dimples beneath his cheekbones. "I am discovered," he said. When Edward smiled he was, at the same time, boyish and so seductively handsome that Lindsay's hand found its own way to her breast, and her madly beating heart.

"I admit to being a little tired," she said.

"Then you must sleep." He took a step backwards.

"I don't think I could sleep if I was left alone." She lowered her lashes and felt her cheeks turn red. "But perhaps if you would stay with me I would eventually rest." He might think her very forward but, after all, they were husband and wife.

Without a word, Edward ushered her into her

chamber. It appeared almost as she had left it, except for the absence of the beautiful wedding gown she'd thrown across a chair. The nightrail intended for her wedding night still lay on the bed.

"I'll await you in your sitting room," Edward said. "If you like, you can call me when you're ready and I'll sit in here. Lindsay, is it because of what I did that you're afraid to sleep?"

"No."

A deep breath expanded his chest. The buff-colored trousers he wore fitted his powerful legs tightly. They left no need for imagination as to the shape and size of every part of him. Lindsay had to look away.

Edward turned away, too. He went into the little sitting room and Lindsay heard the creak of a chair as he sat down.

She set aside her reticule and went to the dressing table. Sitting before the mirror, she let down her hair.

The chair creaked again.

"Edward."

"Yes?" he called.

"Could you come, please?"

She watched in the mirror as he came from the sitting room and crossed to stand behind her. "I find I am more tired than I thought. Would I be keeping you from more important matters if I asked your help in preparing for bed?"

In the mirror, his dark eyes settled on hers. "There are no matters more important to me than you, my lady." He selected a silver-backed brush from the dressing table.

He passed a hand beneath her hair, his knuckles grazing the back of Lindsay's neck. She closed her eyes. At first he wielded the brush tentatively, as if afraid of catching snarls. Gradually he gained confidence, lifting heavy locks to brush each length with long, smooth strokes.

And with every move, his fingers found some new, tingling spot of skin to tease.

"Your hair has always reminded me of polished silver," he said, low and soft. "It shines in the firelight like silver satin."

He attended to the curls that fell about her shoulders, and found fresh skin pulsing, awaiting his touch. Then he stood close and eased her back against him.

Lindsay's eyes flew open. He was smiling at her, smoothing the contours of her cheeks with the backs of his fingers. "I think, my lady, that you ought perhaps to have me leave you now."

"Why?" She covered one of his hands against her face. "I do not want you to go."

"I am . . . I am a man, Lindsay. And you are a beautiful, desirable woman. And we are alone."

"And I am your wife," she reminded him.

Edward bent and found the lobe of her ear with his teeth. "Yes, you are my wife." Next he flicked his tongue into her ear in a way that brought a shocking, aching weight to her thighs.

"Did I ever tell you," he whispered, "that you have a voice made to drive men mad?"

She bent her neck, offering him easier access. "You may have said something like that." She shivered.

"Are you cold?" he asked, his breath warm.

"I don't think so."

"Shall I finish brushing your hair?"

She nodded.

With every stroke of the brush, the fine strands of Lindsay's hair sprayed up. Edward stroked them down, stroked them over her back, her shoulders and, finally, the swelling tops of her breasts.

Lindsay ran her tongue over her lips, and in the mirror she saw Edward study her mouth. His fingers stayed where they were, spread, lightly pressing her breasts through the veil of her hair. Lindsay

put her hands over his, moved them, sighed at the
sensations that wound through her. Anxious to feel
him touch her, really touch her, she brushed aside
her hair. Edward bent over her once more, kissed
her neck, her shoulder, the full rise of one breast.

"Edward," she breathed. *"Edward."*

"Yes, my dear one." His kisses continued until
his lips and tongue found the very edge of her neckline.

Lindsay shifted restlessly. He had only to . . .
"Aah." As if he heard her thoughts, the cries of her
body, Edward sent his tongue beneath the edge of
her dress to caress a nipple with rough, sweet force.

Deep in her belly, in her legs, a liquid weakness
spread, hot and heavy.

Edward supported her breasts, used his thumbs
to pull her briefly cut bodice below her nipples. "My
God," he whispered. "Lindsay, you are so fair."

She closed her eyes again.

"No," he said, his voice harsh. "Watch, sweeting. Learn. About yourself and me. You are a very
passionate woman."

Obediently she looked in the mirror at her own
white flesh tipped by stiff pink buds and drawn up
like an offering by Edward's tanned hands. The feelings that raced along her limbs made her almost
faint. Edward's eyes glittered and he passed his fingers back and forth, back and forth, until Lindsay
tried, ineffectually, to grasp his wrists. He laughed,
caught her hands and held them beneath his own
on her straining flesh.

"Perhaps I should help you undress." His smile
was broad and wonderfully wicked. "You will want
to wear that delightful confection on the bed—
eventually."

A pulse began to throb. It pounded all over her
body. They would do again what they had done the
other night. Lindsay quelled a rush of fear. There
had been pain.

"What is it, Lindsay?" He was watching her face. "You're frightened, aren't you?"

She shook her head. Then nodded.

Edward left his place behind her. He pulled out the stool where Lindsay sat and knelt before her. "You have nothing to fear. Trust me."

"I trust you," she said, willing her smile to convince him.

Reaching around her, Edward deftly undid the row of small buttons that closed the back of her dress. He slipped it from her shoulders, removed her arms from the sleeves and pulled the garment beneath her. Lindsay lifted her feet and Edward tossed the dress aside.

She sat, clad only in a flimsy, white lawn chemise trimmed with clusters of tiny embroidered silver flowers, and lacy white stockings decorated at the ankles with matching flowers.

Edward gathered her to him, cradled her face against his shoulder. "I will never hurt you again, Lindsay," he said. "And I'll never allow anyone else to hurt you." While he spoke, he pushed up the chemise, smoothed fine cotton over the silken stockings. The fabric swished. Lindsay clung to him, trembling, and dared to put her hand inside his shirt. She couldn't feel enough of him. Fumbling, she undid the buttons and pulled the shirt free of his trousers. Muscles in his shoulders flexed beneath her hands.

Lindsay held Edward's face to her breasts. He kissed her softness, murmured, trailed his tongue. And his firm touch found the inside of her knee, the inside of her thigh.

Edward raised his head and kissed Lindsay's mouth, a strong, deep kiss that tipped back her head. He looked at her and smiled. "Remember the lesson?" When she nodded, he said: "Now it's time for more of the lesson. Put your tongue inside my mouth. Reach for me, Lindsay."

She did as he asked, and while she did, he bunched
the chemise around her hips. Never taking his lips
from hers, Edward began to wriggle the stockings
down her legs. He sucked her bottom lip gently between his teeth—and pulled off one stocking; nuzzled
up her chin—and pulled off the other stocking. The
next kiss was placed over a seared nipple—and Edward delved between Lindsay's legs, into soft, moist
folds that quickened at his touch.

"You are ready for me, my love." The chemise
fell about her waist and Edward explored her naked
breasts like a starving man finally about to be sated.
"Almost ready." Firmly, he opened her legs and
dropped his kisses to the part of her that leaped at
his every brushing stroke. With demanding darts his
tongue curved around the deliciously aching nubbin
he had the power to entice to ecstasy. Lindsay's hips
slid forward on the stool. He grasped her bottom,
licking at her until she cried out. The world became
a dark, boiling place and Lindsay threw herself over
Edward's back, drove her fingers into his unyielding
buttocks while waves of exquisite agony rocked her.

"Edward!" She felt strong enough to shout and
laugh, yet, at the same time, so deeply vulnerable.
"Edward, I want . . ." What did she want? "I want
to hold you."

Gripping her hips, he sat back on his heels and
looked up at her. In the stark lines of his face she
saw a mirror of the joy she felt, and something else,
some question.

"Edward, tell me," she said simply. There was so
much she didn't understand.

"Tell you?" He stood and pulled her to her feet.
"What should I tell you, sprite? That you are the
best part of me? That what I never thought possible
is true? And I know it because you have shown it
to me?"

"You speak in riddles." She stood before him,
naked, but unashamed, aware that he studied her

body, a small smile hovering about his mouth. "I want to know what I've shown you. You've done everything and I feel so wonderful. Do you feel wonderful? Is that what you're telling me?"

"I feel wonderful. But I shall soon feel more wonderful. I want to take you to my bed, Lindsay. Do you understand?"

She shook her head.

Edward raised his chin. "How could you?"

"I expect you still have a great deal to teach me."

"And there is no need to teach it all at once," he said.

Lindsay breathed deeply. The part between her legs throbbed and there was a shivery, bright feeling low inside her. "I do think there is more I need to know right now, Edward."

He had begun to stroke her—everywhere. Fleeting, gently insistent grazing over places still exquisitely sensitive from what he had already given. "What do you think you need to know right now, Lindsay?"

She moved close and he slipped his hands around her waist. He rubbed his thumbs over the small dips at the base of her spine and Lindsay squealed. "Edward, I think I need to know why I still feel there is more I want to do . . . with you . . . now. It isn't that what you did already wasn't absolutely wonderful. It was. And I hope you'll decide to do it again—when you feel like it, of course. But still there is this sensation that there might be . . . Edward—oh, Edward."

"Hush." He silenced her with a sound kiss that made her mind whirl. "Sometimes you talk too much. Tell me, in a very few words, about this sensation."

She was naked and he still wore his clothes. Lindsay reached up and pushed his shirt from his shoulders. Feeling very bold, she pulled it down his arms, smiling at him from beneath lowered lashes as he offered her first one hand, and then the other, to allow her to pull the garment completely off.

"Tell me about the sensation, Lindsay."

She kissed his chest, rested her cheek on springy black hair, concentrated on an experimental stroking of her own over his flat nipples.

Edward drew in a sharp breath. "Madam wife! I asked you a question. Much more of your wanton behavior and I fear I'll be beyond awaiting an answer."

She kissed a nipple and Edward promptly flattened her against him, trapping her arms between them. "I think there is something more I want to do. In fact I'm sure there is," she said in a rush. "It's probably something like the thing in the closet—only—only— Will it hurt again?"

Edward made a sound that was mostly growl and swept her up into his arms. "You, my dear one, show signs of learning much too quickly. And of being much too inquisitive. Now you will leave matters to me."

He strode with her through the sitting room, threw open a door on the other side and closed them into another bedchamber.

"Oh," was all Lindsay could say. The room was large and quite strange. But opulent.

Edward bent to brush his lips along her cheek. "Oh? Is that what you think of my bedchamber? Simply oh?"

"It's beautiful. Are all these things from the East somewhere?" she asked of black-lacquered chests set with boldly jewel-eyed creatures, of gilt-and-red tables with legs that ended at clawed feet, of a huge bed with no canopy and covered with a black counterpane and a heaping of brilliantly colored and tasseled pillows.

"Yes. Do you like them? Or should we return to your chamber?"

A delicious shudder passed through Lindsay. "I

think I like it here.'' Velvet draperies, black and red, were looped back from deep casement windows with gold satin ropes.

Edward laughed. It was the wicked laugh she was coming to enjoy in a way that made her wonder if she were two people in one, the second having been hidden until Edward arrived to set her free.

''I'm glad you like it here,'' he said, tossing her on the counterpane and smiling down at her. While she waited, balanced on her elbows, he pulled off his boots. ''I like it here, too, Lindsay. Particularly with you lying on my bed looking as you do now.''

Lindsay glanced down at herself and blushed. Unconsciously, she had stretched out a leg and curled the other beneath her. The hair Edward had so carefully brushed tumbled over her breasts but did not hide the fact that they were flushed and showed the effects of having been thoroughly kissed. *Kissed—there.* She wiggled and felt Edward stop moving. He'd stopped, because he was watching her. He'd kissed her breasts and every other bit of her and she . . . She wanted him to do it all again and more.

Now Edward was taking off his trousers.

Lindsay watched. The dark hair on his chest continued over his flat stomach and downward. She rested back on the pillows and passed her tongue over her lips. For an instant she let her eyes close. That part of him she'd known only in darkness had sprung free of his trousers, vigorous and . . . ''Oh.'' She wanted to watch and did so, her heart pounding.

When he'd thrown aside the last of his clothes, Edward stood, hands on hips, regarding Lindsay. ''You are not, I think, typical, my loved one. But I would not have you any other way.''

''There is something I'm not doing correctly?'' Lindsay frowned and made to sit up.

Edward, coming down on top of her, thwarted her efforts. ''You are doing *everything* correctly. And now it is my job to instruct you in a few more details."

His hand between her legs startled her, but she tried to relax and await that wonderful sensation he'd caused before. "I do like it when you do that, Edward," she told him.

"I know you do." His mouth closed off any reply she might have made and he moved over her, worked with his hands, his mouth, his tongue, the weight of his legs, to bring her to the brink of what she knew she wanted, again and again.

Then he stopped.

Lindsay's eyes opened wide. "Edward?"

"This is the next step of your lesson." His voice sounded funny. Lindsay couldn't think properly. She raised her hips from the bed, mutely begging him to finish what he had begun.

Edward slipped his hands beneath her. His eyes glowed and he pulled his lips back from his teeth. "This will hurt, but only a little this time." He rolled himself between her legs and pushed up her knees. "This is what you wanted, Lindsay. This is what you need to make you feel complete. It's what I need."

She grabbed for his shoulders and opened her mouth to cry out. The hardness was at the opening to her body again, then sliding, pushing, forcing inside. Her cry became a moan, low in her throat and she closed her eyes.

"Are you all right, Lindsay? My love, please—" He broke off and began to move within her, to glide deeper and withdraw slightly, only to thrust farther. "Lindsay?" His voice rose.

"Wonderful," was the one word she could form. His skin was hot and slick to the touch. Muscle and sinew rippled. Lindsay wrapped her legs around his waist. Sensations—burning, aching, searing sensations—darted from his flesh to hers. "One," she managed to gasp. *"One!"*

His mouth opened on hers and his driving rhythm jarred every nerve. "Aah," he groaned, surging into her one last time. "One?" he panted, dropping to bury his face in her neck. "You mean one with me?"

"Yes," she whispered before she cried out again. He was still inside her and there was tightening about him that closed her eyes and mouth and sent her fingernails into his shoulders.

"My God," Edward said. "Thank you."

A final burst of raw heat sailed into Lindsay, ebbed and left her weak and clinging. She turned her face aside and pushed her fingers into Edward's hair. She held his head against her throat. "Why do you thank me?"

He rolled slowly to his side and drew her against the length of him. "I thank you for showing me there is love."

Lindsay drew back to see his face. Tousled hair clung damply to his brow, his eyes were gentle now, soft as a summer's moonless night sky is soft. She studied his full mouth and decided that, like hers, it bore some signs of having kissed and been kissed. "I've always known there is love," she told him gently. "But I'm glad I could teach you something."

He sighed and pushed her to her back. "You've taught me a great deal. I love you, my lady."

Tears crowded Lindsay's eyes. She swallowed and laughed. "And I love you."

"I came for you in Cornwall to use a marriage to gain vengeance. You do know that?"

"Yes, Edward. As soon as you explained about your brother, I knew."

"And you aren't angry with me?"

"I love you. And you love me. There can be no anger between us."

"No." He settled beside her. "No anger. Only love."

A soft tap at the door might as well have been a pistol shot. Edward jerked up. "What is it?"

"Stoddart, my lord," came the tentative response. "I thought I should bring you a message."

"Tell it to me," Edward said in something very like a snarl.

"Yes, my lord. A man was here. A rough person who said his name is Kertz. He said you would know him."

Lindsay sat up and found Edward's hand. "Ask—"

Edward's fingers, gently pressed to her lips, silenced her. "What did he say?"

A scuffling sounded. "He said he has information you will want to hear," Stoddart said as if reciting a poem. "You are to meet him at six in the evening on the day after tomorrow. Someone will come and take you to him . . ."

"Go on!"

"He said there is new evidence that will be worth a great deal and you should bring, ah, funds. He said that if you do not do as he asks . . ."

"Finish, man!"

"He said that you must do what he asks or . . . or someone you love may die."

Chapter 25

❧❧

"If Lord Hawkesly says it will be all right, then, of course, it will be all right." Sarah Winslow blew upward at the dainty black curls framing her hairline. "I do believe Lord Hawkesly is the second most handsome man I've ever met." She reclined on a green brocade chaise in the drawing room of the Cavendish Square house.

Lindsay continued to trail around and around a mahogany-topped gaming table with legs painted gold and balanced on feet shaped like the Sphinx. She wanted Edward to come home—*now*.

Sarah put down the novel she'd been pretending to read. "Lindsay! Did you hear me?"

"Mmm. Who is the most handsome man you've ever met?" Despite her own anxiety, she watched Sarah's reaction with amusement.

"I shall not tell you," Sarah said, sniffing. Her thick black lashes lowered to hide her eyes. "But you need not fear. Lord Hawkesly is *almost* as handsome. And you should believe what he tells you."

"I'm trying," Lindsay said. "But he should not have gone alone."

"Gone where alone?" Sarah examined painted flowers on her fan with apparent preoccupation.

"You know I am not at liberty to tell you," Lindsay said. "And you promised you wouldn't pry."

''So I did. However, when a girl is rushed from
her bed to *distract* her best friend for a few hours . . .
Distract, Lindsay. That was Lord Hawkesly's footman's word to the countess's butler, not an invention
of mine. And then I was told by Lord Hawkesly himself that he was concerned about your state of mind
whilst he was gone. So, naturally, I do *wonder* what's
going on.''

''I don't know,'' Lindsay said, not exactly telling
an untruth. ''And if you're supposed to be quieting
my nerves then I suggest we don't continue to discuss the matter.''

''As you wish.'' Sarah settled her hands in her
lap. In a gown of honey-colored muslin decorated
with embroidered knots of seed pearls, she was
stunning.

''You look radiant,'' Lindsay said thoughtfully.

''Thank you.''

''I hardly think four in the afternoon could be
termed *rushing* from one's bed, Sarah. Perhaps you
were out especially late last night?''

''I'm enjoying the Season,'' Sarah said with hauteur. ''The countess has insisted that I go about a
bit. After all, I am already in London and you may
yet need me as a companion from time to time.''

Lindsay forbore to mention that she was now
married and, except for today's unusual circum-
stance, very unlikely to need a companion. ''I believe Edward and I shall have a small dinner party
whilst we're still in Town,'' she said, suddenly inspired. ''We'll have Aunt Ballard bring you. And
Lady Sebbel and Isabelle must come. And of course,
Mr. Lloyd-Preston.''

Sarah clapped her hands together. ''Oh, how
lovely. I know the countess will be delighted for us
to come. And I know Julian will . . .''

Sarah blushed so beautifully that Lindsay laughed
aloud. As quickly, her laughter faded. Edward was
somewhere meeting the man Kertz. And he had re-

fused to say if he'd discovered where the meeting was to be or who was to be his guide. He'd left at six, as ordered. That had been almost an hour since. She was very afraid for her husband's safety.

"Lindsay," Sarah said in the vaguely wheedling tone Lindsay knew very well. "Lindsay, is it . . . is it *pleasant* being married?"

I believe it is criminal for a girl to go to her husband with absolutely no knowledge. Edward had been quite correct. He was correct in so many things. "Yes, Sarah, it is pleasant. Very pleasant." Sarah was also without mature feminine influence but Lindsay didn't feel adequate to address such a delicate subject as married life, not quite yet.

"You seem most involved with your Lord Hawkesly," Sarah noted. "The two of you together seem entirely involved, in fact."

Lindsay crossed her arms and thought of Edward's arms, closed around her, in the private haven of his bed. "Married life can be quite marvelous," she said, unable not to smile. They had scarcely been out of the haven of Edward's bed for the past two days and nights. Lindsay had yet to sleep in her own new chamber and Edward had announced that he had no intention of allowing her to do so.

The drawing room door swept open to admit Garrity, who still showed signs of reproach for having been banished from his duties for several days.

"There is a . . . *gentleman* to see you, my lady," he told Lindsay. "He says you know him. A Mr. Antun Pollack?"

Lindsay looked from Garrity to Sarah and back again. "Antun? Show him in at once. At *once*, Garrity."

Already on her feet, Sarah rushed to Lindsay's side in time to greet Antun. "Antun Pollack! How wonderful! Lindsay, isn't it wonderful to see Antun?"

"Yes, of course." But Lindsay was looking into gray eyes she knew as well as any feature on her own face and she saw nothing resembling pleasure or tranquility. "What brings you to London, Antun?"

His big body filled out a well-cut blue coat and buff-colored doeskin pantaloons. He had attempted, unsuccessfully, to tame his unruly red hair with the result that it curled even more ferociously than usual.

"Antun?" Lindsay prompted. The beginnings of real trepidation were growing stronger by the second.

He inclined his head significantly toward Garrity, who raised a questioning brow at Lindsay. "I'll ring if we need anything," she told him, and he withdrew.

Immediately, Sarah ran to clasp Antun's hand and pull him to the center of the room. "What news from home?" She bounced at his side. "Have you seen my father?"

"Not recently," he said. "Me not being a man to attend services."

Lindsay decided he sounded surly—which didn't bode well. "Are you in London on business?" she asked him, noticing how he held his lips together and darted glances at Sarah.

"Aye. You might say that." He looked at Sarah again and seemed to make up his mind about something. "I've a desperate message to give you, Linny. I'd thought to find you alone."

"Anything you can say to Lindsay you can say to me." Sarah pouted. "We don't have any secrets."

Lindsay met Antun's eyes again. How very many secrets she had kept from both of these special friends. She reminded herself that she had done so from necessity.

"Linny, I need you to come with me."

"Come? Where? I must wait here—" She paused.

Edward had said she must give absolutely no indication of the true nature of their problems to anyone.

Antun turned and took both of Sarah's hands in his. "Sarah, help me. You know I wouldn't do anything that wasn't in Lindsay's best interests?"

She nodded.

"Tell Lindsay to trust me and do as I say. There's no time to waste. We've got to leave."

Sarah nodded again. All color had drained from her face. "I believe you," she whispered. "Lindsay, something's wrong. I can feel it. Do what Antun asks."

"Edward said I'm to remain here," Lindsay said stubbornly. "I cannot leave."

Antun shook his head and some inner pain etched the lines of his face deeper. "Sarah, you'll say nothing of this? You'll wait here until we return? And you won't alert any suspicion?"

"Yes."

"Very well. Lindsay, I came as quickly as I could. A man whose name is known to you and Edward has set out on an evil mission."

Lindsay pressed her palms together. "Roger?" she whispered.

"No." Antun frowned. "Lindsay, the man's name is Kertz. It was Edward who sent me. I'm to take you to him."

The boy slipped ahead of Edward like a flurry of dirty rags. Through alleys and lanes, in the deepening darkness, the small figure dashed on without stopping to ensure his man continued to follow. Appearing when Edward had left Cavendish Square on the dot of six, the urchin had rushed up and whispered urgently: "Follow me, the gent says." No more. And for close to two hours Edward had followed.

"Hold up," he called.

The boy hesitated, but scurried away when Edward made a move to get closer. The first part of the trek had taken him to an abandoned storehouse on Upper Thames Street. After an hour of waiting—the boy in one corner of a barnlike room, Edward in another, the child had fled again as if receiving some signal Edward could not hear.

"Hold up, I say," Edward shouted. "I won't come near you."

"Watcha want?" The boy hovered in the curved entrance to a big drainage pipe. "The gent'll be waiting'."

"Why have we taken this route?" Edward asked. "Where exactly are we going?"

"I'm only doin' what 'e says. Through 'ere now."

Edward considered turning back. He could smell the river and knew the stone-faced pipe must lead there. At this time of night the river was no place to be—unless one was a rat.

Damn it all. He couldn't risk *not* going on.

His guide dodged through inches of slime on the bottom of the pipe and Edward followed, his stomach clenching at the stench.

Then there was at least some measure of fresh air again. But they had emerged onto the towpath beside the Thames and a bevy of new scents assailed the nostrils. Grateful for his hardy boots, Edward strode in the boy's wake, trying not to breathe the river's aromas too deeply. Tar, rotten fruit and vegetables, rank fish carcasses and other even less tolerable waste from the overcrowded slums of the city formed the sickeningly pungent sludge that sucked at the river's muddy banks.

Through the gloom, Edward made out a structure spanning the river. "Is that Black Friars Bridge?"

The boy made no answer.

Edward oriented himself. If he was correct, New Bridge Street lay slightly ahead and to his right. They were definitely coming to Black Friars.

"Over 'ere, your *lordship.*"

Edward stopped. This new voice came from some- where close by. "Over where?"

A hand closed on his arm and pulled him into even deeper shadows. When he glanced back, there was no sign of the boy.

"Bring the money, did you?"

Edward rested his hand on the pistol he'd pushed into the waist of his pantaloons beneath his cloak. "Perhaps I've brought money. Perhaps I haven't." He backed against a wall and braced his weight on his toes.

The other man came nearer. "And perhaps you'd better 'ave. If you want to get out of 'ere alive."

"Tell me your name," Edward said. He was fa- miliar with another scent that came to him: Fear. This man was afraid.

"You know me name."

"Tell it to me."

"Give me the money."

"Tell me your name."

"Kertz," the man said. Spittle hit Edward's face. "Now. Give it to me."

"You give me something of worth and I'll pay for it," Edward said.

Silence folded around them. Edward willed him- self not to speak. Playing on the other man's uncer- tainty could only be an advantage.

"I didn't ask for enough when I came to yer the first time," Kertz whined. 'I'm only askin' for me due."

"Are you telling me you have no new information to sell?" Without awaiting a response, Edward stalked off and set out toward the bridge and wel- come glimmerings of lantern light.

" 'Ere! You wait!" Kertz caught up. "I've got news for yer. 'Ave a bit of patience."

Edward saw the other man now. He hadn't im- proved in the months since they'd last met. If anything, Kertz had grown even more emaciated, his hair even more gray, his clothing and person filthier. "Give me your information and let's complete this transaction. I'm a busy man."

"Er, yes. 'Course you are, my lord. It was your brother what told me to come to you."

Edward took a deep, angry breath. "So you told me."

"And 'e said as how the other man what was wounded told about Roger Latchett wantin' what was 'is."

Edward grabbed a handful of cloth at Kertz's neck. "You are wasting my time. I have already paid for this information."

"Your brother got 'is because he interfered." Kertz's voice rose.

"Damn you." Edward shoved Kertz away."My wife will be worried out of her mind by now and for nothing."

"I'm sure there's something I can remember that'd be worth something." A break in Kertz's voice suggested he was close to tears.

Edward drew back his lips in disgust. He pulled out his watch and peered at the time. "You said we were to meet at six. It's now close to nine. And you've brought me here on a fool's errand. I ought to—"

"Where'd you get that?"

"I beg your pardon?"

"That." Kertz grabbed at Edward's hand. "The watch. Where'd you get it?"

Only this afternoon Edward had decided to wear the watch Lindsay had given him. With grimy fingers, Kertz turned the golden timepiece in Edward's palm—and instantly pulled back as if burned.

"What is it, man? What's the matter now?"

"The watch. Where'd you get it? Tell me. Did 'e come to you? The one?"

"Damn it to hell. What *one*? What is all this non-sense? The watch was a gift."

Kertz gave a snorting laugh as he backed farther away. "A gift from the devil. I know who had that watch last."

"It belonged to William Granville. The man my brother died trying to save."

"You're right." Kertz half turned away. "And it was taken from Granville's body by the man what killed 'im."

Edward advanced. "No." He thought frantically. "You must be wrong."

"I ain't wrong. I saw the cove what did the killing. And I saw 'im take that watch from Granville. I never knew 'is name, but I'd know 'is face if I saw it." Kertz broke into a shuffling run and called over his shoulder: "Big 'e was. He 'ad eyes like the blade of a knife—gray ice they was—and the reddest hair I ever seen."

Chapter 26

‹‹ **G** arrity!'' Edward flung coins at the hackney driver, tore up the front steps and into the house. ''Garrity! Where the hell are you, man?''

The butler appeared at a rapid trot. ''My lord?''

Edward pulled off his gloves and cloak and thrust them at Garrity. ''I've business in Cornwall,'' he told the startled man. ''Lady Hawkesly will remain here. And *no one*—mark what I say—*no one* is to be allowed admittance here without Mr. Lloyd-Preston's express approval.''

''My lord—''

''That reminds me. Send a footman to Mr. Lloyd-Preston's lodgings and ask him to come here directly.''

''My lord—''

''Is Lady Hawkesly still in the drawing room?''

''My lord—''

''*What* is it, man? Can't you see I've no time to waste?''

''Mr. Lloyd-Preston is already in the drawing room, my lord.''

''Ah.'' Running a hand through his disheveled hair, Edward sidestepped the butler and approached the drawing room. ''Might have known Julian would be here by now.'' He didn't add that

Julian appeared to be drawn to Miss Winslow like a
drunken moth to a particularly intoxicating flame.

The gentleman in question chose that moment to
appear in the hall. "There you are, Edward," Julian
said. "We were hoping all the commotion was you."

Edward brushed past and into the drawing room.
"Where's Lindsay?" Miss Winslow stood beside the
gaming table looking, Edward thought, a trifle pink.
He cleared his throat and heard Julian enter the room
behind him. "How are you, Miss Winslow? It was
good of you to agree to come over and sit with Lindsay." And it was inventive of her to use the visit as
an excuse to spend time alone with Julian. No doubt
Lindsay, ever the romantic, had discovered something she *had* to do elsewhere in the house.

"I stopped to pay my respects to the countess,"
Julian said. "She told me Sarah—Miss Winslow—
had been summoned here to attend Lindsay so I
thought I'd drop in and make sure all's well."

"All's perfectly well." Edward lied for Sarah
Winslow's benefit. As soon as she was dispatched
to Bryanston Square he'd tell Julian what must be
done. "I had a little business to take care of and I
thought it might be nice if Miss Winslow and Lindsay spent some time together."

His deliberately engaging smile at Miss Winslow
brought no more than a pained twitch of the lips.
She appeared anxious to watch the door behind him.

Edward turned to look at Julian . . . who also
spared glances in the direction of the door. "Julian,
I wonder if I could prevail upon you to escort Miss
Winslow home." He raised a brow significantly.
"And then to return here immediately. I have a fa-
vor to ask of you."

Julian neither moved nor answered.

Damn it all. Just because he'd caught the two of
them together without a chaperon they were behaving like naughty children. Miss Winslow's behavior

could be excused. Julian was hardly a blushing choirboy.

Suddenly he knew how he could loosen their tongues. "Look, this is dashed awkward, but I've a need to clear up a few things in Cornwall. Lindsay isn't going to appreciate my leaving her again so soon." He avoided meeting Julian's eye. "Perhaps you could also be of assistance here, Miss Winslow. If you and Julian could keep Lindsay amused for a few days I'd be much obliged." Amused and safe. He could not banish this sense of impending danger.

Damn, but these mute responses were beginning to anger him. "May I rely upon you in this matter, Miss Winslow?"

"Lindsay . . ." The girl's high color had drained. "I'd be happy to stay with Lindsay. . . . Um, where is she, Lord Hawkesly? Did she retire?"

Edward drew an exasperated breath. "Retire? If that had been her intention she'd have told you as much. I'll have Garrity ask her to join us."

He approached the bell cord, but Julian blocked his path. "Edward, Sarah meant that she wondered if Lindsay retired as soon as she came into the house."

Edward stared, bewildered. "Came into the house?"

"Just now. With you."

He threw up his hands. "Will one of you tell me what you're talking about?"

"Antun Pollack came," Sarah said, sounding breathless.

Muscles in Edward's legs locked. "Here? Pollack? When, for God's sake?" His heart began to pound.

"Not long after you'd left evidently," Julian said, smiling reassuringly at Miss Winslow. "Sarah tells me he seemed somewhat disturbed."

Edward started for the door. "How long ago did he leave? Did he say where he was headed? Perhaps

I can get to him without going all the way to Cornwall.''

"Edward—"

"I must see Lindsay."

Julian's hand shot out to clutch Edward's sleeve. "Evidently Pollack arrived here shortly after you left. He stayed but a few minutes."

"Did he say where he was going?"

"My God," Julian muttered almost inaudibly. "Something's very wrong here. Edward, did you send a message with Pollack asking that Lindsay go with him?"

"No!" Edward faced Julian and held his shoulders. "Why do you ask?"

"Because he came here and persuaded Lindsay to leave with him. He said you'd told him to take her to you."

Edward reeled. He felt as if he'd received a physical blow. "Julian . . . Gad! Julian, tonight I was drawn out to some hellhole by that man Kertz." He no longer cared what Sarah Winslow heard.

"The seaman?"

"The same. I happened to use this"—he produced William Granville's watch—"and Kertz behaved as if he'd seen a ghost. He said the man who killed James took this from William Granville's body. That man had bright red hair and gray eyes."

Sarah let out a startled cry. Edward bowed his head. "Sit down, dear lady. And if you love Lindsay, keep what you hear this night close to your heart."

"Where did you get the watch?" Julian asked.

"Antun!" Miss Winslow's voice skated to a squeak. "Antun said he heard about William's death and went to the place where the ship docked. He brought back the watch and gave it to old Mr. Granville. When he died, Lindsay had it."

"And she gave it to me," Edward said, willing himself to be patient. "Julian, Kertz gave a description of the man who killed William and James and he could only be Antun Pollack."

Miss Winslow screamed and sank into a chair.

Edward rang impatiently for Garrity and ordered him to send hartshorn.

"Roger Latchett hired the murderer," Julian said slowly. "That's what you told me."

"Precisely. Which may mean that Latchett has decided to get at me through Lindsay. Who better to lure her away than his own assassin, a man whose cooperation he could buy, a man my wife trusts implicitly."

"Chelsea," Julian said, standing back to let a maid attend to Sarah Winslow. "We'll go there at once."

Voices sounded in the hall, one of them female, raised and persistent.

"What now?" Edward said, the instant before he was confronted by Mrs. Felling. For once he was dumbfounded into silence.

"His royal high and mighty here didn't want to let me in," Mrs. Felling said, hands on ample hips, tilted head indicating an exasperated Garrity. "Tell him I'm a friend of yours, Hawkesly."

Edward gestured vaguely to Garrity.

"I should think so." Mrs. Felling, unusually demure in dark brown wool, stood squarely in front of Edward. "Listen to what I'm going to tell you. Then act on it. Don't ask questions, just act."

"Are you sure this person—"

"You can leave us, Garrity," Edward snapped.

"Our friend," Mrs. Felling said significantly. "You know who I mean. Anyway, he's gone. That mother of his is still there giving me orders, but he's taken himself off. Ranting he was. Before he left he talked about you and your lady and said how he was going to finally get what was his."

Edward met Julian's eyes. "Remember every word he said, Mrs. Felling. Quickly, I beg you."

"Don't worry. I'll be quick or I've a notion it'll be

too late." She handed Edward a piece of paper. "He didn't know I got that. Copied it from the instructions I overheard him giving to that red-haired gent."

Edward tried not to react to Sarah Winslow's cry. "Carry on, Mrs. Felling!"

"The man said he had Linny outside in a carriage. That's what he called her, Linny. I worked it out as that was a name for your lady. Anyway, our friend told the man to take her to the place on that piece of paper. He said that later he'd send you a ransom note and you'd pay dearly for what you done to him."

"We'd better take blunt," Julian said.

"You'd better hurry," Mrs. Felling retorted. "And be careful. Our friend said he'd enjoy taking your money . . . and your life. He laughed at that. Thought it was a rare joke that you'd be paying for goods he'd already have used . . . and disposed of."

Heading in a generally easterly direction, the carriage they'd taken through the city had soon passed from the areas Lindsay recognized. Grand establishments had given way to the cluttered dwellings of the less fortunate and, eventually, the driver reined in his team at the edge of what appeared to be a densely forested area.

The coach door was flung open, but no word was spoken by the coachman.

Antun had been silent all the way, sunk into a corner, his eyes downcast, his mouth firmly set. Now he stirred and passed Lindsay to climb outside. When she went to the door, he swept her down and immediately strode away.

Lindsay ran to catch up and slipped a hand into his. "Are you sure this is where Edward told you to bring me?"

"We've a ways to go yet," he said shortly.

He seemed to know exactly where he was going.

A few yards into the trees they reached a single teth-ered horse. Without explanation, Antun lifted Lind-say to the animal's back and mounted behind her.

The night was blessedly dry, the temperature moderate. A full moon gave plenty of light. With one arm firmly circling Lindsay's waist, Antun urged the horse through the trees.

She didn't know how long they'd been traveling when she decided she could no longer be silent. "Antun, where are we going? How did Edward come to send you to me with a message?"

"Be patient, Linny. You'll find out soon enough."

"I've been patient. I don't understand any of this."

"Whoa," he said softly, pulling up the horse. "Linny, do you trust me?"

"Of course!"

"Hush. Not so loud. I've done some things I'm not proud of. But I intend to undo what I can."

She wished she could see his face. "Don't talk in riddles, Antun. What has all that to do with Edward or me?"

"Please know that what I'm doing . . . I'd rather not do what I'm about to do. But there's no other way. I'll do my best to put matters to rights, Linny. Just keep on trusting me."

Her stomach twisted unpleasantly. "You're frightening me, Antun."

"I know." He dismounted and pulled her down beside him. "That was one thing I never wanted to do. Come on."

What choice did she have? Surely Antun would keep her safe. And Edward wouldn't put her in dan-ger's way. "Why are we here? Where's Edward?"

Antun's response was to lift her into his arms and walk rapidly through dense undergrowth.

"Please, put me down," she said. "I'm well able to walk."

"Not in what you're wearing. Not here."

They broke into a clearing. To their left stood a low-lying cottage. Only one dim light showed through a window but the moon silvered white-washed walls and a roof made of stone slabs.

Without pausing, Antun strode toward the building.

"Why would Edward come here?" Now she was seriously frightened. "Antun, please answer me."

"In good time." He used a booted foot to push open the cottage door. Lowering his head to her face he whispered. "Remember. Trust me."

He closed the door and set her down on a flag-stone floor in a cheerless unfurnished room. No fire burned in the fireplace and the light she'd seen came from a single candle placed on the hearth.

Lindsay wrapped her swansdown-decorated cloak more firmly about her. "Edward?" she called tentatively. "I'm here . . . Edward." His name faded on her lips. Standing in a doorway leading to another room stood Roger Latchett. Behind him Lindsay could see flickering red. She swallowed and heard the dry clicking of her own throat.

"Well, well," Roger said, advancing. "I told Mr. Pollack we'd have no trouble persuading you to come here. Not with your husband safely distracted elsewhere." He wore a robe made of black satin.

Lindsay whirled around. Antun stood between her and the door. He stared straight past her at Roger.

"Where is Edward? Why am I here?"

"All in good time," Roger said. "Come with me, my dear. I have a little surprise for you."

"Is the note ready?" Antun asked, his voice oddly muffled.

"The note will be delivered in good time," Roger said. "My time. Get out until I call for you."

"You said you'd have the ransom note ready as soon as I delivered Lindsay."

"Ransom?" Lindsay backed to where she could see both men. "What ransom note?"

Antun looked away.

"Tell her," Roger said, and laughed. His pale thin hair seemed oiled. Combed to carefully pointed curls about his heavily jowled face, it shone. "Tell her that I discovered her husband would be safely out of the way this evening and that I arranged to have you lure her here. Tell her the truth about anything that pleases you, Pollack."

Antun shook his head slowly. "You gave me your word, Latchett. I said I'd—"

"Yes?" Roger crossed to Lindsay and raised her chin. "Antun will doubtless insist on detaining me from giving you your surprise, but we'll humor him." He kissed Lindsay's lips.

"Don't!" Leaping away, she wiped the back of a hand over her mouth. "Antun, what's happening? *Please* tell me."

"Antun doesn't know," Roger said. "But I'll tell you. I'll tell you everything."

"Latchett." Antun used the name with menace.

"The man Kertz. You know who I mean?" Roger asked. "Yes, of course you do. Edward is clearly besotted with you and will have told you everything—everything he knows, that is. He will have told you that Kertz contacted him and arranged a meeting for tonight. Did he tell you Kertz's little story about how I supposedly had the fifth Viscount Hawkesly murdered?"

Lindsay's legs shook. She held the neck of her cloak tightly.

"I see that he did. Well, we won't waste valuable time on this—*our* time, Lindsay. It's all true, but what does it matter?" He grabbed her arm and he pulled her close.

"That's it, Latchett," Antun said, his voice dangerously low. "Let her go. Now."

Lindsay saw a flash before she saw the knife Roger produced from the folds of his robe. He twisted her around and held her against his body. "I do seem to have trouble with the people I choose to trust." Roger sighed and rested the knife blade against Lindsay's neck. "I did hire an assassin, Lindsay. To kill William, not the viscount."

She closed her eyes. What could it mean that he was confessing this now?

"Unfortunately the man Kertz saw what happened and decided to use the information for his own selfish gain." He tutted. His sour breath moved Lindsay's hair and she stifled a wave of sickness. "I only did what I had to do to get what was rightfully mine. I was older than William. Tregonitha is mine."

"You were not my father's son. You—" The knife blade, touching her skin, stopped Lindsay.

"If Kertz hadn't gone to your dear husband and begged money for his information, none of this would have happened. But, as it stands, he has played into my hands anyway. The fool used the blunt Hawkesly gave him and decided to come to me for more. I told him that if he lured Hawkesly away tonight, I would pay him handsomely. So you see, my dear—here we are."

"Latchett," Antun said, taking a step. "If you want to punish someone, let it be me. I deserve it. Leave Lindsay be."

"Another step, *fool*, and I will be forced to spoil her neck. Such a beautiful neck." With his thumb, he stroked a line from the point of her chin to the neck of her cloak and Lindsay shivered.

"Go, Antun," Lindsay said, suddenly very afraid for her friend. "Go quickly."

Antun would not look at her.

Roger giggled. "He has nowhere to go. Murderers don't, you know."

"You said you wouldn't tell her," Antun shouted.

"Ah, but I've changed my mind—about a great many things. Lindsay, I found out that our friend here is a night runner. Can you imagine anything so shameful? Like father, like son. Poacher. Night runner. Thieves.''

Lindsay dared not struggle. Finally she caught Antun's anguished eye. She tried to will him to find a way to escape.

''It's only fair that I tell you everything, my dear. Your husband married you to gain revenge for his brother's death. He had no other interest in you. By taking you away from me he thought to also take Tregonitha. But it won't work. He'll die and then you'll marry me. And all will be as it should be.''

For an instant she thought she might faint. ''That can never be,'' she said quietly. ''Edward would never allow it. *Antun* would never allow it.''

''*Antun?* Hah! Haven't you guessed anything, you silly girl? Why do you think I was able to persuade a man who lusts after you to bring you to me to-night? He does lust after you, you know.''

Antun made to rush forward. ''You swine—''

''Ah, ah.'' Roger brandished the knife and brought it back to Lindsay's neck. ''I was able to persuade him because I own him. You see, Antun Pollack cared so much for the fishing fleet he hoped to buy that he couldn't risk my telling the revenue men about his little activities in the dark hours.''

''No!'' Antun covered his face with a hand.

''Yes,'' Roger said softly. ''Antun is no different from any other man. He has his price. It wasn't money. It was my silence in return for a little job he did for me. Lindsay, my sweet pure one, Antun Pollack wasn't away discussing fishing boats when William died. He was *with* William. Antun murdered William.''

Everything before Lindsay's eyes made an insane circle. She clutched at air with both hands and gasped, before Roger's hand, intimately cupping her breast, jerked her roughly against him.

''No, Antun,'' she whispered, grappling ineffectually with the foul hand that probed her flesh. "Not you."

"Yes, him," Roger said serenely. "And now he will simply go back to his hovel by the sea and never come near us again. Go, Pollack. I am ready to share Lindsay's surprise with her. And later, as I have already arranged, a ransom note will be delivered to Hawkesly. When he arrives, I shall be waiting and after he sees what the nature of Lindsay's surprise has been . . . he'll die." Once again his crazed giggle soared.

"No!" The sickness ebbed, to be replaced by fury. "No!" With all the force in her small body, she slammed the heel of a slippered foot onto Roger's instep.

He sagged, howling his pain.

And Antun, bellowing, launched himself. "You son of Satan!" he yelled.

With arms outstretched he blanketed Roger, fell with him to the stone floor. There was the cracking sound of bone on bone.

Lindsay flinched.

A gurgling cry sent her to her knees. There was blood, a spreading pool of bright, frothing blood. The knife had been between the two men.

"Antun!" On hands and knees, she crawled, not caring that the blood soaked her cloak. "Antun?" He could not have killed William. Her brother had been Antun's best friend.

She put her hand on a big shoulder and pulled. And, slowly, Antun moved, rolled away—onto his back.

The knife handle trembled. The blade was buried in his chest.

Lindsay touched his face.

"He's dead." Roger, blood-soaked black satin clinging to his belly, turned on his side and propped his head on a hand. "And he did kill William. But, no matter. Everything is going beautifully now."

Slowly, her head cleared. She saw Antun's wide, glazed eyes, the pool of blood from a wound that no longer pumped. Dead.

Like a woman in a trance, she rose to her feet and looked down on her old friend. *Friend?* She closed her eyes. "Edward, where are you?"

"Come with me," Roger said. He got clumsily to his feet and held out a hand. When she crossed her arms, he laughed and pulled her to him. "Still so pure and untouched. Exactly as it should be." With an arm around her shoulders, he half dragged her into the room from which he'd emerged.

The center of the room was dominated by a huge four-poster bed draped in red—blood red. Lindsay swayed and Roger dug his fingers into her arm. Candles inside red-glass chimneys flickered on tables. Atop the bed lay a transparent white nightrail.

Roger led Lindsay to the bed and picked up the wisp of fabric. "You will wear this," he said. "Virginal white for my virgin bride."

"You're mad," Lindsay whispered. "Mad, mad."

His hand, connecting with her cheek, snapped her head back. She pressed her lips together against a scream and tasted blood. Her teeth had punctured her lip.

"That's better," Roger said, raising his chin. "No more naughty words. Put on the gown."

She shook her head.

"Come now. I'm losing my patience." He grabbed at the fastenings on her cloak and ripped them open. When he'd flung the cloak aside, he sunk his hand between her breasts, under the bodice of her gown.

Muslin tore.

Lindsay flailed. She fought, kicking and scratching, grasping for Roger's face. His laugh shot along her nerves, but her nails found his cheek.

"Fight, my beautiful virgin. Fight for your virginity." With both hands, he ripped her gown to her waist. Cool air rushed over her naked breasts. Then he dragged her backwards and pushed her down on the bed.

"My God!"

Dimly, her vision a wash of red, Lindsay registered that the voice was not Roger's. She felt him grope between her legs and open his mouth on her breast.

Then he was gone. Dazed, she gathered the tattered shreds of her bodice to her and struggled to sit up.

She saw Julian first—trapping Roger against a wall while he pummeled him with both fists. But then there was Edward. Breathing hard, he braced his hands against the doorjamb before striding to gather her into his arms.

"My dear one," he murmured. "Oh, my dear, sweet wife. What has he done to you?" He pulled off his cloak and wrapped it around her.

"Nothing," she whispered. "But he told me about . . ." She could not go on.

"Latchett's done his worst," Edward said through gritted teeth, looking at the man's form sagging behind Julian's weight. "Don't finish him, Julian. It would be too—"

The shot that rang out silenced Edward. In slow motion, Julian twisted away from Roger, who grinned broadly, happily, a small, smoking pistol held aloft.

"Mine," he caroled. "All mine, you fools. I told you I'm going to get everything I want."

"Julian," Edward said. "Are you hurt, man?"

"You might call it that." Twisting his mouth into a pained smile, he slid to sit on the floor. And Lindsay saw that he used both hands to staunch the flow of blood from his left thigh.

Roger sighed theatrically. "I've always been a man other men should treat with caution," he announced. "Over there, Hawkesly. No, on second thought, kneel beside your friend. No doubt a man of honor, such as yourself, will find some symbolic satisfaction in dying beside a friend." He brandished the pistol.

"And who do you intend to die beside, Roger?" a new voice asked. "After all, you never did have a friend, did you?"

Lindsay refused to believe what she saw.

"Surprised, Roger?" the newcomer said, coming into the room. A tall, fair-haired man, he walked with a pronounced limp. His clothes were rough and worn, his boots badly scuffed and dusty.

"No, no, no!" Roger backed away, crossing his wrists in front of his face. "You're dead!"

"Am I? Look at me, Roger. Am I dead?" Thin as the man's face was, there was no question but that he was handsome. Even a jagged white scar from temple to jaw managed only to increase his masculine vibrancy.

"You're dead!" Roger screamed again.

The man opened his shirt and pulled it free of his pantaloons. Lindsay drew in a sharp breath. The scar on his body drew a puckered line down his breastbone and around his ribs to a livid cluster of badly healed puncture wounds at his side.

"I should be dead, you mean," he said, slow— and low. "And perhaps I am. Perhaps I've only come to escort you to hell."

Roger dropped his arms. His drooling lips hung open and tears streamed from his pale little eyes. "No," he moaned, shaking his head. "No."

Before Lindsay guessed his intent, he raised the pistol to his temple and pulled the trigger. More blood flew and he crumpled soundlessly.

With one hand, Lindsay reached for and found Edward's steady grasp. "He's dead," she said. "Roger's dead."

"Yes," Edward said soothingly. "And you have nothing more to fear. You're safe. We're all safe, my love."

Lindsay held out her hand to the weary-looking man who had just arrived. "We're safe. Edward, God knows how this can be true, but meet my dear brother—William Granville."

Epilogue

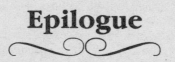

"Sometimes I'm frightened, Edward," Lindsay said. "I awake terrified I have only dreamed my happiness."

"I know, my darling one. You awake in my arms, remember?"

She smiled up at him. "How could I forget? Look at them." She nodded to the lawns sweeping down behind Tregonitha where William and John rolled and scrambled together. "William will not easily forget Maria, but John is bringing him so much joy."

Edward rested a hand on her neck. "Even after months of knowing William I can scarcely believe he survived," he said. "Left to die. Taken by the French. Imprisoned. Escaped! Sent by Mrs. Felling and Sarah barely in time to . . . It is an extraordinary story."

"A wonderful story," Lindsay said. She slipped an arm around Edward's waist and urged him toward the terrace steps. A late summer breeze bore scents of roses, stocks, carnations and the myriad other blooms in well-tended beds surrounding the house. "Thank you for bringing me here to visit, Edward."

He arched a brow at her. "Did I have a choice? You threatened me with tears. My brave, reckless little wife would never resort to such measures over

370

something that wasn't of great importance to her."
His fingertips moved soothingly on the sensitive skin
behind her ear. "What is important to you is important to me, Lindsay."

Lindsay ducked her head to hide her face. He did
not yet know why she had wanted to come here at
exactly this time. "Aunt Ballard seems to be enjoying herself."

"Hm." Edward strolled with Lindsay down the
steps to the lawn. "I am still surprised that she came.
She has always said she hated the country."

The countess, parasol in place, sat on a bench with
Reverend Winslow beside her. From time to time
the sound of their laughter drifted on the breeze.

"Remember that this is not Aunt Ballard's first
visit here," Lindsay commented. "She came to
Cornwall initially to persuade Reverend Winslow to
allow Sarah to visit London regularly."

"I know the story," Edward said, not quite ac-
complishing a bored tone. "Including the Reverend's return visits to London. Now there would be
a strange couple."

Lindsay looked at him sharply. "You think Aunt
Ballard and Reverend Winslow . . ."

"I think I'm glad my aunt has discarded her
mourning clothes at last. We will not speculate further."

"No," Lindsay agreed demurely, aware that Edward would not stop her from discussing whatever
she really wished to discuss. "Edward, could we
take a little ride?"

"Now?" He frowned.

"Yes. I took the liberty of having horses made
ready."

"We aren't dressed to ride."

"Does it matter?"

Edward shook his head. "No, my unconventional
bride. If you wish to ride, we'll ride."

Waving to William and John, they strolled on toward the stables. Passing an opening in a privet hedge, they were afforded a view of Julian and Sarah. "Convalescing, hm?" Edward said of Julian, whose leg wound had taken some weeks to heal.

"Resting," Lindsay said, pulling Edward on. "And Sarah is merely helping him recover."

"I suppose reclining on the grass could be a good place to convalesce," Edward said. "And it is quite possible that kissing Sarah will help him recover."

"Exactly," Lindsay said smugly. "I think they'll marry."

They entered the stable yard. "And I think," Edward said with laughter in his voice, "that you should concentrate on your own affairs and allow others to decide their own fates."

Within minutes they were mounted and riding toward the hills. "Don't you love it here?" Lindsay called. Edward kept his mount behind hers, allowing Lindsay to lead the way.

"I suppose it's a fair second to Devon," he said grudgingly.

Lindsay laughed and spurred her game little gelding into a gallop. The wind bore a salt tang and she raced to reach a ridge where she could see the ocean. With Edward only strides behind, Lindsay tore along, her hair flying free of the ribbons that had bound it.

"You ride like a wild thing"—Edward drew level— "like the wild, reckless thing you are. Where are you going?"

Deep green and spume-laced, the sea roared over rocks far below. "Just follow me," Lindsay shouted. "It isn't far."

When Point Cottage came into view on its headland, Lindsay slowed the pace. Without speaking, she and Edward trotted, side by side, the rest of the way to the pasture surrounding the cottage.

Without waiting for Edward to help her, Lindsay jumped down from her saddle and tethered the horse. She entered the cottage and stood, waiting for Edward to join her.

He came in, his handsome face glowing from the wind, his dark hair falling rakishly over his brow. "You, my girl, are an impossible romantic."

"Why do you say that?" Lindsay asked innocently. She went to sit on the faded satin couch before the fireplace.

"Because"—he came to stand behind her and braced his hands on the back of the couch—"because you wanted to come to the place where we were first together—really together, I mean."

"True," she agreed. "But I shall have to correct your interpretation of that meeting . . . soon. First I'd like to tell you that I've been assured we may expect our first child in about six months. But, to return to our first meeting—"

"What did you say?" Edward straightened slowly.

"To return to our first meeting. We were not *really* together, as you put it, my lord. You tricked an innocent girl into believing herself compromised."

Edward walked around the couch, sat beside Lindsay and framed her face with his warm hands. "A child? *Our* child?"

"Who else's child would it be?" she asked primly.

His black eyes echoed the smile that curved his lips. "In six months I shall see you hold our baby."

"The thought doesn't displease you, then?"

"I have never been more happy." Very gently, he brushed his lips across hers and gathered her into strong arms that trembled slightly. "I did trick you, my dear one. And I shall never be sorry."

"Nor I. But I do think it would be appropriate to see if I have learned more of what we discussed on that first night here."

Edward frowned. "What did we discuss?"

Lindsay sighed. "*Men*. What would they do without women to remind them of important issues?"

Very deliberately, she put a small distance between them and began to unbutton his shirt.

"And what do you think you are doing, madam?" He leaned back and regarded her from beneath lowered lids. When she tugged his shirt from his breeches, he shifted to accommodate her.

"Why, Edward," she said, running her fingers through the hair on his chest. "I'm practicing erring, of course."

Avon Romantic Treasures

*Unforgettable, enthralling love stories,
sparkling with passion and adventure
from Romance's bestselling authors*

FIRE ON THE WIND *by Barbara Dawson Smith*
76274-9/$4.50 US/$5.50 Can

DANCE OF DECEPTION *by Suzannah Davis*
76128-9/$4.50 US/$5.50 Can

ONLY IN YOUR ARMS *by Lisa Kleypas*
76150-5/$4.50 US/$5.50 Can

LADY LEGEND *by Deborah Camp*
76735-X/$4.50 US/$5.50 Can

RAINBOWS AND RAPTURE *by Rebecca Paisley*
76565-9/$4.50 US/$5.50 Can

AWAKEN MY FIRE *by Jennifer Horsman*
76701-5/$4.50 US/$5.50 Can

ONLY BY YOUR TOUCH *by Stella Cameron*
76606-X/$4.50 US/$5.50 Can

Avon Romances—
the best in exceptional authors and unforgettable novels!

L. G

If you enjoyed this book, take advantage of this special offer.
Subscribe now and get a

FREE
Historical
Romance

No Obligation (a $4.50 value)

Each month the editors of True Value select the four *very best* novels from America's leading publishers of romantic fiction. Preview them in your home *Free* for 10 days. With the first four books you receive, we'll send you a FREE book as our introductory gift. No Obligation!

If for any reason you decide not to keep them, just return them and owe nothing. If you like them as much as we think you will, you'll pay just $4.00 each and save at *least* $.50 each off the cover price. (Your savings are *guaranteed* to be at least $2.00 each month.) There is NO postage and handling – or other hidden charges. There are no minimum number of books to buy and you may cancel at any time.

Send in the Coupon Below

To get your FREE historical romance fill out the coupon below and mail it today. As soon as we receive it we'll send you your FREE Book along with your first month's selections.